THE Friday Society

THE Friday Society

ADRIENNE KRESS

DIAL BOOKS
NEW YORK

DIAL BOOKS
A member of Penguin Group (USA) Inc.
Published by The Penguin Group
Penguin Group (USA) Inc., 375 Hudson Street, New York, NY 10014, U.S.A.
Penguin Group (Canada), 90 Eglinton Avenue East, Suite 700, Toronto, Ontario, Canada M4P 2Y3 (a division of Pearson Penguin Canada Inc.) | Penguin Books Ltd, 80 Strand, London WC2R 0RL, England | Penguin Ireland, 25 St. Stephen's Green, Dublin 2, Ireland (a division of Penguin Books Ltd) | Penguin Group (Australia), 250 Camberwell Road, Camberwell, Victoria 3124, Australia (a division of Pearson Australia Group Pty Ltd) | Penguin Books India Pvt Ltd, 11 Community Centre, Panchsheel Park, New Delhi - 110 017, India | Penguin Group (NZ), 67 Apollo Drive, Rosedale, Auckland 0632, New Zealand (a division of Pearson New Zealand Ltd) | Penguin Books (South Africa) (Pty) Ltd, 24 Sturdee Avenue, Rosebank, Johannesburg 2196, South Africa | Penguin Books Ltd, Registered Offices: 80 Strand, London WC2R 0RL, England

Designed by Jennifer Kelly
Text set in Goudy Old Style MT Std
Printed in the U.S.A.

1 3 5 7 9 10 8 6 4 2

Library of Congress Cataloging-in-Publication Data
Kress, Adrienne.
The Friday Society / by Adrienne Kress. p. cm.
Summary: Cora, Nellie, and Michiko, teenaged assistants to three powerful men in Edwardian London, meet by chance at a ball that ends with the discovery of a murdered man, leading the three to work together to solve this and related crimes without drawing undue attention to themselves.
ISBN 978-0-8037-3761-7 (hardback)
[1. Adventure and adventurers—Fiction. 2. Criminals—Fiction. 3. London (England)—History—20th century—Fiction. 4. Great Britain—History—Edward VII, 1901-1910—Fiction. 5. Mystery and detective stories.] I. Title.
PZ7.K8838Fri 2012 [Fic]—dc23 2012005364

BECAUSE IT MAKES SENSE TO DO SO WITH THIS BOOK,

A THREE-WAY DEDICATION:

To my mom

She inspires me to be confident expressing my thoughts,
and proud of being smart, enthusiastic, and weird.
Also totally unashamed to crash open houses.

To Farmor

She had class, athleticism,
a great sense of style, and great taste.
She was also one of the bravest women I've known.

And to Zadie

Because behind every great woman is a great man.
He sent his daughters to college, and loved to cook.
And encouraged his grandchildren to follow their dreams.

* * *

London

1900

When the nations of the world are in crisis,
they turn to our city for aid.
But to whom do we turn in our moment of desperation?
On whom does the great city call in its hour of need?

A fog lifts.
A new brand of hero is born.

How shocking.
Truly.
One simply doesn't do such things in polite society.

PART ONE

Three Helpful Girls

Cora Bell

AND THEN THERE was an explosion.

It was loud. It was bright. It was very explosion-y.

Cora dove under the table and held her breath, waiting for the tinkling sound of glass to cease. It could have been a nice sound, actually. If it didn't reflect her total incompetence.

Stupid tinkling sound of glass.

She'd fixed the calculations, she'd double-checked the equipment. How was it possible to change everything about an experiment and still have it result in the same thing?

Kablooey.

That was the technical term for it.

Cora crossed her legs under the table and pouted. Pouting didn't really solve anything, but she was annoyed. She was also covered in green goo. And it was hard not to pout when covered in green goo.

Now, it wasn't that she didn't love explosions. Quite the opposite. She even remembered her very first explosion. (Some girls remembered their first corset or first grand ball, but she wasn't "some girls.") It had been seven years ago. Lord White had her put on the goggles he'd had custom made to fit her tiny ten-year-old features, handed her the strangest-looking gun she'd ever seen, pointed it in the right direction, and told her to pull the trigger.

Just like that.

So she had. And the dummy's head in front of her had exploded into a million pieces.

"Great aim!" Lord White had laughed enthusiastically for a good five minutes after the destruction.

She had been in love with things exploding ever since.

What she didn't love was green goo.

And failure.

Cora noticed her notepad and pencil floating beside her. She extracted both from the gloop and examined her calculations. She knew she'd only have a few moments of peace before—

"Cora! You all right, love? Cora!"

Cora sighed.

"Yes, Mrs. Philips, I'm fine." She maintained focus on the paper in front of her.

"That was a loud noise. . . . Where are you, pet?"

"Over here." She rolled her eyes and glanced up, watching Mrs. Philips's skirts sweep toward her.

"What a mess." Cora watched the feet of the housekeeper as they maneuvered carefully through the broken glass and goo on the floor. "I'll send for Barker."

"Please do."

Mrs. Philips's round face appeared beneath the table. Her normally pleasantly plump countenance was distorted by gravity into something slightly grotesque. "Why are you hiding under here?"

"Just trying to gather my thoughts."

"What happened?"

"Well, I don't know really. That's why I'm trying to gather my thoughts."

"Looks like something exploded."

"Yes, I know." Cora finally made eye contact with Mrs. Philips. Mrs. Philips shook her head, which looked really odd at that angle.

"No need to get all huffy. Just sayin' what I see," replied the housekeeper standing upright. "Come off the cold floor, love. That ain't healthy for a person."

Cora grabbed the pencil and pad, pushed herself out from under the table, and stood up. She got a head rush when she did and had to hold on to the edge of the table for a moment to steady herself. Then, regaining her balance, she swept the wrinkles out of her long lab coat and pushed her goggles up onto her forehead.

Mrs. Philips was surveying the general damage in what appeared to be a pretty dejected manner. But Cora knew her attitude didn't have much to do with the mess she'd created. Messes occurred—let's just say—a lot, in his lordship's top-secret lab. It wasn't anything to get upset about. No, Cora knew the real reason Mrs. Philips seemed so sad.

"It ain't right. What with all the work Lord White makes you do keeping track of his schedule and such . . . but also helping him out down here? That's too much."

"No it isn't," replied Cora. How many times had they had this argument? It'd been years of the same thing, as if somehow one day it would sink in and Cora, in a flush of realization, would say, "My word, Mrs. Philips, you're right! It *is* too much. And not only that, it turns out that after all those years of saying I loved working in the lab, I actually meant I hated it. How can I ever thank you for showing me the error of my ways?"

She knew the housekeeper would never give up trying, though. Just as Cora would never give in to her. But there were days that Cora wished Mrs. Philips would be just a little bit more understanding. After all, she was the closest thing Cora had ever had to a mother, and even though she hated to admit it, Mrs. Philips's opinion did matter to her.

Lord White's housekeeper had been so wonderfully understanding when his lordship had brought Cora home seven years ago, a tiny little urchin. She'd looked much younger than her ten years, but he'd given her a chance to work as a chambermaid. Mrs. Philips had taught her how to be the perfect servant, and cared for the girl when she caught cold or hurt herself. The hurting-herself thing happened a lot. She'd even supported Lord White when he started taking Cora under his wing, showing her how to do basic math, keep accounts, how to maintain his timetable . . .

How to blow things up.

But Cora had noticed Mrs. Philips's concern when he'd begun bringing in a tutor to teach her the classics, and a linguist to help round out that thick East End accent of hers. It had been a fear, Cora knew, that she would grow beyond her station, and though the precocious girl had learned how to pretend to be of the same class as her boss, Mrs. Philips had cautioned Cora on many occasions that this would only make her unsuitable for any job but being Lord White's assistant.

"A creature of both worlds is a creature of none," she'd warned late one night, sitting on the edge of Cora's bed.

Cora knew the danger. She also knew that she'd probably never find someone willing to marry such a creature. She was too good now for the boys she'd grown up with in the street, and yet would never be good enough for any of his lordship's peers.

Deep down, Cora had wondered if it had been a plan of Lord White's from the beginning. To keep her for himself, his personal assistant until the end of time. But she knew he had acted toward her as he had only because he cared about her. His intentions were usually good. He laid them out, one flagstone at a time, along the road from the proverb, and she walked along them obediently.

So she'd decided to simply appreciate the moment, not think of her murky future, and throw herself into work. And what she loved most was working in his lab. She loved mixing chemicals and playing with electricity. She loved winches and gears and clockwork pieces. She loved how things came together, and she loved taking stuff apart.

It made her happy. Even just unpacking boxes for his lordship made her happy.

Shit. The boxes.

"When's the shipment arriving?" Cora asked, following Mrs. Philips to the winding wrought-iron staircase that circled up toward what appeared, from this angle, to be a closed domed ceiling.

"Soon. An hour. Maybe two."

Cora opened the panel beside the stairs and pushed a large brass button. The dome slowly began to open, revealing a large well-lit room above.

"And I assume his lordship has returned home to greet it?"

Mrs. Philips took a step onto the stairs and stopped, not actually answering the question. Cora knew the housekeeper so well that she could understand her silences as if they were sentences.

"Mrs. Philips?"

"Aw, love . . ."

"Mrs. Philips, Lord White hasn't returned, has he?"

"Not yet, love, though I imagine soon. . . ."

With a rush of energy Cora crossed the room, removing her gloves, lab coat, and goggles and tossing them all in her cubby. Then she returned to the stairs, where Mrs. Philips stood with her arms folded across her ample chest.

"I asked you," said Cora to the formidable bosom before her, "to get me if he hadn't returned by three. He has a very important event tonight."

"I know that but—"

"But nothing, Mrs. Philips. I need to fetch him, even if you don't approve of my doing so. I don't have time to argue about it. Now, would you please bring me my pistol from my room and meet me at the front door?" Cora slid past Mrs. Philips and made her way up the stairs and out into Lord White's vast library.

"It ain't right, it ain't right," muttered Mrs. Philips, coming up behind her.

Cora just ignored her. In trying to protect her from visiting what Mrs. Philips called "a most unhealthy neighborhood," the housekeeper always wound up utterly ruining Lord White's schedule. Sometimes it frustrated Cora that Mrs. Philips seemed to care more about the welfare of her master's personal assistant than the welfare of her master himself. Lord White mattered more than all of them put together. As a highly influential member of Parliament, he was quite likely to be Prime Minister someday, if he played his cards right.

And boy, was his lordship good at cards.

Despite her disapproval, Mrs. Philips fetched Cora's "pistol." Though it had the same shape and purpose as your typical firearm, it was, in fact, one of Lord White's more successful experiments. It was a fair bit smaller than the average, yet it had twice the power. Energy was stored up every evening when she placed it into the "electricity container" by her bed, and the charge, which sent bullets flying at twice their normal speed, lasted a full day. The bullets themselves were tiny, but they carried within them a highly pressurized acid that exploded on contact.

Lord White had invented the weapon especially for her, out of concern for her general safety, and also because he knew she liked destructive things. It had been her gift a few years ago in honor of her fifteenth birthday. He'd even had her name engraved on it.

Cora loved her present and made sure to take it with her wherever she went. Just in case. Mrs. Philips also kind of insisted on her doing so. Cora placed the weapon snugly in her purse, and in no time at all, she was out on the high street in her coat and hat, hailing a cab.

And Introducing Lord White

CORA ARRIVED IN the East End after thirty frustrating minutes in a hansom cab negotiating London foot traffic. This stupid city, for some reason, simply refused to acknowledge any form of transportation other than walking. The narrow streets helped with that. Next time she'd spend the extra cash on a steam cab. They were smaller and more agile than those pulled by horses.

Rescuing Lord White had become as much a part of Cora's job as working in the lab. It really wasn't meant to be one of her regular duties, but apparently she'd become the only person able to convince him to leave his hobbies and get back to work.

Hobbies.

She didn't judge Lord White for having them. He had a stressful career, and relieving tension in whatever manner he could made him far more tolerable at home. Sometimes even fun.

But why did his hobbies have to get in the way of *her* work?

Of course, she knew she wasn't being fair; she was, after all, his servant. Still. She sometimes forgot that. And who could blame her with the way he treated her, often almost as if they were equals? It got to be rather confusing at times.

The cab pulled up to the mouth of a narrow alley, and she jumped out to take the rest of it by foot. His lordship had left a few instructions on how to find the Red Veil, in case she had to rescue him. "In case." Hah. More like "when." She'd never been to this particular opium den before and had been a bit surprised that he'd changed venues.

Despite her current position in high society, Cora knew these streets well. Things a person learns as a child have a habit of sticking. She'd grown up here, learned all the shortcuts and secrets over a decade of picking pockets, selling flowers, and stealing food from windows. Yes, it was easier to negotiate the streets in flat thick shoes and a simple skirt, but even in her tweed and more refined footwear, she followed her boss's instructions easily enough.

The entrance to the Red Veil was at the far end of the bustling south market set up in the shadow of four teetering tenement buildings. It was a relatively small market that specialized in foreign goods because it was just a few blocks from the docks. The crowd was always thick, and full of recent immigrants. Walking through it, Cora felt what it might be like to be in a land where you didn't speak the language.

Isolated and alone.

"Flower, miss?"

Not so alone, evidently.

"No, thank you," she replied.

She didn't need to look at the girl; she knew exactly what

she'd look like, how dirty her clothes would be. Big hollow eyes in a drawn face. She knew it because she'd seen that reflection of herself in the smudged windows of the high street so many years ago.

There was a hand on her arm, and Cora pulled away without turning around. She told herself she simply didn't have the time to engage, but she knew the truth. She didn't want to see this girl, the look of desperation. A look that translated into a sad resignation deep inside.

"I said no thank you."

There was a small gasp. "Are you . . ."

"Very busy? Yes. Good day." Cora resumed her journey through the crowd, desperate to brush off the encounter. She would not go back there. Even if she had to physically, now and again, she would never go back there in her mind.

Though, "Are you . . .?"

Cora turned, but the girl was nowhere to be seen.

She hoped upon hope that the rest of the sentence hadn't been, ". . . Cora Bell?"

Only a few steps more and she was facing the door to the Red Veil, a plain wooden thing with a small dragon carved into it at eye level. Cora pushed the brief encounter with the flower girl from her thoughts and focused on the task ahead.

Deep breath.

She didn't bother knocking, just burst her way inside. Maybe it was a little overly enthusiastic of her, but her nerves were on edge.

She found herself in a small vestibule where a short, pockmarked Chinese man, his flesh sagging off his face, stood staring at her, clearly shocked by her sudden arrival.

She approached him and, as casually as she could, said, "I'm looking for Lord White."

The way the man's eyes widened instantly told her that her boss was definitely here. Where he was precisely, though, she had no idea, as it looked like there were no other rooms or hallways off this one.

"Where is he?" she asked, turning back to the man.

The man suddenly launched into a speech in his native language, but of course Cora couldn't understand a word of it. He gesticulated wildly, punctuating his thoughts with his finger thrusting into her face. Cora nodded, growing impatient.

"Yes, yes, I see," she interrupted loudly. "Now, as to Lord White . . . ?"

"Lord White?" asked the man as if it was the first time she'd mentioned the name.

"Stop pretending. There's no need for secrecy. I know for a fact he's here. Where is he?"

The man shook his head vehemently.

"No Lord White," he said.

"Don't be difficult; just show me."

"No. No Lord White here. Now go."

He pointed toward the exit. Cora noticed the man glance for a brief moment at a faded tapestry hanging on the wall beside him, and then glance back at her. It was the smallest of moves, but Cora had seen it.

"Yes, fine," she said slowly, "I'll go." And she turned her body slightly to give the impression she was leaving.

The man relaxed, and Cora knew that finally his guard was down. It didn't take much effort to push beyond him to the tapestry. He'd clearly had no idea she was going to just whip past him like that, and, as she pushed her way through the tapestry and into the dark stairwell beyond, he stood totally still, paralyzed with confusion.

She was already halfway down the stairs when he finally came rushing down after her, shouting, "No, no!" When he put his sweaty palm on her shoulder, Cora had had enough.

"Sir," she said, turning around abruptly and aiming her small pistol between his legs, "I am *not* the police. I am *not* here to make a scene, nor to report any activity to anyone. I am merely here to find my boss and bring him home so he can prepare for an event this evening for which it would be best if he were sober. You have been most unhelpful, and if you don't let me take care of my business, I can assure you I will do away with yours."

The man offered a weak "No," but it was clear he took her threat seriously. Cora raised an eyebrow at him, and he took two steps back upstairs.

She lowered the pistol and tucked it back inside her small purse. "Good." Then she turned and continued her descent into the dark.

She wasn't feeling half as confident as she pretended to be. This place freaked her out. Though she'd rescued Lord White many, many times, this was the first time she'd been anywhere quite so . . . skeevy. Usually opium dens were simple places. A front room for money to exchange hands, a back room to get high. Really a very straightforward business model.

This place was different, though. For one thing, it was huge. Far too huge to house an opium den alone. And it all made her feel slightly uncomfortable to think what else might be hidden away down the dark, damp passages.

Cora made her way down the hall, past several doors on either side with small square windows cut into them. She decided to avoid looking through the windows. She knew that his lordship was not likely to be in one of those rooms. Such proclivities just didn't suit his taste. Also she really didn't need to see anything that might keep her awake at night.

Finally the hall opened up onto a room a lot like the ones in smaller opium dens, a simple square open space with pillows strewn about and pipes littering the floor. It was here she spotted Lord White, lying surrounded by half a dozen or so women. All of them appeared dead to the world, including his lordship, and Cora wondered why he'd bothered to come to this particular den only to pass out. Seemed impractical.

The room was pleasant, though, artfully decorated with fabric that draped across the ceiling, down the walls, and over the bodies strewn about. Chinese lanterns lit the scene most ineffectively; they seemed to be more for atmosphere than anything else.

"Very picturesque," she said as she approached Lord White.

His glasses were askew, falling across his face, and he was hugging a silk pillow. He opened his eyes a crack.

"Miss Bell," he said, the words drooling out of his mouth.

"Indeed. Come; it's time to go."

"Five more minutes."

"No, now." *Don't make me sift through all these bodies to pull you up, sir. Please.*

"I don't want to."

"Well, we all have to do things we don't want." Cora considered pointing out that the things that most people had to do that they didn't want to do were probably a little more unpleasant than his not wanting to go home and get ready for an extravagant gala.

But of course she didn't.

"This is intolerable," he said, shifting himself up onto his elbows. "Where are my glasses?"

"On your face."

"They're clearly not." His voice was getting louder, a little too loud.

"Well, no, I mean . . . You aren't wearing them properly, true, but they are lying across your face."

"No."

"They are . . . right on your . . ." Cora sighed hard and leaned over, plucking his glasses from his face and showing them to him.

"Oh, look, my glasses!" said his lordship with great pleasure.

"I know. What a wonderful magic trick. Up, now."

It was Lord White's turn to release a sigh. He reached out his hand, and Cora, with much effort, helped him to stand. For a small man, his lordship's body mass was awfully dense.

Lord White teetered dangerously. He finally looked at her. He squinted. Then the squint slowly turned into eyes closing.

Dear God, sobering him up was going to be a task.

"Time to go home," she said, giving him a firm shake. It took a lot of work to get him up the stairs, but fortunately she met a helpful Chinese man carrying a tea tray who gave her a hand dragging him.

When they arrived in the foyer that led back through the tapestry, Cora gave an indulgent smile to the man she'd met earlier. Then, reaching into his lordship's breast pocket, she pulled out a sovereign and passed it to him. He stared at it in surprise.

"For your discretion," she said.

The man nodded in silence and helped them to the door. Once more Cora's hand flew inside Lord White's pocket and she withdrew a pair of dark round sunglasses. She exchanged his normal glasses for these, and then, with a sharp nod, she directed the man to open the door to bright daylight.

An Unexpected Guest

"LET HIM SLEEP it off," instructed Cora as she and Lord White entered his darkened foyer. Barker nodded and took over escorting duties, leading his lordship up the grand staircase.

Cora sighed and slowly removed her hat, gloves, and jacket. But she didn't have time to relax yet. She still had to unpack that shipment which might or might not have arrived, and which she was obviously now doing alone, considering that his lordship could barely carry a conversation, let alone heavy boxes.

She made her way along the dark hall to Lord White's library.

A modern addition to the Tudor home, it stood two stories tall, with bookshelves packed with every book imaginable covering all walls. It had a huge fireplace at one end opposite an equally huge double set of doors. A giant-domed, stained-glass skylight lit the place by day, and nearly a hundred lanterns by night. Rugs from all corners of the earth lay wherever they damn well felt like, covering one another and the floor. And in the center of the room was a giant globe that spun slowly on its axis.

Cora loved his lordship's library. Who could blame her? For someone who loved reading as much as she did, it was pure heaven.

But what she loved even more was the lab beneath it. Only a handful of people knew of its existence, and of Lord White's private business operation: his staff, obviously his lordship himself, and Cora. Anyone who commissioned an invention from his lordship did so through a third party.

Cora made her way over to the stack of books at the foot of the globe. It looked like they'd been piled there without much thought. Hidden underneath a volume of *The Origin of Species* was an oversized copy of Dante's *Inferno*. She opened the book. It was hollow and empty except for the giant brass button that stared up at her. And, as most giant buttons tended to do, it invited her, by its mere giant buttonness, to push it.

She did.

The globe beside her slowly stopped its rotation.

There was a moment of nothingness.

And then.

A seam appeared in the middle of the globe, cutting the top hemisphere in two. Light poured out of it, up toward the darkening skylight. Slowly the seam grew wider as each side of the top hemisphere pulled apart and sank into the lower hemisphere until the latter was all that remained, open, like a giant punch bowl.

Cora climbed up the stepladder that stood conveniently to the globe's side and looked down into the depths. A curling wrought-iron staircase wound deep into the ground, leading to a white marble floor.

Cora skipped lightly down the steps.

Then she pulled her pistol from her purse and placed it firmly between the fifteenth and sixteenth vertebrae of the stranger standing in the middle of the room.

"Is that a pistol you've placed firmly between my fifteenth and sixteenth vertebrae?"

The young gentleman's voice was surprisingly calm, Cora thought, considering the situation.

"It is indeed," she replied.

The young man didn't say anything for a second—Cora assumed probably because he hadn't been expecting the person who was threatening him to be, you know, a girl.

Then:

"I ask only because there have been occasions when an individual might pretend to be threatening a person with a pistol when really they are using something far more mundane. Like a finger, maybe."

"I suppose that could happen."

"And if I spin around and use a spectacular set of moves I learned while at school, and I disarm you of this instrument of death, I will indeed be removing a weapon and not, say, pulling your finger."

"I can assure you, sir, this is no finger."

There was a sudden flurry of activity as the young man spun on the spot, his arms a blur, and Cora found herself no longer holding on to her pistol. Why did he underestimate her like that? I mean, who threatens someone without a backup plan? Honestly. She removed the knife from its sheath at her waist and placed it at the young man's throat as he came at her in some kind of attack. He froze in place.

"Ah, well, now I know for certain you've got a knife to my throat because I saw it," he said, tensing his neck against the blade pushing into his skin. "And can feel it. Very bladelike."

"No mistaking this for a finger now, is there?" Okay, so now she was kind of having fun with this.

"No indeed. Very well played."

"I'm good at games. I always win."

"Well, it's easy to win when you cheat."

"I don't cheat!" Maybe Lord White would hide a card or two up his sleeve, but she'd never do that. . . .

"You did approach a man with his back turned, you did reveal a secondary, previously undisclosed, weapon. That's not playing fair."

Cora thought about this for a moment. Okay . . . fair point . . . "A burglar with a sense of propriety. How interesting."

"I'm no burglar, miss."

"No?" Actually, with his accent and his clothes, he didn't seem likely to be one. Then again, with her accent and her clothes, he'd never have thought her to have been a common street urchin once upon a time either.

"I am a legitimate employee of Lord White, as a matter of fact."

A lie. She knew all of Lord White's employees—both at home and at the office. "How legitimate?"

"It depends. I've been legitimately hired, with a contract. However, having perused his lordship's inventions now, I can see that some of them might cross the line of what is considered legal. And so possibly there is a degree of illegitimacy in being such a man's lab assistant . . . Ow!"

"Sorry." Cora lightened the pressure of the blade against his skin, revealing a small red mark on his neck. With her heart pounding in her chest, she asked, "Did you say 'lab assistant'?"

"Yes."

She lowered her arm. It was starting to ache from holding the knife to his throat anyway.

It wasn't possible that after all this time Lord White had just decided to replace her. Not now, not when she was really getting into the whole inventing thing.

She made her way over to the far end of the room. Barker had done his usual remarkable job and there wasn't a trace of her earlier disaster, or goo. Though . . . she reached up to her hair and felt a dried clump of the stuff. Great. She'd gone out looking like this. *Next time, Cora, maybe glance in a mirror before you step outside.*

She collapsed into the chair at Lord White's desk, feeling small and insignificant surrounded by the large ticking machines.

"I say, what's made you so sullen?" said the young man.

"Nothing." A jet of steam exploded from the pipe to her right and just missed the top of her head. She didn't flinch. She was used to jets of steam exploding around her at unexpected intervals.

"Nothing?" asked the young man, finally coming over and leaning against the desk, looking down at her. "I'd say there's a sudden lack of enthusiasm for killing me. Here," he said, returning her pistol and standing back. "Threaten me."

"I'm not in the mood." Cora replaced her pistol in her purse and crossed her arms over her chest.

"Oh, come now . . . where's that little knife of yours . . . ?"

Cora sighed. His charm wasn't helping the situation. She had to hate him. After all, he was replacing her.

Why didn't his lordship think she was good enough?

She could feel her throat tense. *No*, she scolded herself, *I will not cry. Crying is what other girls do. I am not "other girls."*

"Fine, I'll just have to find . . . where's that cabinet . . . ?" The young man had crossed the floor to Lord White's armory and opened the door before Cora registered what was happening.

"No!" she said, standing up abruptly.

The young man turned to face her, holding a gear-covered gun so large that his lordship had crafted a device to wear around one's waist to support it.

"How about this?"

"Not the Chekhov!" Cora rushed over to his side and very gently pried the weapon from his hands. She returned it to its position in the armory and stared down at it, feeling short of breath.

"Is everything okay?" the young man asked, coming up from behind.

"What the bloody hell is wrong with you?" she said, turning

to him, her rage bringing back traces of her old accent. "You don't touch anything in the lab unless you've been instructed to. And you never, ever, go into the armory. The danger you just put us in—"

"Well, why's it unlocked, then?"

"Why should his lordship lock up anything in a secret lab? The whole point of having a secret lab is that it's secret. There's no fear of stupid young men coming along and grabbing at whatever shiny object suits their fancy without any consideration of the considerable destructive power of said object." *This? This was the person Lord White wanted to replace her? This fool?*

"I . . ." The young man was speechless.

"Yes, very well articulated. Now move out of my way. I have work to do." She pushed past him and crossed to the rear of the room where the loading doors were located. There were four large crates waiting for her to unpack. She grabbed her brass goggles and leather gloves and put them on as she made her way to the long table beside the wall next to the doors. It was a mess of tools, and Cora sighed hard as she looked for the wrenching instrument.

"Can I help?" asked the young man, appearing at her side.

"No."

"Are you trying to open the crates? I can help with that." He showed her the crowbar he'd found.

Cora found the wrenching instrument, a small piece of flat metal attached to a square box with a crank, and moved past him silently.

"Look, I think this will be a bit better," he said, following her to the crates. "I think you're more likely to break that thing you're holding than open up these boxes." He stepped in front of her and held up his hands to stop her.

"Move," she ordered.

"Come on, let me help. You shouldn't have to do such hard labor, not a pretty thing like you."

The fact that he thought a compliment hidden in condescension was the right tactic to get her to listen to him confirmed what a perfect idiot he was. Once more she decided to ignore him and, pushing past him roughly, made her way over to the first crate.

She heard him sigh and glanced up. He was standing over another crate and examining it closely. Then he whipped off his jacket, rolled up his shirtsleeves with great purpose, and with a wink in her direction, began, with great effort, to pry the lid open with the crowbar.

She took the opportunity of his distraction to give him a once-over. She decided his good looks only made him more annoying. In her anger, she started to turn the crank of the wrenching instrument, possibly a little more vigorously than usual.

At least if he'd been a poor creature that Lord White had taken pity on, all brains but hopeless in society, she could've felt bad for him. But this guy with the fancy accent and perfectly square jaw, dark hair that fell just so over his forehead as he pried the lid of the crate up, in a suit clearly made on Savile Row . . . , well, it was obvious he'd never wanted for anything.

He didn't need such an incredible opportunity as being Lord White's assistant.

There was nothing to feel for such a person but contempt.

With a final grunt from him, the lid of the crate popped off its nails and landed to the side in a loud crash. The young man looked at her with a victorious grin.

"I'm Andrew Harris, by the way," he said, as if the grand accomplishment of opening a box was worthy of adding his signature to.

Cora raised an eyebrow and stopped turning the crank on the wrenching instrument. Then, without breaking eye contact with those stupidly clear blue eyes of his, she slid the now-charged flat piece of metal under the lid of her crate. The lid exploded off the box almost instantly, flew high, and landed several feet away in two pieces.

Andrew Harris's mouth fell open.

"Cora Bell," she said. "And you've stolen my job."

Nellie Harrison

AND THEN THERE was an explosion.

"Bloody hell!" Nellie jumped back and started to laugh as the room filled with smoke. "Ha! That was . . . perfect . . ." Trying to find the window by sweeping her arms through the thick haze, she made her way to the far wall. She fell against the frame and pushed hard on the dusty surface. The smoke quickly vanished through the open window and into the sky above the bustling square.

Nellie sighed in relief and leaned back against the wall. She stared at the small tin on the floor before her, its innards black as pitch.

That'd never happened before.

"Did you see that flash, Sherry?" She grinned at the parrot, who was sitting in her cage looking annoyed. "Don't give me that look. I just thought . . ."

She'd just thought that maybe she'd give extra flash to the flashcube, and it had worked, too! Wait till they did it at the show tonight. But obviously, in this small space things got a little smoky. Though there was something to that . . . so much smoke in a small place could be a perfect screen for something.

"Bloody hell!" squawked the parrot.

"Oh, come on." Nellie crossed the room and freed the bird, who flew instantly to her shoulder and gave her ear an affectionate nip. Nellie laughed again. "You should try holdin' a grudge a wee bit longer. You don't fool anyone." She scratched under the parrot's chin, and the bird purred like a cat.

"Pretty Polly," said Nellie softly with a grin. Scheherazade was a gorgeous creature with her red, yellow, and blue feathers, and also incredibly bright. She'd learned the cat-purring trick when they'd been shopping and Nellie had stopped to scratch a stray. All it took was one meeting and Scheherazade could imitate anyone or anything. And she always seemed to use her tricks at exactly the right moment. In fact, the timing of her outbursts was so often precisely appropriate that Nellie was pretty sure the bird knew what she was doing.

If anyone understood Scheherazade, it was Nellie. Yes, it had been the Magician who had rescued the bird from a traveling circus in his homeland and brought her to London with him. But when, several weeks later, he rescued Nellie as well, the bird and the blonde had taken an instant liking to each other. Possibly because they'd gone through a lot of the same troubles. Possibly because they were both gorgeous and knew it. Whatever the reason, the two of them just had this instant bond.

"We'd better clear up before Raheem sees." She wasn't supposed to be playing around with the flashcubes. She was supposed to be gathering all the props together for the show tonight and choosing which outfit to wear.

Nellie packed the flashcube back in its case with the others and grabbed the bottomless table and the large cage holding Arsalan and Esta—two of the most stuck-up rabbits she'd ever met. If they'd been back in Ireland, they'd be dinner, not celebrities.

After she'd placed everything in a pile by the door, Nellie walked over to her costume trunk and opened it. She took a moment to gaze at its contents. She really did have some beautiful outfits. And why shouldn't she? Wasn't that why the Magician hired her in the first place? To dazzle? Okay, yes, like Scheherazade, there was more to her than just her "feathers." The Magician had taught her how to escape any bond, how to work every trick, how to bend into impossible shapes inside tiny boxes. But really, Nellie knew that her biggest selling point was her looks.

Men came to the shows to see the Great Raheem, of course, but they also came to see her: the hot young blond assistant who sparkled in the footlights. She knew it because they told her as much. They also gave her presents. That was the good part. The bad part was they'd get grabby. That part was disgusting.

Not that she hadn't encouraged male attention in the past, flirted her way to the position of top performer back at the burlesque house at such a young age (okay, she was only sixteen and a bit now, still fifteen felt so long ago to her). But she was also damn proud that she'd never done more than flirt. So many of the other girls had. She didn't blame them—some weren't quite as good as she was at making the older men think that, in time, they'd be rewarded for being nice to her. And then never actually rewarding them.

A tease. That was her reputation. But she couldn't help how she looked, could she? That was her ma and da's fault. Two good-looking people who never should have hooked up in the first place, hooking up. "I'd wanted to get rid of you," her ma had told her when she was six. "But yer da, God bless 'im, thought you'd be the prettiest babe, and so here ya are. And there he went. And yer the prettiest burden there ever was."

A pretty burden.

She'd tried to be less of one by making herself as helpful as possible. Getting top billing at the burlesque house was just part of showing that she could be useful, earn her keep. Pay the doctors when her ma took ill. She'd passed on before Nellie started making any real money, though, before the Magician had come into the picture a year later. Probably for the best, really. Ma had never trusted anyone from the "dark races."

Which Nellie found a little funny to think of now, as the Magician had been the kindest man she'd ever known.

Wow, talk about a trip down memory lane. Nellie let her mind return to the task at hand and reached into the trunk. She pulled out her pink and green outfits and laid them out on the bed.

"Which one for tonight, Sherry?"

Scheherazade ruffled her feathers at the question, so Nellie decided to be more specific. "Pink?" She pointed to the first outfit. "Or green?"

Scheherazade thought about this, examined both outfits carefully, and then finally, with a squawk, said, "Green!"

Nellie nodded. "I agree. Thanks, Sherry."

She put the pink costume back in the trunk and gathered the accessories to her green one, including the fabulous peacock feather she wore in her hair. She carefully packed it all into the other trunk with the props and sighed contentedly. Then, with Scheherazade still on her shoulder, she went to find the Magician.

And Introducing the Great Raheem

"I THINK THAT'S Lord White just stepping out of the Red Veil."

Nellie noticed the silhouetted figure of the Magician standing over at his window as she entered the room.

"What?" Nellie skipped across the room and was at the Magician's side in less than a moment, Scheherazade flying to the top of one of the bedposts. Nellie peered through the dusty window at the overcrowded square below. "Look at that. So it is! Ha!" She turned and looked wide-eyed at the Magician, who shook his head at her with a slight smile. Nellie rolled her eyes. "You pretend I'm the one who gets all bothered by gossip, but aren't you the one who called me over?"

"Are you calling me a hypocrite?" asked the Magician. His low, resonant voice was tinged with humor, as well as his usual light accent. So light he probably could have gotten rid of it, but Nellie was pretty sure he kept it in order to maintain his whole exotic-persona thing. Hey, it'd worked on her, that's for sure.

"'Course I am." She grinned, flattening her tongue between her teeth as she always did when she was feeling a bit playful.

"Well, you would be correct." His smile grew and he turned back to the window. "How fascinating. I never would have thought it of him."

"It's them quiet types that you've got to watch out for. Look at him. He's in a bad way."

"Or a very, very good way." The Magician glanced at Nellie out of the corner of his eye, and she returned the look. Then they both started laughing.

"Come, we'll go over the checklist," said the Magician, turning from the window and crossing the room toward his desk. Nellie glanced one last time at Lord White. He and the girl who was propping him up had managed to make their way out beyond the low arch that led toward the high street, where she assumed they'd hail a cab. Looking at how well they were dressed, she imagined it might even be one of those new expensive steam cabs. Nellie sighed wistfully.

"Are you sighing wistfully?" asked the Magician. He was seated now, looking over some papers. With a flick of his wrist, the sleeve of his intricately embroidered robe slid down his arm, and he picked up a pen.

"I'd love to ride in a steam cab," replied Nellie, crossing to the front of his bed and sitting at the foot.

"We don't need a steam cab; we have our wagon. A cab could never handle all the equipment."

"I know."

The Magician glanced up at her. "I had no idea."

"It don't matter much."

"I'll tell you what: Tonight, after the performance, you shall return home in a cab."

"Don't be silly . . . ," Nellie said with a laugh.

"No arguments. It's done. Now, have you collected everything? The ordeal over choosing what to wear is over?"

Nellie nodded. She stood up and walked over to where he was sitting. Then she bent over and grabbed him in a big bear hug.

"It's just a cab," he wheezed as the air was squashed out of him.

"Thank you all the same," she replied.

He waved off her gratitude as he always did, and as they started going through the checklist, she returned to the bed, which was a much fancier version of the one she slept in.

Everything about the Magician's room was, in general, a fancier version of hers. It wasn't as if he hadn't tried to help decorate her room. He'd given her some silks from his native Persia to use, and she had tried her best, hanging them from the ceiling and tacking them up to the wall, creating a sort of swath across the room. But she had none of his wall hangings, his rugs from India, his ornamental lamps from the Far East. Nor did she have the atmospheric haze that always lingered in the air of his room.

The Magician had exotic tastes and exquisite style, and the means to support both, which made it all the more surprising to some that he and Nellie lived in the rough part of the city that they did. But it made sense, once you got to know him. Part of the reason was that the square was near the docks, where the Magician could pick up his shipments, which arrived weekly. It also kept them pretty well hidden from any of the Magician's competitors.

But Nellie knew the biggest reason they lived there was that the Magician had a fantastic relationship with his fellow immigrants in the neighborhood and felt a huge sense of responsibility to them. Nellie didn't know why, but shortly after they'd moved in, the people from the area had begun coming to him with issues that needed to be resolved. He'd become like a judge to them, listening to debates and helping resolve disputes between neighbors. He'd also become the man to go to when you needed something a little unusual. Like maybe if you were looking for some infinity vines from Patagonia, or jewel-encrusted cockroaches from Tanzania, he could get them for you. And he never asked for anything in return. He was marvelous like that.

He really just wanted to help. This was his little kingdom, and he was determined to protect it. Nellie thought it was awfully sweet of him.

At last, they were done with the checklist. As usual she hadn't forgotten a thing.

She thought back to the first time the Magician had complimented her on the quality of her mind. The first man, like ever, to have done that. It had been after one of their first rehearsals. She'd been utterly terrified. After all, this dark older man had approached her, offering her a job, and she'd accepted, just like that, not knowing exactly what he expected of her. She'd seen his magic show, sure. Everyone had. He'd been the act-one closer at the burlesque house for a week at that point. A prized position. Almost as important as her act-two closer.

But she'd never seen the inside of the tricks before. The first time he showed her how the "sawing the lady in half" trick really worked, she'd been kind of disappointed. It was so straightforward, no magic at all. Just a girl bent up in a box and a pair of fake legs sticking out. And yet there was still something mystical about Raheem, even though he was always so unpretentious, never claiming he was anything other than an illusionist. Maybe it was how he looked. Maybe it was how he spoke. Maybe back in Persia, where everyone looked like that, he was nothing special and he was only something unique here in London.

Still.

So he'd shown her a card trick, and she'd pointed out that it was impossible for him to be holding the seven of clubs because she'd seen it fly by. He asked her what else she'd seen, and she counted off all the cards back to him. This is what led him to create the memory trick that she performed. Quite the crowd-pleaser. Especially as it meant that one of the men from the audience got to come up onstage and interact with her.

Of course, there was a downside to having the mind she did. It meant, first of all, that she remembered everything. And if people weren't accurate in recalling a story or something, it would seriously irk her. It also meant that the Magician had to do his hypnotizing trick on someone else. Most of what they did was just pretend, but he actually could mesmerize people. He'd tried to do it to Nellie, but he needed a mind that was willing, open. Not already full of facts and figures.

Yeah, her head was a very busy place.

Her brain could also distract her from what was going on around her—like now for example. The Magician had left and she was alone in his room.

Shite.

She crossed the hall to her room, where she saw him picking up cases to put into the wagon.

"No, let me!" she insisted.

She knew the Magician always hated when she insisted, but she wouldn't stop. Even though he'd just turned forty, he was still very strong. He kept fit through a strange set of exercises he called "yoga," during the performance of which he'd bend himself into weird shapes. Nellie had tried it a few times, but she just couldn't get into it. She was lucky that she was naturally flexible. After all, some of the positions she had to assume in the boxes, especially for the "sawing the girl in half" trick, were pretty twisty.

But Nellie didn't care how strong he was. She was constantly trying to prove he'd made the right choice in choosing her as his assistant. She would not be a pretty burden, even if that meant lugging around trunks twice her size.

"Okay," she said, when it was clear the Magician was not about to let her haul everything down to their wagon on her own. "How about I help you?"

She was awfully helpful.

An Unexpected Guest

THEY ALWAYS HAD dinner together. It was very civilized, sitting at the small table in the kitchen, a full place setting for each of them. The Magician had insisted on this from the start. It was how he always ate, even if he was alone. Dining was as much of an art as anything else. And it needed to be appreciated like anything else.

The Magician was what Nellie called totally obsessed with art. He collected everything. Paintings, sculptures, books. They went to plays all the time. Concerts. Even lectures, which bored Nellie out of her mind. He always forced her to come along to these events, saying, "You will learn to appreciate these things."

Not likely . . . how was she supposed to find some fat guy singing with a superhigh voice romantic? He looked ridiculous.

On top of everything else, the Magician was an amazing chef. This was a good thing, because Nellie stank at cooking.

The Magician could do anything, it seemed to her. How this was possible she wasn't exactly sure. She knew a bit of his history, but he always left stuff out when he spoke of it. Even when she pointed out that he had left stuff out. She knew he'd been poor. It was something he'd told her so that she could relate to him.

At first, they'd seemed so different from each other. She didn't know what to say to him, how to speak to him. Finally, he started to share his stories from back in Persia: how he grew up with nothing, but had been taught that hard work would get him where he wanted to go; how he'd watched his first magic show; how he'd spent many long hours teaching himself the tricks.

He hadn't been the Great Raheem in his homeland. He was just a young man performing little shows on street corners. One day, he volunteered to perform outside the tent of a passing circus, and it was there that he'd been spotted by the princess who had come to see the show. Nellie always thought a great love affair had happened then, but the Magician never said anything about that. Only that he was hired as a kind of court jester, a court illusionist, she supposed, performing his magic at royal balls and banquets. . . .

Why and how he'd come to London was still a mystery to her. Again, Nellie was sure it had something to do with this princess girl. Anyway, when the Magician had arrived with his strange pets and exotic appearance, he immediately landed work in the music halls. To make extra cash, he'd worked the burlesque house—which is, of course, where she'd met him. The rest was history. When he and Nellie eventually teamed up, real magic happened. She knew she was the missing link, the special ingredient that had brought the word "great" to the Great Raheem's name. And she knew he knew.

Which was why he treated her so well.

Almost like a daughter.

So odd, being appreciated. Even back when she was performing her very popular "breeches part" (dressing as a boy so that the men could stare at her legs) in the burlesque house, the owner had taken all the credit for her success since he had discovered her.

Now she and the Magician were famous. They were given gifts by royalty—she jewelry, he a painting or other piece of art or historical artifact. They were also hated. By fellow illusionists.

And she'd never been happier.

Even when he made her eat really weird stuff.

"You need your strength for tonight," said the Magician, watching her push the snails around her plate.

"Meat and potatoes. That gives a body strength, not slimy garden creatures." She picked one of them up in her fingers and looked at it closely.

"The French consider them quite the delicacy."

"Exactly. What does that tell you?"

The Magician laughed. Nellie couldn't help but grin back. She liked that he would just laugh at her jokes like that. Boys had always found it necessary to comment about how peculiar it was that she was so funny. Like girls couldn't be funny or something?

She offered the snail to Scheherazade, who was sitting on her shoulder. The parrot made a gagging sound and turned away.

"See?"

"I don't consider the opinion of a bird the last word on good taste," replied the Magician.

"Nah, but maybe on what tastes good?"

Their conversation was suddenly interrupted by a loud banging at the front door.

"You expectin' someone?" asked Nellie.

The Magician shook his head. "Strange."

The Magician started to stand, but Nellie took the chance to escape from this revolting dinner by beating him to her feet.

"I'll get it, don't want to be interruptin' your feast, now," she said. "Come on, Sherry, let's see who it is."

She walked down the dark narrow hall, past the two Turner paintings that the Magician had received last fall from the Earl of Essex, toward the small, plain front door. The banging was getting more persistent, and Nellie picked up her pace, more out of frustration than anything else.

"Keep yer shirt on," she said.

"Shirt!" agreed Scheherazade.

The banging continued as she started on the first of half a dozen intricate locks that had been custom-made to the Magician's specifications. By the time she reached the last one, Nellie was so annoyed with the nonstop knocking that she was beginning to think that she should just lock them all up again and walk away.

"What the hell do you want?" she asked, flinging the door open wide.

The man fell past her into the hallway, and she jumped out of the way just in time. Scheherazade let out a screech and flew off her shoulder, landing on the top of the door. The man convulsed on the floor, his arms and legs twitching in spasms. As he rolled onto his back, Nellie saw white foam at this mouth and finally got her voice back.

"Raheem!" she cried out.

In an instant the Magician was at her side, kneeling down to examine the man, whose eyes had now rolled into the back of his head, revealing just the whites. Nellie couldn't see what the Magician was doing, but then, suddenly, she heard a snap and the twitching stopped.

"What did you do?" asked Nellie, her voice rising in pitch.

"He was poisoned, suffering an excruciating death," replied the Magician.

"Did you . . . did you . . ."

"I broke his neck." Lost in thought, the Magician stood up and stared down at the man.

"Broke his neck—"

"Death!" interrupted Scheherazade.

"Do you, did you . . . know him?" asked Nellie, watching the Magician. Her hands were shaking, and she hid them behind her back so the Magician wouldn't see. She always tried to follow his example, to stay calm in the face of danger, but she really wasn't that good at it. Her temper especially got her in trouble. The Magician had said he'd always enjoyed her fiery personality, but she wished that in moments like these she could be cool and thoughtful, and not in a complete panic like she was now.

"I did not." He bent over again, this time going through the man's pockets. He found a few pound notes in a clip and a large square ring. He stood up. "Look at this."

He handed Nellie the ring, and she looked at the engraving on the top. It was of a bird, slender, with an elegant long neck.

"What's that?" asked Nellie, returning the ring to the Magician.

"I don't know. But I'm going to find out." Without another word, he moved past her through the open door. "Lock it shut behind me," he ordered.

She nodded and watched him as he swept down the hall. Once the last of his robes disappeared around the corner down the stairs, she closed the door and fastened all the latches as quickly as she could, realizing only after she had done so that she had just locked herself in the room with a dead body.

Michiko Takeda

AND THEN THERE was an explosion.

"You stupid, blasted Jap! What the hell did you think you were doing? You've gone and created a right mess now, haven't you? You stupid, stupid girl!"

Michiko didn't understand much of what Callum was saying to her in his sudden eruption of anger, though she understood the cause. But really. Was it her fault that she'd been taught to practice and practice until her fingers bled? Until her joints were so sore she could hardly move? Until a weapon became an extension of herself, not just something she was holding?

No. It wasn't. Just because Callum didn't share her philosophy, and the philosophy of her masters back in Japan, that did not mean she shouldn't still follow her strict regime. And it certainly wasn't her fault that Callum couldn't tell well-made weapons from crap ones. That putting crap weapons through rigorous practice might cause them to break. Even quality weapons broke every once in a while.

What she did know was that Callum was angry. She also knew why he was angry. They needed the rapiers for the demonstration that night, and she'd gone and destroyed not just one, but both.

Michiko pointed toward the arsenal.

"No!" yelled Callum. "No more. Those were the last."

That she understood. The last? No more?

What an idiot he was.

"Apologies, Callum-kun," she replied, the words coming out in an annoyingly thick accent. Why was it so hard to speak English properly? She'd been here six months already, and she was usually such a quick study.

Callum stormed out of the room and Michiko sighed. This was not what she had signed up for, all this abuse. Maybe it was a good thing that nine times out of ten she had no idea what he was yelling at her.

It hadn't always been this way. When she'd first met him, she'd admired him. She remembered the moment as if it was yesterday, even though it had been over a year now. A whole year. She'd been practicing in the yard, fighting against two of her fellow samurai apprentices. When she defeated both, boys who were several years older than she and twice her size, she'd looked up to her sensei to see if he approved. But he was deep in conversation with some foreign man. And the foreign man was staring right at her.

She remembered what it was like to look into those eyes for the first time. Those incredibly round eyes that were so unnerving. They were so open, so wide, as if they were absorbing the smallest of details about her. Not that she wasn't used to being looked at.

Men had been staring at her for years, ever since she'd been a young girl. Of course, back then their stares weren't as obvious. There was too much respect for her family and its position in society for men to just gawk at her. But the attention existed.

She saw it when her father's friends came over to play cards. And she more than noticed it the day she watched the men enter her father's study to speak with him. One after the other. It was time to begin marriage negotiations. Her mother gave her other reasons why all those men were coming over. But she wasn't stupid. She'd seen it happen with her sister. With her best friend. Even at eleven years old, she knew why they were going in to talk to her father.

That's why she'd had to get out of there.

She'd crossed the country all on her own, and was lucky to meet an old retired geisha in one of the carriages she was traveling in. The old woman took her in as her servant and spent time teaching her how to play the *shamisen* and other instruments. She'd even shown her how to perform many of the geisha dances. She took Michiko with her everywhere, almost like a pet. In fact, Michiko was nicknamed "Kitten" by the men at the teahouses. Everyone expected that someday soon she would begin her geisha training. But then one day she saw a secret underground demonstration of the now-banned art of samurai combat, and everything changed.

She ran away. Again. She was good at doing that.

What she wasn't as good at was convincing a samurai master to take a girl on as an apprentice. She knew her age wasn't a problem. The great Kyoshi Adachi had students younger than thirteen studying with him already. It was the whole girl thing.

He tested her. Over and over again. Made her do things that none of the boys had had to do. Stay out all night in meditation during the winter and then perform her *kata* when the sun rose, her body blistered from the cold.

She had to serve tea, and play music for them as they ate, as well as study and practice. She had to work twice as hard as any of the boys. But finally, on her fourteenth birthday, she was officially welcomed into the school.

When she had met Callum the next year, she hadn't been sure at first what she thought of him. Of course, he fascinated her. And when he'd ask to train with her, to have her teach him, she had been flattered. Not that she could blame him, really. Of all of Adachi's students, she was by far the best. Even if Adachi would never admit it.

Even if he refused to present her with her sword.

So when a year later Callum suggested she come back with him to England to help him teach self-defense to English ladies and gentlemen, Michiko was intrigued. Aside from the fact that she was getting tired of living a life in fear of the authorities discovering their training camp and being thrown in jail or worse, it had been pretty obvious that her sensei was not going to let her get much further in her illicit training. And here was a man who could take her to a country where she could fight openly, who, moreover, respected what she could do, so much so that he thought she could be a teacher.

How naive she'd been.

And Introducing Sir Callum Fielding-Shaw

THEY ARRIVED AT the market twenty minutes later. Michiko knew Callum probably would have preferred to go on his own, but whenever he went out in public, she went along, too. She was *his* "kitten" now, but not treated with half so much love or even respect as the old geisha woman had given her. Everyone knew that Sir Callum Fielding-Shaw had a young Japanese assistant. She was an accessory, like the customized walking stick that he'd had Japanese characters engraved on. Though Michiko was pretty sure that "a pig is a small pie" was not what he thought the characters meant.

He led her under the archway that bridged two teetering tenements and into a small bustling square.

Callum cut an impressive swath through the market. Everyone in the square knew the great fight instructor Sir Callum Fielding-Shaw. It was hard to mistake that swagger and that thick curling mustache. They knew he'd traveled the world to become a master of his craft, even returning from Japan with an ethereal-looking, exotic young female protégée. They knew he trained everyone from princes to actors and had had an audience with the Queen. More importantly, everyone knew he had money to spend. Or, at least, they thought he had money to spend.

Like everything else, the whole rich thing was just a front. Not that he couldn't have been rich. Michiko knew this. If he didn't waste his money as he did, he'd have been fine. Instead, he hosted huge parties that put him in the hole, and bought new gadgets for his physiotherapy business. He was in debt to many merchants around the city, including several tailors along Savile Row.

Michiko was pretty impressed by his ability to spend the huge fees he charged for his teaching, especially because not much of it wound up in her pocket, or the pockets of any of his servants. It was one of the reasons she was stuck working with him. All she wanted to do was to leave, but she just couldn't afford to do it. Not yet. Besides, what other job could she get, a girl who didn't speak the language? Certainly not one that allowed her to fight, and fighting made her happy.

So she'd been saving her money. Not buying the weapons she so desperately wanted. Not buying new clothes that she really needed. Just saving and saving.

So that once more she could run away.

But no one else knew about Callum's poverty, and so, as he made his way through the crowd, people would either step aside in reverence to let him by or accost him with their wares. The many Chinese would bow their heads as he passed, and he always had sweets for the beggar children who swarmed briefly at his feet and then vanished back into the crowd. Michiko stayed back, watching him, as she always did. He was completely enjoying being the center of this little world, and he had no idea that they were all just taking advantage of him.

There was a loud bang as a door at the far end of the square was flung open. Michiko turned and stared across the square. The most magnificent-looking man she had ever seen stood in the doorway. He was tall, with dark skin. He had long, thick black hair that fell down his back and a trim beard, both of which were peppered with gray. His robes—yes, he was actually wearing robes—were a deep midnight blue with an intricate abstract pattern embroidered onto them in a dark silver. They were cinched at the waist with a thick black belt. He stood for a moment, looking around the square. Michiko couldn't look away. His eyes were so bright and, even from some distance, appeared clear and sharp. Penetrating.

A small skinny man approached him with a concern, and Michiko watched the magnificent-looking man kindly but firmly send him away. She then noticed that everyone else had stopped doing whatever they were doing to watch, too. Callum was the only person still moving through the crowd, totally confused about why he was no longer the center of attention.

A neat path was cleared immediately for the dark man as he made his way through the square, directly past Michiko, and out onto the high street.

"Michiko!" She turned and rushed over to join Callum at the edge of the market by the weaponry stand run by the old

Japanese samurai. Callum yelled something at her about having his grand arrival so rudely interrupted, and she bowed her head.

"Forgiveness, Callum-kun," she said. She caught a movement out of the corner of her eye and realized the old samurai sitting in the corner had looked up as she spoke. It startled her, as typically he didn't pay any attention to her. Or really to anyone. Usually he just sat, smoking his pipe, staring into the space before him, as he let his assistants make all the deals.

Callum made a strange, exacerbated puffing sound and then turned to the old samurai's young assistant to bargain over a new case of rapiers. They began haggling over prices, and Michiko, as stealthily as she could, made her way to the far end of the table to examine the other swords. She noticed one in particular and gaped. Quickly closing her mouth tightly, she glanced over at Callum, but he wasn't paying any attention to her.

She returned her focus to the sword in front of her. It was so beautiful, and she'd never seen it at the stall before. A *katana*. The samurai's sword. The one she had never been presented with at her school, even though all the boys had one. Unable to hold back, she reached out and touched the hilt.

"*You called him Callum-kun*," said the old samurai.

Michiko's head snapped up. She was shocked to see the old samurai looking right at her, almost as if he had been looking at her the whole time. What struck her even more was the feeling that overwhelmed her at hearing her own language spoken. It was such relief to be able to understand, such a comfort.

Too bad the words were spoken to shame her.

"*Yes.*" She could feel the redness rise in her cheeks.

"*That is extremely disrespectful.*"

Michiko nodded. "*I know.*" She lowered her eyes and kept her gaze on the sword. She was feeling completely ashamed of herself at the moment.

"*Unless he is your husband.*"

"*He is not.*"

"*And even then . . .*"

Michiko nodded. There weren't that many people in this country whose opinions mattered to her. The old samurai was the rare exception. After all, no matter what he looked like now, withered and small, he'd once been a great warrior. He probably still was. He was deserving of respect, and she really wanted his respect in return. Though she knew she wasn't likely to get it.

She understood the importance of respect; it had been ingrained into her at a very young age, and it was driven home even more to her with her old geisha mistress and, of course, her sensei. She didn't want the old samurai before her to think she didn't understand how important respect was. She did. Which is why she'd decided to call Callum "kun" in the first place.

When they'd first met in Japan, she had called him "Callum-san" with all due politeness. But as she'd gotten to know him here in England, her opinion had changed drastically. And the only way she could handle her inability to express her true feelings for him without losing her job, and the security that came with it, was to undermine him in a way he would never understand. So she had switched to "Callum-kun."

The change from "*san*" to "*kun*" really didn't seem to affect him. He had no idea that "*kun*" was a term used for an inferior. He also didn't know that a woman would almost never call a man that, even one who was her equal. Plus it had made her feel so good, so like herself again, that she hadn't seen the harm in addressing him as one would address a young boy. After all, he behaved like a young boy. And he was, technically, her inferior in almost every way: class, education, and even ability. The fact that he hadn't noticed the change from "*san*" to "*kun*" was enough to make her feel she'd made the right choice. He claimed to be an expert in all things Japanese, but he didn't even know the difference between the two honorifics.

Still, she knew that none of these reasons would excuse her behavior to the old samurai. None of it mattered. She was a girl. And girls should not be so disrespectful toward men. Not even if the men were disrespectful toward them.

"*I'm sorry,*" she said, her eyes still lowered.

There was a long pause and finally he spoke.

"*Look at me, child.*"

With great effort she looked up. The old samurai took a long drag on his pipe and then exhaled slowly.

"*There is no excuse for your impropriety.*"

"*Yes, I know . . .*" and in a bold moment she added, "*It's just that he's . . .*"

The old samurai interrupted. "*No need to explain. I under-*

stand your motivation, as wrong as you might be to act on it. That man is a great fool. He talks of Japan as though he was born there, but speaks no Japanese and understands nothing of our traditions. He holds himself up as a great warrior, a fighter, a teacher even, to the people here in this city. And yet he bargains for weapons worth half of what he is offering."

Michiko didn't say anything, though she had an overwhelming desire to just pour out all the feelings she'd been bottling up for six months.

"And you, a young woman, almost still a girl, you come and see this sword and understand its worth."

"Yes."

"How?"

"I studied with his honor Kyoshi Adachi-sama."

The old samurai's expression stayed the same, but she sensed a shift in his energy.

"You?"

"Yes." Her heart was racing. How she'd longed to share that secret with the old samurai since the first day she'd met him.

"And you serve this foolish teacher?"

"I do."

"Why?"

Michiko wasn't sure she could remember the answer to that question. Adventure had been the reason once. Escaping persecution another. But after half a year living this life, her heart was aching. It was a means to an end, she reminded herself, not a permanent situation. Occasionally, too, when they traveled the country to give demonstrations of Callum's fighting technique, or performed before dignitaries, there was some fun in that.

"*It's complicated.*"

"*Did Kyoshi Adachi-sama present you with your sword?*"

Michiko shook her head. She thought back to that moment, when all the boys had gotten their swords and she hadn't.

"*What point could it possibly serve?*" Adachi had asked. "*You will marry soon. Do you intend to carve fish with it?*"

The other students had laughed. So had Michiko. She always laughed with the others. It was so easy for her to hide her real feelings. She'd been doing it since before she could remember.

"*I see.*" The old samurai was silent again.

Michiko was grabbed violently from behind and whipped around to find herself nose to nose with a red-faced Callum. He shouted something at her. He shouted it again. Then he shouted it slower in that strange accent of his. It sounded like "WAT WEH U TAWKING ABOWT?" but even at the slower pace she still didn't know what he was talking about. The best she could do was bite her bottom lip and keep silent.

Her cheek was stinging before she even registered the slap. She stared at Callum, stunned, and he seemed pretty shocked himself. It was one thing to hit her in private in his studio; it was another to do it where everyone could see.

"I'm sorry," he stammered. "Forgive me."

That she understood. Callum apologized a lot. His apologies were never sincere, more like a way to sweep the past under the rug, as if somehow an apology erased the bad behavior.

Aware that he was still watching, even if he appeared otherwise, Michiko glanced at the old samurai. He was sitting deep in thought as usual, puffing on his pipe as if they'd never had a conversation. But then, just as she was about to look away, she noticed him nod. It was such a small gesture. It seemed like . . . like he was giving her permission to do something.

Michiko looked back at her boss. Then, with downcast eyes and a humble voice, she said, "Yes, I forgive. Callum-kun."

An Unexpected Guest

MICHIKO SAT ON her bed. Her eyes closed. Trying to empty her mind. Trying to let the thoughts flow in and out like waves in the ocean. This letting the thoughts in was the easy part. But letting them go? Letting them out of her brain? That was a bit trickier.

There was only a short hour to go before they would be heading to the gala to demonstrate Callum's self-defense technique. It was how they got clients—showing them how impressive they would look. Michiko knew Callum got clients best by showing them how impressive *she* looked, that she was his secret weapon. She also knew how much he hated that this was the case.

Still, she always tried to meditate before a performance. Tried to focus on the moves she would do, her *kata*. But today all she could focus on was the old samurai. He'd talked to her. He'd been . . . impressed by her. Not that he had any reason to believe what she'd told him was the truth. But it was.

She was a warrior. A samurai.

No.

No, she really wasn't.

Stupid brain. It sometimes liked to build her up, make her feel more special than she was. But the fact was, she wasn't a samurai. She'd never been presented with her sword; she'd never completed her training. Most of all, deep down, she didn't feel like one. And she had to damn well accept that.

Meditating wasn't working today. Clearly.

Michiko rose from her bed and opened her wardrobe. It still looked odd to her, her clothes hanging as they did, and not folded neatly in a chest. She sighed and reached for her robe. Might as well get ready for the demonstration and do something productive.

Getting changed really didn't help improve her mood much. She always felt ridiculous wearing the outfit Callum insisted she wear. It basically consisted of a silk bathrobe. He'd bought it for her at the market on Canal Street. Silk, yes, and embroidered with a large yellow dragon, but it was nothing like a kimono, which Callum was clearly hoping to copy. But kimonos were expensive. Silk bathrobes were not.

It was a simple thing, flimsy, that she put on like a jacket and tied at her waist. There was no way to keep it firmly shut and there were no pieces that hid her legs when she would spin. After trying to fight with the thing on, and seeing how high it flew up and open, she'd insisted on wearing her samurai training gear beneath, a black tunic and thin trousers that were tapered and tied midcalf, to achieve some level of decency.

Dressed now, and feeling ridiculous, Michiko moved on to makeup and hair. Which was very simple. Nothing compared to what she'd seen her old geisha mistress do. A little rouge to the cheeks, red on the lips, black around the eyes, and she was done. The hair was even easier. Callum always insisted that she wear her hair down, which meant it would whip into her face when she fought.

There was a quiet tap on her door. So quiet she almost didn't hear it, and it took her a moment before she said, "Come in."

One of Callum's footmen opened the door slowly and peered around it. Callum only had two, an older man, over sixty, and this one, a boy younger than even she was. Michiko had taken to nicknaming them "Shuu" (dried meat) and "Koukou" (baby chicken). Of course, nobody knew the meanings of the words, they just put up with her calling them that.

"Yes, Koukou?"

Koukou always tried his best to communicate with her, pairing words with hand motions. It worked a little bit.

"Someone is in the alley to see you."

She understood most of the sentence except for "alley."

"Me?" No one came to see her. No one was allowed to come see her. "Who?"

"I don't know." He shrugged at the same time as he said the words even though by now she'd learned what "I don't know" meant.

"Show me." She stood up and followed Koukou out into the dark narrow hallway and down the servants' staircase to the delivery entrance. They stepped outside into the alley behind the row of terraced houses. Ah. So "alley" meant alley. Good to know.

"You can come out now," said Koukou toward the corner.

Michiko watched a boy turn the corner. She was confused. It was one of the old samurai's apprentices from his market stall. He carried something over his shoulder.

"*You are the girl from before?*" he asked. Once more Michiko found hearing her native tongue spoken such a relief. But she couldn't let this common boy know how much she appreciated it.

"*Well, clearly I am. Or do you know any other Japanese fight assistants?*"

"*What are you wearing?*"

Michiko pulled the bathrobe closer together. How embarrassing.

"*I know. Please, let's not talk about it.*"

"*Okay.*"

"*Look, either tell me why you're here or leave. I'm not allowed visitors, and really I don't need some lowly assistant judging me.*"

"*I'm sorry, I wasn't judging you, really, I just . . .*" The boy stopped talking and furrowed his forehead in thought. Then, after a brief moment, he knelt onto the ground. He removed the parcel from over his shoulder. It was narrow and long.

No. It couldn't be.

Michiko felt her heart beat so fast she thought it might burst out of her chest. This wasn't happening. And yet . . . *oh please, let this be happening.*

"*My master wanted me to give this to you. He would have come and given it to you in person, but he is old and cannot travel around as he once could.*"

The boy pulled out a sheathed *katana* from within the package. Looking at the fine decoration on the sheath, Michiko knew exactly which sword this was.

But she couldn't . . .

"I can't accept this. I just . . . your master doesn't know me. I could have been lying to him. He hasn't seen me fight. He feels pity for the girl who was struck in front of everyone in the market."

The boy held out the sword toward her. With his head bowed he said, "*Forgive me, miss, but you greatly dishonor my master speaking like that. He can see into the soul of any person. He sees the warrior in you. And any girl who could convince the great Kyoshi Adachi-sama to train her must be a true warrior. He wants you to have your sword.*"

Michiko looked at Koukou, who clearly had no idea what the hell was going on. He just stared back at her wide-eyed.

She approached the boy, her legs shaking, and knelt in front of him. He laid the sword on the ground between them, and she bowed low, feeling the gravel from the pavement on her forehead. The cold soothed her, calmed her nerves. Then, with a deep breath, she sat upright and took up the sheathed *katana* carefully. She slowly removed the sword itself, and yes, it was the one she had admired at the old samurai's stall. Her eyes welled with tears.

True warriors did not cry.

But she was not a true warrior. She was a girl being given a gift that was far too good for her. She was a girl accepting her samurai sword in a dirty back alley, with horseshit and broken glass around her. There was nothing warrior-like about any of this.

"My master says you must do everything you can to live up to the honor of being a samurai. He says that this is more than just being a good warrior; he says that this is living an honorable life and using your skills wisely. That you must help others before you help yourself. That you must bear adversity gracefully."

"*Of course . . .*" The words barely escaped her mouth. She knew what the old samurai was trying to tell her. Especially about adversity. "*Tell your master I will do everything I can to live up to the honor of his gift. And, while I don't expect I ever will, that I shall spend every moment of my life striving toward that goal.*"

The boy grinned.

"*What?*"

"*He said you might say something like that.*"

"*He did?*"

"*Yes. So he told me to tell you to not let your devotion keep you from enjoying the pleasures of life.*"

"*In other words . . .*"

"*Don't forget to have fun.*"

Michiko laughed. It felt good to do it, a release. She started to rise, when the boy held up his hand.

"*Aren't you forgetting something?*" he asked.

Forgetting something . . . "*Of course.* Koukou, money!" Koukou turned in a full circle for some reason at that order, and then looked at her, panic-stricken.

"*No, no,*" said the boy. "*Well, yes, thank you. But no. I haven't told you the name my master gave this sword for you.*"

The name. Of course. She felt emotion well up inside her again.

"Oh, yes. Please. What is its name?"

"The name of the sword reflects the soul of the warrior."

"Yes, yes, I know. Get on with it . . ."

"The Silver Heart."

The Silver Heart.

Well, that did it. No stopping her now. And the tears flowed freely.

So Isn't It About Time for That Gala Everyone's Been Going on About?

SEE CORA ANGRY.

See Cora tired.

See Cora in a bright red dress that makes her look super hot but not giving a shit.

"Miss Bell, you look charming, as always." It was that guy. That guy who was always first to seek out Lord White at these events. Yet for some reason his name always slipped her memory. Marley? Masterson?

"Mr. Marshall, a pleasure." She extended her hand and he kissed it. Or rather pressed his open mouth to it, leaving a nice wet ring of saliva behind.

Yuck.

Quickly she was forgotten as Mr. Marshall set to wooing her boss. It was just a pleasantry, the whole "complimenting Lord White's assistant" thing. Like answering those "questions three" to the troll at the bridge in the fairy tale. Humor the assistant; get to the man.

But the fact was, she did look charming. She looked smokin'. Head to toe in red satin, her wavy dark hair piled high on her head. A diamond necklace around her neck worth more than what most of these men earned in a year. She knew his lordship had ordered her an outfit that would make her stand out like crazy in a crowd. She was a representation of his awesomeness. His beacon. And there was no missing her tonight.

Even the Prime Minister, such a shy stuttering man, had to say something about her appearance.

"Miss . . . Bell. You look . . . lovely."

"Thank you, Mr. Prime Minister. And thank you so much for inviting me to this wonderful gala. I look forward to the demonstrations of modernity."

"Me . . . too."

So, yes. She looked good. No question. But she was still upset. Things hadn't ended too well with Mr. Harris. She'd taken him up to meet with his lordship in his room, and yup, it turned out Lord White had hired him all right.

After Mr. Harris left, Lord White had tried to placate her by giving her the dress and the jewelry. But that only made her angrier. "Clearly this is all you think of me, some life-size doll for you to dress up. It's obvious you don't think there's much else going on inside."

So, possibly she radiated beauty tonight. Or possibly she radiated rage and everyone was mistaking it for something else.

She and Lord White took their tour around the home. It belonged to . . . someone. Some fellow from the House of Lords.

It was big. It was baroque. It was silly.

It was also very crowded.

Lord White was very popular—of course he was. So they had to stop to chat with everyone. He was so good at seeming genuinely interested in every gentleman, even though it was Cora who whispered the name of each one into his ear. She couldn't stand most of them, but you never knew when one would suddenly become important. It was totally unpredictable who would rise up and who would fall. She'd have thought intelligence, at least, would have been an important quality in a member of Parliament, but really it seemed that breathing was the only requirement.

They finally made their way to the huge glassed-in conservatory where the exhibits were being displayed. This she'd actually been looking forward to, though she knew Lord White wasn't as keen. Being an inventor himself—okay, a secret inventor—he was never that impressed with "modern" ideas. He'd scoffed when he'd seen the invitation: "The Prime Minister invites you for an evening of modernity." Since his brain seemed to mostly exist in the future anyway, she guessed "modern" to him was practically outdated.

Twisted logic that.

But Cora loved this stuff, and she released his lordship's arm in order to have a closer look. Her eye was immediately drawn to half a dozen toy-size mechanical men. They were made of copper and trapped in some kind of tiny corral. They walked around, eyes glowing red. When they walked into one another, they'd get into little fights. One tried bopping another over the head, but this attempt just made the bopper fall over. It was very cute.

She moved around to the side of the room, where there was a screen with moving images of two clowns projected on it. Clowns made her uncomfortable, so she continued to the model of a dirigible with a box in front of it that said, "Place your card inside and win a ride!" Cora had never had the chance to go up in a dirigible, though she'd always wanted to. They weren't exactly common. Only royalty were legally allowed to use them for travel. Other than that they were used for aerial warfare and emergency services. Some international agreement had been reached a couple years back preventing everyday citizens from piloting their own. Chaos. Cora remembered hearing that word a lot at the time. She slipped one of Lord White's cards into the box.

There were other neat things to see. Moving instruments using clockwork pieces. A mechanical sculpture that did nothing but shoot steam every eighteen minutes, for some reason. And there was a glowing piece of cavorite on display, that strange green mineral that had been unearthed the year before. It floated in its glass box, totally oblivious to the laws of nature. "Courtesy of Dr. Welland" was inscribed on the brass plaque beneath it.

By the time she'd made it around the whole exhibit, Cora kind of understood why Lord White was never that excited by modern displays. Nothing she'd seen was really anything better than what she saw daily in his lordship's lab. And certainly there was nothing that compared to the weapons he'd invented. Though maybe others were doing weapons, too, and it was just that no one wanted to share that kind of information. After all, inventing weapons is one thing, but letting someone get their hands on them is another.

Stupid rich young male lab-assistant replacements were dangerous enough with such weapons, let alone, you know, evil people.

A bell sounded and a footman instructed everyone to congregate in the ballroom.

Cora hurried over, but all the seats were already taken, so she leaned against one of the pillars dividing the room in two. In front of her was a makeshift stage with curtains hiding a backstage area on either side. There were footlights along the bottom and a couple of theatrical lights hanging above. How lovely. Their own tiny theater. Cora hoped the entertainment would begin soon. She was starting to feel a little restless, and anything to distract her thoughts from the intolerable Mr. Harris would be very welcome.

The Show

NELLIE WATCHED THE Japanese girl lay out all the weapons on the table before her. It was a strange combination of items. There were swords she recognized, but then there were also odd-looking daggers and sticks on chains that looked pretty threatening. Then there were the parasol and gentleman's walking stick that seemed totally out of place.

The girl noticed her watching and looked at her suspiciously.

"Hi there!" said Nellie with a wave. The girl just looked back down at her weapons. "Nice to meet you, too," muttered Nellie to herself.

She returned to unpacking, which was pretty much what everyone backstage was doing. There was a manic energy in the air that Nellie found energizing. But she knew the Magician hated it. That's why he was in the corner currently, meditating. Adorably, so was Scheherazade, standing on the floor beside him, her eyes shut tight.

Ridiculous bird.

Nellie looked herself over in the mirror. Her makeup was

perfect, her hair gorgeous, and yet . . . there was a dead body waiting for her at home. Okay, so maybe that had nothing to do with how she looked, but that's how her mind was working right now. Change into her costume. Dead body in living room. Set up the props. Dead body in living room. Flirt with the cellist from the quartet. Dead body in living room.

They'd moved the body from the hall to the large sofa in the living room when the Magician had returned. Nellie had insisted they cover it with a sheet. She just didn't think it was right to have a body lying on the sofa, like it was some friend staying overnight or something.

As to their investigation of who the mystery man might be, the Magician had learned only one thing from his contacts. He'd learned that the bird on the ring was the emblem of the Society of Heroes, a group of science-minded gentlemen who met on occasion. To what end, the Magician had not been successful in determining.

"Heroes? Well, they think highly of themselves, now, don't they?" Nellie had said.

"It's actually very interesting. They are named after an ancient Greek scientist, named Hero or Heron. A gentleman who evidently invented the steam engine centuries before our time."

"Heron . . . so that explains the bird, then."

"Exactly."

So the guy was a scientist. Or liked science. Or liked societies. Fantastic. Still didn't change the fact that there was a dead body in their living room!

She glanced at the Japanese girl in the mirror. Maybe she should ask to borrow a weapon.

Yeah, like she'd know what to do with one of those things.

And like a weapon would be much use against an already dead guy.

Sigh.

THE BLOND GIRL was staring at her again. Why did she keep doing that? Probably for the same reason everyone stared at her. She was "different." None of them seemed to understand that, to her, all of them were different, too. That they all looked a little wrong to her. And so many of them in one room totally freaked her out. The tall pasty one who was speaking with Callum at the moment looked particularly unpleasant and sweaty.

Focus on the task ahead. Michiko looked at the weapons now laid out in front of her on the table and started to put them in performance order. The *katana* was placed last, and for a moment she thought of the far more elegant and deadly version of the weapon hidden in her wardrobe at Callum's. She would never dare use it in a show. Even with Callum's stupidity about weapons, he would recognize one he didn't own. And there was no mistaking the Silver Heart.

She felt a great welling of emotion fill her up again, and she had to close her eyes for a few moments to calm herself. She'd noticed that the dark man from the market was actually meditating. But she felt too vulnerable to do the same.

There was a sudden quiet, and Michiko opened her eyes.

The show had started. Five acts were scheduled to perform. She knew that she and Callum would be last, so she moved over to the wings, from where she could watch the stage.

The show began with a musical number, something very funny, it seemed, because the audience laughed often. Michiko liked the melody. It was happy, and it raised her spirits. She should have been filled with joy after being given her gift this afternoon, but the moment had been so confusing. And she couldn't help but feel unworthy. Worse, the pressure to be worthy of it all was daunting. She'd gone from pure joy to pure panic pretty quickly. Now she was just feeling depressed. So the happy music was more than welcome.

Next was some kind of scientific demonstration. An older man with white whiskers sticking out of his chin was holding on to a small box with two small wheels on it. When the man pressed a button on the side, a model of a bird sitting center stage took off in flight around the room. There was something green glowing deep inside it, causing a green light to follow it along the ground wherever it went. When the bird was sent out over the audience, the eager faces of the spectators glowed green, too.

After that was a dance presentation. Not very exciting after the mechanical bird, and really, really weird. The music seemed to be a combination of many different styles. She even recognized some Japanese-like melody lines. The dancers also seemed to be doing every different style of dance, from ballet, to Chinese opera, to something reminiscent of the dances the old geisha woman had shown her. None of it worked well together. And the dancers just didn't seem that good. Maybe Michiko was being a bit judgmental, but as she once again took a peek at the audience, she didn't think she was the only one thinking this.

Then. Then was the magic show.

CORA NOTICED THAT the audience got extra quiet all of a sudden. The orchestra started to play a strange exotic melody, a tune that evoked sand dunes under a red-hot sun. Then a young woman stepped through the curtain, and the audience began to applaud. If they were that impressed by a girl walking out onstage, what would they do with themselves after the first trick? Cora wondered. She assumed, rightly, that many in the audience had already seen the Great Raheem perform with his stunning blond assistant and that she was pretty popular in and of herself.

Cora could see why. It wasn't just her startlingly bright hair that drew attention; she was pretty much just perfect-looking in general. She wore an emerald green sleeveless dress with a skirt that went just below her knees, and matching green stockings like the dancers wore in Paris. The whole ensemble was covered in a glitter that, from the audience's point of view, made her look like she had an angelic glow. Her hair piled high on her head was accented by a marvelous peacock feather, and on her shoulder was the most beautiful bird Cora had ever seen. With a squawk, it flew off her shoulder and, imitating the mechanical bird from earlier, did a full tour of the room, until it landed on a perch to the side of the stage.

The Magician's assistant wheeled a large box into the center of the stage and opened its side to reveal its emptiness to the audience. She closed it again and covered it with a thick cloth of deep silver that sparked and flickered in the candlelight. Then, after turning the box around in one full circle, she climbed up on top of it, pulling the cloth up to her chin as if she was about to change behind it. Cora imagined that most of the audience would have been quite happy just to watch that. But then there was a huge bright flash that caused a collective gasp, and the assistant pulled the cloth high to cover her whole person, held it for less than a moment, then dropped it, revealing the Great Raheem himself standing in her place. Going from a petite blonde in green to a dark man over six feet tall wearing a turban and gold robes was pretty amazing.

There was a huge round of applause at his appearance, and after he jumped down to the stage, the applause turned into cheers when he revealed his attractive assistant lying on her side, knees up to her chest, in the previously empty box.

"*How on earth did he do that?*" Cora asked herself, absolutely amazed.

MICHIKO WATCHED THE man from the market. She had never thought she would see him again, let alone twice on the same day. When she'd seen him the first time, she'd almost thought he was some kind of vision; he had appeared and vanished so quickly. But here he was again. And there was nothing remotely mystical about him. He was, it turned out, nothing more than an illusionist.

How disappointing.

And yet.

Michiko couldn't help but be impressed with his opening trick. Even standing to the side with a view the audience couldn't see, she'd no idea how he'd done it. The fact was, even if he wasn't anything more than a magician, at least he was a skilled performer, and there was something to respect in that.

She watched as the Magician and his assistant went from trick to trick. Every move was choreographed, she could tell. But only once did she get a fleeting glimpse of the inside of a trick, when she noticed the ear of a second white rabbit hidden in the small black table.

She worried that there was no way she and Callum could top this performance. She also thought it was odd that they were going last instead of the magic show, which would have been a much grander finale. Then the thought struck her that it was probably Callum's fault. He'd probably pushed for the last spot. Michiko sighed. There was no doubt about it. Callum was just the sort of man to do something so stupid.

The Great Raheem's performance was over after twenty minutes, though it seemed like he'd been onstage for much less time. He'd even brought the Prime Minister's son onstage to help him with one trick. The boy had turned a deep red when it was explained that he'd have to tie the assistant's wrists together.

Michiko could feel the familiar fluttering in her stomach as the Great Raheem and his assistant swept offstage, the applause still loud and appreciative from the other side of the curtain.

"Death!" came an abrasive squawk, and Michiko looked up at the Great Raheem's parrot, now resting on some trunks. It sat, in profile, looking at her through one eye.

"*Death*" was one of the few words Michiko understood. A word that she'd learned very early on when practicing the art of combat.

Startled, she stared back at the bird, and it, unblinking, returned the gaze. Was it a threat? Was it a sign? Was it a coincidence?

The Magician's assistant called out, and the bird spread its wings and took off with a few labored flaps in the air. Michiko watched it fly over to its cage and stroll inside.

"Michiko!" Her name. She turned to see Callum gesticulating toward her wildly. She imagined that meant she was on. She grabbed her parasol and double-checked that her daggers were secure at her waist.

And then, in what seemed like a magic trick itself, she was on the rickety stage in front of a crowd of one hundred or so and in the middle of demonstrating a fight. She and Callum always began with props belonging to the typical English lady or gentleman so the audience would be able to relate and understand right from the start how useful Callum's self-defense system was. Michiko never much enjoyed fighting with the parasol, but she could fight with anything, and the freedom she experienced in any fight made her feel most like herself. It made up for feeling totally stupid fighting with a lacy umbrella.

Soon it was time to move on to other weapons—"real" weapons—and then, finally, Callum presented her to the audience. This was Michiko's favorite part because this was when she got to do her *kata*, albeit with his very cheap *katana*. She loved this moment for two reasons: First, and most importantly, the *katana* was her weapon of choice.

Second, it was a solo act. No Callum.

CORA WATCHED THE young Japanese girl perform a strange, dancelike routine with the slender sword. It was one of the most beautiful things she'd ever seen. Of course, the girl herself was beautiful, her thick, long black hair flying across her face as she moved across the stage. She was such a slender creature. Cora had been impressed at how effortlessly she'd managed to fight off Mr. Fielding-Shaw's aggressions toward her earlier in the demonstration. But now the girl was on her own on the stage, and Cora could see that she didn't use fighting just to protect herself. It was an art. It was . . . spiritual.

It occurred to Cora that possibly the girl was more than just an assistant. She'd noticed that whatever weapon the girl picked up, even the parasol, it had instantly become an extension of herself. Fielding-Shaw was pretty skilled with the weapons as well, but they always appeared gripped tightly in his hand, as if he was afraid he might lose them at any moment.

He'd introduced her as "Michiko." A fellow student in

Japan. Cora wasn't so sure that this was the truth. Or if it was, Fielding-Shaw and the girl certainly hadn't been in the same class.

The sword dance was over, and Michiko bowed low. There was a silence as she did so, a collective breath held by the audience. And then she stood upright and gazed out at the crowd with a defiant expression.

The audience erupted into cheers and rose to their feet. Michiko bowed again, and Mr. Fielding-Shaw joined her. Whether he'd meant for her dance to end the demonstration, it was impossible to know. The fact was, there was nothing he could do now except bow with her.

And, with that, the show was over.

Cora decided it was time to seek out Lord White. She glanced around the room and found him sitting just down the row next to her, slumped in his chair, eyes shut tight. Cora could hear the rhythmic breathing from where she stood. Instantly, she was at his side, giving him a firm shake.

"What? What?" Lord White's eyes popped open in their usual startled fashion.

"You were asleep," Cora hissed into his ear.

"Hardly criminal," replied his lordship, blinking hard a few times.

"You missed some truly spectacular presentations."

"Were they startlingly modern?" asked Lord White, rising as the crowd began to file out of the room.

"Stop it." She wasn't in the mood for his sarcasm.

"I've no idea why 'modern' has become such a catchphrase of late, but I have no interest in it." He nodded to Mr. Williams, one of his fellow MPs, who said a brief hello.

"I know. There's no one quite as modern as you, but do keep your attitude to yourself. You were the one who wanted to do business this evening, not me." She had little patience for him tonight. Especially not after her whole encounter with Mr. Harris.

"Yes, yes." He gave her hand a pat and took a survey of the room. "Mr. Carter," he called out. A tall pasty man standing in the doorway looked his way. "I say, cigars and brandy in the library?"

Mr. Carter nodded. "It's about time." He led the way, and Cora and Lord White followed.

"Do behave yourself," whispered Cora.

"Behaving myself defeats the purpose, Miss Bell. No man earns success by behaving himself."

"So I have come to understand." They stopped outside the library. Cora shook her head. "Well, have fun, then."

"But not too much." He gave her that smile that always calmed her down a bit. There was nothing special about it, really. It was just that it was so totally sincere.

She reached up, adjusted his tie, and brushed the lapels of his jacket flat. "Just get done what you need to."

"I always do, Miss Bell." He gave her a wink and opened the door to the library.

As always, Cora got a peek into the forbidden world of men.

A place where decisions were made, dirty jokes were told, and fantastic whiskey was drunk.

Then the door closed and Cora was back where she belonged.

She sighed.

It was that time of night.

Time to escape.

After the Show

NELLIE WAS STARVING. She was always starving after a performance, but she was extra-starving now. After all, no matter what the Magician said, snails were just not filling. And she hadn't even been able to eat any of the buggers with the arrival of the soon-to-be dead body. Mr. Foamy Scientist Guy.

Now it wasn't that she hadn't expected the attention. A large crowd of mostly older men had gathered around her in an instant, giving her no time even to change out of her costume. Not that she imagined they minded her being still in costume. She seriously needed food, and instead she was being offered glass after glass of champagne. One had been more than enough. Even just a couple sips had caused her head to feel light and fuzzy.

Food. Anything for food.

"Has anyone ever told you how stunning you are?" asked a pimply boy, the only guy who was around her age in the crowd.

"Yes." Of course, she'd been told that. That's all anyone ever told her.

The pimply boy laughed kind of like a donkey.

Someone else grabbed her elbow and wrenched her around to face him. By now all these men were starting to look alike, pasty, hair matted to their heads with sweat. The degree to which each man was old, fat, and drunk varied, but if any of them wasn't in one of these conditions yet, there was no doubt that in a short time he would be. The man who had so violently assaulted her elbow was in the later stages of all three.

She jerked her arm free from his death grip and almost gave him a good smack across the face, but she knew that the Magician would definitely not approve of that. Well, he'd approve of her motivation, just not of her action.

"I'm going to find food," she announced loudly, and pushed her way violently past the gross man.

Many hands attempted to stop her from leaving, making her feel hot and uncomfortable. She tried to flick them off with a shake, like when a horse shudders to get rid of a fly. There were too many of them. She pushed and pushed and finally was free of them all, practically running away from them. The laughter that followed her exit made her feel so angry and so . . . small . . . that when she turned the corner, she stopped and kicked the wall.

Why couldn't she get used to that kind of attention? Sure she'd been pretty for forever, but this whole "guys coming up to her and even touching her" thing had only really started happening in the last two years. It was one thing to be a superstar onstage, but being so "popular" offstage still totally freaked her out. Her breathing always got shallow, her face hot.

Nellie stormed off to find the kitchen. She couldn't make

herself feel better, but she could make herself full. It was a maze downstairs, but eventually she found the huge room, which was full of chaos and wonderful, wonderful smells.

The cook didn't seem to like her at first, probably because of the way she was dressed, but after a few quick minutes of conversation, Nellie won her over. The line about how the food had been so popular upstairs that she hadn't gotten a chance to try it worked particularly well. In the end, she was begrudgingly given a Cornish pasty. It was better than nothing.

She wandered back out into the hall, inhaling the pasty, aware that she looked hardly ladylike. Then again, she wasn't really a lady, now, was she? She turned a corner as she finished it, not really feeling full, but at least feeling better. The hall she was in was different from the one she'd been in before, narrow, low-ceilinged, poorly lit. Damn. She'd got turned around somehow.

She needed to get back upstairs soon. She didn't want the Magician to worry, plus he'd promised she'd get to take a cab home, and she didn't want to miss out on the chance. She turned back the way she'd come.

"Hello, there."

Standing in her path was a footman, some young guy who looked like all the other footmen.

"Hiya," replied Nellie, walking forward. He took a step to the side to block her way. Nice.

"Ain't you pretty."

Nellie sighed. "Uh, thanks." She kept her eyes lowered.

"Tomorrow's my day off."

Nellie was starting to feel uncomfortable. It was creepy standing alone in a strange hallway with this guy. "Good for you."

He took a step toward her, and she took a step back.

"Come to the pub with me."

"No, thank you."

"No?"

"I'm . . . busy tomorrow."

The footman reached up to push a stray curl away from her cheek. It made her flinch. He started to laugh. "You scared of me?"

Yes. "No."

He laughed some more. And took a step closer. Nellie found her back against the wall. How'd she get turned around like that? Her heart was racing, and she could feel herself start to panic. The footman could obviously sense this.

"Hey, just sayin' you're sweet. Ain't nothin' to be all fussed about."

"I know. But could you back off?"

The footman smiled. "I think you like it."

"I think I don't."

"I think you do."

"No. I really don't think she does," said another voice. And then the footman got it—right across the kisser.

CORA HAD ESCAPED from the din of small talk by hastening down the servants' staircase, much to her relief. Okay, sure, several servants she'd passed had given her some pretty filthy

looks, but Cora really didn't care. All that mattered was that she wasn't upstairs anymore.

The downstairs was considerably larger than it was at Lord White's, though probably that had something to do with a secret lab taking up most of the space at his place. She thought it was interesting, the difference between the atmospheres in homes. Even in the servants' part of this house, there was a general air of superiority.

She'd made her way down the wide hall toward a narrower one that branched to the left when she heard voices. Normally she'd try to avoid any voices that were emanating from around corners, but there was a quality to this conversation, combined with a strange shuffling sound, that made Cora curious. She took a moment to steady herself and then turned the corner. One of the footmen had the Magician's assistant backed up against the wall. The girl looked really scared. Who could blame her? What a sleaze.

Cora didn't know why, but seeing this footman attempting to take advantage of the assistant made Cora's blood boil.

"I know. But could you back off?" the assistant was saying.

"I think you like it," replied the footman,

"I think I don't."

"I think you do."

Cora approached the footman from behind. "No. I really don't think she does." He turned in surprise at the new voice, and she punched him in the face.

"Bugger and hell!" she said, holding on to her fist. She'd

never punched anyone before, and prior to this moment, the concept that her hand might hurt as much as his face had not occurred to her.

The footman massaged his jaw for a second, looking at her in total shock. Cora backed off slightly as he walked toward her. *Oh shit.* Then he struck her, palm open, across her cheek. Now, *that* was a feeling she was very familiar with, from her days on the street.

"You arse!" This time he turned back to look at the assistant, who kneed him in the groin. Quite firmly. So firmly that he let out a high-pitched squeal, much like a mouse might do if it had been squashed underfoot. He doubled over.

Cora was about to express her gratitude when the Magician's assistant kicked her leg up high and then brought her heel across the footman's head, putting him out like a light. She stood over the body for a moment, then looked at Cora.

"I think maybe that wasn't necessary," the assistant said, biting her lower lip.

"Maybe."

"When I get mad, I go a bit overboard."

I know the feeling, thought Cora. She knelt down and examined the footman. He was still breathing, thank goodness. The heel of the assistant's boot was a formidable weapon and could have gone clear through the man's skull if applied with enough force. "That was an impressive kick."

"Never used it for violence before. Normally just kick high in the show."

"Yes, I saw that earlier. You're very skilled."

"Thank you." The assistant smiled broadly, brushing one of her blond curls from her forehead. "And thanks for the help."

"Well, I hardly think my blow even bruised him." Though *her* knuckles were still sore.

"You distracted him good and proper. Wouldn't have had the confidence to do what I did without you takin' charge like that."

"Well . . . glad I could help, then." Then she added, "I'm Cora Bell." She extended her hand.

"Nellie Harrison," replied the assistant, taking it firmly. Almost a little too firmly. She pumped Cora's arm up and down with great enthusiasm, and though, yeah, it was a slightly painful experience, Cora liked her general level of energy. Having spent so much time with the upper classes, Cora had grown familiar with the accepted tradition of never demonstrating passion about anything. It was nice to meet someone so artless.

There was a moan, and they turned to look at the footman. He pushed himself up to his elbows and then noticed the two of them staring down at him.

"Get on with you!" ordered Cora, with an edge to her voice that she saved for such characters. The footman took to his feet like a newborn foal falling over himself. Once standing, he lumbered off down the hall.

The girls turned to each other again.

"It's very nice to meet you," said Cora.

"Likewise. And cheers for the rescue," replied Nellie.

"My pleasure. Though I think you'd have done just fine without me."

"Like I says before, not so sure about that."

"Well, you're welcome, again." There was a slight awkwardness, the kind that always came when saying good-bye to someone one had just met. Ought one to be familiar, formal . . . they had just shook hands. Should Cora extend hers again? A little nod? Her thoughts were interrupted by:

"Say, how you gettin' home?"

Oh. Well . . . "Probably with his lordship in his carriage. Though"—she thought of Lord White getting drunk in the library—"when that might be, God only knows."

"I'm takin' a steam cab," Nellie announced. She said it with great pride, though Cora could hardly understand why.

"Well . . . that's good."

"You want to share it with me? Could drop you off at home."

Cora was about to say no automatically when she realized that the suggestion was actually a good one. She'd be able to leave this horrible party, getting home at a fairly reasonable time. She might even be able to do a bit of reading, something that had become a luxury of late.

"That sounds like a very good idea, actually."

"Wonderful!" Nellie linked her arm in hers. "We can get to know each other better, and the best part, of course, we'll get to ride in a steam cab!"

"Uh, yes," Cora replied as she led the two of them down the hall to the servants' staircase. "How thrilling."

The London Fog

"GO HOME, MICHIKO."

Sit, Michiko. Beg, Michiko. Play dead, Michiko.

It hadn't been her fault that everyone had wanted to speak with her after the show. Though it was pretty intimidating having all these people crowd around, talking loudly at her. A huge wall of sound. Well, maybe it was a bit her fault. But she'd just been doing her job, after all. Just doing the fights like they'd practiced. Her *kata* was the same one as always. Hadn't Callum wanted this kind of attention? Watching him exchange cards with person after person was proof that his plan had worked. He ought to be thrilled.

"Go home, Michiko." Blunt. To the point. A hiss in the ear.

He was drunk. Already. Pushing his way through the crowd, laughing loudly. Giving big hugs to some of the men.

"Now, aren't I good teacher? If I can teach a Jap like her, I can teach anyone. Your wives, daughters, yourself."

Again, she had no clue what he was talking about. Until: "Go home, Michiko."

He handed her the satchel of weapons. More like threw it at her.

And that was that. Apparently he thought the best way for her to get home was to walk. Carrying all the weapons with her.

Well, she was fine with that. She was done with the loud, claustrophobic party. Besides, she could use the alone time, and it wasn't that late anyway. She liked walking, and she had grown so used to lugging around the weapons that they were hardly a burden.

So she had left. Many people had tried to convince her to stay, but Callum had helped her to the front door. Had also slammed it shut behind her.

"Go home, Michiko." How she wanted to. She missed Japan—the countryside, the food. Understanding what the hell people were saying.

As she started the long journey back to Callum's, the air was damp, as it always was. The fog was thick. As it always was. London at night, Michiko had quickly learned, was nothing like London during the day. During the day, the streets were crowded, the city teemed with people, like maggots feeding on roadkill. But at night . . . at night the streets grew quiet. The fog unrolled itself over the Gothic towers, smothering the city in an eerie silence. The light from the streetlamps created halos in the white. Figures appeared and then vanished as if they'd never been at all. And you could find yourself walking right into a wall or the river if you weren't careful.

Shadows would appear in the distance. Shadows that could be anything, that could tease the imagination.

Like the one looming before her now.

Michiko wasn't scared of illusion, but still. She felt unnerved. She rarely felt unnerved without cause. She trusted her instincts. Something was off about this giant shadow.

She approached it carefully.

The giant shadow turned out to be a carriage. Motionless. No driver. The horses standing still, ears twitching as if they were waiting for something.

"Hello?" she called out. Her voice sounded loud in the empty street. One of the horses snorted at her. This wasn't right; this was so many versions of what wasn't right. She put down the weapons as softly as she could and pulled out the *katana*. Then, preparing it for use behind her back, she approached the carriage.

"Hello?" she said, more softly. She was close enough now that she could see that one of the doors was standing open, the dark purple window drapes pulled free at one side from their hooks. She took a few more steps and her foot accidentally kicked something. She looked as the something rolled a few feet then stopped. She leaned down to examine it more closely. On the ground staring up at her was the old, whiskered face of the man from the gala. The one who'd flown the mechanical bird around the room. His eyes were expressionless. His head . . . bodiless.

Michiko felt numb. She was staring at a head. A head. That looked to have been divorced from its body surprisingly cleanly. A very clean cut indeed. The arteries and cartilage severed as if sliced with scissors.

Then.

There it was.

The sound she'd been waiting for.

A footstep in the dark and fog.

She tightened her grip on the *katana* and spun, her opposite knee on the ground and her other leg stretched out to the side. She blocked the blade coming for her jugular. She rolled to one side and was instantly up on her feet. The blade of her assailant came fast and furious, and each time she parried an attack, she tried to get take a peek at the man she was fighting. All she caught a glimpse of was a bowler hat and a long dark trench coat.

And then her sword shattered. One piece flying up and embedding itself in her cheek.

Pain. Just a little.

And anger.

Damn you, Callum. Damn you for being so cheap.

And so stupid.

As the figure circled her like a lion examining its prey, Michiko cursed herself. Why hadn't she just brought the Silver Heart with her tonight? If she had, its blade certainly would not be in pieces at her feet. Who cared what Callum thought? Even if he noticed the new sword, what would he do? Yell? Hit her a couple times when they got home? Nothing significant.

Now she was about to die.

That was significant.

A samurai enters every duel expecting to die.

Another sign that she really wasn't one. She had not expected this outcome. Well. If she was going to face death, she was going to do so with honor.

"Do it fast." She fell to her knees and held her chin up high. She could see more of the figure now, a face hidden in shadow, but she could see he had a thick beard.

Oh, who cared.

The figure walked around behind her. Then he started to laugh.

And suddenly Michiko didn't feel like a samurai at all. She felt like a little girl. She couldn't accept death, she just couldn't. She feared it. She feared it with every fiber of her being. Hot tears filled her eyes. You're weak. You're weak and not worthy of the Silver Heart.

In a rush of feeling, she sent out a stream of Japanese at her assailant. It was some of the nastiest things she could think of calling him. She ended it with "coward," the nastiest of all.

Then the world went black. But even as it did, she understood.

Not death, then.

Not this time.

Three Girls, Together at Long Last

"THERE'S A *WHAT* in your sitting room?" Cora jumped in her seat, but not from alarm, just the nasty pothole they'd just gone over. Scheherazade squawked at the same moment, and Nellie saw Cora eye the bird with uncertainty.

She reached up and scratched the parrot sitting on her shoulder. "A dead body," she repeated. "And it's really not right for me to be tellin' you all this, but I just can't keep it in sometimes, you know? When I feel things, I just got to say them. You know? And I'm headin' back there right now. I know he's dead and all, but I don't mind tellin' you, it gives me the heebie-jeebies."

Nellie knew she shouldn't be saying any of this to a stranger, but after all, the stranger had saved her, and so she couldn't be all that bad, now, could she?

"I don't blame you for your concern, but you really ought to know that the biggest problem with having a dead body in the house, I imagine, is the smell. Really, of all the bodies in the world, a dead one is the least offensive, when you think about it," replied Cora.

Nellie thought about it.

"Still scares the shite out of me."

"Well . . . yes . . ."

"Not sayin' it makes sense."

"A lot of what we feel isn't rational. I, for example . . ." Cora stopped speaking. Nellie watched her think something over. Then: "Well, hang it all. You've shared with me, I can share with you. But this is top secret, okay? My reputation, indeed my job, depends on your discretion."

Nellie nodded. She loved secret stuff. Anything, even the simplest gossip, excited her. Unlike some, however, she had no need to spread the news about. She just liked knowing for her own sake.

"Cross my heart and spit in yer eye," she said.

"My eye?"

"What's the secret?"

She listened as Cora explained about her boss and his lab. About how she got to work with all kinds of cool equipment and assist with all these crazy experiments. Then she started on about a someone named Mr. Harris:

"And it's not his fault that Lord White hired him—after all, he was just applying for a job. But I hate him for taking something that I thought was special to me away. Not that it's even been taken away. You see? Emotions aren't rational. I ought to be happy that there's someone to share the workload, and instead, all I can think of is punching him in the face."

"Do you fancy him?"

"What?"

"Oh, is he that ugly, then?"

". . . No . . . I mean, that's not the point . . ."

"No you don't fancy him, or no he's not ugly."

"Uh . . . well, both."

Nellie nodded.

Cora rolled her eyes.

"Ugly!" insisted Scheherazade.

The cab lurched to a violent stop, tossing both girls and parrot across to the opposite seat. After fighting away a flapping Scheherazade, whom Nellie plucked out of the air and held tightly on her lap, Cora opened a window. She leaned out, letting in some of the hot steam that was quickly dissipating now that they'd stopped.

"Do be more careful now, would you!" she called out.

"Sorry, miss," returned the hoarse voice of their cabby. "Just there's a carriage up ahead, and it's blocking this side of the street. Came right out of the fog, it did. Didn't hardly see it till we come upon it."

"Yes, well, fine. And how are you planning on remedying the situation?" Cora asked.

"Back in a tick," replied the cabby. Nellie watched him jump down and make his way over to the other carriage. She looked over at Cora, who'd brought her head back inside, and sighed.

There was a strange sound from the street.

"Did our cabby just cry out?" Cora asked.

Before Nellie could answer, Cora was out of the cab and heading over to the carriage.

"Shite," said Nellie under her breath, and went to join her. Scheherazade remained unusually quiet on her shoulder as they walked over, and Nellie could understand her silence. The air was still and thick. The fog danced around her in thick white waves. There was a tingle running up her spine, an instinct that something wasn't right. The carriage up ahead looked too black, almost like a slain beast.

Nellie watched as the cabby tried to hold Cora back, but there was no stopping the girl. She was a determined one, that was for sure.

"No, young miss, don't . . ." said the cabby as she flew past him. Nellie saw Cora hunched over something . . . No. Not something. Someone . . . It was . . .

"That Japanese girl from the show. She's out cold," said Cora quietly as Nellie knelt beside her.

What in the world . . .? "Is she all right?"

"I think so. Yes, she's still breathing."

"Well . . . not sure why the cabby was so freaked out, then, just a girl on the ground . . ."

"No, I think he found *that* slightly more upsetting," replied Cora pointing. Nellie turned to look, and saw a head lying on its side staring up at her, eyes empty, face bloodied, neck . . . dripping. It was maybe all of three feet away.

"Mary, Mother of God." Nellie stood up and covered her mouth, looking back at Cora wide-eyed.

Cora said nothing, but carefully pushed the Japanese girl's hair from off her face. She reached out and gently touched a piece of metal protruding from her cheek.

Nellie was shaking now. She also felt sick to her stomach. A head. A human head. A vaguely familiar human head. Oh God. "I've decided a head is far worse than a dead body."

"Good," said Cora, rising. "Because we ought to take this girl back to your flat so she has a safe place to recover. Maybe she can tell us what happened."

Nellie looked at Cora. For the first time she could tell that the girl wasn't nearly as calm as she sounded. She could see the fear hidden just under the surface. It was another thing Nellie had learned from the Magician, how to read people's expressions. Helped with the psychic bit in the show.

Fine. Of course. "Yes, come on, then. Yes."

"Oi!" Cora called out, and Nellie started. Weird word choice for a high-class girl like that. "Carry this girl into the carriage and let's get to this young lady's flat as quickly as possible. When we arrive, you must then notify the police of this beastly situation."

"Yes'm," replied the cabby quietly.

"Well, come on, then!" Cora was sounding more exasperated now as she bent to pick up the satchel of weapons that the Japanese girl had used in her performance. As they returned to the cab, Nellie heard her mutter something about having to do everything herself.

Cora sat on one side of the cab this time, with the Japanese girl lying across the seat, her head in her lap, and Nellie took the other side with Scheherazade firmly on her shoulder, her talons holding on maybe a little too hard. They lurched slightly as the cab started moving again.

There was a moment of silence.

"Well, this is what I'd call an eventful evening," said Nellie quietly.

"Indeed." Cora sighed and looked out the window.

"And it's not over yet." Nellie, too, glanced out the window, watching as the carriage and its severed head disappeared into a combination of fog and steam behind them. "Fact is," she added, "I've a funny feeling that this is just the beginning."

Cora looked back at Nellie just as Nellie turned to look at her, and they made eye contact.

There was a squawk that broke their silence, and both girls looked at Scheherazade.

"Death!" said the parrot helpfully.

PART TWO

The Beginning

A Spot of Tea

"NICE PLACE YOU have here," said Cora, easing herself into a chair.

"Uh . . . thanks?" replied Nellie. She carefully placed the tea tray on the table between them.

"No, no, I mean it! I do. It's very nice. Sometimes the way I say things comes across the opposite of what I mean. I don't know why."

"Maybe it's your tone. Sugar?" Nellie dangled the tongs over the sugar bowl.

"No, thank you, I take it black."

Nellie nodded and took two cubes for herself.

"Maybe it *is* my tone. It must be. People think I can be awfully harsh."

"People think I'm stupid." Nellie sat down in the chair opposite Cora and handed over to her a cup of tea. "Happens."

"Doesn't it frustrate you, though?"

Nellie thought about it for a minute. Yes. And no. It didn't really matter to her that much. The Magician respected her and that's all that really counted.

"Sometimes. But of all the things I gotta put up with, I find dealin' with boys by far the most trying."

"I don't see why. They seem to just adore you."

"That's the problem."

Scheherazade interrupted the conversation with a squawk and a gymnastic attempt to grab herself a sugar cube, resulting in the entire bowl being turned over along with the milk.

"Blasted bird!" said Nellie, jumping to her feet as Cora did the same. "Bad Sherry!" Able to do little else, as Scheherazade had flown up to the top of the cabinets with her prize, Nellie admonished the parrot with a wave of her finger.

"Tasty," commented the parrot in response.

"Sorry 'bout that." Nellie sighed. She didn't know why, but for some reason she was really intent on impressing Cora. Didn't seem to be going too well at the moment. Cora gave her a nod with a tight-lipped smile. Then Nellie noticed her focus shift to a point beyond her shoulder.

She turned.

"Excuse please. Where am I?"

The Japanese girl was standing in the doorway to the kitchen, her hand absentmindedly stroking the stitches on her cheek. Cora had done quite a decent job as nurse to the girl. Evidently, as she'd explained to Nellie, she herself had had her share of accidents and had lots of experience with fixing a broken body.

"Michiko, right?" said Cora, walking over to the girl and giving her a soft smile.

The girl pointed to herself and nodded. "Michiko."

"I'm Cora, and this is Nellie."

Nellie gave a little wave. "Hiya."

Michiko nodded again. Then: "Where am I?"

"Do sit down," said Cora, escorting her to the kitchen table while Nellie drew up a chair for her. As Michiko sat, Cora explained. "We found you on the street. On the street? Yes?"

Michiko looked at her with what seemed to be great apprehension. "Street. Yes."

"We"—Cora gestured to herself and Nellie—"found you." She pointed to Michiko. "You were . . . God, 'unconscious' is such a complicated word." She looked at Nellie for help.

"Asleep?" suggested Nellie. She looked at Michiko, closed her eyes, and cocked her head to the side.

"Yes. You were . . . sleeping," Cora said.

"No," replied Michiko, shaking her head.

"Yes; yes, that's what happened."

"No. Not sleeping. I . . ." She looked frustrated with herself and clenched her fists. Then she touched the back of her head tenderly. She apparently found what she was looking for because she turned around to show Cora what she was touching. She pulled at her hair so that Cora could have a closer look.

Nellie came over to look, too.

"A bump," said Cora, examining her. "Dried blood, too. Someone attacked you? That's why you were . . . asleep."

"Not asleep!" Michiko was obviously getting angry.

"No, not asleep. You were unconscious. Hit on the head. Hit. And then you . . . black. Everything went black. Not asleep. Unconscious."

Michiko appeared to calm down then. "Not asleep. Un . . . con . . . shus."

Cora glanced up at Nellie and Nellie gave a small smile. They were on the same page at last.

"Who did it?" Nellie asked. "Who hit you . . .?"

Michiko looked at Nellie, and Nellie was pretty sure that in that moment she recognized her from the show. Michiko shook her head. "Fog. Thick. Don't . . . don't . . ."

"Don't?" asked Cora. "Don't remember? Don't know, is that it?"

"Don't know." Michiko nodded. "I fight him. Lost." She touched her cheek again.

"Uh, yes, I did that. Hope that's okay. Here." Cora reached into her purse and pulled out the small piece of metal she'd extracted from Michiko's cheek. She handed it to Michiko.

Michiko shook her head. "No, thank you."

"You fought him?" interjected Nellie.

Michiko nodded.

"Wow. And you lost to him? You? He must be good."

Michiko sighed hard. "Good yes. *Katana* bad."

"What's '*katana*'?" Nellie asked Cora, who shrugged in response.

Michiko sighed again.

"This is all so odd," said Cora, leaning back in her chair. "Why would this mysterious man in the fog kill Dr. Welland? And why would he leave her alive?"

"Dr. Welland? You knew him?" Nellie sat down next to Cora quickly. Well, this was news!

"Not personally, not really. He was the one who went onstage before you, with the cavorite bird."

"Yes! Now I remember. What kind of bird?"

"The one that flew around; the one fueled by cavorite."

"What's cavorite?"

"It was only discovered last year. A glowing green metal that defies gravity. It can be used as an energy source to lift something otherwise not able to fly up off the ground, or you can melt it and cover an object with it and make the entire object lighter than air. Of course, doing that means you have to have a way to tether whatever the object is to the ground or it will just keep flying up and up. So most people just use the metal as an energy source. The air force has made a rather large order for it, and they've started outfitting their ships. It's a much more reliable means of lifting something into the air, you see, than, say, the hydrogen used in dirigibles, and it seems to sustain itself infinitely. Though, of course, that's not really possible."

"So that's what that glowing green business was."

"Indeed. In any event, Dr. Welland was one of the men who helped isolate and refine it. I say. That could be meaningful, I suppose."

"You mean like rivalry, or something. Jealousy?" Nellie was all too familiar with that. How many times had rival illusionists attempted to sabotage one of the Magician's shows?

"Possibly." Though Cora didn't appear entirely convinced.

"Or not."

"It's just . . . I don't know, none of this makes sense. But I suppose the police will investigate."

Nellie felt a bit disappointed that Cora was so willing to let the matter drop. It was exciting, all this murder business. And, yes, sad, terribly sad, she supposed . . . but it wasn't like she'd known the man. *Wow*. She was terrible.

"I think it's time to move on to the harder stuff," said Cora, examining her empty teacup.

Nellie grinned. "Yeah, I'm all for that. But Raheem doesn't drink."

Cora reached into her purse and produced a silver flask. "Yes, but I do."

Just Your Average Turn-of-the-Century Slumber Party with a Dead Body.

You Know How It Is.

CLEARLY CORA WAS the kind of girl who could hold her booze. Nellie was feeling downright drunk after two sips from the flask. It was scotch. Good scotch. Or, at least, strong scotch. She really wasn't the kind of person who could tell quality scotch from not.

Even tiny Michiko appeared only mildly tipsy. Or, at least, that's what Nellie assumed. The few shy smiles that broke the Japanese girl's serious expression seemed to suggest that she'd let her guard down a little.

"No!" said Cora with a laugh. "And stop saying it!"

"I'm only sayin' it because you keep on going on about him."

"I keep going on about him because I hate him. Because of the unfairness of the world. I'm just as good as he is, probably better, but because I'm a girl—"

"You're in love with Mr. Harris."

"Am not!"

"Are, too."

"Yes!" insisted Michiko, even though both girls were pretty sure she had no idea what they were talking about.

"Let's play a game," said Cora, obviously trying to change the subject. The three of them were now in Nellie's room, sitting on her bed. Cora had escaped from her gorgeous red satin gown and was now wearing nothing but her undergarments, sitting cross-legged at the foot. Nellie was in her nightgown under the covers, and Michiko was still in her costume, sitting on a chair to the side.

"Don't change the subject!" said Nellie.

"I damn well will. Do you know any games?"

Nellie sighed. She thought back to her time backstage at the burlesque house with the other girls. They had gotten up to all kinds of mischief, but they usually required a theater and rigging . . . But, oh! "Let's play 'answer the question or do the deed'!"

"What's that?" asked Cora, taking another sip from her flask.

"Well," said Nellie, hugging her knees up to her chin, "you have a choice. Either you answer any question we ask, or Michiko and I get to make you do something."

"That's it?" asked Cora.

"That's it. Not good enough for you, is it?"

"Just very simple. No points system, no rules?"

"Rule is, you can't lie, and you can't back out of doing the deed."

Cora passed the now much lighter flask over to Nellie. "Okay. Let's play."

Nellie took the flask and a swig of scotch. It burned for a moment, then she passed it on to Michiko, who took a tiny sip.

"Who's first, then?" asked Nellie.

"I'll go."

"Right. So. Which you want to do?"

"I'll answer a question."

Now, in all fairness, Nellie knew she should consult with Michiko over what to ask, but it didn't seem like the poor girl was really going to be able to contribute to the game. Still, she turned to her and said slowly, "What should we ask her?"

Michiko furrowed her fine eyebrows. "Ask her?"

"For the game."

"Game?"

"Okay, I'll ask. Why does your accent slip, like when you're angry, or now, when you're toasted?"

Cora smiled. "That's an easy one. I was born on the street, grew up in the East End until I was ten, when Lord White hired me."

"Really?"

"Yeah. I've worked at changing it, but sometimes when I'm not totally in control, I slip up a bit."

"Neat."

"Is it my turn now?" asked Cora, sitting herself up on her knees. She looked excited, and that made Nellie nervous.

"Okay. I guess we can't really include her," said Nellie,

glancing at Michiko, who was taking another sip of scotch. "So just do me."

"Which do you want?"

"I guess . . . do the deed."

A wide grin spread across Cora's face and Nellie's heart sank. Okay, so she'd chosen the wrong option.

"You have to go into the sitting room . . ."

"No," said Nellie right away.

"You said the rule was you had to do whatever I told you to."

"But—"

"You have to go into the sitting room and kiss the dead guy on the forehead."

"Cora!"

"You have to do it!"

"I refuse!"

"You can't!"

Nellie pouted for a moment. "Fine. I'll do it, but only if you admit you have a crush on Mr. Harris."

"That's not the rule!"

"I think you really want to see me do this, and I can tell you I just won't unless you admit to it. So it's up to you."

"You can't break the rules."

"Look. When it's your turn, either I'll make you tell me if you choose 'do the deed' or I'll ask you if you like him, and I know you do. So why not just get it over with now?"

Cora sighed. Then responded, "I. Have. A. Crush. On. Mr. Harris."

Nellie laughed and clapped her hands. Michiko did the same.

"But it's a very little one," Cora added hastily, "founded on biological impulses. He's clearly meant to be someone that girls are attracted to. It just shows I'm a normal human being. However, pragmatically—"

"Oh, shut it," said Nellie, laughing, pulling the covers off and slipping out of the bed.

"No, really, pragmatically I find him a fool, and I could never be truly interested in someone who—"

"Are you coming or not? I thought you wanted to see this?"

With another sigh Cora climbed off the bed, and she and Michiko followed Nellie into the sitting room. At one point Cora listed toward the wall, and Michiko grabbed her to keep her heading straight.

"Thanks," Cora said. "Who knew walking down a hallway could be so treacherous."

The three girls stared at the body lying on the couch. Or rather stared at the white sheet that covered the shape of the body beneath it.

Nellie could hear Cora start to giggle behind her. Okay. So maybe she couldn't handle her booze as well as she'd initially thought. Giggling just didn't seem right for Cora.

"This is so mean." Nellie crossed her arms over her chest.

"Do it," said Cora.

Nellie inhaled deeply. It was fair play, she thought, slowly approaching the couch. After all, when they'd shared secrets in the cab, her fear of this body had been just as big as Cora's secret about Mr. Harris. And she'd had way too much fun picking on Cora about him. This was payback.

The body seemed to float toward her, even though she was the one moving toward it. The white sheet almost made it creepier. And she had this feeling like all of a sudden the body would sit up, just as she was about to peel the sheet off. She reached out her arms, trying to make them as long as she could, keeping the rest of her body far away from it.

Please don't sit up. Please don't sit up.

She leaned over, her fingers touching the white sheet . . .

"BOO!"

Nellie screamed and whirled around. Cora was doubled over in laughter, Michiko staring down at her as if she'd lost her mind. "Damn you, Cora Bell! Damn you, and your bloody stupid sense of humor! What the hell is wrong with you?"

"That scream," Cora wheezed, "it was so . . . I'm sorry, but your face!"

"You're dead, you hear me, dead!" Nellie could barely hear her voice over the frantic beating of her heart. She turned back to the body and with one swift angry motion peeled back the sheet.

The scientist looked pretty much the same as he'd looked earlier that day. A little less healthy maybe, a little more dead. Gray. *Just do it, Nellie, and get it over with.*

"Pucker up," Cora encouraged from behind.

Nellie shook her head and took a deep breath, plugging her nose. She leaned over. Just one kiss. One quick kiss.

She was pulled back fiercely, and though it wasn't half as startling as Cora's "boo," it still shocked her. She turned to see Michiko standing with a deadly serious expression on her face.

"No," said Michiko.

"What?"

"No. Much disrespect. No."

Nellie glanced at Cora, who had stopped laughing and was looking startled.

"It was . . . just a game, Michiko," Cora said.

Michiko's head snapped toward her. "No," she repeated.

Cora nodded slowly, and Michiko turned to Nellie again.

"I didn't want to do it in the first place," Nellie said, holding up her hands. She really didn't need an insanely talented sword fighter mad at her.

Michiko released a breath, and gave a little smile. "Good."

"I'm getting a little tired. I don't suppose you'd mind having company for the night? It's so late it's almost morning, and I'm certain Lord White will assume I've already gone to bed. I won't be missed," said Cora, leaning against the doorframe.

"You're already in your underwear. Stay over. And who knows when Raheem will be getting back. So he can't say no now, can he?" Nellie grinned. She turned to Michiko. "Stay?"

"Stay?"

"Here. Tonight. Stay till morning?"

There was no way of knowing what the girl was thinking, if she even understood. But she eventually nodded, so it seemed she sort of knew what was going on.

"What was that?" Cora turned and stuck her head around into the hall.

"What was what?"

"I thought I heard a knock on the door . . . but it was so quiet . . . there it is again . . ."

Nellie followed Cora out into the hall and they leaned against the front door to listen. Well, Cora leaned, Nellie kind of fell against it. Michiko stood behind them.

Suddenly there was a loud bang on the door, startling the girls and causing them to bolt back upright.

"What the hell do you want?" yelled Nellie at the solid oak in front of her.

There was a muffled response.

"Louder, please! Can't hear a damn thing yer sayin'!"

The muffled sound got a bit louder with at least one recognizable word.

"Police?" said Nellie. Her heart was pumping again, and she stared at Cora in a panic.

"Probably the whole Dr. Welland thing," said Cora. "Remember, I told the cabby to go to the police. He probably told them about us, where you live and all. Don't worry. But, uh, let's hide the dead body maybe?"

"Shoot, you're right. Good call. Raheem doesn't like it when the police get involved in his business." There was a knock on the door again. "Look, I'm naked, okay, give me a minute!"

There were no further sounds from the other side of the door.

Cora had already grabbed Michiko's arm and dragged her back into the living room. Nellie watched her give frantic instructions to the girl, who didn't seem to understand fully until Cora took hold of the body by its armpits. Alarmed, but clearly aware something was wrong, Michiko took the feet, and the two girls lifted the body.

Nellie was impressed by how strong they both were and let them do the work without her interference. Not that she had any desire to touch a dead body, mind. She watched as they carried it down the hall. It wasn't exactly the smoothest she'd seen people negotiate a hallway. There was quite a bit of teetering, and Cora had started giggling slightly, which wasn't helping the situation in the least. Especially as it was clear that Michiko was trying to be as respectful as possible in carrying the body. But finally they got their bearings and were able to make it down the hall and into, oh no . . . please no . . . her bedroom.

Great. Now she'd have to sleep in a room that had had a dead body in it.

When they had disappeared, she turned to the front door, took a moment to attempt to compose herself, and then answered it.

It was, indeed, a police officer. Though to call him that felt wrong. He was just so young, and the uniform he wore made him look even younger. Like he was playing dress-up. His not-quite-there blond mustache and hair slicked back with a little too much pomade only added to the effect. He looked terrified to see Nellie answer the door, and his gaze immediately fell on the pad of paper in front of him.

"Um, I'm looking for a . . . Mr. Raheem," he said almost inaudibly.

Nellie was finding it hard to remain standing. She grasped the doorframe. "He's not here."

"Oh." The young officer appeared extremely flustered by this sudden turn of events, and made strange faces as he flipped the pages of his pad, until finally, with a sigh of resignation, he looked up and made eye contact with her. Nellie thought his eyes were a very pretty shade of blue.

"Can I help you?" she asked, hoping the words were coming out in the order she wanted them to.

There was a sound from somewhere behind her, and she turned around in time to see a mess of dark hair vanish back into the bedroom.

"Shhh!" she called out

"Is there someone else here?"

"No." The young police officer furrowed his eyebrows, which Nellie thought made him look extra adorable. Poor fellow. She probably shouldn't lie to him. Much. "Yes. My . . . friend." She suddenly didn't think that Michiko, with her sewn cheek, would make a good impression.

"Could you ask her to come here?"

"She's in her underwear."

Instantly the officer's face turned bright red. "Oh, I . . . I see. I . . ." Clearly he was using all of his problem-solving ability to figure out how the situation could be resolved. Finally he hit on it. "Can she put on a robe?"

"I'm here, I'm here." Cora came to her side, wrapped up in one of Nellie's shawls. "What's all the fuss and other, Bofficer?" She thought for a moment, and then laughed. "That came out wrong."

"Uh . . . yeah . . ."

"What can we do for you?"

"Well, this cabby came to the station, and . . . there's been a murder, see . . . so he told us where he'd dropped off three witnesses, and so here I am."

"Yes, you are."

Nellie felt some relief that Cora had taken over communications and resigned herself to watching the young officer and his nervous twitches, which for some reason gave her a slight butterfly feeling in her stomach.

"Uh . . . so . . . can you tell me anything?"

"I can tell you many things—where to go for dinner on Friday nights, what the fashion for hats is this season, which votes are coming up in Parliament. . . . What in particular interests you?"

"What you . . . witnessed."

There was a pause as Cora stared at the officer. So many things to decide. Nellie understood why it took her a moment.

"Miss Harrison and I were returning from a gala hosted by the Prime Minister when our cab came across another cab, which was empty. On the ground, we discovered the unconscious body of another young lady we had met that evening.

Next to her was the head of Dr. Welland, who had, coincidentally also been at the affair. We brought the young lady back here, and she is currently sleeping. Sadly, she doesn't speak English, so questioning her might be a little . . . pointless." Nellie was impressed that, despite a bit of slurring, Cora was able to enunciate her words so well.

"No English?"

"She's Japanese."

"Ah."

"She was injured, and I can only assume it was by the same person who killed Dr. Welland."

The young officer nodded, writing it all down frantically.

"And, uh, is there anything else you can add?"

"No."

"Well, you're awfully cute," said Nellie. She covered her mouth with her hand, her eyes wide. Had she really just said that?

The young officer's face, which had only just returned to its normal color after its first reddening, was instantly a deep shade of burgundy once more, and he stumbled a few steps backward. Nellie looked at Cora, who, she could tell, was trying to maintain her composure, but was awfully close to bursting into laughter again.

"Well . . . if . . . uh . . . that is to say . . . if that's everything . . . good-bye." The young officer disappeared around the corner, and the two girls leaned around the door to watch him fly down the hall and down the stairs.

"I didn't just say that, did I?" Nellie was in a mild panic.

Cora started laughing and pulled Nellie back into the flat, closing the door behind them. "You did. And you scared him half to death. Oh, that was hilarious!" She sighed and put her hands on her hips. After taking a moment to calm down, she said, "Well, you lock up this mess of contraptions you have on this door, and Michiko and I will bring the body back. Guess we didn't need to move him after all."

Nellie nodded and stared before her as she pictured the young officer running wildly through the streets of London. She let her forehead fall against the door.

God, I'm such an idiot.

A New Kind of Morning

CORA AWOKE WITH a start. She didn't know what had prompted such a rude awakening, only that her heart was pumping in her chest and she had to sit still for a moment to allow it to regain a regular rhythm. It was in that moment of stillness that she remembered the night before, where she was now, and, thanks to the sudden sharp stab of a headache whisking its way from behind one eye to the other, just how much she'd had to drink.

She sighed and looked to her right. They'd been lying like squished sardines, side by side on Nellie's bed, the slight Michiko in the middle. Cora was closest to the window, and she slipped out from under the covers as quietly as she could to take a peek outside. The square below was starting to fill up with vendors, and the sky was stuck somewhere between night and day, as if it hadn't quite made up its mind which to go with yet.

Go with night, thought Cora.

It didn't.

There was a sound from out in the hall.

Nellie and Michiko stayed curled up together, and it seemed

likely they'd stay that way, even if a parade took a detour through the room.

Cora decided to investigate. She grabbed Nellie's shawl that she'd used the night before and suddenly remembered. *Oh my God, the police officer.* She'd happily presented herself to him in her underwear with nothing covering her but a shawl, and she was pretty sure she'd made a mess of her conversation. How humiliating.

She followed the noise down the hall to the kitchen and took a peek around the corner. She didn't gasp. She was grateful she didn't gasp. Any other time she probably would have, but for some reason, in this moment she didn't.

It wasn't that she hadn't seen half-naked guys before. In the summers, as a child, she'd sometimes go swimming in the Thames, and there were always older guys there, doing flips off the wall into the murky water. She'd also seen men without their shirts on before, just working, out in the sun on a hot summer day. But seeing some man with his shirt off in his own home after he'd been sleeping in his own bed . . . that just seemed wrong.

Besides. There was something about seeing a man, not a boy, not even a young man her age, but a fully grown man who'd been one for quite some time, in his altogether. Or almost altogether. It reminded her, despite her every attempt to be as mature as possible, that deep inside she still felt very much like a little girl.

The Great Raheem was standing at the far end of the kitchen, wearing nothing more than loose-fitting beige trousers that ended midcalf, staring out the small window above the washbasin. His hair was tied up in a knot on his head, so she had a perfect view of his back. His skin stretched tight across broad shoulders, and his muscles contracted beneath it as he raised a cup of tea to his lips. In fact, Cora considered his back a perfect replica of a drawing she'd seen in one of Lord White's physiognomy books of the ideal human musculature system.

"I see you," said the Magician.

"No, you don't," replied Cora, pulling herself back behind the door into the hall. Her heart, having just settled, was beating fast once more.

There was a low laugh, and Cora felt a mixture of pride at her joke and deep embarrassment at being caught out. She was debating whether or not to go into the kitchen when the man's shadow appeared in the doorframe.

"And who are you?" asked the Magician, looking down at her.

Aware that they were both in their undergarments, and also aware that there was nothing to be done about it at the moment, Cora decided it was for the best to pretend all was normal. "I'm Cora Bell. Lord White's assistant." She extended her hand.

"Ah yes, now I recognize you." He took her hand and kissed it softly. "And I'm Raheem."

"I know. The Great Raheem." *Cora, he knows he's the Great Raheem.*

"Not in the early hours of the morning in my undergarments. In the early hours in my undergarments, I am only Raheem."

Cora smiled. "Well then, in the early hours of the morning in my undergarments, I'm Miss Bell."

The Magician laughed again.

"Thought I heard voices!" Nellie came bursting out of her room in her robe, and skipped to Cora's side. "It's early. What the blazes are you doing up, Cora? I mean, this fool always rises before dawn, but you?"

"I don't know. I just . . . woke up. But I should probably head out soon anyway. Before his lordship wakes up and discovers I wasn't home all night."

Nellie nodded and practically pulled Cora back into her room with her, leaving the Magician to return to his tea.

Michiko was awake and sitting on the edge of the bed watching them closely as Nellie laced Cora back into her gown.

"I . . . I didn't do anything wrong, did I?" asked Cora as Nellie gave the strings a good yank.

"What? What do you mean?"

"Well, you seem . . . rather energetic—"

"Oh, you mean grabbing you. No, it's just Raheem really hates being disturbed in the morning. He needs his quiet time. It's why he gets up so early."

"Okay."

"Also, I'm jealous."

Cora turned and looked at Nellie, who seemed surprised that the progress of her tying had been interrupted.

"Jealous?"

"It's petty. And it's not your fault. I hate seeing other girls get on with Raheem. Especially girls my age. Women are okay, and they make fools of themselves flirtin' with him. But you . . . he seems to like you. And I don't want him likin' you better than he likes me. He's like a father to me, see."

Cora just stared at Nellie, who seemed perfectly relaxed and amiable.

"That's . . . honest."

"That's how I am. But don't worry. I know it's not your fault. And I know it's just me being all insecure and everything. I'll get over it. And I like you too much to let it bug me. Now turn around so I can tie you off."

In a daze, Cora did as she was told, and in short order she looked ready for a night on the town.

At six in the morning.

"I'll be mocked for this," she said.

"For what?"

"Returning in the same clothes I went out in. And everyone in the street will know that I'm wearing an evening gown, not day clothes. They'll all think—"

"Who gives a damn what they think?" said Nellie.

"Go," said Michiko.

The two girls turned to see Michiko at the door, her satchel of weapons over her shoulder.

Cora smiled. The advantage to a limited vocabulary—directness. "Well, that's that, then," she said. She offered her hand to Nellie, but the girl attacked her in a bear hug instead. Cora patted Nellie's back as she felt the air squeezed out of her.

Nellie moved over to Michiko, who apparently considered such a hug a threat, and indicated that she would not like to be touched. Nellie stopped herself short and gave her a broad smile instead. "Last night was fun!" she announced to the both of them. "Well, except for the whole decapitated-head thing. And Michiko being attacked. And the dead body in the other room. And the footman at the party. Oh, and the feeling hung-over now."

"You feel it, too?"

"Oh yeah." She grabbed her head and squeezed it dramatically. "Ow."

"Ow," said Michiko in the corner with a nod.

The three girls laughed.

"Okay, we're off. Thank you for the hospitality, and thanks for letting us stay over. I hope we meet again soon," Cora said as Nellie escorted Michiko and her to the door. Cora made sure to keep her gaze directly in front of her, lest the Magician's naked back slip into view.

After another quick farewell, they were out the door. She and Michiko parted ways soon after, and Cora was left on her own to brave the odd glances and the few choice words that were tossed her way by a couple of boys who, she could see, were vainly attempting to grow beards.

By the time she reached Lord White's, the day had decided to be hotter than usual for the time of year, and her hair had not reacted well. She was sweating through her red satin, and she felt even more constricted than usual in her corset. A great sense of relief washed over her as she entered the cool darkened foyer and she tiptoed upstairs to her room, hoping that Lord White was still asleep. Chances were good that he would be.

The door to her room creaked softly as she closed it behind her, and she put an ear to it to listen for the telltale step of his lordship. A moment passed, and she exhaled a breath of relief.

"Where the hell have you been?"

Cora nearly jumped out of her skin.

"Sir, you scared me!"

Lord White was sitting on the side of her bed, one leg casually crossed over the other, his dangling foot shaking in frustration. His arms were crossed over his chest, and he was fully decked out in his light-blue-and-yellow-checked day suit. Cora was impressed he'd got himself out of bed and dressed all on his own.

"*I* scared *you*? I scared *you*?" he said with great indignation. "Where the hell have you been all night? I haven't been able to sleep a wink."

"You haven't?"

"Well, I slept a bit, but I woke up frantic. And when Mrs. Philips said you hadn't returned all night . . . you had the poor creature in tears, don't you know?"

Poor Mrs. Philips.

"I'm sorry."

Lord White stood in a huff and marched over to her. He wasn't a very tall man. He stood maybe an inch above her.

He oughtn't have been intimidating. But there was something about him that was, despite the receding ginger hair, round glasses, and small stature. "That's all well and good, but where have you been, damn it?"

"It's a very long story."

Which clearly wasn't a good enough excuse for him.

And so . . . she told him everything.

That she could think to make up in the moment.

What Michiko Makes of All This

MICHIKO WAS STANDING in the shadow of the archway that led to the market. Once she'd parted ways with Cora, she'd doubled back, intent on her purpose, but now she was full of doubt. And fear. She watched as the old samurai's assistants set up his stall while the old man sat in his chair gazing into the distance. Absentmindedly she touched the stitches on her cheek. Stupid Callum and his stupid, cheap *katana*.

What a strange night it had all been. Almost dreamlike. A man in the fog, a close encounter with death. Blackness. And then . . . and then the really weird stuff. There was one thing to be said about those girls. They liked to talk. A lot. Though they seemed pleasant enough. And they had really tried to include her.

At times.

She'd never had whiskey before. And she hated the throbbing in her brain now. Still, it almost seemed worth it, really, for the slight relief of anxiety the alcohol had provided. After the encounter in the fog, last night had been . . . dare she think it . . . fun. The girls were silly. And she didn't approve of their lack of respect toward the dead body in the living room. But there was something about Nellie and Cora she had still . . . liked. They were so amazingly independent. Despite their having bosses just like her. They seemed . . . happy.

She wasn't sure what to make of the parrot, however.

It was no matter. She was unlikely to ever spend much time with them again. She might meet them in passing, give them a little smile—she didn't think she could smile so broadly to expose her teeth the way Nellie did—but that was it. The night was over and it was time to move on.

Well.

Not quite.

There was still one piece of business that needed to be taken care of.

Deep in her gut, and more present than ever now that the effects of the alcohol had worn off, she felt a burning ember. It radiated through her and would not go out, no matter how much she tried to extinguish it. The fact remained. She'd been defeated in an unfair fight, and honor had to be restored. Somehow she'd have to find the man in the fog and face him again. And this time she'd win.

She had to.

But first she had to thank the old samurai in person for his gift. And seeing as she had a full day of nothing aside from Callum's curses and possibly worse ahead of her, she had the time now to approach him.

What she didn't have was the courage.

After what had happened last night, she didn't feel worthy

of such a gift as the Silver Heart. Worse, she feared it had all been a terrible mistake. Maybe the Silver Heart had been meant for another Japanese assistant to a self-defense instructor. Or maybe the old samurai had said something like "Whatever you do, don't give that girl this sword," and his assistant, who hadn't been listening carefully at the time, had only heard the last five words of the sentence.

Yes. That was it exactly. It had all been a horrible, horrible miscommunication.

She stared at the old samurai and felt her heart sink. And then the old samurai did his "looking right at her as if he'd been looking at her the whole time" thing. One second she was momentarily distracted by a pale flower girl in a muddy dress scurrying out to the high street, and then she glanced back up at him only to discover that she was the object of his attention.

She didn't move. She couldn't. She was rooted to the spot, and she felt like a perfect fool.

He didn't move either. And then, finally, after what seemed like forever, he nodded that almost imperceptible nod of his: "You're welcome."

"Thank you." Except she said it by pressing her lips together and raising her eyebrows.

And then he was no longer looking at her. As if he'd never been looking at her.

Not a miscommunication, then.

Why did she still feel like it was?

Michiko had barely made her way out onto the high street when she heard a familiar voice call out after her. She placed it immediately. After all, she could count on one hand the number of people who had spoken to her in her native tongue in this country.

She turned and watched as the servant to the old samurai came bounding up to her. He was all limbs, galumphing his way over, a puppy—no more than fourteen—but he had speed. Much speed.

"*Silver Heart,*" he said when he skidded to a stop in front of her. He ought to have been out of breath, but he wasn't.

"*What about it?*" she asked, feeling a panic rise in her throat. Just as she'd felt confident in the old samurai's choice . . .

"*No, that's you. You are the Silver Heart.*"

Me? The energy that flowed through all things flowed through the samurai's sword and into his soul. Just as his soul flowed into the sword. So Michiko supposed it made sense that he would call her by the same name as her *katana*. Still. It sounded so strange to her.

"*What do you want?*"

"*Can we speak privately?*"

"*Why?*"

"*I have a question to ask of you.*"

"*No, I mean why do we need to speak in private? No one will be able to understand us. We could go to a theater and stand in the middle of the stage and yell back and forth to each other, and still, it would be a conversation shared just between us.*"

The young servant thought for a moment. "*Good point.*"

"*What do you want?*"

"*I want to be your student.*"

"What?"

"I want to study under you. I want to become samurai. Like you."

"Why don't you just ask your old master?"

"He refuses. He says his time is past."

"He is testing you."

"No, he's not. I know my master."

"You must be persistent. You must show him your dedication. He will refuse, and you must keep asking. That's how it works."

"I want you to teach me."

"Why?"

"Because you studied in Japan, where it was illegal. You could have died for your passion."

"A samurai expects to die every day, lives his life as if it was his last. The sure sign you are a samurai is that you feel no fear facing your own death." Except, of course, when you *are* truly facing your own death, then you get scared and panic and feel like a child.

"And you're a girl. Girls are rare as samurai. That is special."

Well . . . he made a good point. Nonetheless.

"No."

"Please."

"No."

And she turned and left.

She couldn't teach him. She didn't have the time. Callum would certainly not approve, and she hardly felt worthy of being a samurai herself. She had all but abandoned the ancient teachings since arriving in this new world, and she couldn't exactly become someone's teacher in the tradition.

Besides, she had her own issues to deal with. She had to find the man in the fog; she had to restore her honor. The very day she finally earned her sword was the same day she lost her first fight. And he didn't even kill her. Her head started to throb even harder.

"*Let's try this again.*" The young servant appeared in front of her. Michiko stopped in her tracks and looked behind her. She'd left him to turn off the high street onto a narrow alley that saved her around ten minutes of travel time home. He had appeared at the far end. There was no way he could have gotten from where they'd been talking to here so fast. It was . . . impossible.

"*I understand you don't think I'm worthy . . .*" the boy was saying.

"*What?*" Michiko was far too distracted by his seeming to appear out of thin air.

"*The other day. You said I was just a servant, that you were of a higher class than I am, and you're right. But we're not in Japan anymore. Here, in some ways we are very much equals in status. No one gives us foreigners a second glance . . .*"

Michiko really wasn't paying attention.

"*How did you do that?*" she asked.

The boy stopped midspeech. "*Do what?*"

"*How did you get in front of me?*"

The boy smiled. "*Oh, that. It's a . . . hobby.*"

"*What is?*"

"*If I show you, will you teach me?*"

"*No.*"

The boy sighed. "*Fine. Watch.*"

The boy took off running toward a large overflowing bin full of garbage and looked like he was going to run right into it. Instead he leaped up into the air and touched the top of the bin with his foot, using the slight push to propel himself onto a tattered awning. He continued at the same speed along its supports, never faltering, grabbing a window ledge here, a line of laundry there, until he landed on the roof toward the entrance of the alley. But still he didn't stop.

He rolled across the roof and used a drainage pipe to launch himself across to the other side. And he kept running, leaping over the spaces between buildings, sometimes landing in a kneeling position, other times doing that roll again. Sometimes he used his hands almost as she'd seen monkeys do, pulling himself along until finally he leaped back down in front of her where he'd started.

"*What on Earth was that?*" asked Michiko in awe.

"*I run. I just . . . I run. I go where my body tells me, I use falling to keep me going forward. I don't know. I just . . . run.*"

"*Well . . . you do it really well.*"

"*Thank you. Now will you teach me?*"

"*No.*"

But the boy wouldn't leave her alone. She could sense his presence flying high above her as she walked the rest of the way home. He could have arrived at her place far in advance of her, but he stalked her like some crazy monkey.

She didn't need a pet.

"*Stop it!*" she said as he landed in front of her, blocking the rear entrance to Callum's.

"*Hey, this is where we met,*" said the boy, glancing around the alley.

"*No, we met at your master's stall.*"

"*Oh yeah.*"

"*Look, you can't be here. I'll get in a lot of trouble if he sees you here.*" Michiko thought for a moment. "*I'm already in a lot of trouble.*"

"*Are you?*"

He was trying to stall her. Trying to make her like him. Didn't he understand? This was impossible. She hardly felt samurai herself; she didn't feel qualified to teach anyone. Though, she acknowledged, the true samurai was aware of how little she knew, and if that was the only definition, then there was no one half as qualified as she was.

"*Uh . . . are you okay?*" asked the boy, interrupting her train of thought.

Why did she always do that? Just disappear into her thoughts like that. Maybe it was because she'd been living inside her own head for so many months now that the outside world sometimes seemed secondary, almost like a dream.

"*Really. Are you okay?*" The boy looked sincerely concerned now.

Michiko nodded. "*If I teach you, will you teach me how to run like you do?*"

The boy's eyes went wide, and Michiko was surprised to

hear herself say it. What? Of all the thoughts passing through her brain, she didn't seem to recall that one. How had that happened? Instinct?

Before the boy answered, she added, "*This is not an equal exchange. I will always be your master, even when you show me that running thing you do. This can only work if I am given the proper respect. Otherwise the deal is off.*"

The boy nodded. Nodded so hard Michiko was concerned he might hurt himself. Then he was immediately on his knees, bowing low.

"*Yes, yes, that's great,*" she said. "*But look, you really have to go now. I have to get inside. I have my own 'master' to serve.*"

The boy sat up and made a face. "*That guy's an asshole.*"

"*You're telling me.*" The boy stood up and brushed the dirt from his trousers. "*What's your name?*"

"*Hayao.*"

Michiko smiled in spite of herself. Hayao. The fast-flying man. "*Appropriate.*"

Hayao rolled his eyes. "*Yes, I know. I think my parents knew I'd be quick. They could sense it.*"

"*Where are they now?*"

"*Dead.*"

Short, single-syllable-word answers, Michiko knew, weren't meant to be followed up on.

"*Well, Hayao, I'm—*"

"*The Silver Heart.*" Hayao smiled broadly, seeming truly thrilled by this fact.

Michiko didn't know what to say. He wasn't entirely wrong.

Energy was shared with everything. The soul of the sword, the soul of the warrior, they were one and the same.

And yet.

She was just Michiko.

"You can call me that."

Hayao had to go. She insisted. But now that she was the boy's teacher, evidently he was ready to take her orders easily and without complaint. Soon he had scampered up onto the rooftops where he seemed most at home and disappeared behind a chimney pot.

Upstairs, hiding out in her room for as long as she could before Callum discovered her return, Michiko sat inside her wardrobe. The door was cracked open and the light fell across the blade of the Silver Heart. Her own heart ached holding it. Everything about the *katana* was perfect. Yes, as she admired the skillful detail in the *tsuba* with the intertwining vines of steel, the simple braided rope of black silk along the hilt, the single piece of metal sharpened to a razor edge, she knew she simply had to work harder at her craft. A samurai strove for perfection, in every move, in every fight, in every thought. And here in her hands was perfection. It would serve as a constant reminder of her life's goal.

Perfection in all things. And until that was reached, you could not stop. You would not stop.

She was going to return to the scene of the crime and track down that man in the fog.

And she was going to defeat him.

A Field Trip

NELLIE STOOD IN the corner watching the widow. The woman wasn't crying. She didn't wear an expression of any kind. And her words were few. She simply knelt down beside her husband and took his hand in hers.

"I told him this would happen," she said quietly.

Nellie didn't say anything back. She didn't know what to say.

"What would happen?" asked the Magician softly from his position at the foot of the sofa.

The widow shook her head and rose to standing. Then she nodded, and the two men who'd accompanied her carefully took hold of the body and carried it out of the room. Out of the apartment. Out of Nellie's and the Magician's lives and into theirs.

"Thank you," said the widow, taking the Magician's hand.

"I did nothing."

It had taken some effort, but the Magician had discovered the man's identity and that of his wife. It was why he'd been out so late coming back after the party. He'd been following a lead. A surname: Thompkins.

The widow said nothing further. Face as hard as stone.

When she was gone, Nellie said, "What do you think she meant?"

"I don't know. Clearly the man lived a dangerous life."

"He was a scientist."

"And your point?"

Nellie thought for a moment. She didn't know. But it seemed strange that someone as harmless as a scientist would be in such trouble. That sort of peril belonged to gang leaders, or soldiers. Or theater reviewers. But a man of science? Why would anyone wish such a person harm?

"You're curious," said the Magician, sitting on the now-empty sofa, which Nellie found both brave and gross.

"'Course I am."

"Well," said the Magician, "I have errands to run today. And the Smiths have asked that I witness their daughter's wedding. Why don't you have a bit of fun and investigate?"

"Is this because you're curious, too?"

The Magician smiled. "Maybe."

Nellie smiled, too. It wouldn't be too bad a way to spend the day. Besides, it wasn't as if they were just being nosy. The man had sought them out. Like it or not, they were a part of this.

And by "they," she meant the Magician, of course.

Lunch was eaten and partings were made, and soon Nellie was on her way to the Medical and Scientific Institute. It was the only place she could think of to start her investigation. Even if Thompkins had had nothing to do with the institute, it was likely that another member of the Society of Heroes worked there. And such a person was likely to know at least who Thompkins was.

She'd tried to dress science-y. She opted for a tweed skirt and jacket, even though they were pink. And she wore a pair of glasses, a prop she'd gotten from one of the comics back at the burlesque house. The purse she'd grabbed from her costume box was a plain black thing that she normally used in performance to hide props or some glitter or a flashcube. She'd also tried for a respectable bun at the nape of her neck, though she couldn't resist giving the hair on top of her head a bit of volume, releasing a curl from its bond to dangle by her right cheekbone.

It was clear, however, as she passed through the front doors of the large Gothic building, that her attempt had failed. Evidently science-y meant all black suits and white lab coats. *Oh well.* She smiled as she passed the woman behind the desk, who squinted in suspicion at her from behind a large red book with "Personal Aeronautics" written across the front in gold lettering.

Nellie took a left and found herself in a long narrow hall.

"Can I help you?" A man with a thick mustache skidded to a stop after doing a double take.

Nellie was about to explain her situation in a straightforward manner when it occurred to her that just maybe this Society of Heroes was an underground kind of thing. One of those clubs that men kept secret so they'd feel extra special. If she asked about it, even if he was a member, he might not be honest. He might go further and find other members to warn them that she was coming. No. That wouldn't do at all. Her gaze flitted to his hands and she noted a lack of ring.

"No, thank you," she said. And just in case he was about to ask her to leave, she flashed him what she dubbed "the dazzle." A smile so broad, so sincere, so . . . well, guys seemed to like it.

This guy certainly seemed to, as he turned a deep red and immediately ran off. Nellie sighed. This might take longer than she thought. She'd have to prowl the halls until she saw someone wearing that ring. Who knew how many or how few were in possession of it?

Well, she had all day, after all. No show that night, and nothing better to do. Time to be systematic. She began searching through the halls, one by one.

It was easy enough to look for a ring. Every man she passed on her route slowed when he saw her approaching. Some were even brave enough to say hello, though, as she'd often suspected of science guys, most were ridiculously shy. She kind of liked that. It was way better than the grabby guys at the stage door.

Shy. She thought of the police officer from last night and smiled. What a sweetheart. A bit of not bad as well. And she'd totally embarrassed herself in front of him.

"Can I help you?" again.

"No, thank you, I . . ." Nellie said automatically, glancing at the man's hands. The ring. She looked up at him. This one was bald, with no facial hair. He didn't even have eyebrows or eyelashes. "Oh my, what's wrong with you?" she asked.

"Wrong with me?" he said in almost a whisper, and a thick northern accent.

"You've no hair!"

"I was born this way."

"Really? That's amazing."

He stared at her for a long moment. Really stared. It was as though he was trying to look through her head and into her brain. Finally: "You've got beautiful eyes." That same whisper, though it wasn't as if he was trying to flirt with her or anything. It just didn't seem like his voice got any louder than that.

"Thank you." She'd been told that a lot. She'd also been told her skin was like porcelain, her hair like gold, and, once, that she had divine earlobes.

"I was wonderin' . . ." she continued, "if you could help me with somethin'."

He cocked his head to the side.

"Uh . . . is there anywhere we could talk . . . in private?" She gave a coy smile after that, hinting at something, even if it wasn't anything.

The man looked at her, astonished. She knew he wouldn't say no. Not when she asked him to be alone with her. She felt that familiar flutter in her stomach, the one that reminded her she wasn't nearly as worldly as she pretended. It was a useful flutter. It protected her from making bad choices.

"Okay," he said quietly.

She followed him up a flight of stairs to an empty office with "Dr. Mantis" painted onto the door. It was a small and windowless room, and when the door closed, the only light came from the four electric fixtures humming on each wall. They highlighted, with strange shadows, the jars standing side by side on shelf after shelf. And each individual jar contained a body part. An ear here, a liver there. Nellie didn't look too closely, but she assumed that there were enough pieces to make up a full human.

". . . Nice . . ." she said as she moved into the middle of the room.

Dr. Mantis sat down behind his desk at the far end and looked at her.

"So?" he asked, dropping his hands into his lap and looking at her with the same concern she felt about his collection lining the walls.

"So," she said, and pulled up a chair opposite him, "I just find this the most interestin' room." She smiled. He immediately avoided her eye contact.

"Thank you."

"Whatever do you need all those bits for?"

"I study them."

"You do? How fascinatin'."

"Yes." He was quiet for a moment. "Would you mind if I continued with my work as we talk?"

Nellie nodded. "Oh yes, please. It would be so interestin' to watch."

Dr. Mantis leaned down behind the desk and pulled up a metal tray. It had a lot in common with a tray one might use to serve breakfast in bed. It had a plate in the middle with a set of instruments on either side that sort of resembled a knife and fork. And on the plate was a human hand. It was lying palm up, the skin peeled open and pinned back. In fact, it appeared several layers were pinned back as the white bone was clearly visible.

Nellie observed this closely, unable to look away. She wanted to. She really wanted to. But she just sat there, staring at the hand, as Dr. Mantis quickly picked up the instruments and pulled at the open flesh, and then began to gently cut at something as if he was working his way daintily through a steak.

"Uh . . ." said Nellie. "So . . . I wanted to talk with a scientist about somethin'."

Dr. Mantis nodded but didn't look back up at her.

"My father passed away recently, and as I was goin' through his things, I noticed that he had a letter from somethin' called the Society of Heroes."

"Can't talk about that."

"Oh." She sat silently watching him picking at the hand. His nonexistent eyebrows appeared furrowed in frustration. "Is everythin' okay?"

". . . It's . . ." He sighed hard and leaned in toward the hand.

"Here, let me help," she said, standing and coming to his side. "What can I do?"

He looked up at her, finally making eye contact again. "You hold that muscle open. Use those." He nodded toward two long thin round tools that looked a bit like pencils, but were made of metal and had much sharper points. Nellie picked them up and bent down next to him. She took one in each hand and placed them where he was now stretching the muscle. He let go and proceeded to pick at a tendon between what she held open.

They stayed like that for what felt like ages. Once she'd brought herself close to him so that her side was touching his shoulder, but he'd pulled away as if he'd been electrocuted. She could tell her presence was starting to make him feel uncomfortable, and not in the good way. As she held the hand apart as diligently as she could, she racked her brain for something to say, anything that would help her get to the heart of her purpose.

But not a literal heart. She glanced up at the wall opposite.

"Oh my," she decided to say.

"Yes?" Dr. Mantis didn't look up from his work.

"I think I'm feelin' a wee bit faint." It was an old trick, but reliable.

That made him look up at her finally. He didn't say anything, though. Clearly his mighty scientific brain was at a loss as to what to do about the situation.

She'd have to help him out. "Uh, I was wonderin' if you maybe could get me some water?"

"Oh." He looked down at the hand and furrowed his nonexistent eyebrows again. Then he slowly removed the implements from within the tendon and gave Nellie a nod.

"I'll be right back."

She smiled brightly and watched him shuffle slowly out of the room.

The second the door was closed behind him, Nellie set to work. First she dropped the tools and examined the desk the hand was sitting on. Drawers were always a very good place to start. She pulled each one out and found piles and piles of paper, seeming to be in no particular order. Some were ripped in two, others crumpled into balls. There were many more just stacked haphazardly on top of one another. All of them had detailed drawings of various body parts on them, labeled with an attention to detail not given to the organization of the paper on which they'd been written.

She pulled another drawer open and found a file folder in it. She opened it to a single page with another sketch drawn on it. It was hard to tell what she was looking at. It seemed to be a human figure, but it was in bits and pieces, like a puzzle about to be put together. Or maybe just taken apart.

Nellie didn't have time to examine further. Nothing she'd seen yet had seemed to have anything to do with the Society of Heroes. She slammed the drawer shut in her frustration.

It was then that she heard the buzzing sound. So faint that at first she wasn't sure if it was real or a figment of her not insignificant imagination. But it became clear that the sound came from the thin drawer that ran just under the top of the desk.

She gave it a pull. It was locked. As she'd suspected.

One of the very first techniques the Magician had shown her was how to pick a lock. He did this so that she could perform any number of seemingly impossible escapes from all manner of shackles, cages, or what have you. True, often she just had the key to the lock secretly hidden on her person, but she'd also learned how to pick. How to do it, even when her hands were behind her back.

Compared with some of the extravagant locks the Magician worked with, a simple one on a simple desk was nothing for her. It was as if the drawer hadn't even been fastened in the first place.

She pulled it open and there, spinning in the corner, was a small brass ball. Nellie picked it up, and it vibrated in her hand. She turned it over and saw that one side was covered in glass and she could look right into the middle. Small gears ticked away, and a red light glowed through the cracks. It radiated warmth against her palm. Then something opened, just larger than a pinprick, and the red light could be seen more visibly. It grew. Her palm was getting warmer.

Not good.

She dropped the ball back into the drawer, where it spun furiously for a moment longer and then sat still.

Best to avoid that, then, thought Nellie, and turned her attention to the flat black leather checkbook beside it.

Ah! Now this was more like it. Follow the money. Just what her boss at the burlesque house had always told her.

She picked up the book and flipped through it. The scientist had spent a lot of money on jars. Also on formaldehyde. There were a couple of small checks written to a Messrs. Staunch and Proper that seemed to repeat each month. She flipped to the back of the book, where the scientist kept very orderly accounts of both withdrawals and deposits. It was there that she noticed a lump sum paid to the order of Dr. Mantis. Two hundred pounds? That was astonishing. Better still, in the margin was scrawled "Heron." And the extremely generous benefactor? A one Mr. Carter.

Mr. Carter.

The name sounded awfully familiar.

As she racked her memory, Nellie's gaze shifted, and she noticed a pretty wooden box sitting farther back in the drawer.

The party! Of course. There had been a Mr. Carter at the party last night. He'd come backstage to introduce himself to Sir Callum Fielding-Shaw. Mr. Carter . . . he was an MP. A Tory, if she remembered correctly. Yes, she was a consummate eavesdropper.

Follow the money. Mr. Carter.

Dr. Mantis still wasn't back yet, and Nellie couldn't resist. After returning the checkbook to its spot, she picked up the small box. She noticed the familiar heron carved on the top. This could be something. She opened it.

Staring up at her were half a dozen pairs of eyes. Nellie was frozen in horror. She couldn't look away. It was like the eyes had drawn her unwittingly into a staring contest that she had no chance of winning. And still, despite it all, she stared. The box was lined with lead, and each pair floated in that blasted formaldehyde, preserved as good as new.

"That's private." It was impressive how Dr. Mantis's whispery voice could cut through a room like that.

"Oh, I'm sorry." Nellie quickly stashed the box back in the drawer and closed it shut with a bang. She tried to defuse the situation by smiling broadly at him, but then remembered how he didn't seem to respond to that.

"How'd you get into that drawer?" he asked, approaching the desk as Nellie tried as casually as she could to maneuver herself around to the front of it.

"What do you mean?"

"It was locked."

"No, it wasn't." A quick glance of the room: one door, no windows. Ceiling: one vent, too high.

"It was." They were standing at the foot and head of the desk respectively. The door was behind him.

"I . . . don't know what to tell you. I'm sorry for snoopin', got bored, see. But the drawer was definitely unlocked . . . sir."

Be polite. Be a little stupid. Be pretty.

She took a small step to the right, and he countered it.

"That's my private drawer. That's private."

Each time he said "private," saliva shot out of his mouth on the "*p*."

"I'm sorry." She was now as quiet as he was. She watched his hands tighten their grip on the desk. "It's a lovely . . . collection. Very . . . unique." She took a step back and absently opened her purse and reached inside.

He took a step around to the front of the desk and toward her.

"I imagine it must be a difficult collection to maintain. I mean"—she gave a small laugh—"stamps are one thing; you'll find them on just about every letter. Eyes, on the other hand . . ."

"Nothing rare about eyes. Everybody's got them."

"Good point."

She felt a grainy substance in the bottom of her purse and

recognized it instantly. Thank goodness. Okay, then. For this to work she'd have to let him get closer.

She took another step back, this time bringing herself close to the wall. He took the bait and stepped in toward her again. One, maybe two more steps, that's all she needed. Then she noticed the scalpel clutched in his right hand. He must have picked it up on passing the desk. Great.

"Well, still . . ." she said, "it's . . . very interestin'."

Dr. Mantis took another step and he was right there. So close she could hear his shallow wheezing. He squinted at her. Not good enough . . .

"You said earlier you liked my eyes," she said, her throat getting tight.

"Yes."

"Would you like to take a closer look?" She brought her purse up to her chest. At that offer, he opened his eyes wide. Bloodshot. Not worthy of his own collection, she mused.

She had one chance and one chance only. She whipped her hand out of her purse and tossed the fistful of glitter into his face. It hit the mark perfectly, and Dr. Mantis bent over, thunderstruck, his eyes full of sparkly irritation. For good measure, Nellie gave him a swift kick in the kidneys, which caused him to double over further, and then she was out of there.

She flew along the hall, down the stairs, and out the front doors.

She didn't stop running until she'd turned the corner, and even then she kept walking at a fast pace.

It was at this moment, only when she was several streets

away, that she allowed the shudder to come over her, starting at her tailbone, working its way up her spine and to her shoulders, down her arms, and shaking free through her hands.

If this was what the members of the Society of Heroes were into . . . after meeting Dr. Body Parts Enthusiast, she could see how her dead guy might have gotten dead, carrying on with such characters.

What was with all those body parts? Especially the eyes? And then there were the sketches in the drawer . . . the spinning brass ball . . .

Icky and scary, clearly very dangerous. And clearly she really needed to know what was going on . . .

Making a New Friend

"**BE NICE,**" **HISSED** Lord White as Cora climbed into the globe.

"And you, be good," she said to him in return.

"Just get the work started. I want to see progress by the time I get back."

"Good luck." She paused at the top of the staircase and gave him a smile, hoping that he'd forgive her for not joining him this afternoon. Her head was spinning too much to be useful in a social setting.

Evidently his lordship wasn't in a forgiving mood. "Get it done." With that, Lord White stormed out of the library, and Cora continued down the stairs.

Mr. Harris was there, sitting at the long table, already examining the order his lordship had just received for a new invention. *Be nice*, Cora thought to herself.

Then she thought . . . *Why?*

"Let me see." She snatched the paper from under Mr. Harris's nose and took it with her to her cubby as she grabbed her lab coat and gloves. "Odd," she muttered to herself.

"What is?" Mr. Harris was standing behind her, breathing down her neck.

Cora ignored him and returned to the table.

"What's odd?" asked Mr. Harris again, following like a puppy and sitting next to her.

Just answer the question, Cora, or he'll never shut it. "What's odd . . . is that I've never seen such a specific order before. Usually the client asks for something, a device that shoots fire, a machine to haul the shopping, and then we figure out how to create it. But this . . ."

"Is a set of instructions."

"More like a puzzle." It was a list of components for the device, and suggestions on how to put the whole thing together. At the bottom, there was a question written in an almost illegible scrawl: *But how do we activate it?* "So the client is seeking outside help because he doesn't know how to make it go." Cora immediately felt disdain for this client. Making it go was, after all, the most interesting, even if it was the hardest, part.

"Do we have to follow the instructions to the letter?" asked Mr. Harris.

Cora didn't want to admit it, but she'd been wondering the exact same thing. Making this invention work wasn't just a question of sprinkling some fairy dust over an inert device. It required that the whole object be constructed in such a way that it could be activated. This meant every piece was critical to "making it go," and if these component parts that the client wanted didn't serve that function, they could be considered useless.

"Let's just work on the blueprint and see if we can't do this as the client wants us to. If it's impossible . . ."

"Then we get to have fun?"

Cora looked up at Mr. Harris and immediately heard Nellie's voice: *"Do you fancy him?"* Examining him now, she felt embarrassed for having said yes the other night. Mr. Harris in a lab coat was utterly ridiculous. Like he was playacting "lab assistant."

"Really, Mr. Harris, you don't already find this fun? I do."

He smiled a closed-lipped smile at her which she returned with one of her own.

"Fetch us some paper and pencils, Mr. Harris."

They worked on the blueprint for an hour; however, it seemed pretty clear that "activating" the device was not going to be possible with the information that they'd been given. Fun eluded them. In fact, all that followed was frustration and annoyance with Mr. Harris, who, despite making a few reasonable suggestions, was altogether useless at coming up with a solution.

Then again, so was she.

They were at that point that Cora so hated. The point that required Lord White's input. Cora longed for the day when she wouldn't need his help, and thought she was coming pretty darn close to it. But every once in a while . . . she got stumped.

So they had to set the blueprint aside for now, which she knew meant that Lord White was going to give her a good talking-to about not completing assignments. Instead, she got Mr. Harris to do some busywork tidying up the lab, and she set about working on a personal project. As she fiddled with a screw, she did have a tiny thought in the back of her head that maybe she'd given up a little too easily in favor of working on her pet piece. But then again, she was still hungover from the night before, and not in the mood for serious problem solving. Bad excuse, but one Lord White seemed to use on a regular basis.

"So you're not going to help at all, is that the plan?" Mr. Harris dropped a box of tools on the table right next to Cora. She flinched inwardly, but nothing was going to make her react to his presence.

"Hey, don't look at me," she replied. "You were hired for a job. I have my own things to take care of."

"Like fiddling about with a pair of glasses? You don't even wear glasses." He sat next to her and dumped the tools out onto the table. They scattered about, some sliding right across to the other side and onto the floor.

Cora sighed hard.

"What's wrong now? I'll pick them up."

"I just can't understand why his lordship would hire someone so stupid."

"Hey now!"

Cora looked up at him. "Well, what other conclusion can I draw? You really think these are glasses, do you, Mr. Harris?"

"Look, please, call me Andrew."

"They're goggles. Clearly they are goggles. Glasses look like glasses, goggles look like—"

"Goggles. Fine; I get it." Mr. Harris . . . Andrew . . . stupid name . . . Andrew stood up and bent down to collect the fallen tools. "You know," he said, his voice muffled, "you don't have to be quite so unpleasant."

"I'm not being anything. The fact that you bring out my unpleasant side has more to do with you than with me." Cora returned to tweaking her goggles and Andrew started nattering on about something.

She'd been working on the goggles for months now. Lord White had always given her little personal tasks to challenge her, and his latest was to see if she could invent something that would make it possible for a person to see in pitch darkness. It had been his hardest assignment to date, and as she labored over the two glass plates, she had half a mind to just throw the whole thing on the floor and let it break into several pieces. But that was silly. Her frustration was with Andrew. Not with her invention.

She should just have gone with Lord White as he'd asked her to. He was making the rounds, drumming up support for the vote in the House tomorrow. But Cora had no desire to sit, drink tea, and be ogled by old white-haired men. She also didn't want to spend the day listening to Lord White admonish her for the night before.

So she'd stayed behind. To work on the new order. To take inventory of the supplies from yesterday. Mundane stuff. If only she'd remembered that Andrew would be here, too, she would have totally put up with making the rounds.

". . . with Mrs. Philips," Andrew was saying.

"What?" His voice had ceased to be a buzzing in the background and was becoming too much of a distraction. She looked up at him with an exaggerated sigh.

"I said, I've seen you with Mrs. Philips. With Barker. You're as sweet as all get-out. But with me, the way you just ignore me like now, or tell me off like before . . . You, little miss, are a perfect example of it."

"Of what?" *Resist the temptation to punch him for the "little miss" comment, Cora. Resist . . .*

"What I was just talking about. Before."

"Oh, I wasn't listening before."

"I was talking about duality."

"Were you? What the hell for?"

Andrew laughed. "In the book, the idea is that he has two sides to himself . . ."

"Book? What? Honestly Mr. Harris, I really wasn't listening earlier."

Of course, engaging him like this was a ridiculous thing to do, but she couldn't stop herself. He smiled smugly at her interest, and Cora instantly regretted it. "*The Strange Case of Dr. Jekyll and Mr. Hyde.* You might have heard of it. Rather popular. I think it's really very interesting. It's all about—"

"I've read the story," interrupted Cora. "Didn't really care for it. Found it tedious in the storytelling."

"Well, I think it's interesting. The notion that everyone has two sides."

"Well, good for you."

"For example," he continued, oblivious to her contempt, "your two sides could be sweet and harsh."

Cora rolled her eyes inwardly. "So you think me a Mr. Hyde, do you?"

"To be fair, you've never shown me your Jekyll."

She sighed. It was just like a well-educated boy to want to talk themes and theory to show that the expensive education had been worth it. "What are you going on about?"

"I just find it interesting. How we all have fronts . . ."

She sighed. "And your front would be rich, pompous, intolerable fool . . ."

"Intolerable? I'll have you know lots of girls are rather fond of my front. My back, too."

Cora wasn't really listening again. "I don't know if we're all hiding something," she continued, thinking about it now despite herself. "You might be . . . but everybody?" No. Not everyone hid stuff. She thought of Nellie. So direct, to the point. Even with her admission of jealousy. But then there was Michiko, the opposite, all silence and mystery. And what was she, then . . .?

Well, damn it all. He might have a bit of a point. When it came to her.

But it wasn't two sides to her personality. It was rather the difference between the real her and the fake her. It was the frustration bubbling under the surface. An ocean trapped in a goldfish bowl.

God, now she was depressed. Was she meant to live a life of never being who she was? And did she even know who she really was herself?

"You're quiet."

"I'm bored."

"I'm sorry. Didn't think talking about a book about a murderer was dull subject matter."

"The second you said 'duality,' I tuned out."

"Miss Bell, look at me."

She wasn't aware that she hadn't been looking and did. He seemed concerned. He looked . . . sincere. "What?"

"Can we start over?"

"What?"

"Can we be friends? I hate this tension."

Cora sighed again. This time a silent, internal sigh. "It's difficult for me. I don't really like you."

"You don't really know me." He edged his chair closer to hers. "You judged me from the beginning. And, of course, when we first met, you thought I was a thief. Then you learned Lord White hired me, and you clearly did not approve of that. And I think your judgment was colored."

"You think?"

"Please?"

It was so draining hating him. And it wasn't like they had to be best friends or anything. "Fine."

"So we start over."

"We start over."

"Good." He stuck out his hand and she took it with a roll of her eyes. Then he pulled her into a hot kiss, one hand at the back of her neck, the other moving from her hand up along her arm, holding it fast. Cora neither reciprocated nor pulled away. She was too surprised. All she felt was his hot breath and tight fingers. And a horrible, horrible feeling in the pit of her stomach that she feared might be something like pleasure.

He pulled away.

"And that was what exactly?" she asked.

"I'm really sorry—I didn't mean to do that. It was an accident."

"Weird accident."

"I apologize. It won't happen again. Now can we start over?"

"And if I say yes, what exactly will you do this time?"

"What if I get up and stand at the other end of the room, and then on the count of three, we start over?"

"What if we just . . . act normal?"

"Can you do that?"

"Probably not."

"I'm going to the other side of the room." And he did. He stood with his back to the staircase and held up his hand. "Ready?"

Yeah, so this game was not exactly what her mind was focused on at the moment.

"One . . ." He held up one finger. "Two . . ." Two fingers. "Three."

There was silence. Then, with a smile, he came back over to the table and sat down.

"Hi!" he said, extending his hand. "I'm Andrew Harris. But you can call me Andrew."

Cora shook her head and then, with a little laugh, took his hand. "I'm Cora Bell, but you can call me—"

His lips were on hers again, his hand at the back of her neck once more. This time, though, she didn't leave her hands at her side, but rather brought them up to his head and ran them through his soft hair. It was so . . . soft. She returned the kiss. She wanted to drink in more and more of him, and she just wasn't getting enough. She stood up, still tightly lip-locked, and sat on his knee as he pulled her in more tightly, running his hands down her back to her waist, holding on as if he were scared she might suddenly float up and away. And she kind of worried she just might.

Finally Andrew came up for air, taking in a deep breath and staring at her wide-eyed.

"I'm really sorry about this," he said, panting slightly.

"You should be." Cora leaned in and they were kissing again.

He pushed her away.

"I really want you to respect me," he said.

"I do, I do," she replied, leaning in.

"Oh, good."

More kissing.

Then: "You're just saying that."

God, this fellow was infuriating. "What?"

"You think I'm an idiot."

"What?"

"You do. I don't think I've ever had anyone think that of me, especially not a servant."

"I'm sorry, what?" She leaned back.

"No, it's not that. I didn't mean it like that, I'm sorry. It's just . . . you're very bright. Quite the marvel, really."

Grand, both an insult and praise.

In any other moment she'd have had a word or two to say about that, but right then, in that moment . . .

"Oh, just stop talking," she said, kissing him again before he could say anything that would really piss her off.

He pushed her away again.

"I think you're just using me for my looks," he said.

"I wouldn't know how to do that."

"This is doing that."

"Well, I'm a quick study."

Kissing time.

Pushing away time.

Tossing up her hands, Cora rose off his lap and shook her head at him. "You know, that whole duality thing? I'm starting to get it. Make up your mind!"

"About what?" Mrs. Philips was standing halfway down the stairs squinting her eyes at them.

Cora was grateful she'd stood up. She was also grateful she wasn't prone to flushed cheeks, as some girls were when they were embarrassed.

"Oh, nothing, Mrs. Philips. Just having a disagreement about his lordship's latest commission." She smiled at the housekeeper.

"Hmm" was her response. "Well. I've made you both a spot of lunch, if you'd come to the kitchens." And she made her way back up the stairs.

"A bit of a mother hen, that one," said Andrew when she'd gone.

"Yes." But it wasn't a bad thing.

"How about we skip lunch?"

"How about we don't."

They ate under Mrs. Philips's watchful eye, and then returned to work. It was so hard to focus with Andrew sitting right next to her. Like . . . right next to her. His right leg against her left leg, their arms touching as they worked. When she had finally been able to focus on her goggles to the point where she felt she'd solved the problem of making them weigh half as much as they'd first weighed, he had leaned in and kissed her on the neck. She'd never been kissed on the neck before. Before that morning, she'd never been kissed at all. The feeling was so overpowering that she became light-headed. Honest-to-goodness light-headed.

It was fortunate (and also a little disappointing) that Lord White returned from making visits at around two in the afternoon. He came bounding down the stairs, taking them two at a time. Cora was concerned he would just skip several altogether and fall flat on his face.

He joined them with the energy he reserved for spending time in his lab. Certainly aspects of politics invigorated him, and spending a morning and lunch convincing people of his opinion and why they should agree with him tended to put him in high spirits. But add to that an afternoon of fiddling about with tools? He was like a five-year-old. All smiles and rosy cheeks.

All seemed forgiven now. Cora had expected it. Lord White had a tendency to act all huffy about something until he moved on to the next topic and then forgot all about being upset. It was almost as if he could feel only one emotion at a time. Besides, she knew he didn't particularly enjoy being upset with her.

"Well, well! Let's see what you've done," he said, pulling a seat between his two assistants and not noticing how little room he had to squeeze in. There was a pause as he looked at their work. "Not much, evidently."

"We were stumped, so we worked on other projects." And . . . other things.

It was impressive to watch Lord White work. He solved the problem of how to "make it go" in a matter of minutes, sticking pretty much to the original design specs. Then he set his assistants to their jobs and the day turned out to be rather productive after all.

Andrew left before supper, and Lord White and Cora shared a pleasant meal in the formal dining room.

"Now see, isn't it better when you stay home at night instead of leaving me to go gallivanting around the city by yourself?" asked Lord White, scooping himself a second helping of mashed potatoes.

When she didn't respond right away, he looked at her with large trusting eyes, and she sighed.

"Yes," said Cora. "It is."

He smiled brightly and returned to the mashed potatoes.

And Then . . .

NIGHT FELL OVER London. Lights were lit and glowed cozily from tall windows. Responsible people went to bed. Less responsible people ventured forth into the darkness.

Three girls ventured forth.

Michiko, dressed head to toe in black, the Silver Heart at her waist, tiptoed out the back door and into the alley.

And Nellie grabbed a piece of toast as she said good-bye to the Magician, having to return to the apartment a moment later when she noticed Scheherazade had followed her out the door. "Stay, Sherry. Stay."

And Cora, overwhelmed by the day's events, still a little light-headed from Andrew's touch, and needing some air to collect her thoughts, slipped out through the kitchen when Lord White went to bed.

AND THE FOG rolled in.

CORA WAS THE first to stumble on the body. Her walk had led her back to the scene of last night's crime, though she'd had no intention of returning. The carriage had been cleared and the street was empty. No traffic. No sounds from the city, even. Just quiet stillness and a white blanket over everything.

She didn't know why her feet had carried her to this spot. Clearly she hadn't been thinking about the murder at all, but of her own silly concerns. Like did Andrew really like her? Or was he just trying to win her over because she was particularly tricky, unlike the other girls he knew? And if he did like her . . . why?

Of course, there was also the little matter of her own actions. Was she simply attracted to him because of his looks? Had he been right in that? After all, he'd yet to prove himself intellectually. Though . . . he was pretty good at banter. But could one trust someone who bantered so effortlessly?

And then there she was. At the place where a murder had been committed. Where a man's head had been divorced from its body and a man's life from this earth.

Strange place to wander to.

"Cora."

The voice creaked, pushed its way through the fog, and landed a few feet in front of her. Close enough that she heard it, but only just.

"Yes?" she called out.

A pause.

"Help."

The voice was clearer now, and Cora realized it came from behind her, from where she'd just been. She retraced her steps, squinting out into the fog before her.

"Where are you?"

A pause.

"Down . . ."

Another pause.

". . . here."

For the first time, Cora let her eyes fall to the cobblestone road beneath her feet. She caught sight of the hand first, and as she moved toward it, the rest of the body came into view.

It was a girl. Her age? Younger? Older? It was hard to tell. She had the world-weary face of someone who'd grown up on the street, but her eyes were wide with the fear of a small child.

Cora knelt down beside her and finally saw the blood. The last thing to come into sharp focus. The girl was holding her stomach, a mess of red and fabric, her other hand outstretched and clutching at the stone street beneath it. Reaching out as if it was seeking something. The flowers from the basket that lay at her side fell along her torso and spilled onto the ground.

A small, but strong voice. A familiar voice. "Knew it was you. Knew the other day too." A pause to breathe. "Recognized you right off, even if you wouldn't look at me . . ."

"Oh my God." The girl from yesterday. In the market. It all came flooding back. Cora grabbed the hand and felt it squeeze hers tightly.

"What happened?"

"I were comin' to find you. To . . . get yer help. . . . But 'e found me . . . attacked me. . . ." The girl gasped then, and a trickle of blood seeped out of the corner of her mouth.

"Don't talk. Don't say anything, I've got to get you to a doctor."

The girl closed her eyes. "You sound like a real posh one now."

"Shhh . . ."

"Some don't fancy it, says it's all airs. But me, I always knew you'd end up well."

"Please, you have to save your energy. . . ." Cora placed her hand behind the girl's head and tried to prop it up, but it was a deadweight.

The girl opened her eyes again. "Glad it's you, 'ere now. Beginnin' and the end."

Oh my God.

Alice.

The realization flashed bright across her memory. How could she not have recognized Alice?

Tears welled up in Cora's eyes.

"Now, none of that, Cora. You're the tough one. . . . Ain't right."

And that was it.

That was the last thing she said, and it wasn't poetic or profound. In fact, it was all about Cora, which seemed really inappropriate, seeing as she hadn't seen Alice since she was ten years old when they'd run around together making a nuisance of themselves.

Now Alice was lying still in the street, the red still seeping from her middle, and in it little purple and pink flowers.

"Not again!"

Cora turned at the voice and looked up. Nellie was staring at

Alice's body in horror, and Cora flashed back instantly to the night before when they'd discovered Michiko.

Of course, Michiko hadn't died.

Cora stood. "What are you doing here?"

"I was actually comin' to find you. Headin' to your place."

"You, too?"

"Needed to ask your help. Who's she?" Nellie knelt down and picked up a stray flower that had found its way onto the cobblestones.

"She was coming to find me, too. Her name is Alice. We were friends when I was little, living on the street. She had a home, though . . . well, a room in a tenement. Her parents would take me in a lot. They were nice."

And then I vanished and never told them where I'd gone or why, thought Cora, finishing the story to herself. Her stomach was hollow, and yet despite how empty it felt, she thought she might still throw up.

"Why was she comin' to see you?"

"I don't know." How could she not have remembered Alice?

"Do you want a hug?"

Cora looked at Nellie blankly. "What?"

"You're upset. It don't make sense, but a hug can help."

"Uh . . . no . . . thank you." It seemed unlikely that it would make much of a difference. "I could use some help taking her home, though."

"Well, I'm a right good lifter."

"Excellent."

Cora's stomach clenched. As she reached for Alice, her thoughts went back to last night. She'd been so cavalier about the dead guy in Nellie's apartment, turned it into a big joke. And what about the headless Dr. Welland? She'd barely thought of him since last night. But this time it hit home. The men from last night weren't just bodies; they'd been people, with lives and folk who cared about them. Just as tonight she carried not just a corpse in her arms, but Alice. Quiet, sweet Alice who only got in trouble because Cora got her into it.

And she wondered . . . was it somehow her fault in this case, too?

She shouldn't have dismissed Dr. Welland's murder as she had. Whoever this mysterious attacker in the fog was, he meant business. And Cora wasn't about to make the same mistake twice.

"Hello."

"Good God, what are *you* doing here?" Both Nellie and Cora stood upright as Michiko approached from the shadows. She was dressed head to toe in black, literally, for a hood covered her long sleek hair, so that she appeared to be a ghostly face floating in the fog.

Michiko, of course, didn't say anything; just looked at the body before her.

"We're takin' her home," explained Nellie slowly.

"Home. Yes." Michiko understood. Cora was certain of that.

All three girls bent down and took hold of the girl. She

wasn't that heavy to lift, and Cora wasn't surprised. Alice had been a bit of a frail thing to begin with, and being poor helped keep one's figure trim. Well, that was a nice way of putting it. There was nothing fashionable about starving.

"Follow my lead," she said.

They met few people on their journey, and the one elderly man they did pass nodded sagely, as if he'd long been expecting to see three girls carrying a dead body.

It wasn't until they turned down the dusty alley that led to Alice's front door that anyone took any real notice.

"Blimey, what's that, then?" asked a rough voice, and though Cora refused to answer the man, he came up to investigate anyway. "That ain't Alice, is it? No. Bloody hell!" He ran up ahead of them and was banging on the door before they even got a chance. "Toby! Mary!" He yelled so loudly that windows opened around them, heads peered out.

Cora, Nellie, and Michiko carried the body to the door, which opened as they arrived. Alice's parents stood in the frame. Toby, a short squat man, stood protectively in front of his tiny wife.

"Mr. Foster . . ." started Cora, but he had no interest in what she had to say. Silent tears started streaming down his cheeks the moment he saw his little girl, and without uttering a word, he stepped to one side to allow the three of them to bring her across the threshold. The door shut out the man who'd banged on the door and the rest of the prying eyes.

It was an awkward moment, standing in the small public

stairwell, but soon Mr. Foster scooped up Alice out of their hands and into his arms, and they were following him up three flights of stairs.

The place hadn't changed in all the time that Cora had been living at Lord White's—though, Cora thought, it seemed smaller. The same faded wallpaper peeked out from under several layers of grime. And the stairs creaked as much as they ever had, letting everyone in the building know someone was using them. It had been extra frustrating when the someone who was using them had been trying to sneak in late at night, Cora recalled. And that smell. That same smell of sweat and body odor, of men and women worked to the bone. Of boots tracking in the waste, human and animal, from the street. Of booze and burned meat.

Doors opened as they passed, just a crack, just enough to see what it was this time. And then they closed. As they always did.

The room the Fosters rented was on the third floor, and as they entered it, Cora noticed how it, too, seemed unchanged. Neat and as tidy as Mary could make it, with her hand-sewn quilts covering the walls as artwork. A dwindling fire burned in the small coal stove, a luxury that the Fosters had always been proud of.

Gingerly, Toby laid his daughter on the small mattress in the corner, the same mattress Cora and Alice had snuggled on to keep each other warm whenever she was a guest.

Now nothing would keep Alice warm.

Toby pushed his daughter's hair from her face and sat down beside her, holding her hand.

"Did you see 'im?" asked Mary quietly, setting herself in her chair by the fire and gesturing for Cora to take the other one. She gestured to Nellie and Michiko, too, but they seemed content to stay in the corner by the door.

"No," replied Cora.

Mary nodded. "It started a few nights ago. First Gwen, then Annie. Then Beth. All flower girls. We warned her. Told her not to go. Just for now. But Alice, she—"

"Was stubborn."

"You knew her?"

"Mrs. Foster, it's me, Cora Bell."

Mary covered her mouth with her hand and her stoic expression faltered. Her eyes filled with tears that made them shine in the candlelight. "Oh my. Cora Bell. Now, ain't that somethin'. She said she was going to find you, to ask you to help. That you'd listen. Said somethin' about seein' ya the other day. But I never thought—"

"She recognized me right away. She recognized me through the fog."

"She were always a clever one. Never thought it of herself, though." Mary couldn't hold back anymore, and Cora was astounded to see the woman, who had always been so strong and yet so kind, finally break down. Funny how memories could just come back to you as clear as day after not having thought about them for years. Mary Foster had always been the one to go to if things got tough, if life got hard. Harder than it already was. She could fix any problem, make you feel right again.

So seeing her upset, even though she hadn't seen her in

years, made Cora's throat so tight she thought she might stop breathing.

"I want you to know," Cora said, fighting the tears back with each word, "that I'm going to find the man who did this. And I'll bring him to justice."

It sounded so grand, so noble. She didn't feel either, particularly.

Mary reached out and grabbed her hand. "The police ain't interested in the likes of us. Even though it's a pattern as clear as any, they say it's just coincidence. But they'd listen to you, like Alice said. What with your new . . . arrangement."

Cora wondered exactly what the people of her old community thought that arrangement was. She was pretty sure she knew where their imaginations had taken them.

But she just nodded.

"Now, how about a cuppa?" Mary stood.

"That's lovely of you, Mrs. Foster, but I should be getting back. It's quite late." Cora rose and glanced at Nellie and Michiko. She was impressed how they didn't seem to mind being so inconvenienced. Especially seeing as they'd all only just met the day before. It wasn't as if they owed her anything, especially not loyalty.

"Right," said Mary. "Well."

She looked at Cora, and Cora looked at her, and everything felt so completely odd.

How does one leave a room that had been a second home once, a family one hasn't seen in seven years, and a flower girl growing cold in the corner?

In the end, there's only one way.

Through the door.

Once the door was closed and all three girls were standing on the other side, Cora quietly said, "Bye, Alice." She leaned her forehead against the door. Then, in barely a whisper, added, "I'm an awful person."

"You're not," said Nellie, placing a warm hand on her shoulder.

"Didn't even say good-bye back then. Didn't even come to see them."

"What, you were ten, right? You were a little kid. Now, don't you go judgin' a wee kid."

Cora turned to face her new friends. They were friends, weren't they? It was okay for her to think of them that way, right? Not that she deserved friends, not with how easily she could just forget about people, desert people . . .

She just stared at Nellie and Michiko, not able to articulate what she wanted to say. Not knowing what that was in the first place.

"Let's get you some fresh air, then." Nellie wrapped a protective arm around her shoulder and escorted her down the stairs and into the now-empty narrow street.

Three Girls and Three Men

NELLIE DIDN'T KNOW Cora particularly well. This was because she'd only met her the night before, and you just couldn't get to know a person that quickly. Like the Magician—it had been almost two years now and he'd still surprise her with a new story or a new talent. But she was good at reading people. It was her thing. And she knew that Cora was hurting. Bad.

The street air seemed to calm her a little bit, but Nellie knew a good walk would refresh the senses best. She led her friends back toward Lord White's, a place she'd never been to but had ascertained the whereabouts of that afternoon.

"Uh," said Nellie after they'd wandered out onto the empty high street. Though there couldn't have been fewer people on the road than on the narrower streets they'd navigated, it seemed even more deserted because of its size and the lack of the usual daytime bustle. The fog today was yellower in hue than the night before, and the lamps glowed like little suns at equal intervals along the street. Little creepy suns.

"Did you say something?" asked Cora.

"Well, it don't seem right to ask you for a favor . . ."

"Why not?"

"Well . . . uh . . ."

"What is it, Nellie?"

"You remember that bloke . . . the one in my sittin' room . . ."

"The dead guy, yes."

Nellie turned to examine Cora's expression, but it didn't flinch, so she continued. She explained the story from earlier that day, about the weird Dr. Mantis, and even mentioned the eyeballs, because they were particularly noteworthy. Then she brought up the checkbook and Mr. Carter.

"And I was thinkin', seein' as you seemed to know everyone at the party last night . . ."

"I could talk to him about it. I can't see that being a problem."

Nellie smiled. "Thanks."

"What do you want?" It was Michiko from behind them, an edge to her voice.

"I say, that was a remarkably confident complete sentence there, Michiko," said Cora, turning around, with Nellie following her half a moment after.

"Oh, bleedin' hell," said Nellie.

"'Allo girls."

Three men, three stupidly large and quite ugly men, were grinning at them. Michiko had her hands on her hips, standing protectively before Cora and Nellie.

"Just leave us," said Cora, in a tone of voice that Nellie understood to mean she was not in the mood for this.

The man in the middle with the muttonchops laughed, revealing a large gap where the front few of his teeth should be. Then he stopped suddenly. "No."

The men moved closer, causing Nellie and Cora instinctively to step back, but Michiko stood steadfast, allowing Muttonchops to tower over her.

"What do you want?" she asked.

He stared at her for a moment, then gave a look to his buddies. "Well, seein' as you asked . . . I'll take them purses, and that there sword at yer hip. And then . . . we'll see what else I want."

"Sounds threatening," said Cora. Nellie watched her as she reached into her purse.

She also saw Michiko kneel down on the cold street, her legs still quite wide apart, and the man before her take a stunned step backward.

"What the hell's she doin'?" he asked.

"No idea," replied Cora. Her hand appeared from within her purse, empty. "But I'd be just a little bit concerned."

ENTER EVERY DUEL expecting to die.

That was hard in this case, since it was so clear she'd easily defeat them. They weren't even worthy of fighting, really. If it weren't for the need to protect the other two. The blonde and the brunette.

Stillness.

Calm.

Breathe.

Time to wake up the Silver Heart.

Michiko reached with lightning speed to her left side and pulled the hilt of the *katana* a notch, just a bit, just to let it know it was time. Then it was unsheathed, and she was back on her feet, holding it in both hands before her.

The three strange men looked a little taken aback at the sight of the Silver Heart. Michiko's speed was impressive. She knew this. She could make it seem that the *katana* had materialized out of thin air in her hands.

They looked a bit like children to her, mouths agape, brains not quite up to speed with what had just happened. What was about to happen.

She would not kill them. Who kills children?

Her focus shifted, her mind clear.

First man. Second man. Third man. Like looking through a telescope, her focus examined each up close.

Okay.

She attacked.

THE MEN RAN like wild creatures, holding tightly to their wounds, leaving a trail of blood behind them. If Michiko had been a hunting animal, they'd have been easy for her to stalk, thought Nellie. But there was nothing animal-like in the efficiency with which she'd disposed of her prey.

"One each," said Michiko, turning to them with a small smile.

"One cut, you mean?" asked Nellie.

"Cut. Yes. Arm, arm, leg. Leg for leader. Bad man."

So she'd reasoned the whole thing out, in so little time. In a blink of an eye, it had seemed. In the dark, Nellie had been able to discern very little of what Michiko had done, her black outfit a blur in the fog. Only the blade was clear to see, reflecting the light from the streetlamps, and then, even then, it had seemed she'd made only one move, not three.

"Thank you," said Cora, staring at Michiko with the same awe that Nellie felt.

Michiko nodded.

The silence now was awkward, and then Nellie started to giggle. She couldn't help herself. It was nervous energy combined with the awesomeness she'd just seen.

Cora grinned, too, despite everything she'd been through that night.

Michiko furrowed her brow.

"I think it's time maybe for us to be gettin' on home," said Nellie, calming herself.

Cora nodded, and Michiko, who seemed to understand the word *home*, sighed a little sadly, it seemed.

"Everyone comfortable being on their own?" asked Cora in her take-charge kind of voice. "By which I, of course, mean Nellie. Michiko, I think you'll be just fine."

"I'm good. I coulda' taken them, if Michiko hadn't." Nellie wasn't entirely certain she spoke the truth, but she'd done okay with the creepy eyeball man, and then there was the footman from the other night. Besides, worse came to worst, no one was better at disappearing than she was. "How about you, though?"

Cora shrugged and produced a tiny gun from her purse. "I'm good."

They made their final farewells.

And then they were off.

THREE GIRLS INTO the night.

PART THREE
Investigations

A Lesson

THERE WAS NO light to wake Michiko the next morning.

No physical signal that her body was rested and ready to face a new day.

There was, however, a knock on the tiny window next to her bed, the window that she'd never been able to wrench open.

"*What?*" Michiko pushed herself off her bed, her neck crying out in pain because she had slept on the right side of her face the whole night. Still half asleep, it took her a moment to figure out that the sound was, in fact, coming from her window. But the second she found the source of the noise, she was wide-awake.

Hayao's upside-down face was staring at her. He wore a big smile, and when she finally saw him, he waved happily.

Oh, for crying out loud. Michiko got out of bed and went to the window. Of course, the thought that he was dangling from a roof five stories above the street had occurred to her, but she wasn't too surprised by this fact. His athleticism was, after all, what had impressed her about him. Exactly this monkey business . . .

"*What do you want?*" she asked loudly from behind the glass, for once happy that Callum made her sleep all the way up in the servants' quarters and far away from him.

"*It's time for lessons,*" he said back.

Michiko scoffed at this. "*You're not the one who gets to choose when we learn, little monkey.*"

"*I just thought you'd probably be busy later, and—*"

"*What time is it?*"

"*Five.*"

Michiko was suddenly exhausted. Back when she was studying in Japan, early mornings were a regular part of her day, but early nights were common as well. And she'd spent the better part of last night first carting a dead girl around the city, and then, upon parting ways with those very strange and giggly girls, stalking some fog man who never materialized.

Still, she wasn't going to let monkey boy out-energize her.

"*Fine. Go to the garden. Wait for me. Sit . . . still.*"

Hayao nodded vigorously and disappeared back onto the roof.

She didn't hurry to meet him. Patience was going to be one of the more important lessons for monkey boy. So she took her time dressing in her all-black training gear, thinking that, really, she'd only just removed it a few hours earlier.

Why had she agreed to this, again?

Then she lightly made her way down two flights of stairs in the pitch darkness to the second floor, where all the weapons were stored. She took stock of the shoddy choices available to her and decided on two gentleman's canes. She closed the cabinet quietly and had a look at Callum's physical therapy equipment, lit by the lamp in the street whose light filtered through the tall windows that ran along the far wall. The various devices looked unnatural and the stuff of horror stories to her, but Callum's patients paid good money to be treated with them. Evidently he could ease their pains. Renew their bodies.

It made little sense to her.

She'd wasted enough time. Hopefully the boy had left in impatience, but she doubted it. He was determined, that one. After all, he'd had no idea where she slept, so he had probably spent a good long while investigating every window of the house to find her.

She sighed. Time to go outside.

THE COMMUNAL GARDEN that filled the square between the two narrow streets was locked from nine at night until eight in the morning. A high, wrought-iron fence with spikes at the top was enough to enforce the rule. For most people. For someone like Michiko and, she had no doubt, Hayao, such fortifications were little more than a closed door, a slight obstacle that had to be contended with for a moment and then overcome.

Scaling the fence was nothing for her, and she was quickly concealed from the street in a leafy cover. Michiko had to admit that the garden was pretty nice, a flash of green in the general gloom of the dark, gray neighborhood. Trees and hedges blocked the open space in the middle from preying eyes, and small flower gardens lined the green from one end to the other, all merging under a bubbling birdbath fountain.

Hayao was sitting cross-legged right in the center of the green. His eyes were closed, and clearly he'd taken her instruction to wait for her quite literally. She approached him in silence and took a moment to observe him.

Then she struck him on the shoulder with a cane.

"*Ow!*" Hayao flinched and opened his eyes wide.

"*Why did you react?*" asked Michiko, circling around him to the other side.

"*Because you hit me.*"

"*So?*"

"*It hurt.*"

"*So?*"

"*It surprised me.*"

"*So?*"

Hayao stopped talking.

Michiko started.

"*You feel pain. You feel surprise. An unexpected moment happened and you reacted. But why? We can feel, we can think, we can react without having to share this information. Discipline and control allow the samurai to internalize every moment. Distraction can be deadly.*

"*Distraction is one of the samurai's deadliest weapons. We yell when we attack. We wear our masks to strike fear in the hearts of our enemies. We hit you on the left so we may cut you on the right. Do you know of the story of the samurai who sat for four hours waiting for the sun to rise? Did your old master tell you that one?*"

Hayao didn't respond.

Michiko smiled. Okay, this was kind of fun. "*You may answer.*"

"He chose his position so that when the sun rose, it would be in his opponent's eyes," replied Hayao quickly.

"Yes. An example of using distraction to defeat one's enemy. Also an example of patience. Both are your lessons for this morning. For the next hour you will stay here and sit. You will keep your eyes open and observe the world around you. Your breathing will be slow and measured. Your thoughts will flow in and out of your mind like water, for a sticking thought can be as distracting as a physical threat. You will not lose focus. You will stay centered. Understand?"

Hayao gave a little nod, then furrowed his brow in concentration. Michiko smacked the back of his head. *"Relaxed focus. Your body should be calm, but alert. Not tight. Tight does not win. Tight causes muscles to pull and tear."*

Hayao's brow slowly released. And Michiko nodded.

For the next hour Hayao did his best to follow Michiko's instructions as she practiced different *katas* with the two canes. Once in a while a cane would find its way to Hayao's leg or hand or arm, a short sharp tap. The boy couldn't seem to prevent himself from flinching. He would learn.

Finally the sun rose, and though the leaves sheltered Hayao from its full brightness, the moment wasn't lost on him. He didn't squint. He smiled.

"*No,*" said Michiko quietly. He immediately stopped. "*Not being distracted by the sun this morning is good. But you were still distracted by the memory of the story.*"

With that, the lesson was over. She had to get back to the house before Callum discovered her absence. The last morning she had been lucky. He had not come home until lunchtime.

Where he'd spent the night she didn't know and didn't care. But she suspected one of his many female admirers had something to do with it. She'd been spared the beating she otherwise would have received had he learned that she hadn't come home that night herself.

But he had been asleep in his luxurious four-poster bed when she'd sneaked out last night, and he'd be awake soon. They had a day trip to Cambridge where they were scheduled to give a demonstration in front of an assembly of college students.

"*Come back tomorrow morning. Same time. We shall meet here again,*" instructed Michiko.

"*But what about my lesson to you?*"

"*What?*"

"*My running.*"

Of course. She'd nearly forgotten. And she did want to learn. It would help her so much in seeking out the fog man if she could run along the rooftops instead of navigating narrow streets. She'd intended to go out again that night in her quest, not studying a new skill. But sometimes taking the time to learn, though a seeming step back, could help move a person forward more quickly.

"*Tonight.*"

Hayao smiled and then he turned and bounded up and over the garden fence, using a tree to propel himself upward.

Little monkey.

Politics

IT HAD BEEN almost exactly a year since Lord White had first brought Cora with him to the Palace of Westminster. It was an odd sort of coming-out for a girl, but she was presented to Lord White's colleagues as his assistant in a way oddly similar to the way a girl of means would be presented to society as a candidate ready for marriage. Cora had found herself surrounded by men who complimented her for little more than existing; the main difference was simply that none of them was interested in courting her.

Now a year on, she was a common sight walking down the neo-Gothic halls of Parliament. And, where once she had been mocked as one of the only women in the palace, now others were mocked if they didn't know who she was. She was famous.

She was also being totally ignored this morning. And not in that usual "Oh, it's just Miss Bell" kind of way. There was a heightened feeling of tension this morning—something different from the typical anxiety that preceded a vote. Usually the halls were filled with men trying to make last-minute deals with their colleagues, pretending they weren't remotely concerned about the outcome and sweating through to their topcoats. It was a mix of denial and male bravado. Fascinating in its absurdity.

Today. Different.

"Dr. Welland," whispered Lord White into her ear as they passed between two of the Queen's guards.

Of course. The doctor's murder had been the subject of much conversation in the last day or so. Articles had been appearing in both the morning and evening papers speculating about the murder. The victim had evidently been found by some most clever police officers in the wee hours, his body and head easy enough to recognize. Cora had a faint memory of a young officer speaking with her at the door and wondered if there was a reason her presence at the scene had been left out of the newspapers.

Dr. Welland wasn't an MP. He had never been been involved in any particular political doings at all, from what Cora could tell. She'd only met him a handful of times accompanying Lord White and she'd been more focused on her boss than on the doctor. His lordship had found it so hard to conceal his fondness for inventing things, the internal struggle playing across his face in a series of twitches and short intakes of breath. It had been fascinating and a little sad to watch.

There would be a funeral, of course, and it would be quite the event. Anyone who was anyone would likely be there. Maybe a few anyones who weren't anyone, even.

The bell rang. Like Eton schoolboys, the men in the chambers picked themselves up and, in an orderly fashion, started toward the House. Cora stayed close to Lord White's heels, though she wouldn't be allowed onto the floor itself, of course. She'd go and sit up in the gallery.

"We'll send flowers to Mrs. Rawley, but take John Able off the list . . . ," Lord White said with regard to a completely unrelated matter as she jotted it all down in her notebook. He always just said whatever came to his mind, and she had to sort it all out on her own later.

Cora allowed her eyes to flick up and take quick stock of her company. She had to find Mr. Carter in this mess. He was usually pretty easy to spot, towering several inches above most of the gentlemen.

She turned to look upstream, and finally, as Mr. Low scuttled over to plead one last futile time with Mr. Fish, Mr. Carter and his long limbs came into view. Lord White had stopped speaking, and Cora made the decision that he was finished for now. She could have turned and fought her way up to Mr. Carter, but it seemed like a bit of an ordeal to put herself through. So she simply stopped walking.

Okay, so the man behind her almost fell flat on his face when she did, and she was sworn at as he passed, but it worked remarkably well. In no time, Mr. Carter had floated up next to her and given her a small, tight-lipped smile.

"Bad news about Dr. Welland," she said.

"Indeed."

Cora had to jog to keep up with his long strides.

"A great loss to the scientific community," she added.

Mr. Carter grunted back. Odd that he was so uncommunicative. He was usually quite pleasant to her.

"I met him a few times with Lord White, and—"

"Must we discuss this, Miss Bell?" asked Mr. Carter abruptly.

"Oh, uh, no. I suppose not. I just thought you, in particular, would care, that's all."

"And why is that?"

"Well, I thought you were a financial contributor to the Medical and Scientific Institute. Thought you'd care that one of its top men had been murdered . . ."

It was Mr. Carter's turn to stop the flow of traffic. He seemed unaware of the chaos he had caused and just stared at Cora for a really uncomfortably long moment. Then he grabbed her wrist and yanked her across the flow of men and into an arched alcove.

"What?" he finally managed to say when they were on their own.

"I thought . . . that is to say . . ."

"How would you know something like that? Does Lord White know?"

"I honestly can't remember where I heard it, but I don't think his lordship knows. I don't think he'd mind if he did."

Mr. Carter was a pasty-faced man at the best of times. A bit of a stereotype of an Englishman, with white, almost translucent skin and yellowing teeth. Cora was impressed that he managed to become even paler at this moment. His mustache, a fine waxed line across his upper lip, quivered.

"Mr. Carter, are you all right?"

"This isn't good. Not at all. Who else knows?"

"I couldn't tell you." She really couldn't. She was pretty sure he'd freak out if he knew that Nellie knew, too.

"Where did you hear it from?" His voice was getting loud and he grabbed both her shoulders.

"I don't—"

"Don't tell me you don't remember, little girl. Don't tell me that. You do, and you're keeping it from me. He told you, didn't he? How did you meet him? Of course, he liked you. Look at you. Look at your eyes."

"My eyes?"

"They're stunning."

A moment of total confusion. "Uh, thank you?"

"I've got to go home." Mr. Carter released Cora so violently that she nearly lost her balance, and he made his way up the now-empty corridor in the opposite direction.

"Mr. Carter, the vote!" Cora called after him. But he didn't respond. He didn't do anything but let those long strides of his carry him out of sight.

A Delivery

THE SHIP APPROACHED from the east, hovering several feet above the water on a shimmer of steam and air. It wasn't the biggest ship Nellie had seen, possibly the size of a small frigate, with as many masts and sails, but hovering technology was only a couple of years old, so it was still pretty impressive to watch the ship make berth. She and the Magician stood right at the edge of the dock as the ship gently glided to a stop. The steam passed over them, propelled by hot air, and Nellie and the Magician were showered by a fine mist.

"Refreshing," said the Magician, giving her a smile.

All Nellie could think was that her hair was going to be seriously frizzy now.

The Magician usually had his shipments come in to the London Docks at the Wapping Basin, but today they'd traveled over to the West India Docks off Blackwall Reach. It was the first time he'd ordered anything from Africa, and this was where the *Sunburnt Mary* made berth.

The dock system here was two-tiered, a lower level for vessels that sailed upon the water and an upper one for the hovering ships, the ones that floated just above, using the steam created between the bottom of the ship and the water in the sea to propel themselves forward. The West India Docks were currently the only ones outfitted to accommodate the new technology.

Despite the unusual architecture of the place, the smell of the rotting fish and rancid stagnant water that were trapped under the docks was all too familiar to Nellie. The noise, too. The hustle and bustle of travel, of work, always intrigued her. She watched as a young family boarded a small cutter, the child far more excited about the journey than the mother who held on to her tightly.

There were sailors sitting on barrels and leaning against struts, smoking and eating pale-looking sandwiches. Engineers, wearing large round goggles and holding strange large tools, dangled on ropes alongside the hovering crafts. There were several dock masters running about in their black suits carrying notebooks and yelling at everyone and no one.

And then there was the small group of children that had congregated at a distance to stare at the Magician. While almost everyone tended to stare at him, children were the only ones who did it so artlessly. Nellie respected that.

It took some time before the giant crane began to unload the crates from the ship. Nellie knew she and the Magician could have come a full half hour later at least to pick up his shipment, but the Magician had really wanted to see the *Sunburnt Mary* come in.

"Take pleasure even in the daily tasks of life," he'd say. And that was all well and good if you took pleasure in watching boats. Nellie took pleasure in sleeping in.

The Magician was waiting for a few orders of powders and bottled liquids from Africa for himself, but also waiting for items requested by others. He took requests only if they could be filled by the same local supplier that he was getting orders from, and in this case, fortunately, there were only a few items that had to find their owners.

Finally, they had collected all their goods and traveled back to the south market square in the Magician's open wagon. It always felt a little old-fashioned to travel by wagon now that there were those steam-carriages available. They easily could have afforded such a luxury, but the Magician liked his wagon. He liked Brutus and Caesar, the old workhorses he had to pull it. The fact was, he had no need to show off to others, and considering where they lived, he'd explained, having expensive new things might appear insensitive to their neighbors. The Magician had an odd way of not caring what others thought and yet, at the same time, doing just that.

The crates were unloaded from the carriage by a couple of helpful boys to whom the Magician tossed a couple of shillings. The first large box, the top of which was riddled with holes, was delivered almost immediately to a very round woman who looked beyond thrilled to see it. The package seemed pretty thrilled to see her, too, the contents making a cross between a growl and a purr as she carted it away.

They had to wait a little longer for the other one to be picked up, and Nellie took a turn about the market as she waited, pausing by the Japanese man's stand. One of the two boys who worked for him was fast asleep on the ground, leaning up against the leg of a table, but the old man hadn't noticed. Or at least didn't seem to care. Nellie glanced over the weapons and thought about Michiko's sword from the night before. How quickly she'd moved it through the air.

She returned to the Magician just in time to see two tall and thin gentlemen approach. Nellie marveled at their appearance. They seemed like shadows, so lanky and dark in their attire. Both wore bowler caps and dark, tattered overcoats, and each had a pair of dark, round sunglasses. The man on the left had dark stubble on his chin and dark, greasy hair that fell in curls down to just below his chin. The man on the right was clean-shaven save for an overwaxed mustache, and though it was hard to tell, it being hidden by his hat, Nellie suspected his hair was probably equally overly tended. When they were close enough, Nellie got a whiff of a strange odor. A dense, overripe, stale thing.

"You the Great Raheem?" asked the mustached man, his voice higher than Nellie expected.

"I am. Are you Mr. Proper?" replied the Magician.

"Aye." He paused. Then: "This is my business partner, Mr. Staunch." He made a slight nod to the curly-haired man. Nellie gasped and both men looked at her. She immediately smiled brightly. In unison their heads turned back toward the Magician, and the transaction continued.

"You've given me too much," said the Magician, counting the coins Mr. Proper had produced.

"Finder's fee," explained Mr. Staunch.

"That's unnecessary." The Magician returned the extra coin and nodded to Nellie, who produced a small sealed box with "handle with care" stamped on the side. She held it out before her and Mr. Proper, noticing her again as if for the first time, slowly leaned in and took it from her. The air between them seemed to hum as she passed the package, but that didn't make any sense.

Then the two men turned and disappeared in the crowd.

"Do you know them?" asked Nellie when she felt that it was safe to speak.

"Only one of them. Grave robbers. Fascinating that they would want anything from Africa. Seems like they're branching out. Why?" The Magician gave her that piercing look of his. There were days when Nellie was certain he could read her mind.

"It's just, when I was at the institute investigatin' the society, I came across their names."

"That makes sense. They make their living selling their . . . goods . . . to hospitals and so forth on the black market. Surely someone at the institute would need a body part or two."

Well, creepy eye man certainly would. Made perfect sense, actually, that he'd hire them. Still . . .

"Oh."

"You're not so sure?"

"No, I'm sure. It sits bad with me, that's all."

"Well, they don't exactly come across as friendly and approachable. But I see your meaning. Never trust anyone who smells of death."

"Was that what that was?"

"That was. Also never trust anyone who steals bodies from their graves and sells them for profit and orders strange things from distant lands through a third party."

"That makes sense."

"Yes." He didn't speak for a moment. Just stood, quietly. Then he exhaled so slowly that it could hardly have been called a sigh. Though maybe it was. His version of one. "Come. We have a show to prepare for."

An Afternoon on the Town

CORA RARELY WENT to matinees. In fact, she couldn't recall if she'd ever seen one. After all, she had to work long hours for his lordship, and anytime they went to the theater it was usually not just for the pleasure of catching a show. Negotiations would be made during the interval. Notes passed between men in boxes. And, of course, it was important to be seen.

A silly turn of phrase, Cora thought, to be "seen." As if one was invisible if one was not in attendance at events that someone had decided were important. She wondered who made those decisions. Which event was important, which was not.

In any case . . .

She rarely saw matinees.

She oughtn't to be seeing one today either. She knew that. But Lord White had a late lunch with some of the peers and then . . . well, then she'd been informed of a change to his schedule. Evidently, after all the hard work of securing votes, it was time for his lordship to hit the Red Veil again.

Twice in one week.

Such fun for her, of course.

But it didn't matter what Lord White got up to. She was meant to return to the house and work on the new commission. Or if not that, at least go over the accounts for the tax man.

Of course . . . none of this meant that she had any plans of returning home anytime soon.

You see. There was the small matter of Mr. Harris.

She didn't know why she feared Andrew exactly. She'd tried to figure it out, but in the end, it was all a bit of a mess in her head. Basically, the thought of seeing Andrew terrified her. While other girls thrilled at seeing the boys they had romantic entanglements with, evidently Cora dreaded it. Clearly this was because something was wrong with her.

Or maybe . . . there was a difference between what her heart and her head wanted, and her head was still not entirely convinced that Andrew was someone she should spend time with. He didn't seem to be able to solve problems without her help, had a bit of an ego about his appearance, and that whole "duality" thing. That seemed a little pretentious to her, really, if she thought about it. Even if she'd sort of agreed with the premise.

But he was also really good-looking.

And a great kisser.

Feelings were messy.

She couldn't avoid him forever. But she could today. Especially because she needed to tell Nellie of Mr. Carter's strange response to her that morning. So why not take in a magic show? And how convenient that there happened to be a matinee. As if she was meant to avoid going home.

It was fate.

Yeah, that's it.

Fate.

The Great Raheem had a couple days' engagement at St. James's Theater on King Street. It was a popular theater, done up in a very decadent baroque style. The theater's manager, Mr. Alexander, would schedule the Great Raheem during the dark period between plays, and thus the Magician became a constant performer at the theater while shows came and went. There must have been a friendship there, Cora assumed. And why not? Everyone loved the Great Raheem, and he brought sold-out shows and certain profit wherever he went.

Which, of course, meant that Cora was in standing-room-only in the upper circle.

The show was wonderful. The tricks from the gala were performed again, and Cora was still astonished by them. There was more audience participation. And tricks involving larger set pieces. There was one where Nellie was hidden in a solid iron safe, and somehow she managed to appear moments later at the back of the audience, to loud cheers and applause. Amazing.

When the show was over, Cora joined the throng of fans waiting at the stage door, and in short order, the Great Raheem and Nellie appeared. They were immediately swarmed, and Cora found herself at the back of the pack, jumping to get Nellie's attention. Finally, she gave up being subtle and just called her name out loudly. Blond curls bobbed up above the crowd for a moment, and then Nellie's face appeared as she made her way over to her.

"You were great!" Cora called out by way of encouragement. The crowd was formidable, and more than a bit intimidating.

"Thanks," said Nellie with a big exhausted smile, pushing aside the final few overly excited men and coming up to her side. "Let's go . . . over here." She grabbed Cora by the arm and dragged her down the alley and out onto the street behind the theater. Some of the men called after them, upset at Nellie's sudden departure. "Sorry for pullin' you like that. Did you like the show?" Nellie asked brightly.

"I did. Say, how did you get to the back of the house? That was incredible!"

Nellie laughed. "Can't tell you that! It's magic. Okay, and a body double."

"Really?"

Nellie grinned. "Whatcha doin' here?"

"I talked to Mr. Carter this morning, like you asked."

"And?"

"And nothing. He had nothing to say."

Nellie sighed. "That's too bad."

"Not really. He was acting very odd. Asking who told me . . ."

"Who told you what?"

"Exactly. No idea. And then he ran off, I think to go home. Didn't even get a chance to vote."

"That *is* odd!"

"I'm sorry I couldn't help much more than that."

"That's okay."

There was a natural pause in the conversation. Cora used

it to think about whether she wanted to ask Nellie something. She decided she would.

"I . . . also . . ."

"Yes?"

"Well, I was planning on going to the police station today, to tell them about what happened last night, and thought maybe you'd want to come along with me."

Nellie thought for a moment, then nodded. "I guess I could. I don't think I could help much. You got to the flower girl before I did."

"The company would be nice."

Nellie nodded sagely.

"Of course," she said, placing a reassuring hand on Cora's shoulder.

"Uh . . . thanks."

CONSIDERING THE SHABBY appearance of anyone not in uniform, the girls rather stood out in the dark little station in the Foster family's district. A few rough men who reminded Nellie a bit of those blokes from the night before stared at them as they passed without even trying to pretend that they weren't.

Cora approached the desk sergeant, who was standing up on his platform behind a high solid desk. "Excuse me, please," she said in that commanding way she had.

"Yes?" The officer glanced up, and it was likely he'd intended it to be a brief glance, but upon glancing back down, he clearly had some kind of realization and looked up instantly again.

"Yes, miss," he said with a friendly smile. Noticing Nellie then, he said, ". . . both of you young misses."

"We would like to report a murder," said Cora.

"Oh. Well, that is very important business. What's the particulars, then?" he asked, picking up a pencil and holding it on top of the pad before him.

"A flower girl, near Charing Cross."

The officer carefully returned the pencil to its resting position and took a moment to think. He glanced at the two of them again, his eyes flitting between the blonde and the brunette. He did a once-over of Cora, and Nellie was pretty sure he was examining not the figure but the clothes hiding it. They were formidable clothes, clearly worth a pretty penny despite their practical, simple appearance.

He made eye contact with Cora once again and then called out, "Murphy!"

There was the sound of something crashing to the ground somewhere in back, the skidding squeak of shoes across a polished floor, and then Murphy came exploding out to join them.

"Oh," said Nellie immediately, and Cora looked at her. Nellie didn't say anything else, just looked at Cora wide-eyed, hoping to send her thoughts magically into her brain at this moment. *Let's go now, let's go now, let's go now.*

"Yes, Sergeant! You called, sir?" said Officer Murphy, still oblivious to the girls' existence. For which Nellie was infinitely grateful. Of all the police stations in all of London . . .

"These young ladies need to make a statement about a

murder. Will you take them back and see to it?" said the sergeant, gesturing toward them. Finally, Officer Murphy turned their way.

Pink. Pure pink. Not red, not blotchy, but the pink face of total recognition and embarrassment. "You!" he blurted.

"You know these young ladies, Murphy?" asked the sergeant, a hint of something in his voice. Anger? Jealousy?

"Uh . . . no." A stupid answer and clearly a lie, but fortunately at that moment the front door burst open and everyone turned to see two coppers trying to manage a large barrel-chested hairy man who was flailing around and looking a bit like an overgrown infant. His entrance distracted everyone in the room, including the desk sergeant.

Officer Murphy took the opportunity to signal Cora and Nellie, and they followed him into the larger back room. They passed several desks manned by surprised-looking police officers until they arrived at Murphy's. Of course, as there were two girls and only that number of chairs, Officer Murphy had to take a turn about the room before he could find one for himself, managing, in the process, to knock all the items on a fellow officer's desk onto the floor.

Soon he had returned and was sitting, his face expressing mild panic, little beads of sweat appearing along his brow, just below his yellow hair. Hair that had probably had a bit too much pomade added to it and was sticking up in a few odd directions, likely caused by his running his hand through it in frustration without realizing the aesthetic results.

So cute, thought Nellie.

"So," he managed to squeeze out. "You again. Funny, that."

"Isn't it," said Cora, not sounding particularly amused.

"Right. Of course. So . . . murder, was it?"

Cora opened her eyes wide at him, then turned to look at Nellie. Nellie just smiled back.

"Yes. Murder. A rather serious subject, don't you think?" said Cora slowly.

"Oh yes. Of course. Please, tell me."

Cora sighed. "Last night, near Charing Cross, we came across a flower girl by the name of Alice Foster. She was dying. I think she was stabbed in the stomach. She passed on after a few minutes. . . ."

A back-and-forth followed. Officer Murphy asking reasonable questions and Cora providing as many answers as she could. Finally, there was a lull in the interview, a moment when it seemed they'd been through all the facts and the conversation was coming to an end. Officer Murphy looked over his notes. Then he looked up and glanced around the room. He jerked his chair close to the two of them and leaned in. Nellie and Cora followed his example.

"I must be honest with you girls. There's only one reason the sergeant called me over, and that was because they're not going to investigate this."

"I don't understand," said Nellie. It was the first time she'd piped up, and when Officer Murphy looked at her, she noticed his ears turn pink.

"Uh, well, uh . . . it's just . . . I'm pretty new. And they wouldn't give me a murder case if they actually wanted to solve it."

"What about Dr. Welland?" asked Cora.

"They sent me to interview a couple of girls. That's maybe one step up from paperwork."

"Thanks," said Cora.

"Look, I just want to be honest with you both. And that doctor business is part of the problem. Everyone's on the case. Then there's the British Museum . . ." He stopped.

"Go on."

Officer Murphy didn't look like he wanted to.

Nellie leaned in and placed a comforting hand on his leg. "You can tell us. We won't tell anyone." Officer Murphy stared at the white hand against the dark blue of his trouser intently.

"The museum was robbed last night, an artifact, a scroll from the traveling *Lost Treasures of Alexandria* exhibit," he explained to the hand in barely a whisper.

"Amazing," said Nellie. No false enthusiasm required in this moment. It was impressive that anyone could rob such a building with its formidable wrought-iron fence and gates.

"If they're working on the doctor's murder case, why haven't you asked us for an official statement?" said Cora.

Officer Murphy looked up almost reluctantly. "What's that?"

"We were the ones who found him. Michiko fought the man who is probably your most likely suspect."

"Well, I interviewed you. You said what you had to say, and there wasn't much more to it. . . ."

"For that matter," continued Cora, standing up and starting to look annoyed, "why were none of us mentioned in any of the articles about the investigation?"

Nellie could feel Officer Murphy's leg tense and she realized she hadn't yet removed her hand. She pulled it back quickly, and he seemed to take that as an admonishment and looked at her with great concern.

"It's not that . . . it's just . . . I don't know. I'm not in charge. I imagine it's a matter of you being civilians . . ."

"What leads have you been pursuing? I imagine his work with cavorite?"

"With . . . what?"

"He had a very valuable piece of cavorite with him. Anyone from the party could have told you that."

"People talked of a glowing, flying, mechanical bird. But not this cavorite you're talking about. And nothing was found at the scene."

"Of course not, the man in the fog probably took it."

"You think he was murdered for this cavorite?"

"It's a very reasonable possibility."

"I wonder if this British Museum business might have to do with any of it, then?" asked Nellie, fascinated by the conversation, which had set her mind spinning.

Officer Murphy and Cora both looked at her. Cora nodded and pointed at her. "I wonder . . ."

"Now, let's not get ahead of ourselves," said Officer Murphy, finally rising. "There's a lot of crime in this city . . ."

"But what do the flower girls have to do with anything?" Cora asked, mostly to herself. She sat back down, with Officer Murphy following suit immediately, and Nellie felt a bit like she was watching a French farce.

"Nothing," said Officer Murphy. "Look, someone's murdered almost every night in this city. And that's just the reported crime. It's bad business, but it's the sorry state we live in. And people get robbed. I imagine this cavorite is valuable, right?"

Cora nodded. "Yes."

"Well, then, there you go. Money. Usually the motivation for most crimes."

"How old are you?" Cora leaned back in her chair and crossed her arms over her chest.

"What . . . I . . . twenty-one. Just. Why, what does it matter?"

"You talk as if you've been on the job a long time, but I know the rules, and you can't have been an officer more for than a couple months."

"What's your point?"

"I don't trust your experience, is all. Quite frankly I don't think you know what you're doing."

Officer Murphy sputtered at her candor. He ran his fingers through his hair, mussing it up further and seemed to be having a private conversation with himself, nodding his head about and sighing a few times. Finally: "Miss, you're young. Younger than I am, and not an officer and . . . well, I'd call you a bit of a troublemaker, quite frankly. I've taken your statement about the girl, and I think it's time for the two of you to leave." He rose. This time it was clear that he wouldn't be sitting down again. It was also clear that they should be standing up. So Nellie stood.

Cora didn't.

"Alice."

"What was that?" said Officer Murphy.

"The 'girl' has a name. And it's Alice Foster." She stood finally and slowly began to put her gloves back on. "Thank you, Officer Murphy. And I apologize for my comment. You clearly, in your short time in this job, have come to exemplify all that we expect from the police."

There was another sputter, and Cora turned and left. Nellie took it to be her cue as well, but she felt so bad for Officer Murphy, and she couldn't just leave him like that. He hadn't been mean on purpose. He was just doing his job.

"Thank you for speakin' with us," she said with an apologetic smile.

Officer Murphy nodded.

She turned to leave and heard him blurt out, "Name!"

She looked back at him. "I'm sorry?"

He had a dejected expression on his face, his shoulders drooped, and his hair even seemed to have lost its frustrated enthusiasm. "Your name. I . . . forgot to get your names the other night, and now this time and . . . I just wanted your name."

Nellie smiled. "That was Miss Cora Bell. And I'm Nellie. Harrison."

"Nellie," repeated Officer Murphy. "I'm . . . Jeff. Jeffery. Jeff."

Nellie felt a little flutter in her heart at the name and quickly turned to follow Cora before she felt anything stronger. Not that there was anything wrong with a flutter. But it probably wasn't the time or place.

Cora was pacing impatiently outside the station.

"I'm sorry that he couldn't help," said Nellie softly.

"It doesn't matter. I've been taking care of myself for seventeen years, and I can take care of this."

"Oh . . . good . . ."

There wasn't much more Nellie felt she could say.

They parted ways. It was already past supper time, and the sun had fallen low behind the rooftops, cloaking the city in shadow and giving it its premature evening look as it did every night. Still blue in the sky, but dark in the streets.

As Nellie wound her way home and reappeared in her square, she remembered her meeting with Mr. Staunch and Mr. Proper and thought back to what Cora had said about Mr. Carter. Also about what she'd said about taking things into her own hands. . . .

There were no two ways about it: she'd have to take her investigation to a whole new level.

A Gap Between Two Buildings

MICHIKO STARED BETWEEN her feet at the ground so far below her. Her heart was still racing, even though she'd stopped herself just in time. She couldn't get over the idea that she'd almost plunged to her death. It didn't feel at all like she'd prevented the inevitable. Rather her imagination was so vivid that a version of herself in her mind's eye was falling fast toward the pavement, picking up speed, and then . . . then . . .

"*Silver Heart!*" Hayao called out to her across the chasm. He'd so effortlessly leaped across the space between the two roofs that it had seemed perfectly possible for her to do it, too. But as the moment had approached, as the ledge had gotten closer and the space looked wider, Michiko doubted herself. Gripped with a sudden fear, she'd pulled to a frantic standstill, fighting her own forward momentum and thrashing to a pretty impressive stop just in time. Fortunately, she had years of balance training to help her.

It was the same problem. The same every time. She could never really embrace death, face it head-on. She could never commit herself as much as was demanded of her. It wasn't for a lack of desire. But in the moment she failed herself. Every time.

"*I . . . can't . . .*" said Michiko, truly embarrassed to admit defeat to her student. This had been a bad idea. A master was not meant to seem weak, to seem fearful. She was doing this all wrong.

"*Yes, you can. You are doing very well. Just try it again, and remember to focus on your goal. The ledge, the left hand down, kick out the legs before you, let energy pull your body down. Like we've been doing.*"

This running thing of Hayao's had proven to be far more complex than just taking off and following one's feet. He had a whole philosophy that went with it, one that was very similar to the samurai's and that Michiko assumed had been partially influenced by his old samurai master at the stall in the market. A great deal of it was about mental conditioning. Focusing on self-discipline, being able to take action despite how one felt physically and, especially, emotionally. That same stillness in the center, that same focus on the task. Goals weren't an end; they were what propelled you toward the next challenge.

Hayao saw the world around him in a different way than everyone else, saw paths where others could not, examined corners and noticed the overturned apple crate, the exposed rough brick wall. He created steps out of discarded elements and structural supports. He had explained that when he walked, he didn't pay attention to the people, but to the spaces between them.

Michiko could relate to all this. It made sense to her. And as they'd run along the deserted streets together, at times stopping and examining potentially better ways to launch oneself, only to turn around and try again, she'd thought she was picking the whole thing up quite quickly. She had started to feel confident. So much so that Hayao had taken them up onto the rooftops of the city.

The London skyline was like a forest—no, a jungle. Chimney pots, some decorative, some purely practical, could appear suddenly and unpredictably underfoot. Gothic spires made way for neo-Classical domes, which then made way for a straight clear runway. Round then sharp. Flat then beveled. Hayao saw all these sudden changes as something helpful, not as impediments. And, as he worked out a particular path for them to follow and practiced it a few times before teaching it to her, Michiko could see how much easier it was to run fast with the help of her body weight and different heights than along a flat surface.

Hayao must have been impressed with her, but he was also a boy of fourteen and easily excitable. That must have been the reason he'd thought she was ready, her first night out, to jump between two buildings. Not a small gap, mind you, but a wide alley.

"It's simple because this roof is higher. So you let yourself fall. Push forward and fall down. Much easier than jumping up."

He had yet to teach her that.

Michiko was feeling good. Her heart was pumping, energy was flowing, and she felt this new skill would help her defeat the man she had started to call the Fog. It wouldn't help her in fighting him—for that she would rely on her much more finely honed samurai technique. But the running would help her scour the city until she finally found him.

So she'd agreed to the jump. Hayao had talked her through it, explained the angles, where she should put her hand in order to launch herself. It was all moves she'd been doing for the last couple of hours.

Hayao had gone first, completing the jump perfectly. It had looked easy. He'd grinned at her from across and below where she was standing, and Michiko rolled her eyes at his pride. She'd have to work on that with him.

She walked to the far end of the building and allowed her mind to empty, to focus on nothing but the task before her. It was the same way she'd focused on those three foolish men the night before. This was familiar to her. This was natural.

Running. Running with focus and intention. Not anticipating, but knowing what was to come. In the moment. *Run. Run. Fast. The edge is approaching, the path is clear. Run. Run. Fast.*

I can't.

That's when she'd come to a flailing halt.

"*Yes,*" said Hayao. "*You can.*"

He had such faith in her. This boy who barely knew her. He was in awe of her. You could see it even in the way he taught her, which was always done with reverence. The same way one would teach an elder about a new scientific discovery. She wanted to share his faith in her.

"*How?*" she called out. "*How can I do it?*" *Teach me. Help me.*

"Because I know you can. Trust me. I wouldn't ask you to do something I didn't think you were ready for."

Looking at the boy, his hair sticking up at odd angles, his eyes a little too wide apart, and a grin full of crooked teeth, she saw the least likely person she'd ever have trust in. But then again, those who had once seemed worthy of her respect had proven themselves to be the least trustworthy. Her parents. Her sensei, Kyoshi Adachi. Callum.

Okay, little monkey. I'll trust you.

Giving herself over to the idea, she returned to the far end of the building. *Focus, focus as you know how to focus. Trust.* A deep breath.

She was running again. She gathered strength and confidence as her legs carried her past and over obstacles. She was running fast. So fast. The ledge approached. She felt that familiar fear. Fear of her own mortality. No, she couldn't do it.

Then she saw Hayao, his face screwed up in concentration, watching her every move and nodding at her progress.

Trust.

Run.

Run.

Fast.

Run.

She was in the air, nothing beneath her feet, just her body suspended. Flying. She was flying. And she didn't feel scared. For the first time she could recall, she felt sure and so happy. She felt no fear.

She landed next to Hayao and performed an *aikido* roll as the momentum from her flight kept her body weight moving forward. The roll took her back to her feet and to stillness.

Michiko turned to Hayao, who was smiling even more broadly at her, if that were possible.

"*How did you feel?*" he asked, running over to her.

Michiko returned the smile. "*Free. I felt . . . free.*"

Break and Enter

KENSINGTON GARDENS WAS heavenly first thing in the morning. The picturesque paths were free of nannies and prams, the Round Pond and its surrounds empty except for three sleeping swans, with the only sound the faint wind in the trees. And the morning light danced over everything in a relaxed manner that suggested it was in no rush to proceed with the day.

Nellie made her way contentedly along the Broad Walk to the high street, and eventually turned back up Kensington Palace Gardens Road—a private street nicknamed "Millionaires' Row," gated to vehicles but open to foot traffic. It was a gorgeous street, lined with trees that soared above and canopied overhead. The neo-Classical homes, all unique in their own magnificent extravagance, were protected behind tall wrought-iron fences and white stone pillars, but their height and size still left them susceptible to preying eyes.

Nellie's were rather probing this morning as she wandered down the street, careful not to draw any particular attention. When she reached number eighteen, she stopped and stared at the building behind its carefully crafted number plate. It was, like the palace the street was named after, made of red brick accented with white. It towered, four tall stories, the bottom three displaying tall white windows, and the top, a sloping roof through which smaller windows peeked out and on which five chimneys proudly stood sentinel. There was no sign of life in the house, though Nellie imagined the servants were moving about, preparing for breakfast and airing out the living spaces. She saw a few drapes twitch as she gazed, which confirmed her suspicions.

She knew she was too early. But she'd arrived now on purpose. Her plan was simple, and it relied on her patience. Wait until Mr. Carter vacated the property, then slip inside.

Foolhardy, perhaps, for anyone but her. Your average robber probably would have thought her totally barking mad for trying to slip into such a place during the day, but Nellie was a whiz at making herself invisible. She understood how helpful a shadow could be, how she could make herself smaller by turning one way or the other, or crouching, or bending to mimic whatever she was hiding behind. How many times had she had to slip out of the Magician's boxes, or bend herself up out of the spectators' line of sight, or conceal herself in plain view in the audience? Too many to count. She could hide.

She could also do wonders with a rope. Scale the sides of set pieces, lean out and over, swing across a vast auditorium. And there wasn't a lock she couldn't pick.

So for her, the trick was not in getting into the house or

keeping out of sight, it was waiting for Mr. Carter to head out to the bank for the day.

Nellie had learned a fair bit about Mr. Carter in the last couple days. While Cora had set out to talk with him, Nellie had been asking around town, finding out where he lived and how he made his money. He was an MP. But he was also a banker. And a pretty successful one at that. Knowing he had a day job made life easier for Nellie, who felt quite confident she could then poke about his home office without being interrupted. After all, who went into a man's private office?

Nellie glanced around and, when she was sure no one was about, quickly removed the long black coat she was wearing to hide her dark blue Magician's-assistant costume. She'd been inspired the other night by Michiko's having a special outfit in which to disappear into the shadows. And besides, there was no way she could be sneaky in a long skirt. You needed mobility to break into someone's home.

She hid the coat under a bush and without pause made a running jump at the lowest branch of the large tree before Mr. Carter's estate. She pulled herself up by her arms until she could hook her legs over, bringing herself up to a sitting position. She then reached for the branch above and carefully stood on the one currently supporting her. She swung off it and propelled herself to a higher branch, hooking her knees over it. She continued on this way until she was neatly hidden from view.

Now there was nothing to do but to wait.

. . . But Also This Was Happening

"IT ISN'T ENOUGH TIME," whined Hayao as Michiko ended their second session. She was surprised to hear his frustration. After all, they'd had a very decent first round of sparring, though she'd hardly admit it to him. "*How will I ever learn if I study only a couple of hours every morning?*"

"*Just as I will learn your fast running studying a couple hours every night. We make do with our situation. We do not complain.*"

Hayao sighed loudly and dramatically, and Michiko wondered if he would ever learn how to keep his emotions to himself. Not only was it dangerous to let your enemy know your every thought and vulnerability, it was also just annoying to everyone else.

"*What time do you want to meet tonight?*" he asked, handing her back the cane.

"*Can't tonight.*" She slipped it into the bag with the other weapons, closing the bag quickly so Hayao wouldn't get excited noticing the Silver Heart hidden at the bottom.

"*Why not?*"

Why not? Because I have to find the Fog, that's why. I have a goal, and it must be accomplished. And though the running last night was . . . astounding . . . it means I am now a night behind in my search.

"I can't."

She hated that she felt guilty about leaving him in the small park as she sneaked back into the house. She hated that she felt like she was letting him down. That wasn't the way it should be. He should feel bad for making her feel bad. He should be embarrassed by his histrionics. But the fact was, she did wish she could be the master he wanted her to be. In letting him down, she was letting herself down.

Callum didn't rise until after nine in the morning, so Michiko had some time to sit with Shuu in the kitchen, watch him carefully prepare breakfast in that slow deliberate way of his. She knew Callum couldn't stand his old servant's slowness, but Michiko thought it quite beautiful to watch. Like a dance underwater.

Soon, though, the third little bell to the left over the door began ringing incessantly. Though it rang at the same volume no matter how hard you tugged its cord, Callum always seemed to pull on the rope at the far end of the house in his room with as much vehemence as he could, to make sure he got Shuu and Koukou's full attention.

Michiko had no bell, only—

"Michiko!"

She stood at the foot of his bed and watched him gulp down his breakfast without even tasting it. So much for your efforts, Shuu, thought Michiko.

He'd summoned her to his room, then made her wait until all his food was washed down with hot black coffee. Then he lit a cigarette and exhaled the smoke slowly.

Finally: "We are making a house call today."

"Yes, Callum-kun."

"A private teaching session, a family. And you won't embarrass me."

Most of his words she didn't understand, but "embarrass" she did. I won't, if you won't. "Yes, Callum-kun."

They stared at each other, and once again the gaze of his too-round eyes sent a shiver up her spine. "Well? What are you waiting for? Get packing!"

"Packing," another very familiar word. A little bow, just the head. Nothing more. "Yes, Callum-kun."

She was used to packing. She knew what Callum wanted to bring along to each particular outing. For presentations, it was weaponry that looked showy and exciting. For classes, usually just sticks—parasols, canes, maybe the pair of wooden training *katanas*. So she packed up the latter, thinking fondly of the Silver Heart, now hidden away upstairs in her wardrobe.

She dressed in her all-black training gear, which she had only just removed from her training session with Hayao, and in short order she was joining Callum in his carriage. He was wearing a tweed suit and shiny leather shoes. Michiko sighed inwardly at how impractical an outfit it was for fighting purposes.

She anticipated a very long day.

. . . And Still in the Tree . . .

TIME PASSED. NELLIE remained still. People walked below her, had short conversations about the weather and politics—"I say, isn't the sun bright this afternoon!" "It is indeed, and did you hear about Lord White's latest push in the House?" "He thinks he'll be Prime Minister someday . . ." "What a laugh. And isn't the sky a remarkable blue?" "That it is."

Finally, the wrought-iron gate to the house opened wide and a steam carriage burst out onto the street like a horse champing at the bit just set loose in the yard. For a moment Nellie was enveloped in the white-hot vapor, then the carriage disappeared down Kensington High Street.

There was no time to waste. Nellie climbed across the long branch until it almost reached the roof of the house. From her belt, she took the long thin rope that the Magician had designed especially for his act. Made of a metal so thin it looked like it would support little more than a feather, the rope, in reality, could haul something as heavy as a piano quite effortlessly. It was so fine that, with the correct lighting, it could make a person hanging from it appear to be floating. This rope was Nellie's good friend.

She'd attached a small hook to one end, which she now tossed toward one of the chimneys. The hook just missed its target, and she tried again. And again. And again. By the fourth time, she was getting angry, and her hands were shaking now. *Calm down. Breathe if you can. Breathe.* She tried to do some of that yoga-breathing thing that the Magician had taught her, but she didn't have the patience for it.

And, just as she thought she would have to give up, a little squawk came from above. It was so quiet. A little "psst" in bird form—meant just for her.

Nellie glanced up.

"Well, bless my stars! Sherry," she said in a bemused whisper. "What are you doin' here?"

"That's a laugh," replied the bird, and flew to her shoulder.

Nellie wanted to scold the bird for following her. And to praise her for keeping herself so well hidden. It wasn't easy for a creature as brightly colored as Scheherazade to keep out of sight, but she'd done a remarkable job of it. Come to think of it, it was really the first time the bird had ever followed her like that. Nellie was a little proud. And honored.

Then she had an idea.

"Hey, Sherry, do you think you could fly this rope over to the chimney and hook it around?" She realized after she said it that, of course, the bird didn't understand a word. So she showed her what she meant, hooking the fine rope around a tree branch. Then she released it and tossed it toward the chimney, this time without any intention of getting it to hook on. Just to show the bird what she meant.

Scheherazade watched the whole display intently, but it wasn't altogether clear if she had any idea what Nellie was going on about.

"Here you go, Sherry, open wide." The bird knew that order and opened her beak. Nellie carefully placed the rope inside, the hook dangling down to one side. "Now go!"

She gave the bird a little push in the right direction, and Scheherazade took off toward the roof. Nellie crossed her fingers.

The parrot landed on the roof right by the chimney and looked at it. Then she looked at Nellie.

"Go around," mouthed Nellie, and drew a large circle in the air with her finger.

Scheherazade looked at the chimney again. Then looked at her. Then at the chimney. Then she hopped along around the chimney until she'd made a full circle and dropped the hook on the other side of the rope so it caught it fast. The bird looked at Nellie again, and then at the hook, and then at Nellie.

Nellie tugged at the rope from her end. It was holding fast. She smiled at Scheherazade and said, "Good Polly!" as loudly as she dared so the parrot would hear.

Now all she had to do was swing. Swing so that she was standing on the top-floor window ledge—the servants' quarters and the one place Nellie knew wouldn't be occupied this time of day.

Nothing to it.

Nothing at all.

She'd performed such a move a thousand times before on-stage.

Though, of course, in the theater she had trained stagehands in charge of the rigging, and here she had only a parrot . . .

This is what they called a leap of faith . . .

. . . And Back to Michiko Again . . .

THE LITTLE GIRL wouldn't stop crying. It horrified Michiko to hear this wailing sound from such a little creature. The girl was sitting in the middle of the large ballroom, mouth open so wide you could count her tiny teeth.

Her mother was alternating between frantic apologies and violent pulls on a long red rope in the corner. Eventually, a frightened-looking young woman maybe only a few years older than Michiko came running into the room. She wore a white bonnet and apron, and she scooped the small child off the floor and exited the room so quickly it was as if she'd never been.

At last there was calm again, and the mother gestured to Callum that they should continue. It had been a basic demonstration: Callum with his cane, Michiko with her parasol, but the small child had found their choreographed fight evidently too traumatic to witness in silence. Now they began again, and Michiko barely focused on the steps she was performing—they were so familiar that she didn't have to—and instead made plans for the night ahead. She'd definitely be using the rooftops as her highway, but where to begin? That same spot where both the doctor and flower girl had been killed? It didn't seem likely.

"Michiko!"

Michiko snapped back to attention and saw that Callum was giving her a stern look. "Yes, Callum-kun?"

"Show. Show them." He pointed to the two girls, around ten and eleven respectively.

"Yes, Callum-kun." She hadn't spent much time working with children. To be honest, they kind of scared her. These two, in particular, had very haunted expressions. Their black eyes, which stared at her from under an almost pure white fringe of hair, made Michiko pretty sure they could read her thoughts. Their sad little faces seemed to suggest that they didn't much like what they were finding.

She gave them each a child's parasol, objects she hoped they were familiar with, and set them opposite each other. Immediately the younger one whacked the older over the head.

Michiko ran between them. "No," she said, holding up a finger. "No." She waited a moment and then took a step away.

The older one whacked the younger one.

Both girls started to giggle.

"Michiko!" called Callum from across the room. She had a sudden urge to throw one of the parasols, spearlike, right between his enraged eyes.

The mother placed a hand on Callum's shoulder and smiled gently. Michiko didn't like the look of this woman at all. She was like one of those English desserts with whipped cream and berries and sugar all over the place. A sweetness masking a lack of real substance. She seemed held together by her corset, so cinched she looked ready to burst. Her cheeks a little too red. Her voice a little too high.

She leaned in and whispered something in Callum's ear. Her red lips grazed his skin. He glanced at her and nodded. Instantly the mother was ushering her children out of the room and Callum came storming toward Michiko.

"Go," he said.

"Home?" she asked, confused but relieved.

"No, not 'home.'" He did one of his delightful imitations of her accent in repeating the word. "Somewhere else. In the house. I'll find you later. Just . . . get the hell out of here." He hissed the last bit at her, spit flying into her face.

Oh. She knew what was going on now. She had to stay in the house so that she could leave with him. Keep up appearances and all that.

Fine. She'd wander.

Does a samurai warrior peek into private closets?

Oh, who cares?

Michiko was feeling distinctly grumpy.

She made her way down the wide main hall and toward the grand staircase, following it as it twisted upward. The second floor, she hoped, would have bedrooms and the like. She tiptoed past the nursery, where all three girls were now playing happily with their nanny, and crossed over to what was clearly the grown-ups' part of the house. First she entered what she assumed was the mother's bedroom. It couldn't have been anyone else's—all pink flowers and pillows everywhere. It even smelled pink.

Michiko did a little quiet rifling through the woman's large closet and couldn't help but be astounded by the yards of fabric she'd consumed for her clothes. Silks and thick woolen blends, and sheer fabrics that had almost no texture to them. Then there were her fantastic undergarments, made of French lace with bows sewn on all over. And so many different kinds of corsets, all looking rather frightening with their ropes and metal fasteners.

She moved on from the room into what must have been the woman's husband's. This was a room that intrigued Michiko much more than the woman's. It wasn't the rich green velvet of the curtains or the rather intimidating bearskin rug complete with bear's head at the foot of the bed that fascinated her. Rather it was the glass case of curios at the far end.

She approached it and peered inside. The man had all manner of objects locked away in there. Two ancient books, so old that they clearly were only held together by gravity, sat side by side with what was . . . well, it had to be, a shriveled monkey's head. Poor creature. There was an open box with several different stones that glittered inside. A letter that, of course, she couldn't read, but that must have been written by someone of significance. And more things—some unidentifiable artifacts with sculpted faces on them, a row of buttons, a snakeskin, and at the very bottom, lying flat so that she hadn't noticed it at first, a silver mask.

It hadn't been taken care of, was horribly tarnished, so that at first Michiko didn't even realize it was silver. But when she knelt down to take a closer look, she could see the odd brightness peeking through. Her first thought was of a samurai mask, though this object clearly wasn't one. It was far less expressive than the mask of the samurai. There was no indication of a mouth, no indication of any expression whatsoever. It only had holes for eyes and and for nostrils, and the skillfully carved decoration over it was not meant to represent a human face. Instead it looked like a face that was covered by delicate sweeping vines, a face that hadn't been entirely overtaken by nature, but had become one with it. It made her think of O-Ryu, the goddess of the willow tree.

There was a sound from the room next door.

Michiko quickly escaped back into the hall, determined that her nosiness not be discovered. Though she was a little sad to part with the mask. She heard the noise again. It sounded like someone was in the next room. Maybe it was the master of the house himself, but that was odd. She had seen him leave through the front gate directly after she and Callum had arrived through the back.

It was probably just a servant, then, but for some reason, her gut told her to check it out. She approached the room quietly and peered carefully around the open door.

Nothing.

No one.

But she'd heard . . .

She entered what she assumed was the library, or someone's study, and closed the door behind her. There was a large oak desk at one end, framed by two tall windows. Bookshelves lined the walls, and at the right, there was a large unlit fireplace with a mantel that displayed yet more interesting objects from around the world.

She heard a small sound. This time it didn't sound human. It sounded . . . like a bird?

And just as she heard it, a curtain twitched.

Okay. Now she just had to investigate. She crossed the room and pulled the curtain back in one quick movement.

It was the blond one. Nellie. Her parrot sitting on her shoulder. Both looked completely dumbfounded.

Why were they here? And why were they hiding behind a curtain?

"You're probably wondering why I'm hiding behind a curtain," said Nellie quickly. Michiko understood the gist of what she said and nodded.

"It's a . . . long story."

Michiko didn't know what to say. Or how she'd articulate anything she'd wanted to say in the first place.

"Okay, see, I found out that the dead man, you remember, not the one in the street, the other one, from my place, was a member of the Society of Heroes, and then I found out that Mr. Carter gave a bunch of money to another member of the society, and I was thinkin' that maybe he had somethin', some papers or . . . somethin' . . . that would help me find out what was goin' on and such."

Michiko raised her hand to silence her. "Mr. Carter's house," she said, pointing down to the ground.

"Yes. I know."

Michiko nodded. "Heroes?"

"There's a secret group of scientists. And it's got somethin' to do with the dead man in my flat." Nellie spoke more slowly and Michiko could distinguish each word. It was still difficult to understand. Something to do with science. And Mr. Carter. And a dead man. The dead man Michiko had found on the street? The dead man in Nellie's apartment? There were too many dead men.

Whatever it was, Nellie clearly thought there was a connection with a dead man and this house and was investigating. But in the middle of the day? And in her underwear?

"Why dress like that?"

Nellie looked at herself then back up. "It's easier to climb when you've got your legs free. And I'm used to doin' this sort of stuff in my costume, seemed to make sense . . ."

"Costume?"

"Yes. My costume. Or . . . one of my costumes."

It still didn't make a lot of sense that she would be in her costume, but it didn't make sense for Michiko to mistrust Nellie either. What other reason could she have for being in Mr. Carter's study in her underwear . . . well . . . actually . . .

"Mr. Carter here?"

Clearly the look she gave Nellie was enough to make the girl gasp and then giggle. Nellie gestured for Michiko to come over to the window, which she opened. Then she motioned for Michiko to stick her head out and look up. Michiko leaned out and looked in the direction where Nellie had pointed. At first she didn't see anything, but she kept looking hard until she saw a fine rope or wire or something dangling down over the roof.

Michiko pulled herself back inside.

"See? I broke in. I wasn't . . . invited . . . if that's what you were gettin' at," said Nellie with a wink.

"Broke in . . ." *Oh!* She broke in! A bit criminal, but not anything more . . . illicit. She broke in because . . . she wanted to find information about the dead men. Yes, that was it! "Did you find?" she asked.

"Nope, nothing so far," said Nellie a little sadly. "No papers. At least, nothing important."

"You think he know? Maybe he know." It was hard work having this conversation, but for the first time in a long time, Michiko wanted to try. Maybe that had been the problem all along. Not that she couldn't learn English, but that there hadn't been anyone she'd been all that interested in having conversations with in the first place.

"He knows something. He got scared when Cora talked to him." She paused. Then repeated: "Scared."

"Scared." Mr. Carter was scared. Yes. He must be. Mr. Carter had hired Callum to teach his family how to defend themselves. He *was* scared. What did scared men do with information . . . "Fire."

She pointed at the large fireplace and Nellie's eyes opened wide. Together they flew across the room and crouched, staring into the cinders. Likely all they'd find was ash, but it was worth looking, wasn't it?

"Son of Mary and Joseph, look at that." Nellie extended a black-gloved hand and gingerly pulled out a piece of paper that had fallen to the side of the iron cradle that held two charred pieces of wood. It was covered in black, but still whole. Still existed in its paper form, not turned to ash and dust. It was all that was there, but it was something. Something that wasn't meant to be found and so probably exactly what they were looking for.

Nellie examined it closely.

"You see?" asked Michiko. What had Nellie noticed?

Nellie shook her head. "No. That is to say, I see somethin', but I can't tell what. But I can discover what." She grinned and stood. "Thank you, Michiko."

Michiko bowed.

And then Mrs. Carter let out a bloodcurdling scream.

NELLIE ALMOST DROPPED the paper in shock and turned, as did Michiko. The scream had come from downstairs, but it was so ear-piercing that it startled both girls. "What in the name of all that's holy . . ." Nellie skipped quietly to the door and opened it a crack. A maid flew past just at that moment, but fortunately she was so distracted she didn't notice Nellie peeking through the door.

"What?" asked Michiko at her side.

Nellie shook her head and opened the door wider. "Go," she ordered Scheherazade on her shoulder. Miraculously the bird seemed to understand and flew across the room to the open window. Then Nellie and Michiko slipped through the door and, staying flat to the wall in the hallway, made their way to the staircase. Like children sneaking out of bed while their parents had a party downstairs, they peered through the railing.

Mr. Carter's bloodied body was lying on the marble floor. Mrs. Carter was next to him in a flowing dressing gown, and Sir Callum Fielding-Shaw was standing off to the side, looking so casual he might as well have been whistling.

"Why did you bring him here?" screeched Mrs. Carter at the two men standing in the shadow of the doorway. "Why didn't you take him to the hospital?"

"'E said take 'im home. So we did."

Nellie thought the voice sounded very familiar, and she crouched lower to try to see the man's face.

"Besides," said the other one, "there ain't nothin' for 'im. 'E's as good as dead."

"Yes, well, thank you, gentlemen," said Callum, finally speaking up. He walked over to the door and made to close it in their faces when one of the men stuck his foot in to prevent it.

"I don't suppose 'e'd be willin' to contribute in the name of science . . ."

"Whatever are you going on about . . .?"

"'E'll be freshly dead, see, and such bits of a person could be right 'elpful to the scientific community . . ."

"Get out!" wailed Mrs. Carter. "You vultures, picking off pieces of him . . . Get out!"

This time the door was properly closed, and Nellie knew exactly who the mystery men were. Messrs. Staunch and Proper. Again.

"Hey, you! What are you doin'?" Nellie looked up and saw one of the butlers at the far end of the hall staring at her and Michiko.

Nellie stood and ran; so did Michiko. "Madam!" called out the butler. "There's thieves about!"

Michiko grabbed Nellie and pulled her into the nearest room, which happened to be Mr. Carter's bedroom. She saw Michiko close the door and lock it behind them. They ran to the window and opened it wide. Scheherazade almost flew right into their faces.

"Scared," the bird squawked quietly into Nellie's ear as she came to rest on her shoulder.

"I know." She gave the bird a scratch under the chin, then turned to Michiko. "Coming?" she asked.

"No." Of course, "no." Michiko had been admitted into the house. It was Nellie who was trespassing. With a quick thank-you and a wave, Nellie slipped out through the window and heard it close behind her as she stood tentatively on the narrow ledge. She was now several floors lower than her rope. Glancing down, she noticed the retreating figures of Mr. Staunch and Mr. Proper and hoped that they wouldn't think of looking up. They were deep in conversation, though, and didn't seem interested in anything in the vicinity.

Then, an idea.

She took Scheherazade off her shoulder, placed her on her forearm, and pointed at the thin dangling line. "Fetch," she said. *Please fetch, oh please.*

Scheherazade flew off Nellie's arm in the direction of the rope and, like a very good bird, unhooked it and carried it back to her. The parrot got another solid scratch under the chin for her efforts before being sent with the rope back to the tree with

Nellie holding on to the far end. This time the parrot seemed most confident in the task, almost excited to be performing it, and easily hooked it around a thick branch.

Nellie called Scheherazade back to her and handed her the piece of burned paper she and Michiko had found. "Careful," she said. "Gentle. Take it over there." She pointed to the tree once more. The bird took the paper delicately in her sharp beak and flew to the branch to wait for her mistress. Then without any hesitation, but with a silent prayer, Nellie swung on the rope to the tree. Her legs wrapped around the branch, and with very little effort she was safely sitting. She unhooked the rope herself this time, wound it up, and attached it to her belt. Then she waited till the coast was clear, jumped to the ground, put her long coat back on, and retrieved the paper from the parrot.

She had no idea how to find out what had originally been written on it. But she was certain Cora would be able to. First, though, she needed to go home and change.

And, with Scheherazade on her shoulder, Nellie strolled as casually as she could down the street and into the afternoon crowd.

And What Has Cora Been Up to This Whole Time? . . .

"ARE YOU IGNORING me?"

"I'm working. We need to get this done by the end of the day. The delivery boy comes at nine." She was so close to finishing this device, no thanks to Andrew, who was apparently all thumbs when it came to such intricate work.

"Where were you yesterday?"

"With Lord White."

"All day."

"Yes."

"Why are you avoiding me?"

"Not everything revolves around you." Except, of course, that he was perfectly correct in his assumption. She had been avoiding him yesterday. She'd returned just in time to see him walking along the street in the opposite direction and had felt both relieved and a little disappointed to have missed him. And yes, she'd been ignoring him since he'd shown up—late—this morning.

Today had been entirely devoted to working on the device, as a delivery boy was coming to pick it up after supper. A very hungover Lord White instructed her to put on the finishing touches and had locked himself up in his office for the rest of the day, only occasionally letting Barker in to see him.

After the initial problem-solving issues, Cora had been set right on track, and she had spent the early hours of the morning putting together some of the larger brass elements. The hollow glass ball that went into the middle portion had cooled overnight and was ready to insert, and she'd been in the very middle of that very delicate task when Andrew had burst into the room.

She hadn't made eye contact with him since.

So she finally did now.

Immediately she felt flushed, even though she knew it didn't register on her face.

"Can I ask you something?" she said, putting down the device for a moment.

"Anything." Andrew pulled up his chair eagerly and took her hands in his before she had a moment to react.

"How did you get this job?"

Andrew gave her a sideways glance and then said, "Well, to be honest . . . it was all a bit of an accident."

"Accident?"

Andrew rolled his eyes. "Some of the lads and I were bored one night. We were wandering down the mews that backs onto this house, and one of them pointed to the delivery doors and said that that's where Lord White lived. He said he'd seen deliveries made and always wondered what Lord White got up to. After he said that, I thought a lot about it. Finally, I returned later that night, and . . . well . . . I broke in."

"That's probably why he installed that new locking system two weeks ago." Cora remembered overseeing it. Why on earth had Lord White not told her about any of this? Probably, as with many things, he just didn't think to. Some days she practically had to read his mind, he could be so uncommunicative.

"Lord White was, of course, working and caught me right away. But we were in a bit of a predicament. See, now I knew about his secret lab, and if he reported me . . . I'd probably be going to the nick."

"A posh boy like you . . ." Seemed unlikely.

"The lads and I like to have fun. I've been caught more than once."

"Not very clever, now, are you?" This story really didn't impress.

"My parents have said I could use a bit of a lesson and told me if I ever got in trouble again, they wouldn't be bailing me out. Well. Lord White and I struck a deal. He wouldn't report me if I wouldn't tell anyone. The thing was, it all looked so interesting that I asked him for a job. And here I am."

"Do you really want to be an inventor?" she asked. It didn't seem like he did. All he'd done in the afternoon was reorganize, yet again, the tools and update the stock sheet. He hadn't even touched the device, which Cora hadn't minded one bit. And she had it on good authority from the glass blower, who was still on the premises when she'd gotten in last night, that Andrew had spent most of the afternoon napping in the corner.

Andrew sighed. "I thought I did. On the surface, it all looks marvelous. But after these past few days, I've realized it's a lot of dull work. To be honest, I don't know what I want, and I don't think it really matters. Why should someone like me work?"

Cora thought that an odd question. "Because it's satisfying, because . . . of passion . . ."

Andrew pulled his chair in close at that, and brushed a lock of hair from her forehead. "I have passion . . ."

Cora's heart was pounding fast again. She didn't understand how he could have such an effect on her when what he was saying was so pathetic. "Look at Lord White . . ."

"I'd rather look at you . . ."

"He's rich. He's a lord. But he gave up his seat in the House of Lords so that he could run for Parliament. So that he could follow his passion of someday being Prime Minister. He didn't need to do any of it. And this, this laboratory . . . he works just as hard here and only charges for the pleasure so that people don't figure out he's someone that can afford to do without. He gives away all the money he earns here to charity, and . . ."

Andrew's fingers had made it to her neck and were gently caressing it. She lost her train of thought.

"You really like to talk about Lord White," he said, leaning in and kissing her cheek.

"Well, he's my boss . . ."

"Not everyone speaks of their bosses like you do."

"He took me in . . ." She could feel his hot breath on her ear and she closed her eyes.

"What do you think he wants from you?"

That made her open her eyes.

"Wants from me?"

"You know what I mean . . ."

"No," she said, gently pushing him back so they were face-to-face again, "I don't."

Andrew shook his head. "Oh, come on, Cora. Look at you. You're lovely. And you worship him . . ."

"I don't worship—"

"He's trained you well. What else could he possibly want from you?"

Her passion had changed drastically into hot rage. It was an easy transition to make. "I don't know, maybe he wants my talent. Maybe he wants my company because I'm interesting. Maybe he can't live without me since I organize every facet of his life, know his dietary restrictions, keep track of every penny in his bank account, all his plans for the future."

"Now, don't get angry . . ."

"Why not? Why shouldn't I get angry? You've just said my value as a person is wrapped up in my appearance and—"

"I'm sorry, I'm sorry! Look, just stop, okay? Let's not fight again. Besides, you have a lot of work to do." He tried to smile, but she gave him a look that prevented it.

"You're right. I do."

Typically, anger distracted her from whatever she was doing, but there was something in this particular brand of rage that suited the task at hand perfectly. It had something to do with proving to Andrew that she was more than just a pretty face.

"I'm really sorry," he said quietly a few moments later.

"No, you aren't."

"I'm not sorry for thinking what I did; after all, you *are* beautiful. But I didn't mean there wasn't anything else to you. I just didn't think Lord White was aware of it."

"Well, he is."

"Good."

She hadn't stopped working, but she directed her focus back where it belonged.

"So we're friends again?"

She looked up at him and gave him a look of death.

"I'll take that as a yes?"

. . . And Back to Michiko . . . Again . . .

THEY WERE BANGING hard on the door. Michiko closed the drapes to the window and took a deep breath. Then she crossed the room and unlocked the door.

It burst open and she took several steps back into the room.

The butler who'd spotted her and Nellie was in front, followed by Callum and Mrs. Carter. Clearly thieves were of far more importance than the dying man downstairs.

"See, ma'am! I told you!" said the butler, very proud of his clever ability to spot individuals who were already in plain sight.

Callum sighed hard, and Mrs. Carter stormed over to her. "What are you doing in my husband's room?"

The good thing about not being able to speak the language: You don't have to answer questions. "No understand."

Mrs. Carter grabbed Michiko by her shoulders and shook her. That was unpleasant. "WHY ARE YOU HERE?"

Yes, because shouting and shaking will make understanding easier. "You tell Michiko go. I go."

"Why are you in his room?"

Without pause for thought, Michiko pointed to the cabinet of curios. "Pretty," she said.

Mrs. Carter turned and walked over to the cabinet. Michiko followed and pointed at the mask on the bottom. She looked up at the woman and saw a single tear roll down her cheek. "He bought it for me, but I thought it was ugly. So he kept it here. He bought me so many ugly things." She started to cry harder. "He'll never buy me another ugly thing again."

Then she did something most extraordinary. She turned to Michiko and pulled her into a tight, sobbing hug. Michiko could feel the woman's ample chest heave against her and her tears run down the back of her neck. She didn't know what to do except to tentatively hug her back.

They stayed like that for what seemed forever until finally Mrs. Carter pulled back and looked at Michiko closely. She cradled her face in her hands and shook her head sadly. Then she released her and moved to the cabinet, opened it, and removed the mask.

"For you," she said, handing it to Michiko.

Michiko really didn't want to take it. It felt wrong to be given a gift at this time. Especially because the real reason she was in the room was to help someone steal a private document and escape through the window. She glanced at the butler, whose eyes were flitting about the room, clearly searching for the blonde he'd seen in the hall.

Michiko took the mask. It was lighter than she'd expected, and as she turned it over, she could she just how finely crafted it was. She bowed at Mrs. Carter, who bowed back. Bowing really looked weird when English people tried to do it.

She was sent off home on her own while Callum stayed to watch over Mrs. Carter and her family. Michiko enjoyed a relaxed early dinner while Shuu, very slowly and deliberately, began to shine the silver mask. It was a task he did most every day with their cutlery and other household items, and he was quite adept at it. After a quiet hour, the mask's true beauty was revealed, and Michiko thanked him profusely.

The vines were so much more defined, so much more delicate. Little details of shadow and light, with the asymmetrical way a leaf curled by the right eye.

Michiko wondered . . .

She looked at herself in the mirror. Head to toe black except for the silver mask covering her face. Utterly unrecognizable. She'd worn samurai masks in the past, during her practices, and was used to how little vision such a thing allowed, but it would still take some getting used to.

She liked how well it matched the Silver Heart.

This was meant to be.

A Piece of Paper

THE MAKE-OUT SESSION was interrupted by the bell that signaled someone was at the front door.

"He's here," said Cora, taking in a deep breath and pulling herself off Andrew. She'd told herself one kiss, one celebratory kiss for a job well done. The device was finished, and it hadn't been easy going. (Not, of course, that Andrew would know it. What he had done was little more than pass her tools and make inappropriate comments.)

The kiss had turned into a little more than that. Even though she was still annoyed with him. And she wasn't entirely certain how they'd wound up on the floor, but there they were.

And then the bell had rung.

The device had been neatly packed up into a small wooden box. Cora grabbed it quickly and escaped the lab to the front door. Andrew followed her. Barker was at the door and Cora dismissed him as she approached.

The boy at the door took the package with a nod and handed her a packet of cash, the remaining payment that was to be made upon receipt of the device. She watched as he hopped on his bicycle, then she closed the door and turned to Andrew, who was lounging on the small bench in the vestibule.

"I think you should go home now. Your working day is more than over," said Cora, finding his presence in this part of the house unnerving.

"I don't mind this kind of work," he said, grinning at her.

"Well . . . you should probably still go." Was it that she didn't trust him or was it that she didn't trust herself with him? It didn't matter. Either way, it was time to call it a night.

Andrew stood up, walked into the foyer, and glanced up the dark stairs. He looked back at her. Gave her one of his supposedly "knowing" looks. "Or maybe I should stay."

Cora felt her breath catch and a mild panic rise. Normally it was so easy for her to refuse any such suggestions. She had perfected the art of the withering stare and the slight laugh that implied, "You think there's even the remotest of possibilities I'd do that with you?"

But this was different. For one thing, he wasn't one of those old ugly guys. For another, she kind of wanted to. But she knew what it meant to go through with it, what kind of reputation girls who did such things had. Men, young and old, could do it without anyone giving it a second thought.

But if a girl did it?

Not only would she be risking her own reputation, she'd be risking his lordship's as well.

It was unfair.

And there was another thing. Another thing that went along with the butterflies in her stomach and the deep longing just to stop all the thinking for once and go with what her desires were telling her.

It was another form of instinct. A gut thing. A simple, quiet "no."

All this she thought in less than a moment, and chose the casual laugh this time, not the withering stare. She shook her head and opened the door for him as he rolled his eyes at her.

Barker materialized out of nowhere with Andrew's hat, coat, and stick, and Andrew gave him a look. Then he took his things, passed through the door, giving her a wink as he did, and disappeared out into the early evening.

"That one . . ." Barker began, then stopped.

Cora closed the door and looked at him. Barker wasn't a man of many words. Silent. Formidable.

"Yes, Barker?" she said. *What do you think? Tell me, I need someone to tell me.*

Barker shook his head and turned and left.

There was a knock on the door.

Cora turned, fearful of who was on the other side. *Don't let it be Andrew coming back to try to convince me . . . because he just might . . .*

She opened it slowly.

"Was that Mr. Harris I just walked past? Because if it was, no wonder you fancy him." Nellie passed into the vestibule without invitation and removed her small pink gloves, giving the place a once-over.

"Hi, Nellie," said Cora, closing the door and escorting her

into the foyer. Barker was there, of course, and Nellie smiled brightly as she passed him her coat and gloves.

"This is a nice place you got here, Cora. A bit dark for my likin', but still . . . a bit of all right, as me ma would say."

"Well, it's not really *my* place . . ."

"So was that him, then?" Nellie asked after Barker left again.

Cora nodded.

Nellie cocked her head to the side and looked at her. "What's wrong?"

"I don't want to talk about it."

"Okay. So let's talk about this instead." Nellie made her way into the formal sitting room, which was lit by a single lamp on a table. She sat on the love seat next to it, and Cora followed her, mildly amused by how quickly Nellie was able to make herself right at home. Nellie gingerly pulled out a blackened piece of paper from her purse. "I was thinkin' you could maybe help me figure out what's on this." Cora sat down next to her and looked over her shoulder.

"Where did you get this?" Cora asked, carefully taking the paper from Nellie.

"Found it at Mr. Carter's house."

Cora looked up from the page. "How did you get this from Mr. Carter's house? Or should I not bother asking?"

"I snuck in."

Of course you did.

Cora scratched the paper delicately. Black soot came off on her fingernail. It might just be possible to see what was written underneath if the very foundation of the paper hadn't been burned through. She flipped the page over. The back was much lighter.

"Well," she said, standing up, "let's try. Go upstairs, turn left, then left again. My room is the second door on the right. I'll meet you there."

Nellie nodded and made her way up the staircase.

When Nellie was out of sight, Cora slipped into the lab and collected a few bottles from Lord White's chemistry station, then joined her friend in her room.

"Let's sit at the desk." Cora picked up a footstool that normally sat by the fireplace and placed it near the small oak desk beneath the window. Nellie took a seat as Cora sat in the desk chair and lined up the bottles before her. She placed the paper on a tin pan.

"You've got a nice room," commented Nellie, watching her.

"Thanks."

"It's a lot like you, serious but warm."

Cora glanced at Nellie, who smiled at her. *It's a compliment*, she reminded herself. *She's being nice.*

"Okay, Nellie, this is what I'd like you to do. In that drawer, there is some paper. Would you mind writing something on it?"

"Like what?" asked Nellie as she opened the drawer.

"Anything. It's just a test. We'll singe it after, and then see which one of these liquids is the one that'll do the trick."

Cora was a little disappointed in herself that she didn't already know precisely which liquid to use. There were still so many things for her to learn. But she had observed his lordship do something similar to what they were attempting and she remembered that he had used an odorless, colorless liquid. That left only these three bottles as possibilities.

"Shall I singe it?" asked Nellie, having completed her task of writing.

"Please."

She returned moments later with the paper held in the fireplace tongs and placed it on the pan.

"Now what?"

"We experiment."

First liquid.

Second liquid.

Third liquid.

As if responding to the dramatic nature of the situation, and the general intensity level of the two girls huddled together and bent over a small piece of paper, it was number three that proved to be the correct liquid.

"This is a test ta-da!" appeared in Nellie's flowery scrawl. Literally. Evidently she liked to replace the dots over the *i*'s with little flowers.

"So we try number three on the real one, then?" said Nellie.

Cora nodded. She opened the drawer to her right and produced a small paintbrush, which she dipped into the bottle and lightly applied the colorless liquid to the paper. But she was maybe a bit too careful in her first attempt, and not enough found its way onto the black ash. She took a deep breath and applied the liquid more liberally.

The ash began to melt away and Cora started to worry it

might melt through the paper itself. But the liquid worked a charm, and though it was still difficult to read, markings and words that had been hidden behind the black began to appear.

"It's magic!" exclaimed Nellie, clapping her hands.

"It's science," Cora said, stunned. She was flabbergasted. She couldn't believe what she was seeing.

"Cora, are you all right?"

Cora nodded. But still found she could not speak.

"What is it? What are you seein'?" Nellie leaned in closer to the page, as if greater proximity would reveal something she'd neglected to notice. "It looks like a map. Or, no, more like a set of instructions or somethin'. Do you know what it is?"

"Yes. I know what it is," said Cora softly. "I just made this."

Nellie looked at her, wide-eyed. "Can I see it?"

Cora shook her head. "We just sent it off." The delivery boy. How far had he got by now?

"Oh." There was a pause as Nellie thought for a moment. Then: "Do you think we should maybe follow it?"

Yes, yes I do. "That's a good idea."

Both girls rose, and Cora cleaned up her desk as quickly as possible, shoving everything into the large bottom drawer. Then they left the room and made their way back downstairs.

"Where's it going?" asked Nellie as Cora opened the front closet and handed her her overcoat.

"The Tower." It struck Cora just then. "Wait here." She sprinted back upstairs to her room and pulled out the paper again. This time she ignored the oh-so-familiar blueprints and examined the small drawing in the corner. Something she'd only just glanced at, being a wee bit distracted by the coincidence of seeing plans for the device she'd just spent days working on. Confident in her conclusion, she grabbed her pistol from the bedside table, burst out of her room, and ran smack into Mrs. Philips.

"My word, Cora Bell, what the devil's gotten into you? What's with all this up and down, and who's the girl in the foyer?"

"A friend. We're going for a stroll. She has the most wonderful gossip . . ."

Mrs. Philips furrowed her eyebrows. "A friend."

"I have friends," said Cora. Though, not really. And Mrs. Philips knew it. "I met her at the gala; she's just delightful. And . . . Mrs. Philips, please let me pass. I won't be long. And Lord White's been locked up in his room all evening. He'll hardly notice I've stepped out."

"Well, it's nice you having friends, I guess. Just don't stay out too late, love." Despite her words, Mrs. Philips didn't seem all that approving, but she let Cora pass. "And stay in the neighborhood! There's dangerous business going on in the city these days."

"I will!" called Cora over her shoulder, and she ran back down to Nellie. "I know what the drawing at the bottom is," she whispered, grabbing her coat.

"What drawing?"

Cora put her finger to her lips and glanced upstairs. Nellie got the point, and they said nothing further, but slipped out of the house into the night.

"What drawing at the bottom, then?" asked Nellie as they walked quickly along, but still tried to look casual as they passed men and women out for their evening stroll.

"There's a drawing at the bottom of the page. Something I didn't realize I'd noticed until I spoke of the delivery boy."

"Well, what's it of?"

"The Koh-i-Noor diamond," replied Cora.

"How on earth do you know that?"

"It's part of the Crown Jewels collection. And seeing as it's on the same page as a device being delivered to the Tower, where said collection is held . . ."

"Wow. That's clever of you."

"Thank you." Cora glanced at Nellie and saw she was deep in thought. "What are you thinking?"

"Oh, it's probably silly. Like Officer Murphy said . . . coincidences . . ."

"What?"

"Well, with Dr. Welland bein' killed and robbed, those flower girls, and then the British Museum. And then Mr. Carter . . ."

"What about Mr. Carter?"

"Didn't I tell you? When I was at his home, he was brought back to the house and he was all bleedin' like. Dyin'. Basically dead. Murdered, I think, though can't say for sure."

"My God." Evidently the man really did have reason to be so scared the other day.

"At any rate, now with your sayin' that this is a jewel in the Tower . . . I'm thinkin' maybe it really is all connected. Maybe it's the same bloke?"

"One night after the other . . . murder and thievery . . ."

"Yes!"

Cora thought for a moment. There was no real link, none between the murders of Dr. Welland and the flower girls, and what Nellie had been investigating with the Society of Heroes. And yet . . . maybe?

"It could all work together," continued Nellie. "And if he's pickin' up a package right at the Tower, now don't you think if you were a villainous type, you might want to kill two birds with one stone."

"One very precious stone, yes. Whether he's the man in the fog or not, whoever's picking up the package is going to rob the Tower."

The Tower

THE TOWER OF London loomed in that sublimely terrifying fashion that it always did. Dark stone, made darker by soot and an overcast night sky, it emerged from the fog like an evil sorcerer's castle. Built for many purposes, it seemed that its primary function was to intimidate. A palace, a fort, a prison, a mint, the war offices . . . and now? It was best known for the romance of its former glory, and so visitors would come to see the scrawlings of prisoners past on the walls. Peek at the former torture chambers. They'd also have picnics in the shadow of the Bloody Tower. And, of course, they'd view the Crown Jewels.

Nellie and Cora had the cabby stop a few blocks away so as not to startle any potential fog men in the vicinity, and slipped out quietly onto the street.

"Okay . . ." said Cora, "I'll track down the delivery boy outside the Tower walls. You, Little Miss Sneaking into Private Mansions, can you get into the Tower?"

"Don't see why not."

"You feel good about this? You feel safe?"

"Safe enough. Besides, I don't mind a bit of danger. Only wish I wasn't wearing so many layers . . ." Nellie paused for a moment, thought, then grinned at Cora and tore off her coat. She began next on her dress . . .

"What on earth are you doing?" asked Cora.

"Can't climb walls in a long skirt." She was down to her corset and bloomers in no time, and Cora shook her head. "I'll just hide this lot over here." Nellie bundled her dress into her coat and tossed both into a dark corner. "And I'm set!"

Cora wasn't sure if it was the smartest idea to have Nellie running around in her underwear, but if anything, it could be surprising enough to cause whoever it was to lose his focus for a moment. Might even be an advantage.

"Okay," Cora said with a shake of her head, "let's do this and maybe one of us will stumble on this guy."

"Good plan."

"Well . . . it's a plan. Not sure if it's that good. Meet back here."

"Right."

She watched the fog as it enveloped the ghost-white figure of Nellie heading off toward the Tower. Then . . . she was alone.

SO, SCALING A wall without her rope? Turned out that was a thing she could do. So long as the stone was rough enough and she didn't think too hard about what it was she was actually doing or how high up she actually was. As Nellie found herself inside the wall staring out at the many different towers that made up the fortress called the Tower of London, she thought to herself, "*If I'm going to keep doing stuff like this, I'm going to need the proper equipment.*"

She'd decided to come at the Tower from the wharf so as to avoid the dry moat. Also because it was the side the Wakefield Tower was on. The fact that she knew where the jewels were held wouldn't, she thought, be much of a surprise to anyone. The second she'd learned that it was possible for the paying public to view such precious and fabulous accessories, she'd insisted the Magician take her to see them. Not that she'd known the name of the jewels, or remembered with such precision as Cora what they looked like. She'd just remembered being dazzled by the sparkle.

She moved around the intimidating Wakefield Tower to its entrance, keeping her back flat to the wall in the hope that none of the guards would see her. She couldn't tell if it was because she was so small in such plain sight that made her feel so vulnerable or because she was in her underwear.

It also didn't help that she was standing in the shadow of the Bloody Tower at the moment. This tower, named for its history—one of murder and imprisonment and lots of other very unpleasant things—loomed over her to her left.

Don't let me see any ghosts. They are free to walk the tower as they wish, but please, just don't let me see them.

Nellie was at the entrance to Wakefield Tower and almost stumbled over the fallen guard on the ground before spotting him. She was able to contain her reaction and looked past the crime scene to the open door before her. Okay. So either the man had come and gone, or she was right on time. Whichever it was, Nellie bent down and picked up the guard's rifle just in case.

She had a very basic understanding of how the thing worked, had shot one once when she'd performed at an estate in the countryside. Not with the Magician. This was before, when a baron of some kind had requested that the cast of the burlesque show give him a private performance at his home. He thought it utterly hilarious to have the girls try their hand at shooting at some targets out back. Nellie was the only one who'd hit her mark, which was dismissed as "beginner's luck."

At any rate . . .

She climbed the narrow stairs, rifle awkwardly held in her right hand, and changed her prayer from not wanting to see ghosts to not wanting to be attacked and killed. It made more practical sense.

Nellie arrived in the vaulted room that housed the jewels. She would have been dazzled once more by their sparkle had they not been obscured from view by a figure standing in a long black coat. As quietly as possible, she raised the rifle and then she gathered all her courage.

"Pretty things, aren't they?" she asked. The figure shifted but didn't turn around. "I can see how you might let your guard down in seein' them. I myself get a wee bit distracted by things that sparkle like that."

There was another shift and she saw the figure drop something into its pocket. "Now, don't you be stealin' the Crown

Jewels. That's just not right." The figure finally turned. In the dark, it was hard to see the face, but she saw a thick beard and a strange leather cup contraption over the nose and mouth, complete with goggles over the eyes. "I didn't arrive unprepared, as you can see," she said, cocking the rifle.

But I did arrive in my undergarments.

She'd run out of things to say, and she was concerned about exactly how this confrontation would end. The figure took a step toward her. "I'm not afraid of firing this thing. I think you know that." *By which I mean, I'm terrified of firing this thing, and I hope you don't know that.*

Evidently the man did know that.

He charged her. Just barreled right for her, and before she had a moment to think, he'd pushed her hard onto the ground. The rifle went off after he'd passed, after he was down the steps, and the bullet careened around the stone room. Nellie covered her head with her hands to protect herself.

When the room fell silent, she was up on her feet, dashing out into the yard after the running figure, which was now far away. There was no way she was going to be able to catch up, not with him having such a good head start, and she slowed just in time to observe the attack from above.

It came as a black blur wearing a mask that glinted in the light. The blur landed directly on top of the figure with a scream, an otherworldly-sounding thing that made Nellie's blood run cold. The two figures wrestled for a moment, and then, suddenly, they were hidden behind orange smoke, or (it felt more appropriate) fog. Nellie watched as the man rose and continued running on his original trajectory until he was out of sight, leaving the masked one lying still on the ground.

With no way to catch up, Nellie waited for the orange fog to dissipate and then approached the masked figure carefully. It didn't move, and Nellie wasn't sure what to do. Just as she'd decided she would kneel down and look behind the mask, there was a coughing sound. The figure raised a hand and pulled off the mask quickly. Michiko. Considering this was the third night in a row of chance encounters, Nellie thought, "*Of course.*"

They made eye contact, and then Nellie crouched and helped her to sit. She continued to cough for a good five minutes, finally spitting out orange goop.

"What . . . ?" asked Michiko finally, and Nellie shook her head.

"No idea. Come, let's get out of here before the guards find us and accuse us of stealin' the Crown Jewels."

Michiko rose slowly and took a few careful steps. She nodded, and the two of them ran back to the wall and climbed up and over. Michiko had, of course, the most amazing technique for doing so, and made it look almost effortless. And it was nice for Nellie to have someone to help her get to the top before they jumped down together.

"Follow me," said Nellie as they ran along the wharf and out onto the street. Michiko nodded.

They ran in silence along the opposite side of the Tower from where she and Cora had left the cab, and came to a screeching halt, arriving at the figure that was lying on the ground before them.

Nellie couldn't be certain, but the way the boy was dressed and the fact that he was near the Tower in the first place suggested to her that this was the same delivery boy Cora had been after. He hadn't been felled by the orange fog, though. He'd had his throat cut.

Her gut clenched.

Where was Cora?

She whipped around to Michiko. "We have to find Cora." Michiko nodded and immediately was running up the street. Nellie took the opposite direction running back toward where she and Cora had parted ways earlier. She didn't care about stealth. She didn't feel clever or tough. All she wanted was to make sure Cora was okay.

"Cora!" she called out loudly. *Damn it.* "Cora!"

HOW LONG HAD she been wandering? Looking? No delivery boy. And certainly no man waiting for a package. She should probably go back to their meeting spot. See if Nellie was back yet.

She heard a sound in the distance, like someone was calling for her. Oh, god, something was wrong. Cora turned down an alley toward her name.

There were two figures in the dark some distance before her.

Nellie?

No.

A struggle.

It was him. It had to be him.

"Stop!" She pulled her pistol from her purse. The figures didn't seem to hear her. "I said stop! You think I won't shoot this? I will. And I've got terrific aim."

One of the figures stopped and stared at her. Just stared at her. The other figure, a girl, ran away, but the first figure didn't seem to notice. It just stared. Cora stared back.

"Is it you?" she asked.

The figure took a few steps closer.

"Why are you doing this? Why are you hurting them?"

The figure stopped walking.

Her hand was shaking, the pistol in it shaking, too. The figure turned and ran the other way.

The shadows did their job. And he disappeared.

"NELLIE!" CORA EMERGED from the shadows of a narrow alley. Her eyes were wide and she looked panic-stricken. Well, as much as Cora could look panic-stricken. "Are you okay?" She approached Nellie and grabbed her by the shoulders.

"Am I okay? Are *you* okay?"

"I'm fine, I'm fine. What's wrong?"

Nellie was suddenly aware of how fast her heart was beating, how shallow her breath had become. Adrenaline had kept her going, but now, seeing Cora in one piece, she felt like she might faint.

"Come, sit down." Nellie let Cora help her to a bench and felt a great sense of relief at no longer having to support her body weight. "What happened? Did you see him? What about the diamond?"

"I saw him. He overpowered me and stole the diamond. Then Michiko, in that way of hers, appeared out of nowhere and fought him. But he had this strange orange fog substance and it made Michiko pass out, and he ran off. And then we saw the delivery boy, and he was dead. And . . . then I thought that maybe you . . ."

"I'm okay," said Cora, sitting next to her. "The boy's dead?"

"Yeah."

"We should take him to Officer Murphy."

Even in her current state, the name gave Nellie butterflies. "Why?"

"Because we should take him to the police. And, of all of them, Murphy's the most tolerable."

"Okay." Another evening of hauling a dead body. Would it never end? Why was this happening to them? What did it mean? "Where were you? You scared us half to death."

"You were right, Nellie, your man and mine. They're the same person. I was searching for the delivery boy, and I saw him, the man, just now, just before coming to find you. He was attacking another flower girl. I yelled at him to stop. I held out my pistol. He stopped and just stared at me. It was . . . unnerving. Then . . . he ran away."

"Is the girl okay?" *Because I really can't deal with another dead body tonight.*

"She's fine. She ran away the second I distracted him."

Nellie nodded. She was flooded with relief, and also physically exhausted. It'd been a full day.

"What is he doing exactly? What does it all mean?" she asked quietly.

"I have no idea," replied Cora.

From the darkness, Michiko emerged, her mask seeming to float toward them of its own accord. She removed it and assessed the situation. "You're alive." In that very straightforward Michiko way, the truth of the situation was confirmed. Cora smiled.

"That I am."

"Good." Michiko thought for a moment. "Boy dead. Fog escape."

"Fog?"

"Man who make Michiko . . . un . . . conshus. Fog man."

"It was the same man?" asked Cora slowly. "Same man from the night of the gala?"

"Yes. Beard. Hat. Yes."

Cora looked at Nellie.

"So that's it then," said Nellie. "That proves it. The man who has somethin' to do with Mr. Carter, who ordered your device, who's attacking them flower girls. He's also the same man who decapitated Dr. Welland."

"Not a coincidence," Cora said softly.

"No."

They rested for a moment longer, each girl lost in her own thoughts. And then it was time to get to work. Nellie put her clothes back on and together they brought the delivery boy to Officer Murphy's station. Though the rest of the officers were none too thrilled to have to deal with some small East End dead kid, Officer Murphy took charge and told them he'd personally make sure the boy found his way to the morgue.

"There's a witness this time," said Cora.

"A witness?" asked Officer Murphy.

"A flower girl who got away. I didn't see much, but maybe she did. You going to ask around?"

Nellie felt that Cora didn't need to take quite that tone with him, especially after he'd been so kind to them. But Officer Murphy nodded. "I'll see what I can do."

It didn't appear to satisfy Cora, but Nellie thought it was awfully lovely of him.

He glanced at Nellie just as she was looking fondly at him. She felt her cheeks warm. Small things, like a glance, could make the rough patches a lot easier to bear.

Maybe the night hadn't been a total loss after all.

A Surprisingly Normal Day

THE FOLLOWING AFTERNOON was extraordinary in that it was so ordinary. It passed in such an uneventful fashion that all three girls at various moments in the day looked up, took pause, and thought: *"Really? Nothing?"*

News of the robbery of the Tower and of Mr. Carter's death had been printed in the morning paper. No mention of any of the girls—or the dead delivery boy whom Officer Murphy had carted off to the morgue in the wee hours. Of course, it made sense that they'd be ignored, as no one had seen any of them in the first place, but as usual, Cora felt a slight twinge of disappointment at the realization that, once again, her part in the drama had been completely ignored by the press.

And so it was that the day wore into early evening, the sun floating along waves of clouds toward its bedtime, and the girls did what the girls did.

Cora, now free of the device, had a minor victory in finishing her see-in-the-dark goggles.

Nellie had another show to perform and, of course, delighted the citizens of London.

And Michiko helped Callum pack; he was going to travel southeast with the newly widowed Mrs. Carter and her family.

He was so committed to his job, to protect the entire family like that. So noble. It was remarkable how he could fool himself into believing his own lie, Michiko thought as she piled a third topcoat into his trunk.

Everyone else, especially the gossips of the city, were very much aware of the truth. Which had something to do with Mrs. Carter's voluptuous curves.

But thank goodness he was going. Michiko would have a few days to herself. There was no way Callum would bring her along for this trip. To be a witness. So she got the house to herself. As did Koukou and Shuu, both of whom seemed so much more relaxed than usual as they waved Callum off in the carriage just after dinner.

Hayao arrived shortly afterward and was allowed, for the first time, through the door and into the rest of the house. He practically ran through it, discovering the excitement of one room only to fly off to another, his attention span comparable to a sparrow's. He did take pause on the second floor when Michiko showed him Callum's therapy room.

"*Weird*," he said as he ran his hand along one of the benches, the one with metal paddles attached by wires to a large generator at the back. "*And . . . creepy.*"

Michiko nodded. "*Look at this.*" She opened Callum's armory. It was another test, though considering that the boy sold weapons for a living, she was pretty sure he'd pass.

"*This stuff is all crap,*" he said, rifling through the swords and canes, Irish fighting sticks and ninja stars. "*And we sold most of them to him.*" He grinned widely at Michiko. Okay. He had a fine eye. But there was still that sense of pride she'd have to deal with.

"*Come, let's train.*"

She knelt in the center of the large room, and immediately Hayao knelt before her.

"*Let us begin with breathing. After your frantic tour through the house, I think you need it. Now pay attention . . .*"

She closed her eyes and felt herself sink. She was leaving the surface, far from the waves thrashing in the wind, and sinking into the deep dark blue of stillness. A cool deep breath in; her lungs expanded; she filled herself with air and then slowly exhaled through her nose. Slow, silent. Calm. In and out, in and out. It took a few moments before she could sense that Hayao was with her. He fell into her pattern more quickly now than he had just a few days ago. A quick study, this one. Very eager. A little too eager, maybe?

They sat for a quarter of an hour, and finally, Michiko opened her eyes, pleased to see that Hayao still had his firmly closed.

"*Now open your eyes and rise,*" she said quietly.

They stood at the same time, slowly, carefully, still facing each other.

"*Let's walk.*"

Teaching Hayao how to float across a floor had been one of the trickier tasks she'd faced. He couldn't seem to grasp the very simple concept of walking, heel toe, heel toe, very deliberately. Not bobbing up and down, not scampering about. Even, measured paces.

She knew she shouldn't get frustrated. She should stay calm, but she sighed hard and walked across the room, grabbing one of Callum's anatomy encyclopedias and placing it on Hayao's head. "*Smooth*," she ordered.

It sort of worked. He stopped bobbing up and down, but his body grew so tense that when Michiko gave him a little tap in the side with her stick, he tripped and stumbled.

"*Not quite there yet, are we, little monkey?*"

Hayao rolled his eyes and stood up.

"*Walking is walking. But fighting is fighting*," he said.

"*Wow. Deep.*"

"*You know what I mean. Come, fight me.*" He ran to the armory and pulled out two wooden training swords. Another test passed. The real swords in Callum's collection could hardly handle their sparring.

Michiko sighed and easily caught her sword as he threw it at her.

Then he ran at her, screaming loudly, his sword raised above his head. He was clearly attempting a typical samurai distraction technique. Except it really didn't work well on the person who had taught it to him. She took a step to the side, and he fell past her into the space that she'd just occupied. He turned around and her sword was at his forehead.

"*Try again.*"

And he did. He tried again. And again. Sometimes coming from complete stillness, sometimes trying to attack her as she gave him a new direction. His technique had improved; his handling of the weapon was much more confident. But he still had a long way to go. She decided she needed to teach him a very basic concept just for his own self-preservation.

"*Run away?*" he said, utterly indignant.

"*Yes. Run away. Run away, and then, when your enemies chase you, turn and fight the one who has caught up to you. Defeat the leader, and then . . . run away again. That way the group will turn into one fighter at a time and you may, just may, have a chance at surviving.*"

"*Thanks for the vote of confidence.*"

"*It's a very common practice, trust me. No one expects a warrior to run away.*"

"*Well, that's true . . .*"

"*And if the danger is too great . . . don't turn and fight. Just run. Run like you are teaching me how to run.*"

The last wasn't a samurai technique. It was her own private suggestion. To protect a ridiculous boy.

And seeing his expression, she knew he didn't like it one bit.

Too much frustration now.

"*Let's have tea.*"

The mood changed almost instantly as they headed down into Callum's formal sitting room. All the furniture was covered with white dust cloths, which they both happily pulled off and tossed into a corner. They sat on the plush, floral-patterned, upholstered chairs, and Koukou brought them English-style tea, despite the late hour. Neither of them particularly liked or understood the milky, sugary-sweet substance, and left their cups half full.

It was clear that there was something about Hayao's youth and energy that brought Michiko out of her shell. He was the younger brother she'd never had. That she never knew she'd wanted to have.

He reminded her a bit of the Monkey-King, Gokuu, all energy and climbing over everything, his talking back, his pride—did that make her the monk, Xuanzang, that tamed him?

They talked a bit about Japan, which Hayao barely remembered and Michiko worried she was romanticizing a bit. She talked of the temples and cherry blossoms. And white screen doors and the simple but expensive decorations in her home. She didn't talk about her parents, about their plans for her future. Of the men she'd met as the old geisha's kitten. Nor of Kyoshi Adachi. Whom she'd never had a chance to defeat, something every student must do at some point with their master. It was all music and poetry, honor and tradition. All good things.

Hayao's eyes got heavy, and he tried to hide a yawn. Michiko told him to lie down on the couch.

"*Rest, little monkey,*" she said, grabbing one of the white cloths and covering him with it like a blanket. "*Sleep for a few hours, and then we'll go out and do some running.*"

He smiled at the suggestion and was asleep almost immediately.

She pushed his hair away from his face and looked at him fondly.

You can't. You can't care. The more connections to this earth, the less willing you are to leave it. To face death without fear. To be a true samurai.

She pulled her hand back quickly and cleared the tea set instead.

Meanwhile . . .

"**WOW, YOU FINISHED** it," said Andrew, sounding a little more impressed than he ought to be. After all, Cora thought, it was pretty obvious that she'd find a way to finish the goggles, just as she had finally finished the other device. This was what she was good at.

"You're surprised?" she asked, leaning back in her chair and holding the goggles up in the light.

They were really quite a beautiful creation, leather straps and molded sockets that held the glass for the eyes. Held by thin metal joints off to the side were two other lenses that, neatly, with an easy flick, could fall in place in front of the glasses and change the view to night vision. Only after they had been secured in place, of course, with the automatic lock, and the gas between the two lenses was released from its small container near the ear. Yet it all looked so compact, almost delicate. It was, well, a work of art.

"Not surprised," he said quickly, though it was clear he was. "Just impressed. Always impressed. You are very impressive."

He was standing behind her and leaned down, placing his cheek against hers, wrapping his arms around her.

Why did she feel like he was holding her prisoner and not just being affectionate?

Still . . . he smelled nice.

"I know," replied Cora, and turned her head. He kissed her gently and then stood up again, clapping his hands.

"Come on! We need to celebrate! Let's go for a drink."

Cora sat upright. "I don't think I can. His lordship . . ."

". . . is out. God knows what he's up to."

Cora knew what he was up to. He was playing cards. Probably gambling away a fortune. And drinking. But of course he called such activities a "business meeting."

"If he comes back and finds that I'm not here . . ." She'd been lucky up till now. He hadn't caught her sneaking back in late several nights in a row. But how long would her luck last?

"He won't. We'll get you home before you turn into a pumpkin, I promise."

"I don't know."

"Look, how is it fair that you have to stay in twiddling your thumbs while he's out having a grand old time just because you don't want him to feel bad that you have a life outside of the one he gives you?"

Cora looked at Andrew and was impressed at how spot on his argument was. It *wasn't* fair. It had just always been that way. She'd always felt she'd had a kind of freedom. But it was only freedom up to a point. Freedom so long as his lordship knew her every movement. Going out this week hadn't prevented her from doing her work or being there for him when he needed her. Why couldn't she do what she wanted to when the job was done?

Damn it all. She was going to the pub.

THE DUKE OF York was not your typical local. It was posh, with high ceilings and vaulted windows, a place where lawyers met after work, and where the high-ranking bankers (no clerks) and gentlemen-about-town could experience the cozy comfort of the neighborhood pub without the usual riffraff.

It was also where a few brave ladies of substance, independently wealthy writers (possibly the odd novelist and those who contributed to ladies' magazines) and the like could feel reasonably comfortable. The carpeting was immaculate. The bar shone in the lamplight. And the electric lights along the long wall buzzed in a superior fashion.

No one seemed to notice Cora as being anything out of the ordinary. Still, she did feel a little out of place, since, aside from herself and Andrew, it seemed the youngest person there was thirty. But when they passed into the low-ceilinged back room and found a large round table surrounded by Andrew's friends from his "Eton days" (his "Eton days," as if they were a far-off memory and he'd not graduated just last year), the whole thinking that she'd be more comfortable around folks her own age thing? Not so much.

Not that they didn't try to be affable, all rising while Andrew pulled out a seat for her, and paying for each round of drinks. But every action they made came across as a kind of mockery almost, as if her presence was the biggest joke of all.

It didn't feel good.

"Cora, Cora, Cora," said Dipper (they all been introduced to her by these nicknames that she couldn't for the life of her figure out), "now, what have you done to our chap here?"

"What do you mean?" she asked. She really didn't like how he took the liberty of using her Christian name so casually, but she chose to let it go.

"Well, ever since he met you, he's been a whole different fellow."

"You mean that his arrogance and pretentiousness are a new affectation?" Cora asked in mock surprise.

Dipper guffawed, and he slapped the table hard.

"Oh Lord, what's he been on about this time?" asked Wibbly, a short, pale-faced boy with a receding hairline who simultaneously looked like he was entering middle age and just leaving middle school.

"Haven't you heard about his Jekyll and Hyde theory?" asked Cora with a grin at Andrew who sighed and shook his head.

"I know that one!" said Mops, clearly not out of the prep school mind-set, his hand flying up in excitement.

"Yes, Mops," said Cora, pointing to him and speaking as if she were his teacher recognizing his raised hand. The boys laughed at that.

Mops just grinned, oblivious to the joke, but happy he'd provoked the laughter. "It's that 'two sides to every person' philosophy of his, the whole . . . oh, damn it all, what's the word . . ."

"Duality?" offered Cora.

"That's it! Duality."

"What's this, what's this?" asked Dipper, leaning forward and looking at Andrew, cocking his head to one side.

Andrew smiled and took a puff on his cigar. "I've told you," he said, blowing out the smoke.

"I dare say I'd remember."

"Yes, Captain, I think we'd all remember. Especially that you'd actually read a novel," said Wibbly.

Andrew leaned back farther, tipping the chair off its front legs, and blew smoke at the ceiling. "It's about embracing both sides of ourselves, including the side that society would prefer we keep under wraps. Cora understands."

He glanced at her, and she rolled her eyes.

"What does a woman know about two sides?" said Pheasant.

"What a stupid question," said Cora looking at the pig-faced boy directly across from her.

"I beg your pardon?" Pheasant's cheeks flushed a deep pink.

"You honestly don't think a woman would understand the restrictions that society places on a person?" She was taken aback. Stunned, really.

"Yes," came a quiet smooth voice from beside her.

Cora turned in her chair to look directly at Iago, the boy sitting directly to her left. Aside from Andrew, he was probably the most attractive fellow there, dark blond curls growing a little long, his suit nicely tailored to fit his broad shoulders.

"You boys think you're all so clever, and that you are the only ones with intelligent thoughts to articulate." Cora spoke as calmly as she could. "That we girls just sit and listen and take it all in, and otherwise marvel at how pretty a flower can look in the morning sun. You think this because we don't say anything. But we don't say anything because no one listens. No one lets us speak, and, if we do, our voices are silenced by an affectionate pat on the head. We have opinions. We can problem-solve. There's much more to us than you think."

"You don't seem to have a problem sharing your thoughts," said Iago.

"I'm unique."

"That you are," said Dipper in an easy dismissal.

"I think you're drawing a false conclusion, Cora," said Iago, with a smile.

"Am I?"

"Not everyone is capable of rational thought to the same degree."

Cora scoffed, "And how do you prove that exactly?"

"Why do you think people end up where they do in society? If they had the capacity of being truly brilliant, they'd not be where they are."

"So you are saying that women are second-class citizens because they can't function at a higher level?" *Calm down, Cora, calm down. He's just trying to goad you.*

"Not just women. Of course, look at the poor. If they were

capable of greater intelligence, then don't you think they'd have figured a way out of their situation?"

Despite her best efforts at staying calm, Cora was becoming upset. What frustrated her the most, though, was that, despite how wrong she knew he was, she couldn't think of a quick enough comeback.

Iago saw her silence as his victory and turned to Andrew. "So what are you hiding from the world, then, Captain?"

"My Hyde side you mean?" asked Andrew, falling immediately back into the conversation as if the recent tangent had never happened. "Nothing out of the ordinary. Just the same passions as any man."

"What are those passions, then?" Cora said sharply. "Go on."

She and Andrew looked at each other for a moment, and Cora wondered just what would happen next. He seemed to be holding back. Getting angry, but keeping it to himself.

Oh, *just show us your Hyde already.*

"You've read the book," he said quietly.

"Yes, and I know it's very careful not to specify exactly what terrible things Hyde got up to, as if reading about it might influence the reader. Except for the murder bit. You interested in that?"

"I believe every man is capable of killing for a reason."

It was a very clearly pronounced sentence that fell on his audience heavily.

"What are you going on about?" whined Pheasant. "Are you murdering people, Captain?"

Andrew shook his head and laughed. "It's all philosophical, Pheasant. Stop being so dramatic. But haven't any of you ever wondered what it would be like to take someone's life?"

"Not really, no," said Mops, his voice cracking.

"I have," said Iago.

Andrew nodded at him. "The energy, the power. Fascinating."

Cora was starting to feel sick. She thought of Alice. There was no energy that had flowed from the dying flower girl. It wasn't fascinating. It just felt awful. Sad. Helpless.

"That's not what it feels like," she said quietly.

Iago raised his eyebrows at her. "Killed someone, have you?"

"No. But I've seen someone die. I've seen someone bleed to death on the street, the life evaporate from her eyes. Have you?"

She knew the answer. The closest thing to death any of these boys had experienced was shooting rabbits on an estate in the country.

"I think you're missing the point," said Iago.

"Am I?"

"Yes," said Andrew. "It isn't about the dying. It's about the killing. And I think there is something animalistic in all of us that would get something out of it. Something . . . primal. We all have these basic instincts, basic desires and drives. To think otherwise is irrational. It's part of the conflict of being human. The duality. Reason versus instinct. Animals don't empathize. Don't reason away every impulse like some in this room might." He gave her an unnecessarily pointed look. "They just act."

"Well, I—"

“You’ve never wanted to do something wrong, that went against what society tells you to do? I find that really hard to believe, Cora.”

“We’re not talking about that. We’re talking about one very specific thing . . .” How many drinks had she had? She was feeling dizzy. And overwarm. And royally pissed off that she couldn’t articulate the thoughts she had on the subject. All she knew was it was more complicated than these boys were trying to make it out to be. She definitely knew that wanting to break free from the restrictions she felt put on her was one thing and that killing someone was quite another.

And she knew it was time to go home.

Cora stood.

“Thank you so much for a lovely evening, but it’s time for me to turn in.” She looked down at Andrew. “Good night, Mr. Harris.”

With that, she pushed her chair back and left the room, the pub, the whole stupid evening, and started on the short walk home.

“Cora!” Andrew ran up beside her and fell into step with her.

“What?”

“Don’t be angry,” he said.

“No, I think that’s exactly what I’ll be.”

He stopped and grabbed her by the shoulders, forcing her to stop, too.

“I’m sorry about all that. I’m sorry about the things I said. I know how it must have sounded . . .”

"You do?"

"It's just thoughts people have, and people can have some pretty dark thoughts, at times. It's safe to share them with your friends."

"They're not my friends."

"Cora, you were the one who brought up the whole concept of duality, not me. I just wanted to celebrate your invention."

Cora thought for a moment. His logic didn't seem right. But he was accurate. She had brought it all up.

He hadn't seemed to mind, though.

"I have to go home."

"Let me walk you."

Cora shook her head. No. It wasn't right. None of it was right. Talk about instincts. Since the beginning, it hadn't felt right.

He was kissing her.

How did that always happen when she least expected it?

Why did it always feel so nice? Even when it tasted like alcohol and cigar smoke.

"See, you like me," he said when they parted, touching his forehead to hers.

I don't think I do, Cora thought, hoping the realization wouldn't be transferred from her brain to his with their foreheads touching like that.

"I think . . . you're wrong for me . . ." she said quietly.

"Well . . . what's wrong with wrong?"

Everything. By definition, wrong wasn't right.

"I . . . can't . . ."

"Yes, you can." He kissed her again. Pulled her in tight. He was so warm in the cold night.

She pulled away from him. "Why do you like me?" It had to be asked.

"Because you're different. You're not like other girls. You're not exactly easy to win over."

"I'm a trophy then? Something to put on the mantelpiece?"

He laughed. "Yes, that's it exactly. I'd like to have you bronzed, if you don't mind."

It was one of his fine jokes. He was so good at jokes.

But he hadn't denied it.

"I'm going home now."

"Let me come with you."

"No, Andrew."

"He'll never find out."

"Who won't?"

"Lord White. I'll be sneaky. I'm good at it. Let me come over. Let me . . ." He trailed off.

She was meant to complete his thought, though she was pretty sure he himself was unsure what came next.

Now he was looking at her in a meaningful way. Yet for the life of her she had no idea what he was trying to communicate.

"I'm not sleeping with you," she said.

He coughed a little and took a step back.

"Well, that's what you've been hinting at, isn't it?" she asked.

"I . . ."

"I'm not. I don't care how drunk you get me, or how much you kiss me. I'm not sleeping with you. I mean, what kind of person do you think I am?"

Andrew pressed his lips together and inhaled sharply through his nose. Then: "I think you're the kind of person who oughtn't hold onto something as meaningless as 'purity,' when it's only natural . . ."

"I know, I know, instinct and all that, right? Like with killing. Lust is only natural. Sex is only natural."

"Well, it is. But you wouldn't know that, would you, you little . . ." He stopped.

Cora felt a flame burn bright inside her. "What? What am I?"

"A tease. So direct. So to the point, little Miss Bell. A servant girl who thinks she's better than everyone. Who thinks she better than me, for God's sake." He turned and spoke out as if he had an audience. Okay, so clearly she wasn't the only one who was drunk.

"I'm going home," she said.

"I'm coming with you." He grabbed her arm.

"No, you damn well aren't!" She pulled her arm back.

"Make me."

"Make you what? That doesn't actually work with what I said before."

"I could hit you now," he sputtered. "I could hit you."

Cora laughed. She couldn't help herself. The way he'd phrased it, it was like a small child's threat.

He didn't hit her. She hadn't really thought he would. He

just stumbled backward and pointed at her. Pointed at her and stabbed the air a few times. Then he spat on the ground. Then he started to laugh. "I don't know why I thought you were any different from the rest of them. You're not."

He wanted her to ask "the rest of whom?", so she didn't.

She was done with this. He was drunk; she was drunk. The night was over. She had more important things to focus on. She really wished Nellie were here to vent to. Or Michiko, so she could give him a good walloping.

The thought of Andrew being walloped made Cora smile, and she turned and walked away. Leaving Mr. Harris to do whatever it was Mr. Harris did when he wasn't being a complete arse.

Also This . . .

NELLIE SAT STARING at herself in her dressing room mirror. She was dawdling. She knew it. The audience had emptied from the theater. The Magician had packed up. She'd insisted he head off, and here she was, still in her bathrobe, just sitting. Staring at herself. Or kind of . . . past herself.

It was like all the events from the week had suddenly hit her, just after the curtain call. There was no rhyme or reason as to why now. But there it was.

She was overwhelmed.

There was a knock on the door.

"Come in," she said, not moving.

The door opened a crack, and the stage manager stuck his head in. "Copper's here to see you, miss."

"What?" She shifted her gaze in the mirror to make eye contact with him.

"There's a copper outside what is requesting to see you," he repeated.

This made Nellie turn around in her chair. "Uh . . . did he say what he wanted, then?"

"No."

"Right, let him in." She gave the cord that held her robe together a quick tug and watched for the door to open.

It did.

Slowly.

And even when it had opened enough so that a person might pass through it, nothing happened.

"Hello?" Nellie called out.

A paper-wrapped bundle of red carnations appeared a moment later, as if it was sent along first to make sure the coast was clear. Finally, a blond head appeared.

"Officer Murphy!" said Nellie, suddenly putting two and two together. She quickly glanced at her appearance in the mirror and realized, well, yes, of course she was as pretty as ever. Then she jumped up and skipped across the room, opening the door wide. Officer Murphy stood staring at her as if he'd been caught doing something untoward.

"Good evening, Miss . . ." He stopped and looked in a panic.

"Harrison. Miss Harrison. But call me Nellie. You know that. Don't be silly! Come in!" She stepped back, and Officer Murphy took a step into the room, leaving just enough space for Nellie to close the door behind him. She took a moment to examine him in his uniform from the back. *Yup, just lovely.* She returned to her seat in front of her mirror and sat facing him. Despite his body being in a new location, his posture didn't change.

There was silence for a moment.

"Are those for me?" she asked, realizing that one of them had to say something. The words were remarkably clear and calm sounding despite the fluttery feeling she felt all over.

"No. Yes." He jerked his arm forward, just enough so that, leaning a little off her seat, she could take the flowers from him.

"They're beautiful," she said, giving them a sniff and thinking cheap carnations more darling than any fancy bouquet of roses. This gave her a moment to look away from him and try to compose herself. It was crazy how he could make her heart race like that. He was beyond adorable. And his cheekbones were just delightful. She glanced up, and he looked as if he might cry, he was so physically uncomfortable. "Oh, for the love of Mary's son, Officer Murphy, sit!"

He did so without taking a moment to see if there was actually anything near him to sit on, and it was just plain luck that there happened to be a seat directly behind him. Clearly, it was a little lower than he'd anticipated, and he bounced a little to the side before sitting himself straight up again.

"So . . . what can I be doin' for you, then, Officer?"

"Oh, it's not like that."

"Like what?"

"It's not official. Well, it is and it isn't. It's not that I'm here officially, but now that you ask, I have some news. Well, no . . . not news, not really, just . . . well, I've been looking into those flower girls for you and your friend, and there's really not much to go on. But it does seem the description's the same from witnesses who've seen him flee the scene."

"Yes?"

"Not that they've seen much. Same coat and hat, mind. But no face. No features. Even the girl last night didn't have much to go on. Grabbed her from behind, Miss Bell came on them before she could see. Said . . . and this was interesting . . . that he smelled nice, with cologne or something. Still, not much to go on."

"Okay . . ."

Officer Murphy cleared his throat. "What it does mean is that your friend was right. It's no coincidence that all the girls have been attacked."

"Well, we already knew that."

"Yes. I . . . yes. You did."

"But now you believe her, is your point."

"Yes. I . . . yes."

"Is there anything to be done?"

"Well, I'm doing the best I can, getting the word out, asking for witnesses . . . but it's all in my spare time and . . ." He petered off.

"That's nice of you," said Nellie, because she hoped it would make him look less dejected and because it was true. It was really nice of him to look into this all on his own.

Officer Murphy nodded once and slumped back into the small love seat. Then, realizing that relaxation wasn't polite, he sat upright quickly again.

Nellie smiled to herself. *Poor guy.*

"So, why are you here, then?" she asked, changing the subject.

"Pardon?"

"You said you weren't here 'officially,' so why are you here?"

"Oh. To see the show."

"Really?"

"Well . . . everyone talks about the show . . . and . . ."

"And?"

"Oh, darn it all, I wanted to see you." Immediately he looked terrified, as if he'd just said something foul about her mother.

"You did?" She hoped she wasn't going to be sick with happiness. Like bells in her head: *He likes me! He likes me!*

"Uh . . ." He squirmed in his seat and finally just stood up. Pacing the room, he said, "Yes. You're . . . sweet. I like how . . . energetic you are. You have a pretty smile." He spoke without looking at her, almost as if he was reciting something to himself. Then he stopped and turned and looked right at her. "Will you go to dinner with me?"

It was so surprising to see him suddenly so bold that Nellie said "yes" before she even had a moment to think. Of course, had she had such a moment, she still would have said yes, so it didn't really matter much.

"Great, so how long until you're . . . you know . . . in clothes . . . ?" He blushed.

"Oh, you mean right now?"

"Yes, unless that's inconvenient for you."

"No! No, it's perfect, I'm starving." It was true. But it was also true that she'd had dinner before the show. Fortunately, another true thing was that Nellie was always hungry.

So he left her to change, and even though usually she'd take a little more time perfecting the picture, she was so giddy with excitement that she didn't have the patience to make sure her hair was perfect or her corset pulled as tight as it could go.

Soon they were out on the street and joined the after-theater crowd seamlessly. Though, because Murphy was still in uniform, a couple of Spanish tourists did stop to ask him for directions. Nellie thought the detailed directions he gave them for getting to Trafalgar Square were wonderfully well articulated. *See, he's smart too,* her brain pointed out.

They wound up in a small café in Covent Garden at a small round table placed on a small terrace on the lower level. Nellie did her best to keep her skirts beneath her to avoid having them stepped on by the passing foot traffic, and Officer Murphy kept apologizing at her slightest shift in her seat.

"I'm fine!" she finally said with a laugh. "Once I'm arranged." She shooed a curious pigeon away from her hem.

"Some of the lads suggested this place. I'm sorry," he said again.

"Officer Murphy . . ."

"Jeff."

"Jeff. Just because a girl needs to shift about some, it doesn't mean she's not happy. You try wearin' all these layers and a bloody corset at the same time and see if you don't find sittin' a wee bit of a maneuver."

Officer Murphy nodded and, having nothing to add to such a statement, picked up the menu and examined it very studiously.

Nellie feared that this might turn into a conversation of fits and starts and suggested wine, but Officer Murphy sheepishly admitted to not being much of a drinker, so they had some Italian coffee instead. The arrival of the food was a marvelous distraction. Officer Murphy was able to relax a bit and shared stories about growing up on the family farm. Nellie shared her tales of Dublin life as a young child, which she hoped would demonstrate that she wasn't nearly as intimidating as he thought she was. And they found they had poverty and a strong work ethic in common. They also shared a love of animals.

"I want to work with dogs," said Officer Murphy energetically, taking a large and very confident bite of his raspberry tart. "We have one at the station, a bloodhound, as a pet, but he sniffs out all sorts of stuff on the blokes carted in. And I was thinking, after they tried them out on the Ripper case back in the day, that maybe it was worth a go again. They're really smart, dogs."

"They absolutely are. And that's a mighty fine idea, I think. Dogs could be a real treat in solvin' and findin' stuff. You know . . . have you thought about using this dog at the station to help you track down the flower-girl fella at all?"

"To be honest, I hadn't." Officer Murphy looked intrigued.

"Not sure how it'd be done, but seein' as you don't have any visual clues and you do have a scent, you said."

"That's true!" He pointed his fork at her and smiled, revealing a bit of raspberry between his teeth that made Nellie smile to herself.

"Maybe he left his scent on the girl or somethin'. At any rate, it's somethin' to think about."

Officer Murphy did appear to agree as he thought about her suggestion quietly for a full two minutes, and Nellie began to fear once again that the conversation would stall. But once he'd taken careful stock of her suggestion, he launched into a story about himself as a kid trying to hop a ride on one of the neighbors' horses, not realizing that one hadn't been broken yet. And Nellie had a perfect story to go with it, about the time she'd rescued a foal from a truly nasty blacksmith just down the street from where she and her ma had lived. She'd sneaked in, in the dead of night, and walked it all the way out into the countryside.

"It took all night," she was enthusiastically saying until she realized that maybe she should stop telling the nice young police officer all about her breaking-and-entering experiences. She changed the subject: "I like your mustache."

"You do?" His hand flew up to it instantly.

"Normally I like a clean-shaven face, but on you it works. It makes you look official."

"Well, to be honest, that was part of the point. Everyone at the station kept calling me 'boy' and even 'kid' sometimes. Thought it might make me look older, and . . . like you say, official."

"And they stopped calling you names."

"No."

"Oh."

"But that's all right," he said. "They put you through your paces when you're new. Make you do all the grunt work and also make you feel right pathetic as often as possible. Everyone goes through it. It's a rite of passage."

"Well, I think it's all a little silly. Men always say about us girls that we need to be taken care of like children, and yet you all play games and make believe with passwords and no-girls-allowed societies." Well, now she was starting to sound a bit like Cora there.

"I don't think girls are like children at all. You're just . . . softer . . . gentler. You think about nice things, is all. You don't see the dark world and you need us to protect you from it."

"Bollocks," said Nellie with a laugh. "You think I don't know about darker things? You think I'm soft?"

"You look soft." And, appropriately, he said it softly.

Nellie realized that he wasn't trying to provoke her. He was only trying to compliment her in his way. "Well, a person can be soft and strong. Looks can be deceiving. I think it's just a matter of boys gettin' to know us girls better. And not in a funny-business sort of way."

"Well, I know I'd certainly like to get to know you better."

"Is that your way of askin' me out again, Officer Murphy?" Nellie gave him her coyest of smiles.

His eyes widened in that familiar horror. "Oh no. I mean . . . I didn't mean it that way—"

"Because if it is," she said, interrupting him, "then I'd be very happy to say yes."

The terror was gone and he sighed with relief. "Oh good. Grand. Good."

Nellie reached across the table and took his hand in hers, causing his face to return to that familiar pink. And she was pretty sure she wasn't exactly snow white herself.

PART FOUR

The Team

• • •

AND THEN THERE was an explosion.

It happened in the morning. Just as the foot traffic was picking up in the city, as those manning the market stalls were greeting their first customers, and as a bright sun fought bravely to make its presence known through a thick veil of gray cloud.

It happened as Cora and Lord White had just arrived at Westminster.

It happened as Nellie and the Magician were feeding the animals.

AND IT HAPPENED as Michiko and Hayao sat on a slanted rooftop and took a break from the marathon they were running across the city skyline.

They had both overslept and were now making up for lost time. And though it was dangerous to run in daylight, it was amazing how easy it was to avoid detection in a city where everyone kept a firm gaze on the street beneath their feet. A city of bowed heads.

Taking a break was a luxury they enjoyed, knowing Callum

was out of town. Michiko had no idea when he'd be back, but it wouldn't be for a day at least, which meant she not only had time to train and be a teacher, but also to hunt the Fog.

She had taken the extra precaution, nonetheless, of wearing her new mask along with her usual black outfit. She was getting used to it now. It wasn't nearly as tricky to see through as it had been that night at the Tower. Though, she suspected, daylight helped.

Right now the mask lay in her lap as she and Hayao sat in silence. She'd said it was another test of patience, but truly she'd just wanted some quiet in order to sit and admire the view, the one that looked out toward the river and St. Paul's domed cathedral roof. She knew that under the layers of soot there was a gleaming white building. But it seemed to make sense that one of the tallest structures in the city should reflect the general dirty gray. She'd never been inside. She thought it might be nice to go visit someday.

She saw the explosion before she heard it. As if to taunt her little fantasy, something like a meteor flew from out of a low-hanging cloud and struck the dome. It was so shocking and unbelievable that Michiko was pretty determined to believe it hadn't happened. Then . . . the inside of the cathedral burst outward, and less than an instant later Michiko heard the roar of destruction.

The moment of the explosion was accompanied by a wave of air that pushed toward Hayao and her, along with dust and debris. Instinctively, she pulled Hayao down against the roof, protecting him, and holding her other hand over her head, a feeble attempt to prevent an injury. Which, really, didn't offer much protection.

But, fortunately, they were far enough away from St. Paul's that they were in little danger. Their greatest threat, really, was the chance of getting some grit in their eyes.

"*Are you okay?*" asked Michiko nonetheless.

Hayao nodded, but didn't look at her; he just gaped at the altered view in front of them.

Michiko gaped, too. Though less obviously. Where moments ago there had been a grand cathedral, now there was . . . nothing. Just a cloud of dust and smoke, and flames licking the sky.

Michiko watched the dark smoke curl upward, and then her ears were drawn to a faint siren far to the east. The fire brigade's airships would be dispatched soon to shower down a heavy spray of water. Turning the heat into a white steam.

"*Can you believe we just saw that?*" asked Hayao, staring in awe at the fire burning bright.

Michiko shook her head.

What a week.

IT WAS AMAZING how easily grown men could turn into young boys. Cora quickly dove into an alcove, pulling Lord White with her as the Members of Parliament collided with one another in the chaos.

"My goodness, Miss Bell. This is all rather frenetic," said Lord White, adjusting his glasses and sitting on the narrow bench below the window, crossing one leg over the other.

"Indeed. What was it? It shook the whole building."

Lord White shook his head and then pulled a small brass box from his pocket.

"Not now," said Cora, assuming its contents to be some means of relaxing his lordship.

But Lord White only smiled and slid the top of the box open so that it was now a long rectangle. "Keep lookout, would you?" He extended a small, metal, strawlike thing from one end, and Cora couldn't help but look over his shoulder. The open box didn't contain any illicit substance, just some gears and a glowing yellow center.

"What in the blue blazes is that thing?" She had been pretty confident she'd seen all his inventions. Obviously, this confidence had been misplaced.

Lord White gave her a wink, turned a dial, and a strange crackling sound emanated from the box. And then . . .

Barker's voice. "Sir?"

"I need more information," instructed Lord White.

"About that sound, sir? And the shaking?"

"Yes. As quickly as possible, thank you, Barker."

"Of course, sir."

The crackling stopped as Lord White turned the dial again.

Cora was speechless. "Where is he? He's not at home, surely?"

Lord White smiled. "Oh yes. Isn't life just like that sometimes? Today is the first long-distance test of my tele-audio device, and it just so happens to be a day that it comes in rather handy. Funny, don't you think?"

"Why didn't you tell me about it?"

"Why do you think I wanted you and Harris to work on the commissions? Why do you think I hired him in the first place? I had to focus all my attention on this."

"Oh." Was that what it was all about, then? Why hadn't he just told her? "I thought . . ."

"What?"

She felt really silly now. "I thought . . . you were slowly trying to replace me."

Lord White looked stunned. "By hiring an assistant for you?"

"An assistant for *me*? What in the world do you mean?"

"Well, he's a clever young man, but he doesn't have your gifts. I thought you could maybe teach him a thing or two. Thought you might need help doing the tedious work while you got cracking at the inventing."

"Why didn't you tell me any of this?" Honestly, sometimes his lordship could be infuriating.

"I thought it was obvious."

"He said he was your new assistant."

"Well, he was mistaken."

Cora was astonished. She had nothing to say. She just stared ahead at the MPs running to and fro, and felt altogether ridiculous. Why had she ever doubted Lord White? Well . . . it wasn't like he went out of his way to let her know she mattered either.

There was a crackling sound again.

"Yes, Barker?"

"Sir, St. Paul's has been completely demolished. There was an—"

". . . WILL LISTEN TO THE WORDS OF . . ."

"... water ships. Seems to have been curtailed, however ..."

". . . ST. PAUL'S CATHEDRAL AND UNDERSTAND THE GRAVITY OF ..."

Cora looked at Lord White, who was staring at the device with deadly seriousness. "What's going on?"

"Something's interrupting the current. Someone else is talking." He twisted the dial and the yellow glow faded out. He gave the device an unhelpful hit on the side with his palm.

"... A MERE DROP COMPARED TO AN OCEAN ..."

Cora turned and stared out the window. The tinny voice emanating from Lord White's device sounded far off suddenly. Not coming from his now-defunct tele-audio machine, but from somewhere else. She glanced back toward the room and noticed that the MPs had stopped their racing about. She stood and looked around the corner of the alcove. The men lined the walls, their heads sticking out through the windows, making Cora flash in her mind to the decapitated body of Dr. Welland.

It was only a moment, though, and she had their alcove window open, her head joining those already sticking out. The voice was magnified, seemed to be coming from the sky. It echoed loudly around the city.

"... ONE MILLION POUNDS AND I SPARE LONDON. YOU HAVE UNTIL MIDNIGHT TO COMPLY. I CAN AND WILL DESTROY YOU ALL."

"Ominous," said Lord White wryly, his head joining hers in the morning air.

"Don't you think it's serious?" asked Cora.

"What? The mysterious voice in the sky? Might be. But I've never responded well to histrionics." He pulled his head back inside and Cora followed suit.

"Didn't Barker say something about St. Paul's being destroyed? I don't think this is an empty threat," she said, bringing herself back to sitting next to him.

"I don't know what it is. But I think it would be best to leave it to Scotland Yard."

"Lord White!" Mr. Fish ran up to them and doubled over, short of breath. "Thank goodness you're here. We're calling a meeting of the House instantly to discuss how to respond to this threat."

Lord White rolled his eyes and sighed loudly. For a man who wasn't a fan of theatrics in others, he certainly made use of them when it suited his purpose. "Don't tell me we're even thinking of giving in to such a demand . . ."

"We need to debate the situation. Come, come now, sir. . . uh . . . your lordship."

Lord White was whisked away, and Cora followed, intending to observe the proceedings from the gallery.

If there had been chaos after the explosion, it was nothing compared with the chaos in the House of Commons after being blackmailed by a voice in the sky. Cora was used to watching the men all standing and shouting at one another. Or at least shouting at the Speaker of the House in the way a brother might passive-aggressively yell at his sister through his mother: "Tell

Sally I never want to play with her again . . ." "Tell Bobby that I don't want to play with him either . . ." and so on. But Cora had never seen anything quite like this before.

"Mr. Speaker! Would you explain to Mr. Weatherington that we can't spend the taxpayers' money on blackmail . . ."

"Mr. Speaker, kindly tell Mr. Cox we have no time to deal with political philosophy . . ."

"Mr. Speaker, will you tell Mr. Weatherington to just shut up . . ."

And more conversations of the same kind, each overlapping the other. And worse, MPs were actually throwing things at one another, a pencil here, a shilling there, to get the attention of someone across the aisle. And then there was the haggard-looking Speaker of the House sitting at the far end, his forehead cradled in his hand, looking like what he needed more than anything was a good cry.

Lord White stayed seated in his prime position in the front row and was having a quiet chat with two other MPs. Cora highly doubted that it had anything to do with the topic at hand.

Cora knew how politics worked. She knew that eventually the Members of Parliament would have to settle down. Eventually, they'd all agree to take some action that nobody was happy with. But God only knew when that would be.

She also knew something else.

Cavorite had been stolen from a murdered Dr. Welland.

The British Museum and the Tower had been robbed.

Citizens were dropping like flies.

Moments ago St. Paul's had been destroyed somehow.

Now this loud, magnified voice was threatening London?

None of this was a coincidence.

Watching the men below her, yelling and red-faced, Cora felt surprisingly calm. She turned and left the gallery.

Left the Palace of Westminster altogether.

She'd never walked out on her job before. Certainly she'd procrastinated between tasks. But mid-job? No, she was a good worker.

But what was the point of doing good work when everyone around you was acting foolish?

The streets were empty. They were never empty at this time of day. But they were now. Quiet and still, and with a strange sensation of discontent, as if the hard stone beneath her feet were distinctly unhappy.

She wandered to the edge of the river and looked to her left to see the smoke and steam rising from the place where a spectacular cathedral had once stood. An airship was still circling the spot, but the fire seemed to have been put under control by the water ships. Cora decided to move along the river's edge toward the chaos.

Still a little dazed.

Even more than a little determined.

She arrived at Embankment, very near the spot where all this had started. At least, for her. In the distance, two figures materialized as she approached. She said nothing even as she recognized one of them when it pulled off the unsettling silver mask. Not until they were face-to-face.

Clearly it made sense that she'd be one of the only other people out and about. It made Cora reason that one other person was likely somewhere to be found as well.

"Michiko."

"Cora."

Cora glanced at the boy at Michiko's side. He was all limbs and at least a head shorter than her friend. And like Michiko, he was covered in dust.

"We saw it," said Michiko.

"You saw what happened?"

"Yes."

"What happened?"

"There. Bright light. Flew to there." Michiko pointed up to the sky, quite near where the airship was circling, then toward the burning cathedral. The boy tugged at Michiko's arm and said something to her in Japanese; he seemed to stumble over his words, and once in a while he glanced at Cora as if his explanation needed to be heard as quickly as possible.

Michiko nodded. And nodded. And then finally gave one sharp nod and pushed the boy behind her.

"He say, come from there." Michiko pointed to the water. "Come up, up, and come from there." She pointed back to the spot she'd originally indicated.

"That's all he said?" asked Cora. The stream of Japanese she had just heard had seemed considerably more involved than that.

Michiko looked at her steadfastly, and Cora decided to drop the subject.

"Do you think," she said instead, "that all of this is connected?" Michiko looked at her, not seeming to understand. "Connected," Cora said more slowly.

Say yes and make me feel sane.

"All . . . connected. Energy. All," Michiko replied.

"Yes, but this, the robberies, the man in the fog, all the . . . death. Is it connected?"

For a moment Michiko looked puzzled, and then slowly said "yes," as if she'd already answered the question and wasn't entirely sure what she'd said wrong the first time.

Cora smiled. Michiko looked just as puzzled as ever. Possibly her smiling didn't make sense to an outside eye, but it was good to know someone else saw things the way Cora herself did.

And there was another one, too, another person who saw the connections.

"Let's go to Nellie's."

Plans

"*WHERE ARE WE GOING?*" asked Hayao quietly, though he needn't have lowered his voice. It wasn't like Cora understood what he was saying.

"*We aren't going anywhere. I am going with Cora. You are returning to your master.*"

"*You are my master.*"

Michiko stopped and so did Hayao. "*Then, as your master, I want you to go to the stall and get to work. You're late enough as it is.*"

"*Okay.*" Hayao didn't move.

"*What?*"

"*Well, it's just . . . we're going the same way, it looks like . . .*"

Michiko sighed and started walking again, faster now, in order to catch up with Cora, but also because monkey boy was starting to get on her nerves again.

It turned out he was right. Not only were they going the same way, they were going to the very same location. Cora was taking Michiko to the blonde's flat, the one she'd woken up in that first fateful night. The one that just also happened to overlook the market stall where Hayao worked.

Michiko and Hayao parted before the arched entrance to the square. Hayao hadn't shared with the old samurai that he was studying with Michiko, and quite frankly Michiko didn't want to find out what the old man thought of her having the nerve to teach samurai. She already knew what she thought of it.

But as she entered the square, it was impossible to keep herself apart from Hayao. The stalls were being manned with all diligence, but very few people were there to buy anything. Michiko had never seen the market so empty before. In a way, it was far more eerie than passing the demolished St. Paul's.

As she followed Cora to Nellie's apartment, Michiko started to feel concerned. This wasn't right, this working with other people. This wasn't what she'd been taught. How could she focus on the task ahead with the weight of other problems, with other relationships in the back of her mind?

Yet, here she was, almost glad to have some help in pursuing what was turning out to be a most formidable foe. Were the Fog and the voice in the sky the same person? She thought they were. There were no coincidences in life. And it was not a coincidence that she had met the blonde and the brunette. Over and over again.

They ran into Nellie on the dark stairs leading up to her flat. That bird of hers was sitting on her shoulder looking concerned, and Nellie was overwhelmingly glad to see them both.

Her lilting voice filled the empty hall with speech so fast that there was no way Michiko could follow it. Then Michiko noticed she was smiling in her direction. "Hi there, Michiko!" she said.

Michiko replied, "Hi."

Soon she was following Nellie back up to where she'd come from and then the three of them were in her all-too-familiar room.

Time for more talking. They really liked to talk, those two . . .

IT WASN'T MUCH of a plan. There wasn't much to go on. But they each agreed to handle a task and decided they'd meet back at Nellie's when their respective responsibilities were complete.

And so it was that . . .

Cora would find out who had placed the order for the device.

Nellie would seek out Messrs. Staunch and Proper.

And Michiko would investigate where that thing that blew up St. Paul's came from.

Thus, three girls made their very first plan together.

What Michiko Did . . .

MICHIKO STOOD AT the edge of the Thames staring out across to the South Bank. Behind her, the wreckage from the landmark formerly known as St. Paul's had turned into a heap of blackened embers.

The object that had destroyed the cathedral had come from underwater; that's what Hayao had said at any rate. Had it really? She didn't think he'd lie to her, but what if he'd simply been mistaken? Then again, if it had come from the sky, surely the pilots of the airships would have seen something.

She sat down to think. She closed her eyes and let her body relax. Her thoughts flowed out and away, and she let the world touch her. It was so quiet. So quiet for this city. She was surprised to realize that she'd grown so used to the noise that she could now be struck by its absence.

She heard a bird cry to its friend. A carriage somewhere passing down a cobblestone street several blocks away. She heard water lapping quietly against the bank of the river. And an echo as water passed beneath her, underground, the sound rising up to greet her through a sewer grate.

She opened her eyes.

What if the rocket hadn't come from *under* the river? What if it had simply passed *through* it, but its origin was somewhere else?

It made sense. A lot more sense than a criminal trying to hide something in a highly trafficked and narrow river.

There was so much of this city she knew nothing about, especially what went on underneath it. It had a complex sewer system, she knew, and then, of course, there were the underground trains she avoided whenever she could. Underground could be a very reasonable place from which to launch a rocket.

Michiko stood and started to walk.

She had been to the reading room in the British Museum during her first week in England. Callum had taken her on a big sightseeing tour, showing her all the landmarks, at least from the outside.

"Everything you need to know is in there," he'd said. Or he'd said something like that; Michiko had known even less English at the time than she did now. But he'd tried to communicate the idea to her. That was when he still pretended to care.

She got herself up onto the rooftops and traveled quickly across the city to the British Museum. She passed between the large vermilion banners with "Alexandria" written on them and found herself inside the large-domed reading room in what must have been record time, had anyone cared to calculate it.

She approached a young man in a tweed suit and tapped him on the shoulder.

"Map," she said.

The young man crossed his arms and looked at her carefully. "What was that?"

"Map."

He shook his head, and it was clear to Michiko that for some reason he was pretending not to understand.

"I'm sorry, your accent . . . say again?"

"Map," repeated Michiko, getting angry now. Honestly, it was one word and a one-syllable word at that. This librarian man was clearly just playing with her, finding her funny or whatever in her non-European way.

"Oh, map!" he said, nodding in an exaggerated fashion. "A map of what?" he asked loudly and slowly.

"Under city."

"Say that again?" he asked.

Oh, for crying out loud . . .

"Is something the matter here?" A short, older woman with shockingly white hair approached the man in the tweed suit.

"Uh, no. She's just looking for a map," he replied.

"Under city," repeated Michiko.

"Well, let's help her find it, then," replied the woman, placing a friendly hand on Michiko's shoulder and guiding her to the center of the room.

The reading room was the sort of uniquely Western space that made Michiko uncomfortable. Too tall, too wide, too round. The dome above her overwhelmed her, and she had to make an effort to keep her gaze planted straight ahead.

"Sorry for my colleague's behavior. He didn't want to be here today, after everything. If one landmark gets it, then maybe this one is next, is the worry. But, I say you carry on no matter what. You don't hold yourself prisoner to some voice in the sky. That's the British way."

Michiko understood half of what the friendly woman said, but nodded as if it all made sense to her.

"Makes for a quiet afternoon, though." The woman put on a pair of thin cotton gloves and pulled open a large wooden drawer. She carefully thumbed through some pages and finally pulled out a big square parchment page with two round wooden sticks attached on two ends. These she held on to as she carried the map to the table and Michiko sat in front of it.

"This half shows a map of all the sewers. And this half shows the underground train systems, including the ones no longer in use."

Michiko nodded. She knew what "sewer" meant. And "underground" and "train" made sense to her as well. She examined the parchment closely. There were lines crisscrossing London, and she recognized many of the stops. Then she noticed a line that ran parallel to Tower Bridge. "What that?" she asked the woman, who put on a pair of tiny spectacles that had been hanging around her neck on a silver chain and leaned over the map.

"Ah, that would be Tower Subway. They tried a train there for a couple months, but shut it down and left it open for foot traffic. They closed it completely a couple of years ago."

Michiko understood the gist of this. But she was still astounded by the proximity of the tunnel to the Tower of London. She had a thought. Scanning the map, she found the British Museum. Sure enough, there was another line at the spot, with a train station marked. And, of course, they had found the first dead body near the Embankment station . . .

It was all coming together. Her hunch was right. She just knew it.

"Need anything else?" asked the librarian.

Michiko nodded. "Paper. Ink."

She had to copy it all. And quickly.

What Nellie Did . . .

Back again, THOUGHT Nellie staring at the Medical and Scientific Institute. She wasn't entirely certain if she'd find Mr. Staunch and Mr. Proper on the premises, but she didn't think they'd be grave-robbing in the middle of the day. If she ran such a business, she was certain she'd rob at night and try to sell her . . . wares . . . in the day. And considering the two men's association with Dr. Mantis, she thought it likely they sold their wares . . . *here*.

Of course, there was the matter of the recently destroyed St. Paul's and the fact that in the aftermath most people had shut themselves in their homes. Still. It was worth a shot.

"Have Mr. Staunch and Mr. Proper arrived yet?" she asked, smiling brightly at the woman behind the main desk.

"Who's asking?" the woman replied, giving Nellie a look of deep suspicion from over the rims of her glasses. She looked exhausted, overworked. She was packing up a small suitcase, as if she was getting ready to head out soon. And not remotely interested in helping Nellie out.

"My name's Nellie Harrison. I work with the Great Raheem. There was a bit of confusion about a recent delivery we made."

The woman nodded. Nellie loved name-dropping the Great Raheem. Especially when it got her stuff.

"In the theater, downstairs," the woman said, and pointed toward a staircase in the far corner of the large, empty, white foyer.

A theater? They had theaters in the Medical and Scientific Institute?

Nellie walked lightly down the steps into a narrow low-ceilinged hall that led in only one direction. She followed it until she came upon a set of ornamented oak doors that looked to have been trimmed slightly to fit the space. Because of their awkward shape, they weren't nearly as intimidating to Nellie as they maybe had been intended to be. Besides, if there was any place where Nellie was comfortable, it was in a theater.

She opened the door.

What she saw wasn't the kind of theater she'd been expecting.

She was standing in a large dark room structured like an ancient Greek amphitheater. Seats in shadow rose up before her on three sides. It was hard to see how high up they went, as they vanished into the darkness. Not that it mattered much. Nellie's attention wasn't remotely focused on audience capacity. Who cared how many rows of seats the theater contained when a dead body, its pale white torso sliced open and its purple innards exposed, was lying on a table on the "stage," the round empty center of the room that was lit with a bright white spotlight. Two figures stood, one at the head of the body, the other at the foot. Both were completely oblivious to her presence.

"Quality," said the familiar voice of the man at the head. "See, you 'appy now?"

Apparently she'd found Mr. Staunch, all right. And, at the feet, judging by the domed head reflecting the bright light, was Dr. Mantis.

Time to back up slowly toward the exit, then . . .

"Oi! Mr. Staunch," came a voice from up in the dark audience.

Oh dear.

"Mr. Proper, I'm a bit busy at the moment."

"I see that, Mr. Staunch, but there's that girl again."

"Girl?"

"Right. Standing by the door. The Magician's girl."

She had her hand on the doorknob just as Dr. Mantis and Mr. Staunch turned to look at her.

"Hi," she said, instantly flashing her smile.

"The one with the pretty eyes," said Dr. Mantis softly, almost to himself, but Nellie heard him. *Not the eyes thing again . . .*

"What you doin' 'ere?" asked Mr. Staunch, taking a step toward her. Nellie marveled that he could be wearing his round sunglasses in a dark theater and still manage to see, though, she supposed, the spot on the eviscerated body was as bright as daylight.

"Just checkin' up on the delivery. Wanted to make sure all was . . ." She stopped talking. No one was falling for it. *She* wasn't even falling for it. The two men moved toward her, and she thought that keeping her back to the door was starting to become just plain silly. She turned around and opened it a crack, but it slammed shut. Nellie looked up. A hand attached to a long pale arm hidden behind a dirty white lab coat was holding the door firmly in place.

She turned back around . . . only to find herself looking into Dr. Mantis's beady eyes again. She had no glitter this time to aid in her escape. *Note to self: Never leave home without glitter.*

Mr. Staunch stood just behind him, and Mr. Proper joined him at his side.

"You know 'er?" asked Mr. Staunch.

"We've met. She was asking about the Society of Heroes," replied Dr. Mantis in that hushed voice of his. He seemed determined to defeat her in some kind of staring contest, and she was terrified at what "winning" might look like. Or . . . not look like . . . *Please don't take my eyes, please.*

"Was she, now? Now, why would you be askin' about such a thing?" asked Mr. Staunch, leaning in. Up close, the smell of death on his person was far more pronounced. *Yes, that's certainly what that smells like,* she concluded. There was something else, too. A strange sort of humming noise, faint, almost undetectable. But definitely present. And familiar.

"I have my reasons," replied Nellie, distracted by the internal debate she was currently moderating. To knee in the groin or not to knee in the groin, that was the question. Would it be better to talk her way out of this or to get violent?

"Beautiful eyes," said Dr. Mantis.

Knee in the groin it is.

Dr. Mantis dropped like a stone.

"What the hell do you think you're doin'!" cried Mr. Staunch, his hands at her collarbone, pushing her hard against the door. He pressed his body close against hers so that her knee couldn't go anywhere this time. The humming got louder as he did it, and she could feel his sweat dripping from his nose onto her chin. Dr. Mantis was doubled up in pain, but unfortunately, Messrs. Staunch and Proper weren't. One knee, three groins . . . *Bad math there, Nellie.*

"This one's trouble," said Mr. Proper quietly.

"Indeed," said Dr. Mantis, recovering himself.

"Shall we deal with 'er?" asked Mr. Staunch.

"Deal with her, yes. But save the good bits."

"She's got an awful lot of good bits," pointed out Mr. Proper.

"Save them all, damn it!" It was the first time Nellie had heard Dr. Mantis raise his voice. Clearly Messrs. Staunch and Proper found it a rare occurrence as well.

"Maybe it'd make more sense if you just showed us what you wanted. We could do it right 'ere, right now."

"No. She has to leave as she came in: whole. Take her to the cemetery. I'll come to you after dinner and show you which bits I want. Till then, keep her fresh." Dr. Mantis made his way back to the table the corpse was resting on.

The two nodded sharply in unison.

"Look, I'm sorry I kneed you, that wasn't nice. But I'm really harmless . . . not sure why we need to go through all this bother. Come on, now. I'll tell you what. You let me go, and

I'll give you each a kiss." The thought turned her stomach as soon as she said it, but a moment of gross kissing was better than a lifetime of dead.

"I'll tell *you* what," replied Mr. Proper. "No."

Mr. Staunch peeled her off the door, and Mr. Proper grabbed her around the waist. Nellie kicked out her legs, but Mr. Staunch deftly grabbed them. She twisted and turned; she was in a hot panic. No thoughts seemed reasonable; everything was crazy instinct. Fight or flight. Or, in this case, both. Adrenaline surged through her, and she figured if she made enough of a fuss, there'd be a bit of a problem in their trying to get her out of the building without drawing attention. For that matter, she'd scream, too.

Like this.

"And the little girl saw the body on the table and let out a horrified scream. Then she fainted, dead to the world." She watched Dr. Mantis loom over her, in his hand a damp white cloth. She twisted her head around, but he caught her at the back of her skull, gripping the cloth in one hand. "Dead to the world," he repeated softly as he placed the wet white cloth over her nose and mouth.

What Cora Did . . .

THE POST OFFICE seemed to be the only crowded place left in London. Cora hoped that tapping her foot might be a not-too-subtle hint that she had been waiting for quite some time now. Not complaining, not making a fuss, certainly not like the other customers in the place, all panic and frenzy, dropping books of stamps as they rushed out of the door and holding their hands over their heads like they were caught in a rainstorm. Yeah, as if that would protect a person from someone blowing up the city.

Finally, the round woman who'd disappeared into the back and, for all intents and purposes, it seemed, into another dimension, returned and beckoned Cora to join her behind her desk and take a seat.

"Right, love, got the records right here. What was the address again?"

For the fifth time, Cora repeated Lord White's address, and the woman gave her a pleasant smile, licked her forefinger, and began turning the pages. One at a time. As if her book of records was on par with Shakespeare's First Folio and required the same kind of delicate respect.

Do take as much time as you want, no rush or anything . . .

"Sorry about the wait," said the woman as she turned the third page. "It's a bit chaotic here, as you can see. Ever since the threat, people want to contact their loved ones . . . and it don't help that everyone's in a panic, not thinking straight."

"You don't seem particularly panicked yourself, though." A little panic wouldn't go amiss right about now.

"Gotta set a good example. But . . ." The woman stopped flipping and leaned in toward Cora. "But I'm right scared. Still, as a government employee, I gotta believe that they've got everything in hand."

Cora thought back to the image of the Members of the House yelling and throwing things at one another, and decided that this was one of those moments in which honesty wasn't the best policy. "I'm sure they do," she said, and placed a comforting hand on the woman's. The woman smiled appreciatively and returned to flipping through the book.

"Ah! There we go. Two delivery times."

"Who placed the first delivery?"

The woman shook her head. "Don't know. Signature's hard to read. Let me call Lucy over. She was on duty that day. She might remember. Lucy!"

A thin, plain-looking girl, her face completely drained of color, ran over with wide, frightened eyes. "Yes, Winnie? Is everything okay?"

"It's all fine, Lucy. Do you remember when this order was placed?" Winnie pointed to the page.

Lucy leaned over and had a look. She thought for a moment, then nodded. "Yes, I remember this one. It was a Chinese man. He didn't speak a word of English, just handed me a note with the address on it and the package. And the money, of course. I think . . . I think I might still have the note."

Lucy disappeared into the back of the room, pushing her way through a thick, new crowd of customers who buzzed with fearful energy. She returned a moment later with a neatly folded piece of paper. She passed it over to Cora, who unfolded it. The note was plain, with little more than Lord White's address written on it, but the symbol embossed at the top was familiar.

"You've got to be kidding me," Cora said.

"Not kidding, that's the paper. I like to collect interesting stationery," explained Lucy.

Cora rose. "Thank you both very much. Here." She passed back the piece of paper to Lucy and quickly left the post office for the empty street. It was quite a relief to be outside in deserted London once more, and Cora hailed a cab easily. Even though there was no one to use their services, London cabbies were evidently a devoted lot.

What a waste of time this trip had been. She should have just gone with Nellie in the first place. Now she had spent time looking into something she already suspected was the case, only to discover that her suspicions were accurate. *From now on, Cora, trust your instincts.*

She arrived at the Medical and Scientific Institute ten minutes later and stared at the dark, looming, Gothic building before her. It was pitch-black from soot, and clearly no one had ever attempted to give it a cleaning. Nonetheless, she could see the large carving of a slender bird with a long neck perched in an oval at the top. The same symbol as the one embossed on the note.

She entered the building and approached a woman who was making her way toward the doors Cora had just passed through.

"I'm looking for a girl. Blond. She probably arrived around three-quarters of an hour ago," said Cora, stopping the woman.

She was met with a foul look. "Yes, I saw her."

"She was looking for Mr. Staunch and Mr. Proper."

"She was."

"Is she still here?"

"No. She left with those two maybe twenty minutes ago."

"She did?"

"They were down in the theater together. She must have fainted seeing the body on the table. They had to carry her out."

That didn't sound remotely like Nellie.

"Where did they take her?" she asked.

"They hailed a cab and drove off." The woman removed her glasses.

"All three of them?"

"Yes." Cora thought hard for a moment. "Is there anything I can help you with exactly?" asked the woman, an edge to her voice.

"Give me a moment to think," replied Cora, matching her tone. There was no doubt in Cora's mind that Nellie had been kidnapped. And it was hard for her to problem-solve when she was starting to panic. *Calm down. Calm down.* She could only think of one thing: "Where do Mr. Staunch and Mr. Proper get their . . . goods?"

There was a moment in which the woman was clearly deciding between pretending she had no idea what Cora was talking about and just answering the question. Finally, she let out a sigh and said, "Graveyards, obviously."

"Obviously. Do they have a particular . . . haunt?" The choice of the word had been unintentional, but was actually rather appropriate.

The woman thought some more. Then she smiled slightly and sighed again. "The Hammersmith Cemetery."

"Thank you." Cora practically ran out of the building. She didn't know what was going on exactly, but she knew that time was of the essence.

Graves and Eyes

NELLIE COULDN'T ESCAPE her nightmare. The walls were high and black; she couldn't move; she couldn't speak. *Wake up, Nellie, wake up. No. Yes.* She was awake . . . she was . . . she flipped herself onto her back, onto her hands, which were tied tightly behind her. She saw sky. Sky up high, far away, farther away than usual. And getting darker, fading into night. She wanted to scream out, but something was in her mouth—shoved into her mouth and tied tightly at the nape of her neck. Her feet and knees were bound together as well. *Help me. Someone help me. Help me before he comes and kills me.*

IT WAS DUSK when Cora arrived at the Hammersmith Cemetery. She'd decided on the District Railway as her means of transportation. After all, it was much faster than taking a cab, and all she had to do was get off at Barons Court and she'd be right around the corner from the graveyard.

She approached the low wall and the gates, which still hung open, and stepped onto the path. It felt as though she were leaving one world and crossing through a portal into another. Instantly the sounds of the city were extinguished behind her, and all that remained were the creak of branches above her and the occasional flapping wings of a startled bird taking flight.

Cora knew enough of her city's history to understand why this would be a cemetery of choice for grave robbers. It was only a few decades old, so there would be fewer layers of human remains to contend with. Furthermore, it was very highly populated, with several burials a day taking place. It also helped that the cemetery was rather isolated from the city, though the land in the area was slowly being developed.

Coming this far west was unusual for her. Aside from the odd trip with Lord White, she was a Central London kind of girl. Funny thought, that. She'd once been so proud of being an East Ender.

She thought briefly then of his lordship, wondering whether he was at all concerned about her whereabouts, whether he'd even noticed she had left.

Another flapping of wings. And then a quiet squawk.

And then she was attacked.

Okay, she wasn't actually being attacked, but when something lands on your shoulder totally unexpectedly, it can feel like an attack. Cora jumped and instinctively made a swipe at her shoulder. Scheherazade flew off for a moment and then landed for a second time. She and Cora made eye contact, and Cora finally surrendered to having the parrot sit there.

"Death," whispered the bird.

"I know," replied Cora. If her bird was here, then Nellie was, too. But if her bird wasn't *with* Nellie, then there was trouble ahead.

She made her way as quietly as she could through the darkening cemetery and turned onto the wide main path. She stopped and had a good look around. If there was ever a day to test her newly finished goggles, this would be it. Pity she didn't have them with her.

Cora noticed the two figures almost entirely hidden in the shadow of the wall. They were lounging, it seemed, leaning against the red brick, having a quiet conversation. Whether or not they had noticed her yet remained to be seen. The good thing about cemeteries was there were plenty of ways to hide yourself.

In a flash Cora was down on the ground, crawling to the nearest tombstone, the parrot hopping along behind her. As she got close enough to see the features of each of the men, she noticed the open grave next to them. Shovel lying to the side. Freshly dug. Scheherazade made a doglike whimper, and Cora surmised that Nellie was probably down there.

"What are you doing?" asked a quiet voice.

Cora turned and looked up as the parrot flew into the air and out of sight. A bald man, no hat on his head, his long black coat undone and a ragged scarf hanging around his neck, watched the bird fly off and then looked down at Cora.

"What does it look like I'm doing?" she asked, standing up and brushing her skirt free of dirt. "I was trying to sneak up on those two men over there, the ones who are standing up now. Clearly you caught me. What are *you* doing?"

The man looked at her closely and then glanced over her shoulder. "Mr. Proper, do you know who this is?" he asked.

"No, I don't," replied a thick East End accent. "Mr. Staunch, do you know who it is?"

"I do not," said the other man.

Three tall men standing around her looking confused, and one girl feeling very scared.

"You think maybe the magic girl knows her?" asked Mr. Proper.

The bald man seemed to think about it, then nodded. He leaned in close, almost as if he was examining Cora. He took her chin in his hand and twisted her head hard to one side. "This one has good bits, too. Let's use this one as well."

Whatever that meant, Cora was pretty sure it wasn't something that was likely to turn out well for her. So she punched the man in the jaw. Grabbed from behind, she stomped on a foot, turned, and punched the face that belonged to the foot, knocking the man's dark glasses clean off.

"Oh my God," she said, and stopped mid-windup. She'd expected to be making eye contact with Mr. Proper, but instead she found herself staring into two red lights glowing in the center of a round glass orb where the eyes should have been. Tiny gears inside the orb rotated at that moment to make the light smaller, more focused on her. "What are you?"

"Men," said the quiet bald man in her ear. "Normal everyday men."

"You don't seem ordinary," replied Cora.

"Well, you lose a leg, you replace it with a peg. You lose an eye, or two . . ."

Cora glanced at Mr. Staunch, who readjusted his glasses as he noticed her looking at him.

"Can they see? Can you see?"

Mr. Proper nodded. "Couldn't before. Got sick, see, went blind. And Staunch there had a pretty bad fall as a lad. But Dr. Mantis changed that. Gave us each a pair of these. I owe 'im. We both owe 'im."

"They don't see quite like we do. They see using infrared. You heard about that?" asked Dr. Mantis, coming around to face her.

Cora nodded. Yes, she knew about that, it was key in how she'd developed her special see-in-the-dark goggles. She also knew that with the distraction courtesy of their current conversation, she was free to take a few steps backward.

"They can see heat or lack of it. It's a completely different color spectrum to what we're used to," continued Dr. Mantis.

"How do they dig up dead bodies?" Just keep him talking. Besides, it was all pretty fascinating.

"They can see when it's cold, just not as bright. Also . . ." He turned and gave Mr. Proper a nod. The fellow retrieved an oddly shaped gun from inside his coat and aimed at the ground just before Cora. Fire shot out in a roar and singed the earth black. "They can warm things up when they need to."

"Holy shit."

"That ain't a ladylike thing to say," said Mr. Staunch.

Cora produced her pistol and aimed it at him. "I'm no lady."

"Whatcha gonna do, then?" asked Mr. Proper. "There's three of us, one of you. Jus' fair warnin'."

"I'll just have to incapacitate you one at a time then."

"Let me make it a bit easier for you." At that moment a shovel suddenly appeared from behind Mr. Staunch's head, and with one swift swipe, he was out cold. Standing in his place was Nellie, covered in dirt, yet somehow totally looking great. Mr. Proper only had a moment to react before Scheherazade landed on his face, pecking at his "eyes." There was a struggle, until Cora saw the eyes start to spark. Then the red light at their center went out and the whirring sound that accompanied it died. Nellie gave him a good whack with the shovel, too, and he was down for the count as well.

"Stupid bird! It'll take me weeks to make a new pair of eyes, and he'll be utterly useless till then," said Dr. Mantis, flailing his arms wildly as Scheherazade flew around his head. Cora took aim at the ground right in front of Dr. Mantis and fired. He stumbled backward in shock and Nellie did her shovel thing for a third time.

"You know, that's actually rather dangerous. You could give them serious brain damage, even kill them like that," said Cora as she watched Dr. Mantis fall to the side.

"They were gonna kill me the second he showed up. And I heard him say he had the same goal in mind for you. I'm not too fussed about brain damage, if I'm honest."

Scheherazade chose that moment to land on Nellie's shoulder, and Nellie gave the parrot a very hearty scratch under the chin.

"Are you okay, Nellie?" asked Cora, noticing the girl's expression.

Nellie shook her head. "No. I'm really not. That was all too close. It's a damn fine thing I've got experience gettin' out of tight situations. You can't tie me down."

"You constantly impress me, Nellie. Come on. Let's meet up with Michiko."

Nellie put down the shovel and came over to her. "We'll meet up, but that's it. Count me out."

"What do you mean?" Cora felt hollow inside, stunned, and almost . . . a little betrayed.

"I'm out, Cora. I'm not riskin' everythin' for this. I'm done."

A Conversation

A WATCHED KETTLE never boils. So why was Cora staring at it so intently? She needed to fixate her mind on something else, something other than the frustrated thoughts and feelings she was thinking and . . . feeling. It wasn't fair. It wasn't. They had a plan. It was going so well. It was going better than well. Michiko had copied two very intricate maps of the sewer and underground system for them. Had managed to deduce that there was a strong possibility the old Tower Subway was where the Fog was hiding himself and also the means by which he'd managed to get around the city so effortlessly. How clever of her. And, okay, so maybe neither Cora nor Nellie had really helped that much in their outings, but they were both still alive. That was something.

That was a big something.

"Thoughtfully making tea, I see."

Cora looked up and saw the Magician standing in the doorway of his small kitchen. He was wearing more clothes than he'd worn during their first encounter, a lovely pale gray robe and matching trousers.

"Yes," she replied, looking back at the kettle.

"Our cultures might be different in many ways, but we both understand the importance and pleasure of a good cup of tea." He moved beside her and reached up into the cupboard, pulling out a very English teapot with purple and blue flowers intricately painted on it. He placed it on the counter. "Why is Nellie so upset?"

"She didn't tell you?" She didn't know why the Magician intimidated her like he did. She wasn't frightened of him exactly, but he always made her feel a little nervous. And very much her age.

"I thought it might be the voice in the sky. I have been to many homes this afternoon offering comfort. But she said it was a secret. I respect secrets. But I think maybe . . . Who's the Japanese girl?"

"Didn't you meet her the other day?"

"No."

"Her name is Michiko."

The Magician made a sound of recognition. "The girl from the gala. The warrior."

Cora nodded. *Yes. Exactly. The girl from the gala. The warrior.*

"So, Miss Bell. Can you tell me the secret?"

It wasn't meant for sharing. All the experiences they'd had, their plan for today. But it was all crumbling beneath her now. And for some reason she trusted that the Magician wouldn't reveal their secret. Besides, even if he did, it didn't really matter anymore.

So she explained what had happened to them. What they

had discussed that afternoon, and their attempt at making a plan. She told him about what had happened to Nellie and that Nellie didn't want to be a part of it anymore. She didn't share just how disappointed hearing this had made her feel.

"You seem sad not to be risking your life to solve this mystery anymore," said the Magician, sitting down at the table.

"I am sad. I don't know why. I'm not particularly fond of risking my life. I just . . . I really believed all three of us together could do this. That we could save the city. Make a real difference."

"That makes sense. I, too, think you could save it."

"You do?"

"I think you're all very gifted, though I don't know you and the warrior girl very well. I think it is a risk. I think most would tell you not to do it. I know that's my instinct as well. But I also feel something beyond that instinct. And it says . . . you're right."

"We don't really have much of a plan," said Cora, suddenly feeling a need to play devil's advocate.

"Then make one."

"And what do we do when we find the guy?"

"It will all depend on the situation. But trust yourself. You'll know what to do when the time comes."

"And how do you know that?"

"Because you've known what to do all those other times."

Cora sighed long and slow. Even if she could do it, she couldn't do it alone.

"Can you convince Nellie to come?" she asked him.

The Magician shook his head.

"It is not my place. Besides, I would prefer she stay at home. She is safe with me. But she can't stay with me forever. You can convince her. You can find a way."

"Why do you have so much faith in me?"

"Because it is clear you have a lot of faith in yourself."

Well, I'm glad it's clear to you. It isn't to me.

The Magician rose and gave her a comforting smile. "Take care of yourselves. And take care of each other."

Cora nodded. She had nothing to say, so she just stared into those dark, kind eyes and was a little mesmerized by them.

"Miss Bell," he said.

"Yes."

"The kettle . . . the water has boiled."

How to Convince a Stubborn Magician's Assistant?

SHE POURED TEA for all three of them and sat down in the chair in the corner. Nellie was still lying facedown on the bed, and Michiko was sitting next to her, gently stroking her hair.

"How're you doing?" Cora asked softly.

Nellie sat bolt upright, making Michiko jump slightly, and stared at Cora indignantly. "How do you think I'm doin'?"

Cora shook her head. "Nellie, this is crazy. You faced the Fog at the Tower, no problem. You broke into a house in broad daylight. You escaped being bound and gagged and rendered three men unconscious. Exactly what are you afraid of?"

Nellie scoffed. "It's one thing to think about dyin' as a possibility, but to face it? That makes it a wee bit too real. Makes you realize just what a damn fool you'd been up until that moment."

"So you're scared."

"Damn straight I am."

"Would it help if I said I'm scared, too?"

Nellie didn't reply. Instead she crossed her legs, balanced her elbows on them, and cupped her chin in her hands.

"Don't you want to follow this through to the end? Don't you want to complete this task? Damn it, Nellie, don't you want to save the city?"

Still nothing, and Michiko just stared at her. Tough audience.

Cora couldn't quite believe it. This was not the Nellie she had grown to know over the last week. That girl wasn't afraid of anything. "Are you seriously saying we couldn't do this? Truly? Do you honestly not believe we're capable of going underground, hunting down that horrible Fog person, and bringing him to justice? Because I know we can. And I think you know it, too."

And now I'm just going to wait until someone else says something.

It took a very long pause, but then, finally, Nellie sighed. "It's not that I don't see your point, it's just . . ." She stopped.

"It's just what?"

Cora could see the feeling rushing up inside Nellie, almost as if she were an empty glass being filled with water. It was rising so quickly, ready to overflow any moment. "Did you see what happened?" asked Nellie, gesturing toward the window. Cora saw that her hand was shaking. Just a little. "A whole building exploded! Did you feel it? The whole city shook. I thought it was going to swallow me up whole. And what about the five dead people? Five! And there were almost seven. You and me.

"We were almost killed. And do you think that we'll just be takin' on the Fog alone? I don't think so. Dr. Mantis and

Mr. Staunch, I bet they'll be off to warn him about us nosing around. And who knows what else? I bet the entire system down there's booby-trapped, just in case some idiots decide to play hero. It's one thing to scale a building, to perform little magic tricks outside in the real world, but I don't think I can take on a person like that. I don't think I want to."

"You're being irrational," Cora said. "You absolutely *can* take on a person like this. You already have. And you already took on his henchmen."

Nellie stood up abruptly in a flurry of blond and pink. "I don't think it's irrational to fear someone with this fella's power. And even if it is, so what? So what if I'm afraid? Emotions exist for a reason. They protect us from doing stupid, dangerous, life-threatenin' things. I've never had it so good in my life, and I'm not about to lose it all now. Maybe a couple years ago it didn't matter if I lived or died . . ."

"Are you saying, knowing what we know, that we should just sit back and do nothing?" Cora couldn't believe what she was hearing.

"We should let the professionals handle it."

"Like who?" Cora stood in frustration. "The police? Your precious Officer Murphy? He's the most competent of the lot, and he's at the bottom of the bloody food chain. Or maybe there's some secret organization that the Queen has, or something. As much as I'd like to think such a thing exists, I'm pretty sure it doesn't."

"Someone else has got to have the skills."

"Who? Who exactly?" Cora was pacing now. "Who has 'the

skills,' as you call it? No one can get out of a tricky spot like you, Nellie; you're practically a cat, the way you just get in and out of places. As for me, well, I'm probably one of the best organizers and problem solvers there is, considering what Lord White puts me through on a daily basis. Plus, I've got a great number of weapons at my disposal. And anyway, who needs my arsenal when we've got the greatest weapon of all right there?" She pointed at Michiko.

"Cora . . ."

"We've already been pursuing this, each of us, in our own way. And somehow we always manage to help each other out. It's fate. It . . . it has to mean something. Everything is connected. Right?" She turned to Michiko, who nodded, but it wasn't clear if she was agreeing with Cora or just humoring her. Nellie still didn't look convinced. Cora sighed and sat down at the foot of the bed. "Haven't you always wanted to just do something yourself?" she asked, her voice softer. "To make a real difference? Not for anyone else. Not an assignment or a task. Something that you made the decision to do?"

"Don't know, really."

"I have. Yes, Lord White is the best thing that ever happened to me, but I don't think I owe him servitude for life just because he rescued me as a child."

"Well, you kind of do; you are his servant."

"What I mean is . . . surely what I'm capable of, my brain, my talent, surely that wasn't meant to be just some assistant. Surely I was meant to be more, and to do more."

"You goin' to quit your job, then?"

"No . . . I . . . I just want to do this. And I want to do it with the two of you. We can help each other. We can protect each other. Like we've already been doing." She pushed herself along the bed, leaned her back against the wall, and felt exhausted. "I can't do this alone. I don't want to. Together we're unbeatable. Apart, we're just . . . assistants to men in London society. In other words, nobodies."

She had nothing else to say. Nothing more that she could think of to use in order to persuade Nellie and Michiko. She closed her eyes.

"Yes."

She opened her eyes.

"Yes?" She looked at Michiko carefully. It was hard to trust the Japanese girl's responses.

"Yes," Michiko said again. Well, she certainly did look confident.

"I don't know if you understand what—"

"I understand," said Michiko. She gave a small smile.

"You do?"

"I need help find Fog. You need help fight Fog. We help each other."

Wow. She really did understand.

"So . . . yes?" said Cora, leaning forward.

Michiko's smile grew and she gave a little bow with her head. "Yes."

Cora glanced at Nellie, who still seemed unsure.

"Oh, come on," said Cora, throwing up her hands. "Seriously?

I don't understand the hesitation. It's not like you're some shy, retiring violet, Nellie. You've already robbed a private residence and infiltrated the Tower. You escaped being buried alive. You did. No one else. You did it all by yourself."

"But it was such a close call . . ."

"Says the girl who allows herself to practically suffocate onstage."

Nellie turned so that she avoided direct eye contact with Cora.

"Come on, Nellie, I can tell you want to. Deep down. You wouldn't be fighting this hard if you were sure of yourself. If you were sure, it would be 'no' and that's it. No debate. No passion."

Nellie said nothing, but concentrated hard on the world outside the window. Then she finally thought of something else to say. Speaking as if she'd never stopped, just continued from her previous thought, she said, "And then there's Raheem's reputation. If I got in trouble, if I got caught . . . well, it wouldn't look good."

"Who cares?" said Michiko, rolling her eyes.

"I do!" Nellie snapped at Michiko. "I do. I know your boss is a right bastard, but I care about mine, all right?"

She spat out the sentence so fast that it sounded almost like one word, even to Cora. It was doubtful that Michiko had understood what she'd said. Still, the girl did appear apologetic.

Cora knew the Magician's mind on the subject. But for some reason, she didn't think Nellie would like learning that Cora and Raheem had had a conversation behind her back. She could tell that Nellie's defenses were weakening. That she was seriously considering joining up with her and Michiko again. But Cora was all out of arguments. She needed another tactic. Another approach.

"Don't you care about Lord White's reputation?" asked Nellie when Cora didn't say anything.

"Of course I do, it's just . . ." Then it hit her. The new tactic. "You make a good point, Nellie. I hadn't thought of that before."

"Yes, see?"

Cora nodded and did her best to look thoughtful. "We do have our bosses' reputations to think of. And we're pretty well known in society as it is. What we need are . . . disguises."

Nellie, who was now sitting with her arms folded across her chest and a heavy frown on her face, glanced up at Cora. "Disguises?"

"Yes."

Cora waited. It was best when trying to convince someone of something to let the person think. To figure things out for themselves and let them speak first.

Which is what happened a moment later: "As in . . . costumes?"

Cora worked hard to hold back her smile. "In a manner of speaking."

"To protect Raheem's reputation."

"And ourselves, of course. Look at Michiko. She's got the

right idea. Impossible to tell who it is under that whole getup and that mask."

Nellie's arms unfolded and she dropped her hands into her lap. "And maybe . . ." She squinted her eyes in concentration. "We'd need new names? Exciting, heroic-sounding names?"

Cora nodded. *Not a bad idea.* "Well, yes, that does actually make sense. We can't just call out to each other as we are now. How silly would that be? Us all carefully hiding our identities and then I just call out, 'Oi, Nellie, give us a hand!' That would be downright silly."

Nellie had undergone a remarkable transformation in the past few moments. Her face brightened, her internal tempo lightened, and she bounced up onto her knees with a big smile on her face. "Our names should match our costumes. That would make the most sense."

"It would."

"Oh!" She clapped her hands together in excitement. "I'd like to be Lady Sparkle!"

Cora choked on nothing in particular. "Lady . . . Sparkle?"

"Yes. It's definitely heroic, wouldn't you say?"

"Uh, yes. Definitely . . . something. How quickly you came up with that name, Nellie."

"Off the top of my head. Jus' like that." She was flat-out grinning now, almost giddy with excitement. "That's the way my head works, things just pop up in there. And . . . oh!" She'd bounded off the bed before either Michiko or Cora could say anything further. They watched her open one of two very large traveling trunks in the corner of the room and tear through the items inside, throwing pieces of clothing over her shoulder as she searched for whatever it was. "Ah! Here we go!"

Nellie spun around and held up a dark blue corseted top with what seemed to be a black shiny pattern of clock gears over it. "And there's a skirt to match!"

"Is there?"

"I liked the clock theme. That's why I got it. Best of all, it ain't ever been seen onstage. Raheem thought it was too dark, not enough color to catch the footlights. It's what I wore when I broke into Mr. Carter's."

"Well," said Cora, "as long as you have some practical footwear to go along with it, and you won't get too cold at night . . ."

"I don't mind a bit of the shivers if it means I'll look good. Anyway, breakin' into that house taught me I need my legs easily accessible, not hidden under anything. Now, Michiko has her outfit . . ." She turned to the Japanese girl. "What's your name gonna be, then?"

Michiko looked terribly confused. Finally and with deep suspicion, she said, "Michiko."

Nellie laughed brightly and skipped over to her, sitting down at her side. "No, not your real name," she said slowly. "Your hero name. Your name for fightin'. For . . . " She noticed Michiko's sword and pointed at it. "For that."

Michiko stared at the weapon on the bed. She didn't seem to be following. Cora could understand. The idea of a secret identity, of this dual-personality thing . . . , it was quite a complicated concept. And now she was thinking of Andrew . . . Great, she so didn't need to think of that jerk at the moment.

"Name Silver," said Michiko quietly. "Silver . . ." And she laid a hand across the left side of her chest. "Here. This. Here." She was frustrated. "Silver," she insisted.

Nellie looked at Cora, who shook her head. No clue.

"Here, right here. This here." Michiko grabbed Nellie's hand and placed it where hers had been.

There was a pause. "Heart?" asked Nellie.

Michiko smiled and breathed a sigh of relief. "Yes. Silver Heart." She pointed to the sword. "For fighting."

"That's a great name!" said Nellie. "Ain't that a great name, Cora?" Cora nodded, trying to match her friend's enthusiasm. Nellie turned back to Michiko and, with deep seriousness, added, "It's so noble."

Michiko smiled, though Cora almost thought it was just to humor Nellie.

"And what about you, Cora?"

Cora had anticipated this moment, yet she wasn't ready with an answer.

"I don't . . . I haven't really thought about it."

Now Nellie was bounding over to her. Cora almost missed the sullen Nellie this wildly zealous version had replaced. "Neither of us did. Just the first thing that comes to the top of your head; trust your instincts."

What was at the top of her head? Well, . . . Andrew really.

Why was he there? *Oh yes, the whole duality thing, right.* His whole ridiculous obsession. Not so ridiculous after all, as things were turning out . . .

"Mr. Hyde." She said it before she could even register that she'd thought it.

Nellie cocked her head to one side. "Really?"

This was ridiculous, Cora thought. Now Nellie was judging *her* choice? After choosing something as absurd as "Lady Sparkle" for herself? "Look, you said the top of my head. That's what was there."

"But . . . it's a man's name."

"No kidding."

"You can't be a man."

"I won't be a man, I'll just have a man's name. It's unique."

Nellie rolled her eyes. "That it is."

Hey now! "I didn't make fun of you for your choice . . ."

"My choice is fantastic. Why would you?"

"Are you saying my choice isn't?"

"I'm just sayin' . . ."

"Fine I'll be just Hyde then. No 'Mr.' Is that better?"

Nellie looked at her in a way that suggested she didn't think it was.

"I want to be Hyde, and that's my final word on the matter." The funny thing was, of course, that Cora hadn't been particularly married to the choice, but now she felt a need to defend her decision.

Nellie raised her hands. "Okay, fine!" And she was back at

the trunk, standing over it, hands on hips, examining the contents. "Any idea of what you'd like to wear?"

Indulge her, after all, this was all your bright idea, and anyway, isn't this better than her wanting to bow out of the whole thing? "Well . . . I know I'd prefer to wear trousers."

"And it makes sense, what with bein' a man and all."

"I'm not being a man."

"So you'll still wear a corset?"

"Well, yes. It's only decent. But look, don't bother about trousers. I'll have to have some custom-made or alter an old pair of Barker's or something. No one has trousers my size."

Nellie turned to face her . . . holding up a pair of trousers in Cora's size.

"Where'd you get those?" Cora stood in shock.

"My old burlesque costume. Played boys so that the men in the audience could see the shape of my legs."

"You played the breeches' part?"

"You know the term?"

Cora nodded and walked over to Nellie. The trousers were indeed short breeches. They'd hit her midcalf. She could wear a pair of riding boots, though, to make up the difference. She reached out to touch them. They were thick, made from a tough brown tweed. *Perfect. Just perfect.*

"Thank you," she said as she took them from Nellie.

"I've got a top I think you'd like, too . . ." Nellie said it kind of singsong, in the way a rider might coax a young horse out into the training ring. It was Cora's turn to roll her eyes.

"Yeah?"

"It's in the other trunk."

There was such joy in the way Nellie opened the other trunk that Cora couldn't help but start to find the playing dress-up game not completely intolerable. It was becoming . . . dare she think it? . . . fun. She glanced over her shoulder at Michiko, who had laid herself down across the bed on her left side looking . . . well, there was no other word for it . . . bemused.

"I wore this while playing a pirate wench. It's real leather. The tanney had a wee bit of a crush on me. Only girl who got real leather. Buckles in the front, makes you look right tough."

It was a full corset made of brown leather, a shade or two lighter than the trousers. There was no boning, but the leather was thick and the three straps that buckled around the waist with three solid brass buckles that looked like they'd cinch a person in well enough. It was something different, though, wearing one's underwear on the outside.

It's a costume, Cora. Like what Nellie wears onstage. Perfectly proper in that way.

"This is a good start," said Cora, taking the corset.

"I've got some feathers if you'd like to glam it up a bit . . ."

"No," said Cora quickly. "No, I think this will be good for now. I can figure out the rest. Thanks."

Nellie nodded and seemed quite content. "We'll have to make sure to hide our faces somehow. Don't forget that bit. You know," she said, closing the trunk, "maybe this isn't a bad idea after all. Like you said, Cora, we've got the goods, and we've been practicin' for this kind of thing for years. And I might have faced death, but as you say, I didn't die. I saved myself. With your usual helpful distraction." She gave Cora a wink. "Now, with these disguises, no one's reputation will get hurt, and we can save the city while we're at it."

"I know we can do it," said Cora.

"We can." Michiko joined them, and Cora had to admit that it was nice to know the girl with the really sharp sword agreed with her assessment.

"Okay, the next step is to collect our gear and meet up at the old Tower Subway entrance. One hour from now. Everyone good?"

Nellie and Michiko nodded.

"Good. I'm . . . really happy we're doing this. You know, getting to know both of you recently has been a real treat and I—"

"Cora?" said Nellie.

"Yes?"

"Save the speeches for when we win."

Preparations

CORA SLIPPED INTO her bedroom without anyone in the house noticing her return. She rifled through her closet as quickly as possible and pulled out her plainest and most practical shirt, a very basic, thick, long-sleeved, off-white cotton. Then she went through her options for outerwear. She'd need something large enough to hide all the stuff that she was planning on bringing with her. She decided on the long leather jacket she'd made Barker give her last year. He'd bought it for himself, but it ended up being a few sizes too small. She knew it'd be a bit bulky for her, but there was something about having a leather jacket like that that had always appealed to her. She'd never, of course, worn it before. She tried it on. It was big. But it would do. For now.

She grabbed her riding boots and bundled everything all together in her arms, then she made her way as quietly as she could to the library and waited impatiently for the dome to open, hoping to remain undiscovered. She didn't want to deal with anyone right now. She'd rather be yelled at upon her return than questioned right now about going out. Anyway, Lord White was quite probably still at Parliament, and she hoped that she would be able to avoid—

"Cora, love! Thank goodness. You're okay!"

Damn. "Yes, Mrs. Philips, I'm fine," she said as she was smothered by the housekeeper in a tight hug.

"I sent Barker to fetch you from Westminster hours ago, but he said you weren't there. Oh pet, I'm so happy to see you all in one piece. What's all that you're carrying?"

My supersecret disguise that I'll be wearing when I become my alter ego, Hyde, and take on the Fog.

"Nothing." She climbed up into the dome and started to make her way downstairs.

"Cora, love, what are you up to?"

She stopped so that her head was just peeking over the edge of the globe. "I can't tell you, Mrs. Philips. But I'm going out tonight. And I really have to get ready."

"Not tonight, Cora. Not tonight," said Mrs. Philips, her voice shaking slightly. "Not when the world might end. Stay in with your Mrs. Philips and have a cup of tea. Don't go out. It's not safe."

Cora knew deep down that as much as Mrs. Philips cared for her, she was also speaking out of fear for herself. She wished she could have stayed for the housekeeper, to keep her company, to tell her it would all be all right. But she'd have to bear hurting Mrs. Philips at the moment so that she could protect her in the long run.

"I . . . can't." She quickly ran down the steps into the lab without giving her a second look. She even closed the dome behind her, just for good measure.

Cora dropped the clothes on the floor and took a good look about the room.

First thing, she'd use her new invention for sure. She walked quickly to her cubby and pulled out the goggles. Not only would they be useful underground, in the dark, they'd serve as an excellent mask. Practical and fashionable. *Excellent*.

Next, she collected some small tools and a tool belt to put them on. But it just didn't seem like enough. She placed her small pistol among the objects, and as she did so, she remembered her experience in the graveyard. Three against one and her little gun. It wasn't going to be enough. Not nearly.

She needed something more, something . . . impressive.

Cora looked toward Lord White's armory. Its doors seemed formidable all of a sudden. But she had to protect herself. She had to protect the girls. She'd promised.

She walked over with a confident stride, trying to convince herself that this was the right thing to do. She flung the doors open wide and stood, hands on hips, examining her choices. The problem with many of the weapons before her was that they were either not powerful enough, little better than the pistol she already had, or too unwieldy to carry. But there was one gun, one that would suit her purposes, if she dared.

The Chekhov was a beast of a weapon. Large, like a miniature cannon. Of all the possible choices that Cora could have made, it seemed, at first glance, the least practical. But first glances don't tell the whole story. The most impressive element of the Chekhov was neither its size nor its awe-inspiring capability for destruction. It was the mechanized system Lord White had invented so that it could be taken apart and stored about one's person, and then, by means of an electromagnetic current, reassemble itself at the push of a button. Thus, despite its size, the Chekhov was the perfect weapon for Cora to carry on this particular mission. But first. She needed to get dressed.

Trousers.

Shirt.

Boots.

Leather corset.

Goggles (the normal setting, not the night vision, not yet).

She examined her reflection in the glass cabinet that held Lord White's more explosion-y materials. Okay, she looked kind of good. Even though that wasn't the point. She grabbed the leather tool belt and strapped it around her waist, her little pistol sitting nicely on her left hip. Next . . . well, next, she had to take apart the Chekhov.

She lifted the massive gun off its pedestal as gently as she could and carried it to the worktable. On the bottom side of the weapon was a very small button that would deactivate the magnet inside. She just had to be careful not to push the large button on the side that might otherwise set it off.

She found the small button.

There was a clunking sound, and, almost with a sigh, the gun broke into lots of smaller pieces.

Cora went back to the arsenal to retrieve the gun's very specifically designed holster and brought it back to the table. There was a folded paper inside the holster that contained illustrated instructions of where on her person she should put each piece so that the gun could fly together properly. It was important that the main section, which housed the magnet, was correctly positioned so that the electromagnetic charge would activate nothing but the other pieces of the Chekhov. It was a complicated set of instructions, and Cora couldn't help wishing she had someone to help her distribute the items about her person. But she figured it all out eventually, and soon she was covered in the shiny metal pieces.

She looked at herself again, and this time she almost let out a gasp. She kind of looked . . . not-human. Like one of those mechanical toy men she'd seen at the gala last week. She lifted her arms. They were much heavier now, and covered in metal. She twisted her torso. She was able to move reasonably well; it wasn't bad. After all, this weapon was meant to be brought onto the field of battle, and Lord White had spent close to two years perfecting the way the gun could be taken apart and automatically put itself back together. Designing the look of the reconstructed gun and its firing mechanism had been relatively easy by comparison.

She'd need to practice moving about in the getup she was wearing. So she'd be better prepared for the next time.

Next time?

What are you planning exactly, Cora? she asked herself.

She didn't know. She didn't have time to know. She grabbed the leather jacket and threw it on over the whole ensemble. It covered all the pieces of the gun very nicely.

She took off her goggles and placed them in the jacket's deep pockets.

Now she was ready to go out into the real world.

MICHIKO HADN'T NEEDED to prepare much. She had a light bite to eat, to keep her energy high, and decided to take two daggers as well as the Silver Heart, which she carried on her back. She took a moment to meditate. To focus on the task ahead and to digest—not so much the food that she'd just eaten but the conversation she'd had with her two new friends in Nellie's room.

This was difficult, being a team. It wasn't what she was meant to do; it wasn't how she was meant to act. But going it alone had not proven to be successful so far. Once this mission was completed, once she'd defeated the Fog with the other girls' help, she could return to her solitary life. She could fulfill her quest to become a true samurai. In the meantime, well, there was something about Cora's enthusiasm that had been almost mesmerizing.

Also, it had been kind of fun watching Cora and Nellie come up with their costumes, which were a little like hers. Granted, the way Nellie wanted to dress seemed silly to Michiko, but the idea of using everything at one's disposal to defeat one's enemy was familiar to her. Loud yells, distraction, the unexpected. And there could be an advantage to Nellie's having her legs free beyond just her ability to climb. It would be very distracting to the opposite sex, and therefore a huge advantage for the three of them.

She still wasn't quite sure what the Silver Heart had to do with anything, why she'd had to reveal the name of her sword to them.

"*Silver Heart!*" Hayao appeared from the shadows in the alley. Speaking of which . . . Michiko had thought he might show up, but had hoped he wouldn't.

"*Little monkey, go home. I'm busy.*" She walked past him, trying to indicate that she wasn't kidding around.

"*Where are you going? What are you doing? Who was that girl? Can I come with you?*" he asked, keeping pace with her.

"*Go home.*"

"*I could help. You know I could!*"

Michiko stopped dead in her tracks and whipped off her mask so that he could see her expression. "*You can't come. You must stay home. Your master orders you so.*"

Hayao's face fell and his whole body deflated. He looked so sad, so pathetic, that Michiko almost wanted to take it all back. But she knew he couldn't come with her. And this would be a good lesson for him. In discipline.

"*Well?*" she asked.

"*Yes, Master.*"

"*Go home now.*"

She started walking again, and after she'd gone a block, she turned to see if she'd been obeyed.

He was gone. The street was deserted.

Michiko glanced up.

She wasn't entirely convinced that the rooftops were as well.

Nellie attached the wire rope to her hip, a little box that held two flashcubes and some matches, and another that contained a special and unique compound: a combination of glitter and a green copper powder that the Magician used for some of his pyrotechnics. It was poisonous, so Nellie handled it with gloves. Then she thought that gloves might add a nice finishing touch to the whole ensemble, so she found a pair of black leather ones she wore in the winter.

She was admiring her whole outfit: the corset, short black skirt, the fishnet stockings (silk stockings would be too slippery to do real climbing), the gloves, the boots, and her various tools at her waist, plus a black mask framed with dark blue feathers—when the Magician walked into her room.

Normally he knocked, but he didn't this time. There was nothing she could do, but just stand there in her getup and stare.

"Interesting look. Is this for the show?" he asked casually.

"I didn't think there'd *be* a show tonight, what with the death threat and all."

"Then what's this costume for?"

Right. She hadn't thought the answer through. Now she had no excuse. She didn't know what to say. She just sort of shook a little.

The Magician smiled and sat down in her chair. "I'm sorry.

I'm being cruel. This . . ." He gestured toward her. "This is all because of Miss Bell's plan, is it not?"

Now she still didn't know what to say and so continued to stand there and shake a little.

"She wanted my advice about you. I said I couldn't say anything. It seems you decided her idea was a good one after all."

Nellie nodded.

"This outfit, it needs a bit of work, but it will do for now. You need better shoes, better gloves. Everything needs to be more durable. Next time."

"What do you mean 'next time'?"

The Magician shrugged. "Maybe you could make a real difference. You like to help people. Maybe this all makes sense."

"You approve?"

"I do."

"You aren't worried?"

"I am."

"But—"

"But we don't live our lives in fear. And we don't stop ourselves from doing the right thing even when it might be risky. Costumes, masks, props—it's not a bad idea to be prepared. You've made wise choices in the past. I trust that this one is wise, too."

"I'm scared." She felt tears welling up inside, though she wasn't sure if it was from fear or from the kind words the Magician had just shared with her.

"Good. Be scared. But still be strong."

Nellie nodded.

The Magician rose and came over to her. "I shouldn't have come in. I should have hidden in my room until you left to meet the others. I just wanted to tell you I was proud, but now you are . . . sad?"

Nellie shook her head. She couldn't speak. She couldn't say anything. It meant the world to her that Raheem was proud of her. That he approved of this madness. But, of course, he would. He was a hero, too, in his own way.

"I'd hug you, but . . ." She looked down at her outfit. It wasn't conducive to hugs.

"It's okay." The Magician smiled. "Hold out your hand." She did. He placed what looked like a tiny brass funnel in it. It was no larger than her palm.

"What is this?"

"I bought it last week, thought it could be hidden up a sleeve. Here, you attach this to it." He produced a long thin tube and a small metal canister. "Very dramatic. It shoots fire. An awful lot of fire. Like a dragon roaring. A nice effect. A nice weapon for you, maybe."

He attached the canister to the small of her back. They re-adjusted her corset so the tube could run up it on the inside and then down her arm, plugging into the small funnel, which she hid inside her glove. "You pull this chain here to activate the fire, and release it to make it stop." He indicated toward a metal hoop dangling from a short exposed chain on her left side by the canister.

"Wear this," said the Magician, handing her one of his black capes. "It'll hide the canister, and a cape can always be useful."

Again, Nellie was at a loss for words. "Thank you."

"You're welcome."

As if she was feeling left out of the conversation, Scheherazade flew to her shoulder and gave her ear a friendly peck.

"Could you watch Sherry for me?" Nellie asked, scratching the bird's head. "She might follow. And she can't this time."

"This time?"

Nellie didn't respond, so the Magician gave a small nod and plucked the parrot from her shoulder.

"Thank you."

"Now go," he said, taking a step back. "Join your team."

And So . . .

IN THE SHADOW of Tower Bridge, three girls met in the dark.

"I love it!" said Nellie when Cora removed her overcoat and put on her goggles. She made her strike a pose. Cora, for her part, put her hands on her hips, but that was all she was inclined to do. "It came together beautifully, and you don't look like a man at all."

"Well, that's good."

There was a pause as Cora adjusted her tool belt. Nellie coughed to get her attention.

"Oh, you look great, too! Love the cape and the . . . mask."

Nellie grinned. "Thank you!"

Michiko just sighed.

"Right. Okay, Michiko, I mean, Silver-Heart." Nellie grinned again. "Lead on."

With map in hand, Michiko led the girls toward the river's edge, just east of the neo-Gothic bridge. She stopped and looked at the map. Then at the building before her. She nodded and folded up the map, hiding it somewhere in her black ensemble.

"Is that the entrance?" asked Nellie, staring the small cylindrical building before her and reading the words around the top. "The London Hydraulic Power Company."

Cora nodded. "Yes. That's it. It used to be the Tower Subway. Then the hydraulic company took over. Should have an automated lift inside. At least I hope so."

The steel door was locked, of course, but Nellie pulled out a thin piece of metal, picked the lock, and they were easily inside. Nellie lit a match and the room glowed for a moment. It was small, only enough space for a lift, and Michiko pulled its grate open as Cora examined the box next to it. It seemed to be a pretty standard winching device that ran on electricity. Nellie lit another match when the first one burned out. Cora examined the box carefully. The power had been turned off, but after a quick survey of the room, she found the generator. Soon she had it humming to life, and a small light in the ceiling turned on. She flipped two of the switches in the box and motioned to the girls to step inside the lift. Michiko closed the grate behind her.

"Well, here goes nothing." Cora pulled the lever on the inside of the lift. There was a loud clunking sound, wheels turning, and the faint smell of burning. *Dust*, Cora told herself. *It's just dust*. Then the cage they were in lurched up half a foot and returned to its original spot.

"Is that it?" asked Nellie, not particularly helpfully.

As if to say, "*No, that's not it*," the cage suddenly started to descend. Faster than Cora had anticipated.

"Here we go," she said.

The ride was shaky and unsteady, and the girls stood in silence as they descended farther and farther from the light. Soon they were surrounded by pitch darkness, and it took Cora a few moments to remember she was wearing her goggles. She flipped down the thick secondary green glass, pushed the button by her temple, and the goggles filled with a gaseous substance. She should be able to see now. But she couldn't. She could see a bit of the grate before her, but that was it.

"Damn it," she said.

"What?"

"They're not working."

"What aren't?"

"My goggles." Cora turned to Nellie and was surprised that she could see her face and its confused expression all in a greenish tint. "Oh. I guess they do work. I guess I was just . . . looking at nothing."

"What are you goin' on about?"

"The goggles I'm wearing. I made them so I can see in the dark."

"You can see?"

Cora nodded. Then she realized that Nellie couldn't see her nodding. "Yes," she said.

The lift landed with a heavy thud and the girls were thrown backward.

"Should I light another match?" asked Nellie.

"Let me have a look around first. We don't want our presence to be known." Cora opened the grate as quietly as she could and stepped out into the wide tunnel. She'd never used the Tower Subway herself, but of course she'd known people who had. And she remembered when the authorities had closed it down, too. People had been upset. Which, of course, she'd found odd. You'd had to pay a toll to use the subway. You didn't in order to cross the bridge above. But some people hated change.

She looked both ways and saw nothing. Just pipes overhead that dripped onto the floor. It was worth the risk.

"Light a match," she said.

It was almost too bright for her when Nellie did so. Nellie and Michiko joined Cora in the tunnel and stood by her, gazing out before them.

"Pretty straightforward. If you hold on to me, I'll take you through," said Cora just as the match burned out.

She led them down the tunnel, not sure how far they were going, just looking for something, anything, that hinted at what they should do next. They walked in silence, just the dripping of the water keeping them company. It wasn't the most comforting of sounds.

They were maybe halfway through the tunnel, probably smack-dab in the middle of the river above, when Michiko squeezed her shoulder and said, "Stop."

They did. Cora's heart dropped, and she quickly looked about to see why they had stopped. Had something sneaked up on them? She should have been looking back more often.

But there was nothing. Nothing that she could see.

"Listen," said Michiko.

Cora strained to hear what Michiko was hearing. But nothing sounded any different than it had a moment before.

"Hollow." Michiko released Cora's shoulder and disappeared. Cora turned and looked down to see the Japanese girl crawling on the ground, her hands outstretched before her. "Yes. Here. Come."

"Where's she gone?" asked Nellie, oblivious to what was going on.

"She's on the ground. She's . . . oh my God. There's a trapdoor." She bent down slowly so that Nellie could stay close to her and examined the door that Michiko had discovered. "I can't believe I missed it. I was looking straight ahead; that was stupid of me."

"How did you find it?" asked Nellie slowly.

"Walking sound. Different."

Cora noticed a slight indentation in the wood, enough for a few fingers to slip into it. She pulled, and when the door opened, a crack, a beam of light hit her knees.

There was as sudden loud clang and Nellie gasped. Cora instinctively held her breath, waiting for the attack.

"Lift," said Michiko.

It took a moment to process the word, and then Cora understood. Someone had just activated the lift. There was no time to lose now.

She opened the door wide. Beneath it was an iron ladder that led to a floor a short distance away. "Go down, go now."

Michiko evidently didn't need the ladder; she just jumped straight to the floor beneath. Nellie swung herself easily over the edge and jumped to a lower step. Then, placing her feet and hands on the outside of the ladder, she slid down. *Show-offs,* thought Cora as she hoisted herself onto the ladder and took each step as she carefully climbed down. She shut the door behind her.

Wherever they were now, it was bright, or at least brighter compared to where they'd come from. Cora flipped up the green glass on her goggles so she could look through the plain glass lens. The tunnel was narrower than the one they'd just been in. It was pretty primitive looking, created not for any regular use or any regular person. Electric lamps were connected to one another at intervals by thick black cables. They went along as far as the eye could see, showing the girls the way down the long winding path that eventually turned out of sight.

"I go first," said Michiko, pulling the elegant sword from its sheath on her back and holding it before her.

"I've got no problem with that," replied Cora. Nellie laughed, and they followed Michiko carefully down the hall.

It was exhausting, anticipating something terrible around every corner, and constantly looking over one's shoulder. Cora was grateful that her adrenaline was surging, otherwise she'd probably collapse from the anticipation.

She glanced over her shoulder again, to see if whoever had called the lift was upon them yet. Nothing. She turned and walked right into Nellie.

"Watch it, Hyde," said Nellie, stumbling forward.

"Sorry, you just . . . stopped."

"I stopped because Silver Heart stopped."

"I stop because light stop."

And it was true. They had come to the end of the trail of lights, and a vast blackness opened out before them.

Cora flipped down the green lenses, pushed the button at her temple, and in a moment she was staring out into a wide, low-ceilinged cavern.

"Interesting."

"What do you see?"

"A door at the other end."

"Good!"

"And trip wires between us and it."

Fine wires crisscrossed the space from top to bottom, and as Cora followed them up to the walls of the cavern, she saw that they were attached to devices that resembled small crossbows.

"Darts maybe, likely poisoned. Clearly he was expecting visitors."

"What do we do?" asked Nellie.

"You do what I tell you. You two should be fine; I'm more concerned about my lack of flexibility with all these metal pieces covering me."

"I go first," Michiko insisted yet again.

"No," replied Cora.

"Why no?"

"Because I need to practice giving instructions so that when it's your turn I will be easy to understand."

She said it a few times, adding gestures, until Michiko understood, giving a sharp nod. "Yes."

"You ready . . . Lady Sparkle?"

Nellie gave her a smile and nodded. She tied her cape tightly around her waist, then she turned toward the blackness and took a deep slow breath, focusing on the task ahead.

"The first wire is low to the ground, so lift your foot up perpendicular to your knee . . ."

"Are all the instructions going to be this detailed?"

"Yes."

"Lord, this is gonna take forever . . ."

And so it began. Nellie was a very good listener and followed Cora's instructions to the letter. Well, except for the few times when she offered her own suggestions, like doing a roll over some wire instead of flattening herself under it. She was remarkably bendy, the way she could twist and turn and lift her legs just so. And when she made it to the end, she did a little cartwheel, just for fun.

"Your turn, Silver Heart."

Michiko didn't move. There was a pause. Then: "Me?"

"Yes. You're Silver Heart."

There was silence from behind the mask and then Michiko took a step toward the blackness.

This was going to be harder. But now that Cora had directed someone through the wires once, she felt more confident in her ability to tell Michiko what to do. For her part, Michiko proved to be a wizard at interpreting her meaning, and, like Nellie, came up with her own solutions. There was a series of wires she could pass under, snakelike, simply because she was so slender. When she got to the other side, she didn't cartwheel. But she was attacked in a ferocious hug by Nellie.

"My *turn*," said Cora to herself. She had been fearing this moment. It was one thing to have a sense of the full scope of the situation, and to guide others across the wires, but to be in it herself . . .

Plus, with all the pieces of the Chekhov tucked around her body, she wasn't nearly as agile as the other two.

"Just take your time," called out Nellie into the dark. Cora wondered what it was like for the other two to be standing in the blackness on the other side. Though they weren't completely blind, she realized; they could see her body silhouetted by the lamps that stood behind her in the tunnel.

"Can you see the wires?" Cora called out, maybe they could help her.

"A bit, but they disappear in and out of the light," replied Nellie. "I'll help you when I can."

Every step Cora took, she made sure to examine everything around her, up, down, side to side. She made herself lie on her back instead of her front so that she could keep an eye on the wires. She hopped over one and nearly lost her balance, and she heard Nellie gasp as Cora tried to stay upright. Once in a while Nellie offered a few suggestions, and at one crucial moment stopped Cora just before she tripped a wire. It seemed to take forever, but eventually she made it to the other two.

"That wasn't fun," she said, panting slightly.

"I thought it kind of was—"

"Move."

Cora pushed Nellie to the side so she could examine the

door they were now standing before. It was a thick, solid metal, no handle, no obvious lock.

"Can you do anything with this?" she asked.

"Let me borrow your goggles," replied Nellie.

Cora passed them over, and after Nellie let out a laugh of appreciation and a "This is amazin'!" she started to examine the door.

"No . . . it opens mechanically, I think. From the other side."

"That's what I was thinking, too."

Nellie passed back the goggles.

"I wonder . . . if we break the seal, if it would then slide open," said Cora, again studying the door closely. "The bullets in my pistol are filled with acid."

"They are?"

"Let me try. Both of you stand back." Cora knew that she could probably use the Chekhov to blow a giant hole in the door, but she didn't want to activate the weapon if she didn't have to. She didn't know what kind of collateral damage shooting it off might cause, and then, of course, there was the fact that once the gun was assembled, she'd have to carry the thing around for the rest of the mission. Sure it could quickly fall apart at the push of a button, but putting the pieces back all over her person? Not so easy. So it made sense to try the pistol first.

She aimed for the stone frame around the door, not the door itself. She wasn't sure what kind of metal it was made out of, and definitely wasn't interested in having acid-filled bullets ricocheting off its surface and back at her.

"If they didn't know we were coming before . . ." she said, and then . . . fired.

She discharged her entire supply of bullets, and when silence fell, she examined her handiwork. The stone around the door had melted away, and she could even glimpse into the room behind it.

"Come on, ladies, let's see if we can pull this thing open." She directed Michiko and Nellie to grab the exposed side of the door. "One, two, three . . ." They pulled. They kept pulling. They pulled some more.

There was a click, and suddenly the whole door just slid to the side.

Standing before them, silhouetted by the blue-green light of the room, was Mr. Staunch. His glowing eyes narrowed when he recognized his visitors. The gears inside spun. He produced a familiar looking gun and aimed it.

Michiko was standing directly opposite him. She took one look at the eyes and punched him across the face. Then she punched him in the solar plexus, and, as he keeled over, she ducked down and tossed him over her shoulder. He rolled past Nellie and Cora, into the trip wires where he flailed about as hundreds of poison darts flew at him, sticking into his flesh. For a few moments he writhed in the wires like a fly caught in a spiderweb. Then his gun fell to the ground. He stopped twitching.

Michiko was lying flat on her stomach. Nellie came over and helped her to stand.

"Good job," she said.

It was impossible to read Michiko's expression, what with the mask and all, but a muffled voice from behind it said, "Machine eyes?"

"Yes, Dr. Mantis has a strange obsession. Shall we carry on?" asked Cora, passing into the room. The other girls followed.

More Fun Times . . .

"KEEP YOUR WITS about you. They know we're here."

"I know this place," said Nellie as they walked to the center of the room.

"You do?"

"It's a lot like Dr. Mantis's office at the Medical and Scientific Institute, with jars of body parts everywhere. But there was no table . . ." They all looked at the white-padded table with leather straps attached to it. Nellie felt a shiver run up her spine. "Can we get out of here?"

"Yes, of course."

They crossed to the other side of the room, where they were met with two doors. Both seemed easy enough to open.

"You take one, I'll take the other. One of them has to be an exit," said Cora, placing herself in front of the door on the left.

Nellie nodded, but after meeting Mr. Staunch so unexpectedly, she found the idea of just opening a door a rather daunting prospect.

"One," counted Cora. "Two . . ." She heard the sound of

a sword being unsheathed behind her as Michiko stood prepared. "Three."

Nellie opened her door wide and . . . found herself facing an empty hallway, much like the one they'd been in before. *Well, that was anticlimactic.*

There was a scream, and Nellie looked to the side just in time to see a monstrous arm reach for and then grab Cora by the throat. The screaming stopped instantly as the hand squeezed, and Nellie watched as Michiko sliced the arm off at the elbow. Cora fell back and threw the arm to one side. Nellie sprang into action, and pushed against Cora's door to slam it closed. Something came up against it, though, and pushed back.

"Help, please!" Nellie called out. Her breath froze in the air, and she realized that whatever was beyond that door was freezing cold.

Cora and Michiko were at her side in a flash, and all three girls pushed hard. But the thing on the other side pushed harder. For a while it was a standoff, a stalemate, with the door neither closing nor opening. "Can you hold it much longer?" asked Nellie.

Cora didn't say anything, just shook her head.

"I'm thinkin' we've got to just let go and run out the door I opened. Just make a run for it."

"I think you're right. Ready?" asked Cora, her voice straining with effort.

"When we let go, head to the door. Got that, Silver Heart?" instructed Nellie. But she had no idea if Michiko got it or not. She just had to hope.

"NOW!"

They released the door then flew out the other door into the hall. Once Michiko joined them, Nellie reached back into the room to close the door behind them. But something got there first and tore the door right off its hinges.

Nellie backed away quickly to join the other girls, who were standing, staring in shock.

Looming in the now-wide doorway was . . . something. For all the world, it looked like a human, but something about it was off, something wasn't quite right. This man-creature was bigger, taller, and wider than a human being, and the bits of him didn't seem to match.

That's because, Nellie realized, they *didn't* match. The arm was a bit larger than the shoulder socket it was thrust into, and the torso and neck held up a strangely smaller head. The eyes were too close together, the mouth too wide. Strange, too, was the fact that despite the creature's forearm having been severed clear off his body, and the black blood seeping from the wound onto the ground, it, or he, seemed to feel no pain, nor even to be aware that he, or it, was missing a part.

"He's made up of bits," said Nellie.

"He's not the only one," Cora replied.

As the creature stumbled into the hall, Nellie noticed what Cora already had already observed: The man-creature wasn't alone. There were more of his kind stumbling their way toward the door, making strange groaning sounds as they lumbered along.

"It's as if they were being stored in a freezer box," said Cora.

"Yes."

"They don't seem to feel pain."

"Yes."

"I think it's likely we're going to have to destroy them all."

"Yes."

Without a word, Michiko charged the creatures. The speed with which she attacked was impressive. She cut and thrust, and spun and jumped, and in the end she cut the first three creatures into pieces.

"She's going to exhaust herself. Can we do anything . . . ?" said Nellie in a strange sort of awe.

"Look," said Cora, pointing to the ground at one of the severed arms.

The arm had started to pull itself forward on its own volition and, at the same time, the legs of the creature found its torso and reconnected with it.

"It's puttin' itself back together. What kind of black magic—"

"Silver Heart, Lady Sparkle, get behind me, now," ordered Cora.

Nellie looked at Cora, who had a very serious expression on her face, and did what she was told, grabbing Michiko.

"There's only one thing for this. You two go on. I'm not sure how powerful this thing will turn out to be."

Cora pulled out a small cylindrical brass object from its holster on her right hip and pushed a button on its underside. There was a moment during which nothing happened. And then . . .

It looked like her costume had suddenly sprung to life. The pieces of metal and gears that decorated it began to move. They turned and then started to travel across her body in a pattern that seemed very deliberate, all heading toward the cylinder Cora was holding. They collected and joined with one another, and, as they slid off her torso toward the growing cylinder, the plain leather corset and white shirt she was wearing were revealed.

Then there was stillness. Even the lumbering creatures had stopped to watch the show. And then, in Cora's hand, supported at her hip, was a large rather intimidating gun.

She looked over her shoulder and, seeing that both Nellie and Michiko were still there, yelled, "*Go!*"

Nellie took a step back and watched as a light started to glow at the back of the cylinder. She took another step back, then another, and another.

Cora fired the weapon at the closest creature. The weapon made almost no sound except for a high-pitched *whoosh* as its projectile—whatever it was—since there was nothing to see—traveled toward the creature.

The creature evaporated before their very eyes. It made a slight *pop* sound, and then all that was left was a fine black mist.

"Oh my God."

"I said go," ordered Cora again, not turning around this time. Just firing shot after shot as the creatures realized they had a new enemy to conquer.

Nellie felt Michiko pull on her arm, and she finally started running down the hall. They were running without any idea where they were going, and their desperation probably explained why neither of them noticed the trip wire, brightly lit, crossing the hall.

Within seconds, a heavy net had fallen on top of them, and they were flattened to the ground. Instantly, Michiko had one of her daggers out and was cutting through it. A shadow appeared above them, and then another and another.

CORA DISINTEGRATED THE last of the creatures and turned around to join Nellie and Michiko only to find them standing directly behind her. They were each being held firmly by two large men in lab coats. The girls' masks dangled around their necks. *So much for secret identities.* A third man, whom she recognized as Dr. Mantis, stood staring at her in disbelief.

"You destroyed my babies," he said softly.

"I'm . . . sorry." Cora pushed her goggles up onto her forehead.

"You certainly will be. Give me that," he said, extending his hand toward the Chekhov.

Cora laughed. "No, I don't think I will."

"Give it to me, or I'll take it."

"Or maybe I'll have to disintegrate you, too. How about that?"

Dr. Mantis took a step toward her. "Do you know the difference between you and me?" he asked in that quiet voice of his.

"Aside from the fact that I have hair?"

"The difference between us is that I have no compunction

about killing people." He walked toward her until he had pressed his body against the Chekhov. "I don't think it's the same for you."

Cora stared into his bloodshot eyes. She could do it. Couldn't she?

Damn.

She gave him the weapon.

And Now . . . the Fog

THE THREE GIRLS were marched into a giant, cavernous space carefully buttressed against collapse by thick iron beams and struts. It had an almost cathedral-like appearance, the lancet arches flying up into the shadows above. Along the walls, there were several large round holes that looked to be tunnels leading . . . who knew where. All sorts of contraptions ticked and hissed away on tables and even on the floor, and as the girls made their way into the room, a dozen or so men, all properly dressed in lab coats, stopped running their various experiments and looked at them.

The girls were ushered down a set of stairs to the main level and toward the rear of a room where a raised platform had been constructed and an ornate wooden desk sat.

And in the chair behind the desk, fingers drumming impatiently on the hilt of a cavalry saber, was sitting . . .

"Who the hell are you?" asked Cora, flabbergasted that the Fog should be a total stranger. After all the novels she'd read, she'd sort of assumed that he would be someone she knew.

Then again, she also assumed he would be . . . well . . . a he.

The woman sitting behind the desk looked mildly insulted by the question.

"You don't recognize me?"

Cora looked at the woman carefully. She was probably in her mid-forties, her face, sharply angled, seemed a little wan, a little drained of life. Her dark auburn hair she wore loose, falling in waves over her lab coat. Hanging around her neck was a very familiar device, the one Cora had spent far too many hours on. Okay, yes, there was something vaguely familiar about her, actually. Still . . .

"Not really, no."

"Do *you?*" the woman asked, looking at Nellie.

Nellie shook her head and almost looked embarrassed that she didn't.

The woman placed her sword to one side and leaned back in her seat. "Well, isn't that typical. I thought maybe someone of my own gender might notice me. But clearly I was wrong."

"Stop pouting and tell us who you are," Cora said sharply.

The woman looked at her and gave her a wry smile. "My name is Jane Webb. And I work the front desk at the Medical and Scientific Institute."

"Oh my God, yes! Now I remember," said Cora in amazement. "But . . . you helped me. You told me where they'd taken Nellie."

The Fog rose and held up a finger. "First of all," she said, moving to the front of her desk, "that whole kidnapping murder thing, that had nothing to do with me. Dr. Mantis has his . . . projects. He's been kind enough to assist me with mine.

As you see, there are many other experiments being carried out down here by various gentlemen, but our interests vary widely. And second, since both of you came in search of those two fools, I thought maybe you were on my trail. Clearly, I thought right. So I had no compunction sending them after you. My hope was that they'd get rid of you. Obviously, they didn't."

Well, that was interesting.

"Why are you doing this?" asked Cora. "I don't see the point."

"Of blowing up the city?"

"Well, threatening to blow up the city."

The Fog smiled. "I think both you and I know that the government isn't going to pay the money."

"So you're really going to blow it up?"

"Yes."

"Why?"

"Glad you asked. Because I can. Because I want to prove that I can."

"But . . ." and again "Why?" Was there an advantage to keeping the fog woman talking? Clearly she wanted to, and to be perfectly honest, Cora did kind of want to know the answer to her question.

"*Why?* Do you know how long I've worked at the institute?"

"No," said Nellie.

"That was a rhetorical—oh, never mind. Anyway, I've worked there since I was younger than you are now. At first I was just a happy assistant. But as I got to know the men, and they me, I was invited to watch certain experiments. It got to the point where I was invited to assist. Even given small tasks to do on my own. You can imagine how it grew from there.

"By now I'd say I've worked on almost every kind of experiment there is. There was even a time when I was considering going to medical college. But the men at the institute convinced me it wasn't worth it. Why go elsewhere and fight to be respected when all of them there knew just how much of a genius I was? Enough to do all the hard work, but not enough to join their super-secret club."

"The Society of Heroes."

"Yes. For no good reason, it was a 'no girls allowed' affair, and nothing I said could convince them I should be a member. Then one day that idiot Thompkins mentioned that the society had come up with a brilliant new invention, inspired evidently by an article about the exhibit from the Library of Alexandria that was coming to the British Museum. Something about some long-lost scrolls. Thompkins realized that if what they hinted at were true, a bomb could be manufactured, one that used uranium, and that could destroy an entire city. It was all a theory, of course. None of those fools knew how to put it together. So I offered to try, in exchange for membership."

"What's uranium?" asked Nellie.

"Something that your magician friend can easily come by."

"What?" Cora glanced at Nellie, who looked utterly bewildered.

"In any event, the deal was that if I could make it, I could be a member. And they would act as my assistants, should I need them. However, it was clear that the society was very divided about the moral implications of creating such a bomb. There were some who helped, who engineered this fantastic space you see here, and thought it so fine that they brought some of their more questionable experiments along with them. There were others, however, like Dr. Thompkins, who thought that a bomb of such destructive power should never be created. He tried to sabotage the experiment."

"I can understand that," said Cora.

"Can you? How . . . empathetic of you. At any rate, Mr. Proper informed Dr. Thompkins about a recent order he'd placed with the Great Raheem for something from Africa. Mr. Proper was as excited about meeting the Great Raheem as he was about picking up the shipment from him. He's a fan, evidently. Well, the second Thompkins heard about this, he decided to go to the Great Raheem and warn him not to hand over the shipment. But I followed him and shot him with a poison dart."

"Why a poison dart?" asked Nellie.

"It was all I had on me at the time. Do you want to hear the story or not?"

"Of course I do."

"We needed more and more money, and the society's principal backer, one Mr. Carter, was getting nervous. Especially after I killed off Dr. Thompkins. He pulled his funding."

"So you killed him?"

"Yes. Because otherwise people would think they could walk all over me."

"I see . . ."

"But last night . . . last night was the crux of it all. Finally, everything had come together. You see, I'd had to wait until the exhibit came to the British Museum so I could acquire the final set of instructions, the final piece of the puzzle. Further, it was important I leave it all till the last minute. I assumed someone would get suspicious about the robberies and killings, and I didn't want to give anyone enough time to piece it together."

"But we did."

"Yes, you did. Aren't you clever?"

"What were all the pieces for?"

"It's complicated science stuff, but to be very basic about it: The cavorite would lift my bomb into the sky, the device I commissioned—which I'll have you know, none of these fools could figure out how to make and I certainly didn't have the time to work on—would operate it remotely. I needed the Koh-i-noor diamond because it was large enough to be placed at the bottom of the bomb's casing to prevent the heat from the cavorite from igniting the bomb."

Fine. "And the flowers."

"What flowers?"

"Why did you kill all the flower girls? What was that for?" Cora could feel emotion rising up inside her as she said it.

The Fog stared at Cora and then shook her head. "I have no idea what you're talking about. You're clearly an insane person."

Cora was thunderstruck. But she believed what she heard. Of everything the Fog had said, this was something she trusted. Then . . . if not the Fog, who?

There was a frustrated sigh, and Cora turned to look at Michiko, who was clearly finding all this talking to be a huge waste of time. "So. Anyway. Back to my story," said the Fog. "We were all here, the remaining members of the society, in my lovely little laboratory. We had dinner. I showed them my work. And you know what they said?"

"What?" asked Nellie, who seemed to understand that Cora was now speechless.

"That I couldn't be a member. That I had no proof that the bomb worked. And even if it did, they had been the ones to come up with the plan in the first place."

"Ouch," said Nellie.

"Yes, that was what it felt like. Very ouch. So I decided I might as well show them."

"But . . . why blow up the city? Surely you'll suffer just like the rest of us," said Cora, speaking up again.

"First of all, I'm far belowground, so I won't get blown up. Second of all, you might say, 'But what about the radiation?'"

"What's radiation?" asked Nellie.

"Unpleasant," replied the Fog. "Well, this series of tunnels follows along the Thames into the North Sea. Where I have a boat waiting."

"That's a long journey underground," said Cora.

"I'm a clever girl. I have the means to travel it. You didn't think I needed all that cavorite just for one little bomb, did you?" She rose from the desk and stepped off the platform. She gestured for them to follow her and they stopped before a strange-looking square device. "You strap it on your back. The rockets help propel you; the cavorite lifts you off the ground."

"It's a personal flying device?" asked Cora, fascinated.

"Yes. And it will make journeying through the tunnels much quicker."

"What about everyone else?" Cora looked at the men in the room. They all seemed utterly uninterested in her conversation with the Fog and focused instead on their experiments, as if three costumed girls were a common occurrence here in their secret underground lab.

"What about them? In any event, when I'm on my boat, I will take the plans I have brought with me and go to Germany, where I already have a scheduled meeting with the Chancellor. He has promised me not only a high position in his government, with the respect I so rightfully deserve, but lots and lots of money to go with it."

"I have a question," Nellie said.

"Yes?"

"How could you have made this elaborate plan to meet with the Chancellor if you were only insulted yesterday?"

The Fog thought about this for a moment.

"I anticipated their response."

"I see," said Cora, rolling her eyes. "Well, I don't know how much of your story is true. I only know none of it's going to work."

"Oh, come on. You're not really going to try to stop me now, are you?"

"That was the plan."

"Why don't you come with me? You're all so very impressive, and I think we girls ought to stick together." *Right. With that one flying device you have there,* thought Cora.

"You tried to kill us," said Nellie.

"To be fair, I only tried to kill you two. That one"—she pointed to Michiko—"I actually decided not to kill. I was impressed with her fighting. And, anyway, you managed not to get killed, and I find that impressive as well. Let's form our own secret society. Only, no boys allowed this time."

"You?" said Michiko, finally speaking up.

"Me?" said the Fog.

"You fight me? You Fog?" If Cora didn't know better, she'd swear Michiko sounded indignant.

"Yes. Weren't you paying attention?"

"Where beard?" Michiko asked.

"Yes, that's a good point. What was with the beard?" asked Nellie.

"What's with these costumes you're wearing? A disguise, lovelies, a disguise. And why not throw them completely off the scent and make them think I'm a man?"

Well, now that they had all the information . . . "Can we see the bomb?"

"No."

"Why not?"

"I've already sent it up."

Cora's stomach fell. "How?"

"Through that tunnel there." The Fog pointed to one of the

large round holes in the wall. Up close, Cora realized that they were rather larger than she'd originally thought. Almost as tall as a she was. "That tunnel," she said, pointing to another hole on the other side of the room, "was the one I sent the silly little normal bomb through yesterday. I know you didn't ask, but I think it's neat."

"Well, thank you so much for sharing all this with us in such grand detail," said Cora.

"It was my pleasure. Now," said the Fog, turning to Dr. Mantis. "Pass me that enormous weapon you took off this girl." Dr. Mantis, who had been following her around obediently, jumped into action and passed the Fog the Chekhov. She examined it closely. "Fascinating thing."

"Wait," said Cora, feeling a sudden panic rise, "you aren't just going to kill us, are you?"

"Well, you don't want to be part of my club, and that was just me joking anyway. Of course I'm going to kill you. I don't trust you. You seem . . . awfully capable. Best to get rid of you, I think. Thanks for listening, though. It was a treat getting to brag like that. Let's see this thing in action, shall we?"

The Fog aimed the gun at Cora and Cora stared down the barrel.

Oh God.

I'm going to die.

The Game Changer

MICHIKO SAW HIM just a split second before it happened. He was hidden up near the ceiling, squatting on one of the iron struts that prevented the cave from collapsing in on itself. He launched himself into the air before she had a chance to act, a chance to step in, to do anything. He landed on the Fog, pushing her hard onto the floor. The gun flew out of her hands and skidded to a stop several feet away.

"*Hayao!*" called Michiko. The boy was back up on his feet just as the Fog rose to hers with the help of Dr. Mantis. Hayao drew a *katana* he had strapped to his back and stood prepared. He was still and calm, waiting to see what happened next.

"*Run, Hayao!*"

He looked at her.

Do it, do what you're brilliant at.

"*Run!*"

Hayao turned and ran. He ran across the room toward the steps. He easily maneuvered around the scientists who were trying to grab at him, and even leaped over one who was still hunched over an experiment. He reached the steps and ran up toward the door, but was blocked by another man. So he instantly turned around and launched himself, with the help of the railing, up onto the lowest strut. He ran along it as easily as if it had been the ground.

The Fog produced a pistol from inside her lab coat and shot him in the back.

"*No!*" cried Michiko as she watched Hayao fall hard to the ground. Wrenching herself free of her distracted captor, she had a dagger prepared before she even had the thought. She threw it at the Fog, and it pierced her hand. The pistol fell as she shrieked in pain and staggered backward. Michiko leaped toward her.

"Michiko, don't!" she heard Cora yell.

She landed in front of Hayao, who was lying on the ground shaking and sputtering, and knelt beside him. She sensed something behind her. She didn't turn around. But her sword was instantly flashed backward, the tip touching the soft flesh under Dr. Mantis's chin. "Stay back," she warned. She turned and made eye contact so he knew she was serious.

She looked back to Hayao and pulled him up into her lap. She could hear noise in the background, the sounds of something happening, but she didn't care what it was. All her focus was on Hayao.

"*I was stupid,*" he said.

Yes. So stupid. To follow when she clearly said not to. "*It's not your fault. I should have been a better teacher to you. If I had been a better teacher, you would have made better choices.*"

"*I didn't follow your rules. I didn't wait. She was going to kill your friend, and I couldn't think of anything else. I thought I could take care of it. I thought . . .*" He coughed, and dark sticky blood seeped from between his lips.

"*No more talking, little monkey.*"

"*I'm sorry . . . for following you . . . for disobeying your orders . . .*" he said.

"*Shhh. You have nothing to apologize for. It's me, don't you understand, it's all me. I'm so sorry.*"

I'm so sorry.

"*Thank you for being my teacher.*"

Michiko shook her head and held back her tears. She had to be strong for him. But it was so hard. He looked so small, so helpless. Who were they, she and the other girls? Children playing at warriors. Look at the two of them now. Covered in blood and looking pathetic. "*I think, in this moment, it's clear that I failed* you."

And stubborn as always: "*In this moment, it's clear to me you didn't.*"

"*Shhh,*" she said again. Why did he have to insist on talking, always talking.

In a whisper: "*I am a real samurai because of you.*"

"*Little monkey . . .*"

He squeezed her hand by way of interruption and gave her one of his big, goofy smiles. "*Don't you see . . . I'm not afraid to die.*"

There was a loud rumble then, and Michiko glanced up instinctively and then immediately looked back at Hayao.

He was gone. Dead.

In such a quick moment. The space of a fleeting glance.

She held him close for a moment. But it seemed pointless. All she held now was his shell. His spirit had flown and was, she knew, content.

Everything became very quiet. Michiko had never felt such control, such certainty before.

It was so clear. Her concern for earthly attachments, her fear of death. It might not make her a samurai, but it made her strong in her own way. Hayao was worth fighting for. These other girls were worth fighting for. Her life was worth fighting for.

Maybe she wasn't a samurai, but she could do this.

She turned and stood up. The Fog was running around yelling at people. Michiko had no idea what the woman was saying.

"Fight me," said Michiko loudly.

The Fog turned and looked at her.

"Now."

The Fog stopped for a moment and then, with a shrug, nodded. She grabbed her sword from by her desk and gave a little bow.

"I've defeated you twice," she said slowly, making sure Michiko understood.

A broken sword and poison gas are not defeating me.

"No," said Michiko. "You have not."

Going Back

THE BOY LANDED on top of the Fog, pushing her hard onto the floor. The gun flew out of her hands and skidded to a stop several feet away . . .

. . . from Nellie.

She didn't need to think. She elbowed the man holding her in the stomach and lunged for the gun. The man came after her, but she reached into her pouch and grabbed a handful of her special glitter. She tossed it into his face.

The yell the man made as the poison hit his skin was very satisfying, but Nellie didn't have time to think about it. She rolled and picked up the gun on her way, rising to a standing position and aiming it at the men, who had gathered before her in a truly menacing fashion. She noticed Cora running at her from where the Fog stood screaming in pain and trying to contend with the dagger that had pierced her hand.

"Nellie, cover me!" instructed Cora, and Nellie, following behind her, discovered that they were now standing by the flying pack thing.

"Listen carefully," said Cora as she strapped the contraption onto herself. She handed Nellie a small box, which, upon closer examination, she realized was the device that controlled the bomb. "You keep that away from them. Don't let anyone get it."

"How did you—"

"When the dagger went through her hand, I took my chance. Just like you did. Fought my way free, then swiped it off her while she was still reacting to the pain. Great minds and all that." Cora grinned as she attached the last strap across her waist. "Look, you can't let anyone push that button, okay?" She indicated a big brass button in the center of the device.

"Can't you just deactivate the device? You're the one who made it!"

"I don't have the tool to open it up, and even if I did, it's such a sensitive task there's a very strong chance I'd set the bomb off."

Nellie nodded. "Okay . . . I'll protect it. What're you doin'?"

"I'm going to defuse the bomb."

"Cora!"

"Don't let anyone touch that damn button. Cover me till we reach that tunnel, and then . . . it's all you."

"What about the Fog?"

Cora glanced over her shoulder. "I think Michiko's got that covered."

Nellie ran with Cora to the tunnel, aiming the gun right at the Fog, who was yelling instructions to her men.

"Cora, I don't think I can kill anyone."

"Then don't."

Cora pushed a button on the pack and activated the cavorite. She floated a few feet in the air and aimed herself in front of the tunnel.

She looked at Nellie and gave her a reassuring smile. "You can do it," she said, and then switched on the rockets. It came to life with a loud rumble.

She was gone into the darkness, and Nellie found herself surrounded by evil-scientist-henchmen types.

"Hiya," she said.

CORA WAS FLYING faster than she'd anticipated, and following the curves of the tunnel at this speed was treacherous, to say the least. She learned quickly how to use the two levers at the base of the pack to control her direction. The tunnel bent and twisted and snaked its way underground until it started to head upward. Cora could see the sky approaching. *Just a little more,* she thought to herself, *just a little more . . .*

And then all I have to do is defuse a type of bomb I've never heard of in my life.

Piece of cake.

She burst into the night sky and was already high above Hampstead Heath before she realized where she was. My God, the tunnels crossed the entire city; it was quite a piece of work really.

Focus, Cora . . .

It was a typical London evening, the sky filled with low-hanging clouds. She flew into their cold wetness and turned off the rockets. She slowed to a stop, the cavorite keeping her levitated.

It was hard to see, and it was so dark.

The goggles.

She risked letting go of one of the steering levers, and pushed the goggles back onto her face, flipping the green glass down. With her renewed ability to see, she stared through the fog, twisting and turning her head in every direction, up, left, right, down . . .

There it was. Floating a little below her. She wondered for a brief moment if anything would have happened had she flown right into it.

She decided that that thought gave her the willies, and so she wasn't going to think it anymore.

Cora steered herself toward the bomb.

THE GUN WAS heavy, and Nellie could understand why Cora had used her hip to support it. She couldn't play keep away with this thing weighing her down, but she could hardly drop it either.

Wait . . . what was that button Cora had pushed to make it all come together?

Nellie tried to look threatening as she felt around the gun . . . she felt something on the side but remembered that was the button Cora had pushed to evaporate the creatures and quickly took her finger off . . . that would not be a good one to push. She felt around some more . . . *wait*.

There was a small button on the bottom, she could feel it. Did she dare?

She looked around and noticed Michiko standing with her sword raised and the Fog taking hold of her sword as well. Everyone was doing their part. She had to do hers.

Nellie pushed the button and the gun fell to pieces at her feet. All that remained was the small cylinder in her hand. That she could handle. She hung the remote device around her neck and took a deep breath. Then she reached into her pouch.

Time for some magic.

She threw the flashcube on the ground and it exploded in a burst of light and then smoke. The moment it hit, she launched herself toward the crowd of scientists and flipped over them as they bent over coughing and sputtering. She was running across the room before they even registered that she'd gone. But they'd be on her tail soon enough. The hall . . . she could take them on one at a time from there.

She changed direction and made her way toward the stairs. There was a very large man waiting for her by the door. She whipped off her cape and wrapped it around his head, pulling on it as she did. He stumbled and fell down the stairs, and she ran up his body and out of the giant cavern. She was flying down the hall in no time, the rest of the scientists coming up fast behind her. *Okay. Time to try it out.*

Nellie stopped and turned and whipped off her glove, aiming what seemed to be an empty hand at the men. They stopped running and backed up a few paces. Then, it seemed, it dawned on them that she wasn't actually holding anything. They relaxed a little.

"Stay back," she said as she felt for the small silver hoop at her left hip. "I'm warnin' you. I don't want to be hurtin' any of you."

Dr. Mantis moved to the front of the queue.

"Now, now, pretty girl," he said in that soft way of his. He took a step toward her.

"Stay back!"

I really really don't want to hurt you.

He didn't stay back.

She pulled the chain. A tongue of fire came bursting out of the funnel at her wrist and shot toward the evil-scientist-henchmen guys. It flooded the tunnel, and they ran screaming back the other way. Nellie released the chain, and the fire vanished. She saw then that Dr. Mantis's jacket had caught fire.

"Shoot," she said. "Why didn't you run?!"

He was screaming in pain, and she approached him as near as she could.

"Roll around on the ground. It'll put the fire out. Do it now, damn it!" She was very familiar with fire safety procedures, having had to leap through blazing hoops and even swallow some flames on occasion.

Dr. Mantis did what she said, and finally the fire was out.

He stared at her.

"Why would you help me?"

"Well . . . I don't know really."

"Run," he said. Nellie was so taken aback that she just stood there. "Run away and out of here. Go, now!"

Nellie finally realized what he was doing and nodded. She turned and ran. She ran down the hall and through the blue-green room. She stopped short when she came to the trip wires in which Mr. Staunch lay tangled. *It's safe,* she told herself. He had already activated all the darts. *Just go.* She took a deep breath and was about to run when she remembered.

"Michiko."

"OKAY, LET'S GET this over with," said the Fog. "I understand the whole honor thing, but really, I don't have the time for this. I'll defeat you, with only one good hand even."

Michiko wasn't listening; she was watching. Where had the Fog learned to fight? In school, maybe. Who knew? But she wasn't the great warrior that Michiko had thought she was. Now that she saw her in person, Michiko realized the truth. It was the element of surprise that had worked in her favor. That was all. Face-to-face like this, the Fog didn't stand a chance. Not with only one hand that worked. She was clearly in pain. It seemed almost cruel.

But she did, after all, kill Hayao.

Wait for the first move. The first move reveals all.

But she killed Hayao.

Patience, little monkey, patience.

"Oh, come on, do something already!" The Fog attacked. It was a more precise movement than Michiko had anticipated, but she defended and deflected, and moved out of the way.

They were still again. Facing each other again.

She examined the expression on the Fog's face. Frustration. *Interesting.*

The Fog attacked again, and again Michiko deflected and moved out of the way.

"What is this, some kind of game to you?"

Another attack, another deflection. This time the next attack followed immediately and Michiko fought back, parrying every attack and then spinning out to the side so that she could be on the offensive. Now she attacked, one two, slice, cut, then stop. She pulled back, took several steps backward, and stood at the ready.

"Why do you keep stopping? Why can't you just fight!" cried the Fog as she launched herself at Michiko again.

Because you want me to.

THE BOMB WAS huge. Bigger than any Cora had ever seen; bigger than she was by a long shot. Cora flew around it and examined it from all angles. It looked like she'd have to take it apart from the bottom, which meant she'd have to take it down to the ground. This would have to happen delicately.

NELLIE RAN DOWN the hall, knowing that soon enough . . .

There they were to greet her, all the evil-scientist-henchmen guys.

Nellie wondered why they were acting as the Fog's henchmen in the first place.

Good question.

* * *

THE SOUND OF metal on metal. And then stopping.

The Fog screamed in frustration and drew her pistol. She aimed and fired.

Michiko deflected the bullet with her sword.

"No," she said.

"Yes."

Another shot, another deflection.

Again.

And again.

Until there were no more bullets.

"No," said Michiko again.

The Fog tossed the pistol to the ground.

"Fine."

"WHAT I DON'T understand," Nellie was saying, her finger in the hoop at her hip and ready just in case, "is why any of you are doin' this. Do you lot really want to blow up London? You know she's not takin' you with her, right? That's not possible. So if anyone survives, you'll all be blamed for this. And anyway, won't you miss London? It's a nice city."

The men all stared at her, mouths slightly agape.

"Yes, okay, I don't want you to kill me, and you're definitely not gettin' this wee device here around my neck, but at the same time, when you think about it . . . you're all bein' a little rash, don't you think?"

A murmur rose up in the group as the men started to talk with one another.

"Aren't you supposed to be some of the brightest minds in the city? I think you're takin' your loyalty to your secret society a bit too serious. And. I'll tell you somethin' else. If you all just stop this nonsense and head on up topside right now, I'll get you all free tickets to one of the Great Raheem's magic shows. Now, what do you say to that?"

ON THE HEATH, sitting where one usually picnics: a bomb.

Beside it, a girl. With her tools. Like she was fixing the chain on her bike.

STILLNESS.

Now Michiko. Now.

It's time to attack now.

"AND ANOTHER THING, don't any of you have families, and a life outside of inventin' dangerous weapons? I think you do. I think you were just enjoyin' the ride so much, you didn't notice when you went over the edge of a cliff."

THE INSIDE GLOWED, and clockwork pieces turned slowly, each influencing the other, every movement leading to the next. *Where is it? The solution. The off switch.* It had to be somewhere. *Think, Cora, think.*

FIGHT, MICHIKO, FIGHT.

Not for your life, not for your honor, but for justice.

It was time.

* * *

CORA SAW. SHE knew. It was time.

"IT'S TIME," SAID a short squat scientist. "It's over. The Magician's assistant is right. Let's get the hell out of here."

"DO IT." THE Fog lay on the ground, her sword far to one side. She'd been so easy to disarm. It had been so simple.

The blade was at her throat, and Michiko stood over her.

"You are bad."

"No," replied the Fog. "Just underappreciated."

That. That I can understand, both the word and meaning, thought Michiko. *But I don't care.*

"Don't," said Nellie from the entrance up the stairs. Michiko looked up at her. "She's not worth it. Let's go."

For the first time since she'd started the fight, Michiko was aware of the bigger picture. The room was empty except for that creepy, bald doctor who stood in the corner. He was staring at Nellie in confusion. He called out, "Why are you still here?"

"I came for my friend," she replied.

Friend. Michiko knew that word. *Friend.*

She nodded. It wasn't right to kill this woman. It hadn't been a fair fight. And revenge, however sweet it might feel in the moment, soured over time.

She sheathed her sword, turned to Nellie, and nodded.

"Where everybody go?" she asked.

"Home," said Nellie. "Like us."

Home.

Too complicated a word for her. Too many meanings, and not one truth.

"Michiko!" cried Nellie.

Cold steel at her throat, a blade digging into her skin, sharp pain.

"Give me the device."

"GIVE ME THE device," the Fog called out to Nellie, holding a dagger to Michiko's throat.

Nellie's stomach fell. Her warning had come a moment too late. What should she do? She couldn't just hand this woman the device. What if Cora hadn't finished deactivating the bomb yet?

"If I give you the device, will you let her go?"

"Yes."

"I don't trust you."

"I don't blame you."

Okay okay okay. You can do this, Nellie. You can do it. Think . . .

"On the count of three," said Nellie, "you let her go and I'll toss it in the air. You'll have to catch it."

The Fog nodded. "One."

"Two."

"Three."

The device flew up into the air, and Michiko was pushed aside.

The Fog caught it. She looked at it. "What the hell is this? This isn't the device. You little monster." And she tossed the silver cylinder to the ground. It rolled for several feet then stopped, landing on its stomach, as it were, depressing the tiny button.

Michiko picked up her sword and walked carefully backward up the steps to join Nellie.

"Give me the device!" screamed the Fog.

Little bits and pieces of metal started to slide across the floor and collect themselves at the silver cylinder behind where Dr. Mantis was standing, staring in confusion at the Fog.

"No," replied Nellie. "It's over. You lose."

The Fog let out a scream of pure, white-hot rage. She turned and grabbed Dr. Mantis, who kicked his feet from under him, struggling for his freedom. By doing so, he nudged the now fully reconstructed Chekhov, which slowly started to roll over . . .

. . . onto the large button on its side.

The Fog placed her knife to Dr. Mantis's throat this time.

"I'll kill him."

"And I have mixed feelings about that." *After all*, thought Nellie, *he did try to have both me and Cora killed. Then again, he did let me go this time* . . . This hero business was complicated.

"Gun," whispered Michiko.

Nellie saw the glow.

"Move!" she yelled at the Fog. "Run!"

"No more distractions, little Magician's assistant. The device or death!"

Cora, I hope you were successful. "Fine, just take it, but run!" She tossed the device at the Fog. Who caught it deftly.

And . . .

Poof.

Like that.

The Chekhov fired.

Dr. Mantis was gone.

And all that remained of the Fog . . . was mist.

After

WHEN LONDON DIDN'T explode, Nellie felt quite confident that Cora had done her duty. But it wasn't until the girl dragged herself to the entrance of the Tower Subway that she knew that Cora herself was truly okay.

"You're alive!" exclaimed Nellie, squeezing her so tightly she could hear Cora gasp for air.

"Well, I was, but not for long if you keep squishing the life out of me," she replied.

Nellie released her. And Michiko gave Cora a little bow, which Cora returned.

"What took you so long?" asked Nellie.

"Well, first I had to hide the flying pack, couldn't very well lug it around with me. I'll go get it tomorrow, take it home and give it a once over. It's rather magnificent. Then, of course, I had to get rid of the defused bomb. So I took it apart, which took some time. Then I hired a cabdriver to take me here to the river, where I disposed of its remains. All except for these." She'd removed one of the pockets from the tool belt.

It was wrapped around something. "It's the uranium. I think we should give it back to Raheem and see what he wants to do with it."

"Good idea," said Nellie.

"And this . . ." She revealed the Koh-i-Noor diamond, which she'd stored in another pocket.

"Ooh, it's so beautiful!" said Nellie, taking it in her hand.

"Uh, we have to return it to the Tower, of course," said Cora.

"Oh yes . . . of course." Nellie passed the diamond back to Cora, who replaced it and the uranium on her tool belt.

"And you're both in one piece, that's good," said Cora with a tired smile.

"Yes," said Michiko.

"What happened down there? Where's the Fog?"

"Well, there's someone who isn't in one piece. She sort of . . . evaporated."

"You shot her with the Chekhov?"

"It was kind of all a big accident, really. But I have that gun of yours all right here—in pieces." Nellie held up the bag she'd used to hold all the moving parts. "I can't believe we did it, we really did it." Nellie smiled a happy tired smile. She noticed that Cora didn't follow suit, though. "Why aren't you happy?"

"I am. I'm . . . happy we saved the city. But this whole thing still feels unresolved. What about Alice? What about the flower girl mystery? I promised her family that I'd solve it."

Nellie wrapped an arm around Cora's shoulders. "And we will. Now that we know the Fog had nothin' to do with the flower girls we'll use a different tactic. All right?"

Cora nodded.

"All right," said Nellie. "But first, I think right now, we need a spot of tea."

The Next Night

CORA STOOD ALONE, clutching the basket of flowers she was carrying close to her. She knew the other girls were somewhere close by. Michiko on a rooftop surveying the scene. Nellie in a shadow somewhere, crouched, ready to pounce. She wasn't on her own.

It just felt like it.

He might not even show up. He might have stopped, decided to take a night off. There were so many variables.

But she had to try.

She shivered. The air was crisp. She could see her breath in it.

To keep her blood flowing, Cora walked up and down the riverbank. A couple walked past, and staying in character, she offered them a flower. They ignored her. She remembered that feeling. That feeling of being ignored, like she didn't exist, was worse than the lack of charity.

She saw him then. A shadowy figure, standing a few yards off. Her breath caught in her chest, and she reminded herself that she had defused a bomb and destroyed grotesque creatures.

She could handle one cowardly murderer. And if she couldn't, Nellie and Michiko could.

"Cora?" asked the figure.

Oh no. Even worse than a murderer . . .

"Cora, I thought that was you! What are you doing in that getup?"

"It's none of your business, Mr. Harris," she said as Andrew approached, his hands in his pockets, his eyebrows raised in disbelief.

"Not Mr. Harris, not back to that . . ."

"Yes, back to that. Could you go away now?" A murderer wasn't likely to show himself if she was standing speaking with a male companion.

"You're not still angry with me, are you? We were drunk. We both said things we didn't mean . . ."

"I beg your pardon; I meant every word."

Andrew shook his head sadly. She knew it was "sadly" because he released a melancholy sigh and gave her a hangdog look. Cora was relieved that for the first time since she'd met him, her head and heart were in perfect agreement: *Ew.*

There was a bark. A single bark breaking the silence, and both Cora and Andrew looked up to where the side street sloped up to the Strand. A floppy-eared bloodhound was galumphing toward them. It stared up at the two of them and barked again.

"Hello," said Cora in response. It seemed as if the dog was making an obvious greeting. She presented the back of her hand to his nose.

The bloodhound sniffed it for a moment. And then seemed

completely uninterested in her. Instead, he barked at Andrew.

"Hello," said Andrew, glancing at Cora as if somehow she understood what was going on and could explain it to him.

The dog jumped up on its hind legs and placed its front paws on Andrew's shoulders.

"Down, boy, down . . . get off . . ." Andrew took a few steps back, but the dog walked with him. Cora smiled to herself; it looked a bit like they were dancing. "Get off . . ." Andrew tried to push the dog away. When he wouldn't budge, Andrew started to flail his arms. "Get down *now!*" He struck the dog hard across the face, and the dog landed back on the ground. Cora couldn't believe her eyes and felt her blood start to boil. Before she could do anything, however, the dog started to growl. Then he jumped on Andrew again. The momentum this time sent Andrew flying onto his back.

"Stop. Police!" shouted another familiar voice.

"Officer Murphy?" said Cora as the young officer ran past to the dog, who was standing on top of Andrew, baring its teeth. Andrew stopped struggling and looked like he was trying to stay very still.

Officer Murphy turned and did a double take when he realized who'd called out to him. "Miss Bell, is that you?"

"Yes."

"What are you doing dressed like that?"

"Well," she said, placing a hand on her hip, "I'm doing your job, quite frankly . . ."

"You weren't making yourself bait, were you? That's very dangerous."

"I'm used to danger." *You have no idea how used to danger.*

"Well, he didn't hurt you, did he?"

"That mutt? No, he does seem awfully fond of Andrew, though."

"What? No, not the dog. Him." He pointed at Andrew.

"Him?"

"Oh, how marvelous!" Nellie materialized from out of the shadows, clearly not able to keep herself hidden with Officer Murphy about. Cora was glad to see that Nellie, with her mask removed and long cape covering her person, looked relatively normal and not too hero-like. "The dog works!"

Even in the dark, it was possible to see him blush. "Oh, Nellie! It's so nice to see you. Yes, isn't it grand! I did what you suggested. Talked to that girl from the other night. She gave me her shawl, and we've been using it to track him down ever since. And now look: We caught him!"

"What are you talking about?" asked Cora, because what she thought they were talking about couldn't possibly be what they were talking about.

There was a fierce bark then, followed by a whimper.

"Cabal!" cried Officer Murphy, running over to the bloodhound. Cora looked and gasped. The dog was lying on the ground, a deep puncture wound in its shoulder. And Andrew . . .

He was running fast. Very fast. Where he thought he could go, Cora had no idea. He'd been identified. They'd catch him eventually.

Or they'd just catch him right now.

A primal scream, a flash of silver in the night.

Michiko.

There wasn't even a scuffle. She landed on top of him, knocked him to the ground, and stood over him, sword to his throat.

"Who the hell was that?" said Officer Murphy, his mouth wide open. Then, immediately: "Oh, excuse the language. I'm so sorry."

Nellie shook her head. "It's okay. How's Cabal?"

"I think he'll be fine . . ."

The sounds of conversation faded behind her as Cora approached Andrew slowly. She felt like she was in a dream, almost floating in his direction. She came up alongside Michiko and stared down at him. He was lying flat on his back, his hands folded over his stomach, as if he was lying out on a lawn in the sun on a lazy Saturday afternoon and not on the cold ground with a blade at his throat.

"You're a horrible person," said Cora.

He looked at her and sighed. "Cora, you'll never understand."

"Damn right, I won't."

"We all have two sides to us. If we don't let the dark side vent, it risks taking over the whole person."

"Bullshit. That's just . . . bullshit."

"Follow the train of logic, Cora."

"It's a theoretical exercise. You read it in a work of fiction. And worse, you're so stupid that you drew totally the wrong conclusion. Don't you even understand that in letting it all out, Mr. Hyde wound up consuming Dr. Jekyll?"

Andrew just shook his head at her, like she was the one who was stupid.

She didn't know why she couldn't stop talking. She just had to convince him, prove to him, through logic, how wrong he was. Or maybe, somehow he'd prove to her that it all made sense. But something, anything, had to give. "Besides, even if it were true"—her voice was rising in pitch—"which it isn't, you can't do what you did. You can't kill people. It's wrong. It's absolutely wrong."

"People? You really see those girls as people? You can't, Cora. Not really. They don't have the same brain capacity. If they did, they wouldn't be flower girls."

"No, that's . . . God, you're disgusting, you're just . . ." There was an arm across her chest, a hand squeezing her shoulder tight.

"Bad man," said Michiko.

Cora looked at her.

That was it. There was no reasoning with him. He was just bad. "Yes," she said, feeling herself deflate. "Bad man."

"Thank you, masked vigilante, I think I'll take over now," said Officer Murphy, approaching from behind.

The three girls stood in the shadows to watch as Andrew was handcuffed and walked to the police wagon. Officer Murphy took the credit for the arrest, and none of them minded.

"I hope Cabal will be okay," said Nellie.

"I'm sure he will be," Cora replied.

The wagon pulled away, and the girls walked over to a bench and sat staring out at the river.

"Well," said Nellie after a quiet moment, "that's the end of that."

Cora nodded.

Then she did something she hadn't done in . . . well, she couldn't remember when. She burst into tears.

Nellie was amazed. She'd never seen her friend cry before.

Cora was amazed. She never cried.

Michiko thought it all made perfect sense.

"I'm so sorry about Andrew," Nellie said. "And after all the teasin'—oh, he was a right bastard, that one."

Cora shook her head. "It's not that."

Nellie thought for a moment. "Is it because of all the danger from last night? Just relief that it's all over?"

Cora shook her head and sobbed harder.

"Well, I'm stumped. Any idea?" She looked at Michiko.

Michiko thought for a moment. "It is over."

"Yes, as I said," said Nellie.

Michiko shook her head. "No." She placed a hand on Cora's arm. Cora looked up at her. "It is over."

Cora nodded, and in an act that no one could have anticipated, she leaned her head on Michiko's shoulder.

"It's over. And I don't want it to be. I want it to be last night, when we were solving the mystery. Saving the city. Being in charge of not only our destiny, but the destiny of others. Fixing things. Making a difference. I want to do it again. And I want to do it with you two." She gulped in air and tried to calm herself.

"A team," said Nellie quietly.

"What was that?" asked Cora.

"Raheem called us a team."

"We make a great team."

"Team," said Michiko. "I'm not samurai."

It seemed a bit of a tangent, but the other girls tried to understand what she meant.

"I am not samurai. I am Michiko. I am part of team."

Cora sat upright and wiped the tears from her face with her hands. "Do you mean it?" she asked, looking at both of them. "Do you want to keep doing this?"

Both girls nodded.

"Brilliant!" Cora was up on her feet in an instant and started talking. "Because I actually was thinking about it when I got in last night, and I had some great ideas. I was thinking we should use the Fog's old lab as our secret hideout, only, of course, I'd rig it out to suit our purposes. And I also thought we should place an advertisement, maybe, something that lets people know we exist, since it's unlikely they'll know we saved them and everything. I also think we need a name. Something impressive, something that people will remember . . ."

She stopped talking when she noticed both Nellie and Michiko laughing at her.

"What?"

"You're brilliant, you are," said Nellie, rising.

"Don't you think a name is a good idea?"

Nellie nodded and then grabbed her into a big bear hug. Cora patted her back. She didn't quite understand what was going on, but that was okay.

"So, names?" she said when Nellie pulled away.

Nellie thought, then brightly: "The Dazzling Trio?"

"No."

Nellie thought for another moment and glanced at Michiko, who gave her a look that said, *"I can barely make complete sentences, let alone be clever with this language of yours and come up with a cool-sounding name."*

"Something with 'society' in it," Nellie said suddenly with a smile.

"Society?"

"Yeah, like all those silly societies the men have. Kind of like what the Fog suggested. No boys allowed. Too bad, really, that Society of Heroes is taken. It'd be perfect."

Cora nodded. "That's a good idea . . ."

"The Dazzling Society?"

"No."

Thus . . .

THERE WAS NO grave. And there were only three mourners. They stood on the bridge in St. James's Park, three bowed Japanese figures—an old man, a young boy, and a girl. All who noticed them politely avoided interrupting.

"An exotic ritual," a young woman in lilac whispered to her beau in pale blue.

Callum had forbidden Michiko to come. He had yelled at her and struck her. She had no idea why it bothered him so much that she was spending an hour, at most, with the old samurai and his remaining assistant.

Who cared.

She knelt down on the bridge beside the burning stick of incense the old samurai had brought, and tossed a small yellow flower into the water. It floated peacefully away.

Good-bye, Hayao. Little monkey. You will be missed.

Thank you for being my teacher.

You made me trust.

But most of all, you made me see the truth.

I am not a samurai.

I am Michiko.

And that is okay.

"LEATHER WOULD LOOK fantastic and be very protective. You could even have a leather mask!"

Nellie shushed the Magician as they waited in the wings for their cue. She appreciated his enthusiasm for her new hobby, but this was not the moment. He nodded and mimed locking his lips together. Then he escorted her over to the large, ornamented trunk and held it open for her, extending his free hand to help her climb inside.

She stepped into it and curled up as she had done so many times before. The lid closed, and she was trapped in the black. It was a strange sensation after having been held prisoner in a grave, but she refused to let those evil men get the better of her. This was her home. This dark, cramped, but wonderful, space. In a moment the music would start, the drumroll would follow. And she would appear.

As if by magic.

Applause would fill the theater.

She felt good. She felt better than good. It was one thing saving the city. But performing? Nothing could top that kind of high.

Though . . . maybe she could add some glitter to the mask . . .

THEY LEFT THE courthouse and passed through a flurry of reporters shouting questions at them. Barker, in front, cut a path as Lord White and Cora slipped into the carriage.

"Well," his lordship said as the door closed. "I've learned my lesson: Never hire anyone ever again. No matter the breeding or connections. There's no one out there I can rely on. Except you, of course."

Cora nodded, but kept her focus out the window as the city passed them by.

"I *can* rely on you, can't I? You're not going to leave me, are you?" he asked when she didn't speak.

She looked at him. He seemed sincerely worried, and she thought his concern was quite sweet. Of course, she wasn't going to leave him.

But things were going to get a hell of a lot more complicated.

She hoped it didn't put him out too much.

Then again, maybe it was time for a little payback? Time for him to be put out, just a little.

"No, don't be silly," she said. And he reached over and grabbed her hand. He almost looked tearful. Almost.

"I'm so glad. Mrs. Philips would really miss you if you went and . . ." He stopped. He sighed. "Oh, hang it all. I'd miss you, too. You're my Girl Friday. You know that, right?"

Cora blinked. "What?"

"Girl Friday. You know the term. 'Man Friday.' Like in *Robinson Crusoe*. A person who's always there to help. A person without whom I'd be lost. Only, of course, you're a girl. . . not some island native . . ." Cora grinned. "Ah!" he said, noticing. "You like the name, then?"

"I do," she said, feeling smugly satisfied. "I like the name a lot."

* * *

THE NEXT WEEK, an ad appeared in the morning newspaper. It was repeated that evening and the following day as well. It stayed in the paper a full week, until the citizens of London began to see it as commonplace. It was remarkable how quickly one could become accustomed to new things. How such things could become part of the fabric of one's society, as if they'd always been.

For even legends must be told for a first time. By someone. Somewhere.

AND SO . . . it began.

TO THE CITIZENS of London and its surrounding Burroughs:

Are you being blackmailed? Does a loved one's untimely demise seem suspiciously tied to a brother's new bank account? Are you receiving threats of a personal and/or physically painful nature? Fear not, for salvation is at hand.

We are a trio of lady heroes. If you need us, we will be there. Respond to this advertisement by post, and we shall come to your aid.

We have many talents and skills. But above all things, we know how to assist.

Yours sincerely,
Hyde, the Silver Heart, and Lady Sparkle
AKA
The Friday Society

Credits

(OR HOW ADRIENNE COPES WITH ACKNOWLEDGING A RIDICULOUSLY LONG LIST OF AMAZING PEOPLE WHO HELPED *THE FRIDAY SOCIETY* GET TO WHERE IT IS TODAY)

Editor—Nancy Conescu
Publisher—Dial, Penguin
Agent—Jessica Regel (and the entire team at JVNLA)

Competitive Writing Colleagues—Joanna Blackman, Lesley Livingston
Samurai Gurus—Scott Leaver & Todd Campbell
Fight/Weapons Guru—RiotACT
Steampunk Guru—J. M. Frey
Naming and Logic Queen—Heather Dann
Brainstorming—Jonathan Llyr

Support Systems—TorKidLit, Steampunk Canada, Toronto Steampunk Society, AbsoluteWrite.com, VerlaKay.com, Backspace Writing Forum

Special thanks to Team Kress, without whom none of this would be possible, and who have faith in me even when I don't. And who give me hugs whenever I need them.

Thanks to my extended family and to my brilliant and talented friends, all with shiny hair (or scalps, depending) who always make me feel special when I just feel like I'm crazy.

Lastly, thanks to my followers/likers and readers on various social media. You make procrastination extra fun.

No animals were harmed in the creation of this book, though Atticus the cat did have to be locked out of the office several times due to his inability to stay out of the garbage can. And not nip at my ankles. And not stop slowly pushing things off my desk. Like my glasses. Just stop pushing my glasses off the desk, little dude. Seriously.